DEADLY
OBSESSION

Also by Nigel May:

TRINITY

ADDICTED

SCANDALOUS LIES

DEADLY OBSESSION

Nigel May

bookouture

Published by Bookouture

An imprint of StoryFire Ltd.
23 Sussex Road, Ickenham, UB10 8PN
United Kingdom

www.bookouture.com
Copyright © Nigel May 2016

ISBN: 978-1-910751-67-1
EBOOK ISBN: 978-1-910751-66-4

ACKNOWLEDGEMENTS

Word Up! Neon-lit thanks to the people who have shared this journey with me underneath the glitterball of glamour and intrigue.

La Vie En Rose. Decades of love to David and Kymme (and Latreena too) who have known me since rhythm was a dancer and would doubtless be spinning around (like a record baby) dressed head to toe in sequins.

To my Venuses: Lottie Mayor, Nush Bellamy and Vicky Mitchenall. You will always be my Goddesses on a mountain top.

Amazing, ah-ah-amazing thanks to the soundtrack of my electropop dancefloor, the fabulous Jen and Rick from Hi-Fashion, for being beyond unique and turning music into art. You Are Gorgeous!

Simply The Best. To the glorious Laura Kilbride, who'd be swaying to the beat in a 'delish little combo' and to Gen, Jacqui J, Loen, Leonie, Hayley and Manc Rach, the girls who make sure the Sun Always Shines on TV. And the So Macho Magic Hands – you know who you are!

My Camera Never Lies. To Matthew Watson for snapping that perfect shot from day one and to Dreamee Carol, Jona and Lolly for craftily cross-stitching a Piece of the Action. Plus to Tina Dolan and Debra Bates for letting me rock the floor in knitted pants.

Automatic High-five to my electrifying friend, the brilliant Terry Ronald, who would be writing the tunes and pumping up the beats – you are an inspiration beyond words. Respect-able! My Disco Needs You.

Nothing's Gonna Stop Us Now. An extended 12-inch remix of gratitude to everyone at Bookouture, who continue to lead the way. Oliver, Claire, Lydia, Jennie and Kim for guidance and for taking my latest drama-soaked romp beyond a catfight and making it roar with obsession! And to my literary Two Tribes, my posse of authors and bloggers, for support.

We Are Family – my sis Deb, Keith, Ryan and Loz. To my dearest Dancing Queen Loulou and to my soul mate and the best mover I know, Alan Roberts. He's The Greatest Dancer. Yes Sir, You Can Boogie. I love you all.

And finally, Nobody Does It Better. To the late, great, Jackie Collins. Legend and a lifetime of wonderful words.

For Sarah and Maddie for taking me to Xanadu with their friendship – "an idyllic, exotic, luxurious place"

CHAPTER 1

Now, November 2015, London

Amy Hart knew the dead couldn't talk. And they certainly couldn't put pen to paper. But there they were. Words from beyond the grave ... In black and white. As real as they were terrifying. As terrifying as they were mystifying.

Her dead husband's writing was staring up at her from the letter gripped tightly between her trembling fingers. The man whom she'd cremated earlier that year and cried a lake of tears for as she'd scattered his ashes. Riley Hart – the love of her life, the man who had helped her gain everything and then been so cruelly snatched away six months ago. Taken before his time. Killed by another – murdered. Leaving her a widow at the age of twenty-nine. But now there was this, a letter from him ... *So how could a dead man write anything ...?*

Her hands sweating, her mind racing, Amy tried to make sense of it. Just as life had finally seemed to be getting back to some sort of blurred normality, the letter had arrived that very morning, falling innocently through her apartment letter box and now she was back to square one, side-lined into a fathomless pit of despair, worry, and fear.

Why now? What would she gain from the words she'd scrutinised over and over again? How could an intelligent woman like her read something that was set out so clearly yet still make no sense of it?

Amy had spent months after Riley's murder poring over countless articles in magazines and ploughing through self-help books about 'rebuilding your life'. She had listened to a string of counsellors and therapists telling her she was on the 'right track', though she was not even sure where that particular track was supposed to lead.

They'd all told her how life would seemingly slot into place as time went by. But not one of them, swivelling in their highly polished leather chairs in their fancy offices with their framed certificates on every wall had prepared her for *this*. Every ounce of strength that Amy had managed to reap since Riley's untimely death had been destroyed in a matter of seconds.

The day had begun as every single day started lately; following another restless night of intermittent sleep in a lonely bed, broken and fitful, peppered with vile images she'd tried to obliterate. It was horribly predictable, as if she'd pre-recorded her dreams from the night before onto a disc and inserted it into the DVD player in her brain before hitting the sack. Like the night before, and the night before that, *ad lib* to fade. Endless and bloody. It wasn't an adventure she would have chosen to watch again if she had any choice. She knew the ending and it was never a happy one. Fairy tales were a thing of the past for Amy. This was an '18' certificate movie, a full blown horror. And Amy was playing leading scream queen.

She had eaten breakfast on auto-pilot; tea and some bland cereal while watching TV. It was another world to Amy, one that still seemed so alien. Crass, trite news stories she'd seen before – disgruntled boybands deciding to 'take a break' and duping their fans into believing that they still all loved each other like the happiest of siblings, collagen-obsessed wannabes spending thousands on fake tits and trout pouts to grotesquely turn themselves from looker to hooker, another Hollywood Z-lister telling the world how she'd shifted the baby weight mere minutes after cutting the umbilical cord ... blah, blah, blah ... words and pictures but none of it wormed its way into Amy's psyche. She had no room. It was still full of her own horrific headlines. The tragic leading stories of her own personal blog. Headlines of heartache.

Before, her world had been full of glamour-packed pap-flashing celebrity sound bites about the popular idols of the day – movie stars like Gosling, Tatum, Redmayne and Efron, the hotties tearing up Hollywood with their poster boy looks and million dollar pay demands or the latest vacuous TV talent judge spouting nonsense about her heartfelt quest to find the next five-minute-wonder. Stars that not so long ago she would have done anything to entice into her laser-lit nightclub world. Back when she was strong, self-assured, when life seemed to have a purpose ...

Amy had switched from the TV to radio, as she often did these days, hoping the songs she heard would transport her to places she longed to revisit, but feared she never could. Pharrell, Sia, Kanye as well as home grown talent like George Ezra, Florence and the Machine and Paloma Faith. She'd been part of their scene, at the epicentre of what was current. And they had been part of Amy's, keen to hang at the trendiest of haunts. As joint-owner of the UK's most respected new nightspot, The Kitty Kat Club, Amy had been the Queen Bee at the honeypot to which they flew, clocking up air miles from around the globe to be seen in the VIP area of choice. But that was then.

It was only when she'd flicked off the radio that late November morning that she'd heard the sound. The swoosh of the letterbox and the gentle slap of an envelope as it landed at her front door. Real post had been infrequent lately, an increasing sign of the twenty-first century. In a world of emails, Tweets and shared Facebook statuses, an actual handwritten letter was rarer than a footballer who could keep his cock in his pants. Amy was used to huge amounts of junk mail; offers of free casino memberships and kebab shops for the south London borough she now attempted to call home, but an actual handwritten envelope that was addressed personally to her ... no, that was rare.

It had been the handwritten envelope that first grabbed Amy's attention. The Christmas stamp featuring a donkey and shepherd had momentarily caused Amy to smile, transporting her to Christmases past. Then she saw the postmark, which read 'Manchester', her former home. This reminder of a life she had tried to forget when she'd headed south had wiped the smile away in a second.

She'd stared at the handwriting for what seemed like minutes. In reality it couldn't have been more than a few seconds. The curling of the letters and the looping of the numbers sparked thoughts inside her brain. There was something comforting about them, yet a vein of dreaded doubt ignited and ran through her. *Why? What was stopping her from just ripping the letter open and reading the contents? Why the fear? Who was it from?* She'd pretty much cut herself off since ... well, since *it* had happened. Since she'd disappeared for her own sanity.

Taking the letter to the kitchen she sat down, her legs like jelly, and began to tear at the flap of the envelope. The letter inside was handwritten too. Her tears had started by the end of the first paragraph. So had the trembling. As she read through, word after word chilling her to the bone, her skin pricking into goose bumps, she tried to take in what was written on the page. It seemed impossible – something incomprehensible like from one of those TV shows – an *X Files* or a *Sherlock*. There was no explanation for it, but there had to be.

Fruitlessly wiping away her tears as they snaked down her nose and dripped onto the letter she scanned her eyes to the date at the top of the page. There was no address, but the date was clear, 26th November. Two days ago. She checked the date on the envelope's postmark – it said the same.

Amy hesitated before looking at the signature at the bottom of the letter again. She'd read it once, but maybe she'd been mistaken, maybe her crazy mind was playing tricks on her. God knows it had been through enough to have a season tick-et booked for the nearest padded cell. But no, she hadn't been duped ... there it was, in his own unmistakable handwriting. '*Love Riley x*'. Marked with a kiss. After all that he'd said in the letter, he'd still marked it with a kiss. *How could he?*

How could he mark it with anything? Riley Hart. Her dead husband. The man she had hoped to grow old with. The other equal half that had made her complete, the person who had ef-fortlessly matched her ambitions and dreams. Back then before his death ... before *all* the deaths.

CHAPTER 2
Then, 2013

Amy loved that moment when she first opened her eyes in the morning –as the clarity of a new day formed into glorious shape before her. Lying in bed, enjoying the soft cocoon of the sheet around her, it was easy for her to count her blessings, to be grateful for what life had given her. To know that life was on her side.

For Amy, it was all about being part of the right team and she knew that she definitely was. As she gazed across at the wedding photo of her, Riley and her bridesmaid (and best friend) Laura, sitting on the dressing table on the other side of the room, a broad unstoppable smile stretched across her face. It was the first thing she saw every morning and she adored it. She'd positioned it deliberately. She'd wake up, spooned by the man she loved, his sleepy breathing hot against the back of her neck, his own awakening leading to the brush of a tender, loving kiss on her skin, the stubble on his chin scratching slightly, his arousal pressing anticipatorily against her back. Often as she stared at the photo, Riley would turn her to face him and they would make love, his expert sexual skills riding her to a crescendo of nerve-tingling orgasms. The prelude to the symphony of another happy day in the life of Mrs Riley Hart.

Some mornings he wouldn't be there, where meetings at work had kept him from her side. But her bed never felt cold. The warmth of their love was evident, even in his absence.

As Amy watched the early morning rays of light seeping in across the bedroom she felt nothing but joy bubbling inside her as she stared at the photo. To her it was everything.

Laura Cash, her bridesmaid, was her closest friend, the girl she shared so much with, the one she could turn to in any crisis. The one who had always picked her up and dusted her down when life had thrown her a mental grenade. Laura had shared her tears and then found the strength to mop them up. They were poles apart in so many ways – Laura was brash, effervescent, an ever-burning flame of excitement, always looking for the next high. She had never done a decent day's work in her life. The basics of survival like finding money to pay your bills or working behind a bar on a Saturday night to fund your next fashion fix had never applied to her. Nine-to-fives were for losers. Who needed a skillset when everything you needed to coax a man into flashing his cash was skilfully set down her blouse and under the fabric of her thigh-skimming skirt? It also helped that Laura's parents, both rich and now living their life out at a villa in the Spanish Costas, were happy enough to foot the bill for Laura's passage through a top boarding school and a swanky studio flat in Manchester's fashionable Northern Quarter.

Amy's humble upbringing could not have been more different, her parents grafting for every penny. She muddled her way through comprehensive school, floating around the middle of the class for all of her six years there and bagged a Saturday job as soon as she could in order to buy CDs and the clothes she wanted to wear. Amy had always been much more diligent and thorough in her ways, thinking things out beforehand. The sensible one. Something that Laura certainly wasn't. Yet despite this, both of them had ambition, a yearning to succeed in their own way. Two different facets on the same gemstone, both shining bright in their own unique ways. And they loved each other dearly.

A nuzzling on her neck interrupted her thoughts, a ripple of desire passing through Amy's naked body as she felt the exploration of her husband's lips. 'Hello, my sweet angel ...' he whispered in between kisses. 'And how is my sexy little entrepreneur this morning?'

Amy turned to face him, allowing her lips to find his, silencing his words. She could feel the hardness of his body, an immediate ripple of warm, lustful expectation flowing freely from the folds between her legs. 'Business is good, my *boss* is looking after me nicely, in every way possible ...' she replied with a playful smile.

Amy wrapped her arms around Riley and pushed back the bed sheets as they entwined their bodies beneath them. Nothing would stand in her way. Riley had taught her that, in all areas of life. He was strong. A force. Someone to respect and admire. Some would say ruthless, but Amy saw his business prowess as a major turn-on. It was petrol to her own burning desire to succeed.

Not that she'd realised he was such a captain of industry when she'd first met him. It was his softer side that had initially melted her heart.

She had been eighteen when she had first met him. Strikingly handsome in a rugged Indiana Jones kind of way, Riley had been the only man for Amy ever since the moment he'd offered to buy her a drink in a dive of a pub in North Manchester eight years earlier.

She was instantly smitten, even if their spit and sawdust surroundings had given no indication of Riley's wealth. The owner of a lucrative plastics business in the north of England, bequeathed to him by his late father, it was only once they'd been together for a good year or so that Riley had actually revealed how monied-up he was. Up until that point, Amy had assumed that when he said he worked for his dad's company he was just helping out with the family business. In fact Riley owned one of the most successful plastics factories in the north. Sexy it wasn't … money-making it most definitely was.

But Amy didn't care about the cash. She would have fallen for Riley if he'd have been an out-of-work bum without a penny to scratch his peachy arse with. At four years her senior, he was charming, caring, dynamic, sexy and had a body that proved he looked after himself as well as looking after those he loved. They'd moved in together eighteen months after meeting, their love shared in a palatial pad in well-to-do Sale in Cheshire.

It was all Amy had ever dreamt of; a WAG-worthy lifestyle that her humble upbringing had only ever allowed her to stare wide-eyed in envy at on the TV. Near to her family, yet a million miles away from the grime and graffiti she'd grown up around. As a child she'd barely had a paddling pool but now she owned a swimming pool of Beckham-esque proportions, a sound system that made her favourite songs, from her love of retro classics by Cyndi Lauper, ABBA and Michael Jackson through to modern beats by Taylor Swift and Rihanna, sound like she was seated front row at The Manchester MEN Arena in her own living room. There was also a hot-tub in the garden that still tickled her skin with delight every time she immersed herself into the frothy bubbles. But beyond the riches, the designer brands and the walk-in wardrobe, it was home. The sanctuary that she shared with Riley. The man who matched her own desires. Made them a reality. The man she loved. Love between them in equal measures.

It was a love that had mercifully proven to be as strong as it was true. Especially when Amy had needed it most. Amy's parents had both been killed in a car crash when she was only twenty. If it hadn't been for Riley's love and support when her parents had died she could have easily spiralled out of control. He was her rock, formed from many layers, each of them attractive in their own way, as if sculpted from the experiences that life had placed before him. He played and worked with an equal zest for life. Daring and dangerous yet puppy-soft and doting when necessary.

'So, I'm the boss, am I?' quizzed Riley as he clasped Amy to his chest, a thin slick of glistening sweat still evident from their early morning love-making. His smile revealed the humour behind his question.

'Yes, oh masterful one ... without you I am nothing,' fawned Amy. 'Merely a poor, helpless woman unable to function without the guidance of a good strong alpha male.' She giggled at the notion, knowing it to be light years from the truth.

'Well you're no use to me then, are you? The woman I fell in love with was strong, intelligent, an individual, someone who wanted to take on the world. How can a poor, helpless woman deal with the day-to-day workings of a nightclub? Monies in, monies out, VIP nights, bar orders, employing workers and security ... no, you're no use to me. Better get a man in ...'

Grinning with mischief, Amy stared Riley straight in the eyes and kept his gaze as she allowed one of her hands to travel down his body and cup his balls. She gave them a firmer than comfortable squeeze. 'Well, for your information, mister high-falutin mogul, this little lady is more than capable of doing everything this club needs and more. The business plan is done, I have agencies scouting for the right staff for me and the decor is going to be cool enough to blow any other club in the country out of the water. Got that?'

'I think me and my knackers are more than aware that you're the woman for the job, if you'd like to give them back to me in one piece!' He indicated her clenched hand and sighed slightly as Amy eased the pressure. 'Your strength and drive are two of the many reasons I adore you. I can't wait to see the club come to life.'

'I'll fill you in on the business plan tonight if you wish. I want to bounce some ideas off Laura today – share some rather fabulous thoughts I have for the club with her. If there's one thing that Laura and I have always loved doing together over the years it's strutting our way across a million dance floors so we know what makes a good one. And seeing as she doesn't exactly have a lot of other things on her plate right now, she is more than keen to help. Plus we work well together. I'll fill you in over dinner this evening.'

Riley slipped his body out from beneath the sheets and stood naked at the side of the bed.

A crease of worry streaked across his face. 'It might have to wait until tomorrow. There's some business at the factory I need to attend to tonight. Trouble with some of the workers. I've had to call an after-hours meeting so I may be rather late. Very late in fact, if they don't play ball. Club talk will have to be postponed. I'm sure you're capable of not fucking it up on your own,' he laughed, turning away from Amy and heading towards their en-suite bathroom.

'You cheeky bugger,' laughed Amy, swiping at his naked ass with her hand as he walked away. 'This club will be amazing. You just wait ...'

It was true, she knew it would be. It was something she had always dreamed of, ever since she'd first gyrated her teenage hips to the dance tunes at her school disco. Music made her happy and more so if it made other people happy. And if Amy could make other people euphoric then she would have fulfilled her mission on earth. She would always remember how she felt as the DJ segued from one up-tempo slab of hi-BPM joy into the next. Her senses would fly and her spirits soar as she realised the tune that she would be dancing to next. Music was the ultimate power as far as she was concerned and the DJ was able to play God. It was a feeling that she still adored today, a sense of heaven, and running her own nightclub, employing the best DJs to play the best music, filling it with the rich and famous, the designer and the decadent was what she had always craved.

When she had suggested it to Riley, he had leapt at the chance, ready to let her realise her ambitions. It would be the finest club Manchester had ever seen. She knew it would work, she wouldn't let it be otherwise. She even had the name for it. In her mind she could already see the neon sign, beckoning party-goers nationwide. 'The Kitty Kat Club'. An homage to her favourite musical film, *Cabaret*, changing it from *Kit* to *Kitty* to give it a more modern and cutting edge feel. It was sassy, frothy and legendary and she was sure that it would have the allure to become the sound-filled destination of choice for those who had the right look.

As she watched Riley's majestic ass move out of sight, Amy pulled the pillows towards her, squeezed them tightly and buried her head into their softness, stifling an excited squeal as she did so. She knew that the club would work.

She wasn't wrong ...

CHAPTER 3

Then, May 2015, Manchester

'Can you pass the loo roll under, Laura? I've used the last piece and I'm sure as hell not risking dripping dry,' said Amy, reaching down to stick her hand under the toilet cubicle wall at what had become Manchester's number one nightclub, The Kitty Kat Club.

'It's yours,' replied Laura Cash, a flurry of lace clothing and unmanaged hair in the next cubicle, as she pushed the toilet roll into Amy's hand. 'We need to get back to the dance floor and work those celebs, have you seen who's in tonight?' I think Eighties Night could be your finest moment yet, Amy. This place is becoming hotter than hell for your A-list celebrity and they appear to love a theme night. Everybody loves the retro vibe, even if most of them weren't born when the eighties slipped into view. Half of soapville's here, I've seen at least three *X Factor* champions and their clingy entourages and enough *Made In Chelsea* stars to make me think that SW3 in London must be a ghost town tonight. It is SW3, isn't it? Chelsea? Oh who cares? London's loss, Kitty Kat's gain. And I suppose you've seen …' Laura paused for effect before finishing her sentence. '… him? O M freaking G – no wonder this place has the ultimate reputation! I am so proud of you, Amy. What was it *DJ* magazine said about it …?'

Amy joined her best friend and the woman who had helped her launch The Kitty Kat Club at the huge mirror screwed to the length of the toilet wall, passing her hands under the tap and then running them through her equally explosive hair. They could have used the office toilets provided for the staff, but Laura was insistent that the best gossip was always heard in the ladies' loo. She wasn't wrong. She'd already heard a winner of a US TV model show bemoaning to her stick-thin pal about how her latest squeeze, a top telly chef, 'would have to go, as his fucking food is too calorific and I've already lost two contracts as I've ballooned to a size two. My agent is livid'. Laura, a woman who believed in the joy of food and curves had wanted to slap her, but Amy would never have forgiven her and the fallout on blogs and websites could have been catastrophic.

Amy's dark roots contrasted in perfect eighties Ciccone-chic fashion with the mass of blonde swirls circling her face. They were both rocking the *Like A Virgin* Madonna look for the monthly step back in time night, a change to their normal 'uniform' of Dior, Prada and Stella McCartney.

Amy cleared her throat and began, pride bursting forth. 'And I quote,' she grinned. '"The Kitty Kat Club has become, in a short space of time, the favoured social haunt and haven for celebrities keen to be seen – a melting pot of models, megastars and most-wanteds with a dazzlingly dangerous air of decadence that the fashionable in-crowd thrive on …" or words to that effect, anyway. I believe *DJ* magazine went on to say, "Owner Amy Hart, and her sharp-suited husband, Riley, make the perfect team when it comes to pushing a club that will go down in the annals of Manchester history as the neon-floored nirvana to hang out at. Their range of theme nights and blistering superstar DJ sets cater for all of the UK's clubbing elite and have made the Kitty Kat the *purr-fect* VIP hangout". I know that quote by heart, but then it has been framed and hanging on my office wall ever since publication.'

Amy adjusted her fishnets – more holes than actual stocking – and sprayed herself with a cloud of Jo Malone perfume, one of the many supplied free at The Kitty Kat. Another reason for Laura not to use the office toilet.

'Anyway ... *him*? I assume you're talking about Grant Wilson? He does look sensational tonight, I must say. If I wasn't married to the sexiest man in Manchester then maybe ... Are you not tempted to wave your cut-off gloves in his direction? He's very you – he has a dick and a pulse after all and that's normally all it takes,' she joked. Make that half-joked, she knew Laura better than anyone. 'God knows you could do with a decent bloke, Laura. Is there anyone on the go at the moment? Someone like Grant Wilson would be perfect for you.'

'The man is divine, but he's such a player,' Laura sighed, not sounding overly convincing. 'I guess being the hot-shot on TV's number one medical drama means you can prescribe any woman you like to satisfy your lust. I really don't think he's after me and I wouldn't want him if he was. I've been with better. Plus, he looked like he was sniffing around Genevieve Peters when we came down here.'

There was a distinct sneer in Laura's voice as she continued. 'There is something about that woman that irks me. She may own one of the best clothes shops in Manchester but she always looks like she doesn't really want to be here. Like someone has just shoved a shit sandwich under her nose. She's welcome to him if he wants her. But yes, he does look pretty good, even if he has ignored the eighties dress code, you should speak to his PR about that ... anyway, don't worry about me, I'm very well catered for in *that* department.' Laura let out a shrill squeak of glee and signalled to the door.

'Oh my God ... move it, girl, the DJ's playing "Automatic" by The Pointer Sisters. Only one of the best tunes of the eighties.' Laura's love of good music was just as great as Amy's. And they both loved music from across the decades. It was one of the rare areas in life in which they were exactly alike.

'Now, excuse me, but me and *these* beautiful Pointer Sisters are heading onto the dance floor ...' She rearranged her sizable breasts within her T-shirt and bra combo, hoisting them into proud position.

Back in the main body of the club, Amy watched as her friend gyrated to the music, lost in its post-disco funk. This is what she loved about The Kitty Kat Club. The heat, the excitement, the joy, the variety. One night it would be all old-skool 'You Spin Me Round (Like A Record)', 'Venus' and 'Girls On Film' and the next it would be back-to-back slabs of banging dance that had managed to explode on the dance floor of The Kitty Kat weeks before they became top five on iTunes. And the Club was all hers. Hers and Riley's.

'Another successful night then, angel, you should be proud of yourself.' The voice came from behind her as a pair of strong, solid arms protectively looped around her waist. Their touch was comforting and familiar. Riley.

'Laura looks like she is seriously enjoying herself as ever. Is any man safe?' He spoke softly, his lips dancing their way across Amy's neck as he did so. 'It seems everyone's having a good time. I see Grant Wilson is in the house ... not letting standards slips are we, Amy?' There was an air of jest about his tone, but it was somewhat outweighed by an obvious layer of dislike.

Amy turned to face her husband. 'Grant Wilson is a big draw for this place, despite what you think, Riley. He's one of the most popular actors on TV and having him shimmy his way across our Manchester dance floor instead of hanging out down south in London will only gain us extra column inches, so bite your tongue, big boy.' She placed two fingers on Riley's lips to emphasise her point.

'Doesn't stop him being a prize twat, does it? Don't like him, never will.' Despite his manly appearance there was more than a hint of childishness in Riley's voice.

'That's your opinion, Riley,' teased Amy, rising on tip-toe to kiss her husband's forehead. 'I know you were school rivals and that you can't stomach him, but business is business. If his PA keeps asking me to give him free membership to here then I am more than happy to have him here. His presence keeps The Kitty Kat Club leader of the pack for kudos. And anyway, he could never be as sexy as you, could he, so why don't you take your adoring wife out onto that heaving sweaty dance floor and show her a few moves of your own?'

It was true that The Kitty Kat Club was a heaving mass of bodies that night. People would look back on that evening for many moons to come and think about what had happened there. Amy herself would analyse it over and over again. But it had all happened so fast ...

She and Riley had danced together for most of the night. As joint owner of the club, it was important for Amy to be seen to be enjoying herself but, as ever, the needs of her customers came first. Especially the famous ones. Even if it meant bending the rules.

'Where do I go to buy some drugs in this place?' A sweaty, obviously drunk and yet still strikingly handsome Grant Wilson was clearly in the mood to party. His teeth were icy white and contrasted against the sun-kissed richness of his skin. Amy guessed the tan was out of a bottle but it suited him nevertheless. His fitted white shirt, damp with perspiration, clung tightly to his obviously sculpted frame. It was Savile Row and definitely this season. Amy couldn't help but notice it. It complimented the black Levi's he was wearing to perfection, a fusion of monochrome magic. But eighties it was not. *Maybe some people are too cool for a splash of retro,* thought Amy, before deciding to voice her opinions.

'It's great to have you here. But the dress code obviously passed you by.'

Grant laughed and spoke with a distinct air of cockiness. 'When my PA told me it was eighties night I did consider a *Miami Vice* rolled up sleeve and a perma-tan but I thought I'd leave that to Colin Farrell and Jamie Foxx. It suited them better.' He grinned broadly, an obvious mixture of alcohol and self-amusement, before adding, 'I may be working with Farrell soon. He's aware of my work, shall we say.'

'I'll be sure to recommend you next time he's in,' smiled Amy, contemplating that only someone as handsome as Grant could namedrop LA elite in such a cocky way and get away with it.

'Yeah, he wants me and Evie Merchant in his next flick apparently,' stressed Grant, proving Amy's point once more by throwing the name of one of Hollywood's top starlets into the mix. 'Anyway, I'm not the only one flouting your dress code. There are quite a few 2015 fashions in here. The likes of Genevieve Peters have been busy. Now, about these drugs?'

Amy knew what she had to do. Growing up on the rougher side of Manchester had taught her about the want for drugs even if it was something that neither she nor Laura had ever been tempted by. They could get high on an extended Britney remix.

But the equation of club culture plus celeb culture equalled drug culture and a streetwise Amy sprang into action. She had already done it for countless celebrities since the club opened two years earlier. 'I trust you're enjoying yourself.' There was definitely something charismatic about Grant. Amy could definitely see why the public adored the cocky actor, even if her husband clearly didn't.

'It's cool. Very. I've partied all over the world but I'll spread the word. Now, is it you I see about getting myself a little wasted?'

Amy nodded. 'It sure is ... follow me.'

She guided Grant to her office, raising her hand briefly on the way to gain the attention of a young woman standing on a mezzanine on the far side of the club. The action was slight but effective. The woman, knowing exactly what was required, followed Amy and Grant to her office.

'Grant, this is Lily Rich, a good friend of mine, part time DJ here at the club and the lady who owns the candy store, if you get my drift?' indicated Amy.

'Ah, I see drug dealers are much prettier in Manchester than the ones I'm used to down south,' smiled Grant, swaying a lot as he spoke, his voice more than a little slurred. Indeed, the woman standing in front of him was gamine in appearance with short, deep red hair close against her face and the largest, most inviting green eyes he had ever seen. She must have been about twenty-two. Her legs seemed to go on for forever, ending in a skirt barely an inch or two wider than a belt. She wore the tiniest T-shirt with a skull and crossbones logo on it and her face was smudged with a hint of make-up. To Grant, she looked strangely pure. 'What an angelic beauty. So what are you offering?' His tone was half-sleaze, half-drama, obviously bladdered.

Amy couldn't help but smirk at Grant's use of the word 'angelic' – she knew exactly what was coming next.

Right on cue, Lily launched into action. 'Okay, cut the bullshit. I'm not interested in your flirty crap, Mr Big Shot Actor off the TV. If you've got the cash then I have the drugs.' She stripped off her T-shirt and unhooked her bra, revealing a small yet perfectly formed pair of breasts, one with a pierced nipple. Grant's mouth fell open. He'd worked in enough theatres and shared enough backstreet dressing rooms before his TV success to have seen a woman undress before but Lily's actions still took him by surprise.

'What's the matter, you never seen a pair of tits before? Don't get excited. It's just where I keep my stash.'

She unzipped the back of the bra which had obviously been padded with her goods. She threw a selection of small plastic bags onto the table in front of the actor.

'I've got uppers, downers, Charlie, pills, Mandy, K and weed. I don't accept sexual favours so if you're thinking a quick bunk up in the bogs is decent payment then do one. Now take your pick ...'

Within seconds the deal was done and a semi-frightened Grant had paid for two bags of coke. He watched as Lily stuck her hand up her skirt and added his payment to a roll of notes she obviously had hidden in her knickers. Tucking the roll back where she found it, she placed her bra and T-shirt back on and marched from the room. 'See ya. Amy, if anyone else wants stuff you know where I am,' she called cheerily as the door shut behind her.

Grant was still stood open-mouthed as Lily disappeared from view. He was struck dumb for a number of minutes.

It was Amy who broke the silence. 'She's fun, isn't she? One of a kind. That was Lily Rich, but we prefer to call her 'Filthy' for obvious reasons ...'

Grant had no trouble understanding why.

As Amy escorted Grant back into the club again she saw Riley seated in one of The Kitty Kat's booths. The scowl that passed between her husband and the actor was obvious. Luckily for Amy, the smile Riley flashed her was sufficiently placatory to show that he didn't seem to mind Amy fraternising with his childhood rival. The customer always came first. And besides, Riley was obviously busy.

He was deep in conversation with a group of men who regularly spent time at The Kitty Kat. All of them were suited and looked darkly serious about their discussions.

One was Tommy Hearn. In his late forties, Amy had met him on many occasions. He and his wife, Jemima, had even dined at their house several times. Tommy had worked with Riley's dad, Cazwell Hart, when he was alive and Riley had worked with him ever since he took over the business.

Their dinner get-togethers were always dreaded by Amy. Riley and Tommy would disappear to talk 'the joy of plastics' while Amy would be left to entertain the exceedingly dull Jemima, whose idea of a good time was extolling the virtues of Tchaikovsky. If Amy had heard her say 'such a troubled man, tried to kill himself, died of cholera' once, she had heard it an overture-lasting million times. After a few hours with Jemima, Amy had often been tempted to join the composer and reach for the nearest weapon of destruction. There was just something about the woman that Amy couldn't gel with. She may have been from a different generation but to Amy she may as well have just landed from a different planet.

Amy had been surprised when she'd spotted Jemima in the club earlier that evening. To say that The Kitty Kat was out of Jemima's comfort zone was a huge understatement. She was definitely more pouty than party.

Alongside Riley and Tommy she could see Adam Rich, father of Lily aka 'Filthy' and husband of famed society glamourpuss, Caitlyn Rich, not that either of them knew of their daughter's narcotic sideline. As far as they knew, Lily was employed by Amy and Riley to garner PR for the club and to make sure everything ran beyond smoothly. Adam himself was anything but smooth. Bald and constantly unshaven he was rougher than a bricklayer's handshake. Amy had never seen him look happy. To Amy he looked like a man who would happily drown puppies with one hand while bottling a happy clapping do-gooder with the other. Amy had once asked Lily what her father did for a living. Her reply was straight to the point. 'Fuck knows, he's a businessman, whatever that means, but he earns enough to keep my mother up to her reconstructed chins in diamonds and designer frocks and a bloody good roof over my head so we're all happy. I could move out given the dosh I earn but I like my home comforts too much, even if my mother's taste in decor is more OTT than the whole of Dubai. She's started collecting mirrored statues for Christ's sake and putting them everywhere. She's always down in London buying them or having them commissioned. She's just moved a full-size *David*, covered in head to toe mirror mosaic into the entrance hall. It has a bloody mirrored cock! But I keep schtum and don't rock the boat. Nothing beats free rent and a team of maids cleaning up after you plus the best chef this side of Tom Aikens and Jamie Oliver at your beck and call.

Mother settles for nothing less and Daddy pays for it all. So who cares what the fuck he does for a living?'

The other man at the table was Winston Curtis, a huge slab of a man with skin the colour of liquorice. An e-cigarette constantly hung from his lips, a plume of swirling vape smoke drifting into the air. Despite the smoking ban that had come into place even before the club opened, Amy had always had to turn a blind eye to Riley's colleagues. Ciggies and cigars were banned but she bent the rules for vaping. Alongside 'Filthy' Lily's illegal stash it hardly seemed so bad.

Amy had always found Winston as charming as he was massive, adoring his bear hugs when he greeted her at the club. He'd worked alongside Riley for the last few years as his advisor. Anything Riley needed, from financial know-how through to the laws of hiring and firing, he was the man. He was rarely away from Riley's side.

Amy glanced at her watch. It was approaching 3am. The club normally started turning out about that time but tonight it showed no signs of slowing down. In fact it seemed fuller than it had done in ages. Maybe it was the mass of people that made recalling exactly what happened a few minutes later extremely difficult.

The first thing Amy heard was a scream. It seemed to be close to her. She spun round trying to locate its source but couldn't.

Suddenly the club erupted, screams pouring from every corner. People started to run across her path, heading nowhere yet everywhere at the same time. Panic reigned. Time seemed to stand still as people circled around Amy. Some fell, their bodies and faces trampled underneath a herd of designer footwear.

A forceful push slammed into Amy and she saw Laura's face in front of hers, her deep ruby lips curled into a scream. She was certain she heard the words 'get out of here' and then a loud crack, followed by another, or was it an echo? The two friends fell to the floor. As they fell, Amy was fairly certain she saw Grant, his animated face embossed with panic, diving behind an upturned table, then a flash of deep red blur passed ... was it Lily's hair or something more ominous? Amy couldn't be sure.

Amy stared across at the booth where her husband and his friends had been sitting. Smashed glass lay across the table. A splash of blood streaked its way up the wall behind the booth. The lifeless face of Winston Curtis stared back at her. Amy felt her throat run dry, all moisture sucked from within.

As the sound of screams still rang in her ears, Amy attempted to move the body that still lay on top of her. Why wasn't it moving? Deep down Amy already knew. As she rolled it away from her she saw a pool of blood stretching across Laura's back. She knew that her best friend was dead. Amy screamed as she'd never screamed before, every fibre of her body tortured.

Staggering to her feet she stumbled across the club to where her husband had been. Genevieve Peters, owner of famed Manchester fashion boutique, Eruption, lay on the floor, her manicured hands covering her face.

Amy needed to locate Riley. She found him face down on the booth table. Cold terror gripped her, its touch arctic. Knowing what she had to do, she lifted his head towards her. His face, what was left of it, was a mass of red, a trough of flesh and bone where her husband's beautiful features had once been. Shot away. Whatever had happened had been close range. It was clear that there had been no intention of missing. She blacked out and fell to the floor again.

CHAPTER 4

Then, after the carnage ...

'Can you identify the body as that of your husband, Mrs Hart?'

It was a line Amy had heard a million times before on TV crime dramas but nothing in life had prepared her for the earth-shattering moment when you're the person stood in front of the body under the ominous white cloth. Especially as it's pulled back to reveal the mangled face of the man who had just hours before shared all of your hopes and dreams. Despite the lack of distinguishing features on the face of the corpse in front of her and the regulation black suit he was wearing, something in Amy's heart had told her that the lifeless form was Riley. There was no alternative. She could give the body no more than a cursory glance, the pain of staring at his corpse stabbing her to her soul. She was looking into the broken shards of the reflection of her own shattered dreams. For a moment she considered looking further around the body, in search of a kidney-shaped birthmark on his toned stomach, the dimple just above his left knee. Signs of the body she loved, landmarks on an adoring journey that she had explored many times. But any desire to look more closely around Riley's corpse disintegrated as the sea of red and disfigurement she witnessed on the mortuary slab drowned her in a surging wave of sadness. Riley was gone, she needed to face the truth.

'It's him,' she stammered, her throat raspy and harsh, keen for the ordeal of what she was witnessing to be over.

That night had been the longest night of Amy's life. What had started as another happening evening at The Kitty Kat Club had ended in three deaths and countless injuries. Her husband, his right hand man and Amy's best friend all lay dead, lifeless mounds of mutilated flesh inside a Manchester mortuary.

The abject shock of it all kept slamming into Amy's brain, the total reality of it impossible to grasp, but for someone the night had obviously gone just as predicted.

Someone had planned this. Such barbarity had to be calculated in advance. Which was something Detective Inspector Daniel Chapman was keen to share with Amy as he stared across his desk at her a few hours after the massacre.

'We believe somebody wanted your husband dead and that unfortunately both Winston Curtis and Laura Cash were tragically caught up in the crossfire. If it's any consolation it would appear that all three of the victims would have died instantly. Do you know of any reason why your husband might have been targeted?'

His words felt hollow, somehow horribly routine. 'Detective Chapman, my husband has his own factory and co-owns one of Manchester's most popular nightclubs. He had money and was well known. Could it be some kind of attempted robbery?' *Why was she telling him the answers?*

'How much did you know about his businesses? Did he ever discuss his affairs with you?' Amy was sure she spotted a furrowing of Detective Chapman's brow and a quizzical narrowing of the eyes as he enquired.

'The club I know everything about, it's my baby. As for the factory, well, he sold sheet plastic, rods and tubing across the globe.'

The words scratched at her soul, cutting a feeling of deep annoyance. Why were they discussing the damn factory? Her husband's killer was still out there somewhere. 'Forgive me if I didn't ask about it on a daily basis, Detective. There's not exactly much to know, is there?' Her words were clipped, annoyance weaving through her reply.

Now, 2015

What was there to know? It was a question which suddenly seemed to ricochet around Amy's mind as she sat in her London apartment the day after receiving the letter from Riley all those months later. *What didn't she know?* Riley's job may have been a fruitful one but on an excitement level it hardly ranked up there with Bear Grylls, did it? Their life had been one of great excitement and glamour. Holidays in the most vibrant of European cities, safaris in South Africa, lazing on the sands of Ipanema, the powdery silkiness caressing her skin as she contemplated her next cocktail … work was rarely mentioned. Theirs was a life of pleasure, of togetherness, of love. There had been business trips, but Amy had never been involved. Why would she be? Who would really want to contemplate the joys of insulated lagging and PVC plastics when there were cobbled streets to explore and designer shopping to be done? Amy's mind took itself back to their first trip away together …

Then, 2006

'*Bienvenue* à *Paris!*' cried Riley, his voice enveloped in a mock Inspector Clouseau accent, as he and Amy walked into the lobby of their Parisian hotel. The large chandelier overhead seemed to twinkle, the golden crystal-covered cherubs hanging off every curving stem appearing to smile down at Amy as she took in the scene around her. It was truly magical.

The hotel – one of Paris's finest, Riley had informed her – was a mass of hot, shining gold and deep, dark, solid woods. Amy fell under its spell straight away. It was pure soap opera glamour. The splendour and sexiness of it all, the tiers of history embedded in each and every corner, the faces of scandalous Counts and coquettish Countesses looking down their regal noses from portraits hung on the walls. It was Amy's first trip to Paris, a place she had always dreamt of visiting when she was growing up and she loved it from the moment their plane had landed. She had always found French such a bewitching language, even with her own basic schoolgirl grasp of it, and to hear it spoken at every corner filled her with a Disney-like glee. It was truly *magnifique*. Didn't everything sound so much sexier in French?

The opulence of the hotel was just the beginning of the joy that she and Riley found together in the French capital over the next three days. Walks to the Louvre, hand in hand as they strolled through the leafy glades of the Jardin Des Tuileries, a Bateau Mouche trip and five star dinner sailing along the Seine, the breathtaking views from the top of the Eiffel Tower, the romance of the city laid out below them like toy bricks. Every moment was one to remember, another jewel in the crown that was their union.

Not that the trip had been all play. Riley was there for business, his empire spreading ever wider. And Amy was happy to show her support. To be by his side. Even when she actually wasn't.

On the second evening of their stay, Amy had spent hours alone while Riley headed to a meeting with some French company bigwig. Amy hadn't caught his name, and determined to make the most of her time in Paris, she hailed a cab and made straight for the Champs Élysées. There was shopping to be done and not *un moment* to be wasted.

As she strolled along the Champs Élysées, taking in the best of Paris's cutting edge *prêt-à-porter* with a wide-eyed excitement, Amy couldn't help thinking about Laura. For a moment she contemplated reaching for her mobile phone and contacting her, wanting to share the joy of the bold, floral catwalk delights she saw in the Tara Jarmon store. Laura would adore their wild, figure-hugging sexuality. Then there were the eclectic delights of Louis Vuitton and the exuberant bling of Cartier. Amy's animation grew with every turn of her head. Shopping in Manchester had always been something that she and Laura adored, Laura always happy to spend her parents' cash, but the high-end luxuries of the French capital were something beyond any of her teenage dreams. A chill of excitement passed through her as she thought about how far she had come. The journey from Manchester to Paris may have only been a couple of hours, but to a girl like Amy it was a million miles away from her humble beginnings growing up. Riley had made this possible. Being his wife was perfection – a role that she adored and she knew that he adored her too. Just thinking about him caused a ripple of carnal desire to pulsate within her. The timing was perfect. Amy was walking past the sensual, sexy shop front of one of the most inviting lingerie stores she had ever seen. She let out a slight gasp of anticipatory excitement as she stared through the window at the beautiful creations on display – sheer tulle and scallop-edged materials in soft pink hues, a provocative display of ribbons, satins and lace forming to create a sexual fairy tale enchantment that Amy couldn't resist. Unable to stop herself, she entered the boutique. She was immediately approached by a tall, bald-headed man, quite beautiful in appearance, dressed immaculately in a tight-fitting crisp white shirt and sporting a cravat around his neck. His look was pure Paris chic and his approach was accompanied by a waft of one of the most intoxicating aftershaves Amy had ever smelt. As fresh as a bouquet of summer blooms yet with a top note of deep masculine sexuality about it. If it smelt that good on the shop assistant then Amy could only imagine how delicious it would be on Riley.

'*Bonjour Mademoiselle, je m'appelle Didier, je peux vous aider?*' His voice was as rich as his scent.

'*Oui …je veux …*' Amy attempted to remember her comprehensive schoolgirl French. It wasn't forthcoming, her mind suddenly blank. Didier smiled, flashing a set of poker-straight white teeth, sensing her confusion.

'Would it be easier if I spoke English, Mademoiselle?'

'Er … please,' smiled Amy, thinking that her school French teacher, Mr Hawker, would be horrified that she had managed no more than three words before crashing and burning. But there was shopping to be done and language could not stand in the way. English it was.

'Thank you Didier,' said Amy. She immediately liked him. His manner was as pleasing as his attire. 'I am looking for something …' She hesitated before adding '… *un peu sexuelle* to wear for my boyfriend. Perhaps a negligee. Something simple yet feminine and frilly. Something *memorable* …' She left the sentence hanging, happy that she had attempted at least some kind of Franglais even if her French was rustier than a forgotten girder on the Eiffel Tower.

'Oh Mademoiselle, I have many delights to show you. If you would like to follow me,' grinned Didier, leading Amy to an army of mannequins located at the centre of the store. All of them sported the most fantastic array of intricate stitch work and iridescent fabrics. 'Now where shall we begin …?'

Amy inhaled again as the blanketing scent of Didier's cologne hit her nostrils. It was like an aphrodisiac, immediately lighting the touch paper of carnality within her. She felt a sense of awkwardness run through her as she felt herself becoming slightly turned on. Were her cheeks flushing in front of Didier? She hoped not, she'd hate to give him the wrong impression.

'Well you can start by telling me where I can buy that aftershave you're wearing too. It's just divine.'

Didier's face lit up at her question. 'I am so pleased you like it. It's "Babylon Pour Homme" by Montana Phoenix, the Hollywood star. It's in stock at the perfumerie my boyfriend runs just around the corner from here. I can direct you there afterwards if you wish. It has been selling like … what is the phrase the British use? We say *se vendre comme des petits pains* … I think you say *warm cakes, non* …?'

Amy giggled, any boudoir-talk awkwardness disappearing at the mention of Didier's boyfriend. 'It's *hot* cakes, Didier, hot … which is exactly what I want to be for my boyfriend tonight in one of your creations. Now, where do we start?'

Didier reached towards a rack of negligees alongside him and took the first one in his hands. The sheer fabric, dotted with ditzy embellished flowers was a work of art and Amy's eyes lit up immediately. Didier could already tell that both he and his boyfriend would be discussing how they had sold items to the pretty British tourist with the lucky boyfriend over dinner à *deux* that night. He was right.

Riley hadn't returned to their Paris hotel suite until the early hours of the morning. When he had, he found Amy asleep, her body seeming somehow tiny in the enormity of the hotel bed, wearing the most beautiful negligee. The flowery piece of femininity, something she had obviously bought in his absence that evening, had caused a lusting between his legs as he stared down at his beautiful wife. He felt his cock stiffen within his jockey shorts. It took all of his willpower not to wake her, lift up the material and work his way across the curves of her body. He felt pumped – business had gone well and making love to Amy would have been the perfect end to a profitable evening. But the serenity of Amy's repose stopped him. Wrapping his body around her, he lay down alongside her and allowed himself to sleep.

As Amy awoke a few hours later, the Parisian daylight already seeping into the room, Riley's body was still pressed close to hers. She immediately smiled, a ripple of intensity working through her. He was so sexy, all she'd ever wanted – *why hadn't he been back in time to enjoy the negligee as she'd intended?* Damn his business. *How much was there to say about plastics?*

Riley stirred and began to speak, as if he'd read her mind. 'Morning gorgeous, I am loving this ...' He tugged at the delicate fabric of the negligee, allowing his hands to move down its wave-like folds, and underneath the hemline, his fingers exploring the softness of Amy's thighs before dipping them into his desired destination of the heat between her legs.

Amy wasn't surprised at how wet she already was, she had been feeling horny ever since leaving the lingerie store the evening before. She let out a murmur of excitement as his fingers probed deeper.

'Where were you last night? I was waiting for you?'

'Let me make it up to you.' He manoeuvred his naked body into position. 'You'd be surprised what there is to know about the ever-turning cogs of business.' Amy was about to answer but her mind blurred as Riley eased his way inside her, the hardness of his desire filling her aching needs and rippling a spasm of nerve-tingling euphoria across her body. She gave herself over to pleasure. Whatever there was to know, she didn't need to bother about it just yet.

An unopened bottle of Babylon Pour Homme sat on the bedside table as the young couple rocked their way to orgasm. As Amy could feel her own release mounting she spied the bottle through eyes blurring slightly with the shuddering force of her oncoming climax. She made a mental note to make sure Riley was wearing it for their next sexual encounter. It would always remind her of Paris and it had definitely been a trip worth remembering.

'Oh my God, I love you, baby,' screamed Amy as her lover released a hot flow of sexual lava into her. She should have uttered the exultation in French but any grasp of the Gallic tongue was forgotten once again, having been replaced by the sweet, sexual language of love. It was a language she was happy to be fluent in.

CHAPTER 5
Now, the letter

Nothing made sense. The rantings of a dead man ... how the fuck ...?

'Amy – I'm writing this because I have to, I want to. I have to say sorry. A million times over. Sorry for the misery you've suffered, sorry for the confusion I'm about to cause, sorry for the heartache. Sorry for all of it. It shouldn't have been this way. You might never forgive me but I'm writing this for you, for *us*. Is there an us? I hope so. One day you might understand, but for now ...? I'm not who you thought I was, who I am. I'm wrong, bad.

I should be dead. It's what someone wanted that night in the club, that's clear to me. But I survived. One day I'll explain how. I've spent months thinking of how I'd say it to you.

"Remember the body you cremated Amy, well, it wasn't me ..." I thought of phoning but they'd trace the call and track my mobile. Hunt me down. They'd find me and realise they screwed up. They think they finished the job, Amy, but they didn't. Somebody's behind all this shit and I need help. No-one else knows, no-one, it has to stay that way, no police investigation ... nobody. The police can't help, they'd just make it worse.

Never doubt that I loved you, angel, never. I always did, right from the start, still do. But what happened at the club that night ... I'd seen it coming, bad things happen to bad people and I was the one who caused the deaths of Laura and Winston. I should have warned you. I shouldn't be here, one day you'll realise, maybe one day you'll forgive me.

You must find out who wanted me dead. I have to hide. I can't be with you even though I want to. I need you so badly, to make love to you, but they'd use you against me. Kill you too. I can't risk that. There's only you, Amy. Whoever killed poor Laura and Winston wants me out of the picture too. I was their target, I'm sure of it.

Laura, such a good friend, such a big part of our life. I'm so sorry. It sickens me.

That body wasn't me. It could have been so easily. I had to be quick, seize my chance. I saw my opportunity and took it. Had to make them believe they had succeeded ... at whatever cost, no matter who it hurt. It was the only way.

I'll explain one day. I'm so sorry. Sorry for it all. Sorry for what will happen. Sorry for making you relive it. Sorry for deceiving you. Someone knows the answer, someone wanted me dead.

Tommy, Adam, Lily, Genevieve, Grant ... none of them can be trusted, they all had their reasons for wanting me killed. Somebody at the club knew something. There's more I could say, but can't ... you will find out why. I want to tell you everything, let you know why this has happened but something inside is stopping me from writing it in a letter. It's so weak. So pathetic. So many secrets and lies. God, I hate myself for doing this to you, Amy. I should leave you alone, but I can't. But don't try and find me. Not yet, it's too dangerous.

I have to go. Can't risk them finding out. I have to post this. A letter, how old-fashioned, but I couldn't email or message. This seemed safer somehow. Less traceable. I need this to get to you before it's too late. One of them knows, one of them, maybe more ... they have their reasons, you see. So many reasons. They all could have done it, wanted me dead. Any of them. I don't know what else to say. Words aren't enough. I love you. So much.

Love Riley x'

Nothing made sense. Nothing. How could Amy have spent the last six months believing that her husband was dead? Why would he do that to her? Cause all of that heartache? Should she believe that he was still alive? Why would somebody she loved do that to her, somebody who professed to have loved her, to still love her? The letter was in his handwriting, but its author seemed panicked, crazed. Like a dog backed into a corner. A man on the edge. Not solid like Riley.

If the body wasn't Riley's then whose was it? Who had died? She tried to think of others that had been in the club that fateful evening. Somebody had lost their life? If it wasn't Riley, then who? But she'd seen it, hadn't she? There, slumped on the table ... a mass of tangled flesh and shot away bone. His image almost unrecognisable. *Unrecognisable ...*

It was then that Amy had her first wave of nausea-inducing 'maybe'. That instant that a spark of 'what if?' came into play. What if the body hadn't been Riley's? What if he was still alive? And if so, where the hell was he? She needed to find him.

A second question slammed her conscience. Why would anyone, especially somebody at The Kitty Kat Club that night, want him dead? Something didn't add up. But someone had killed her best friend Laura and killed a man they thought was her husband. Someone had made the last six months of her life edge-to-edge misery. And now she was being told that she was the only one who had any hope of finding out who. She owed it to Laura, to her friend who had shared so much with her, always by her side through everything, to try and delve deeper. To uncover the truth, no matter what revelations raised their ugly heads.

A third question hurtled into her brain ... *how?*

CHAPTER 6
Then, 2005

'So you think he may be *the one*, Amy?' teased Laura, flinging herself onto the zebra-print throw covering the king-size bed of their Brighton guesthouse room. It was to be their home for the weekend, a girlie couple of days away sampling the seaside delights of one of the UK's happiest towns. Two days of 'kiss me quick' British humour and fish'n'chips on the pier with enough cocktails thrown in to keep the girls' TV hero, Carrie Bradshaw, tottering around on her Manolo Blahniks for an NYC lifetime. And all paid for by Laura's loaded Costa del Sol parents.

As Amy landed on the soft faux fur, a swell of liquid escaped from the pink plastic champagne flute containing her Cosmopolitan, leaving a damp rosy stain on an otherwise monochrome canvas. The two friends had cracked open the glasses and a bottle of pre-mixed Cosmo before they had even found time to unpack their cases. Frivolities first, formalities later. 'He's a total peach in the photo you showed me, I'll give you that.'

Amy drained the last few drops from her glass and reached for a top-up as she considered the question. 'Well it's been three months since we met and I can definitely imagine spending a long time with Riley, maybe even a lifetime, so …' She winked before adding 'yep, I think he's the one!'

'Well I've certainly seen less of you since he came on the scene, Amy. He must be doing something right. I assume the sex is fan-bloody-tastic.'

Amy could feel her cheeks reddening at Laura's question. Even though sex was one of Laura's favourite subjects and a topic which she chose to research with as many men as possible given the chance, Amy still found it strangely embarrassing to discuss, even with her best friend.

A little loose-lipped from the Cosmo though, for once Amy could hear herself being remarkably candid. 'Let's just say that nights in are just as good as nights out, shall we?'

'A quick bunk-up in the back of his car in a side-street behind the plastics factory is working for you then is it?' smirked Laura.

'For your information, Laura Cash, his car is more than roomy but our sexual antics are not happening on the back seat of an Audi, thank you very much. And they're certainly not happening in some grotty road behind a factory. I've not even been there, to be honest. I'm channelling *Sex In The City*, not sex in an alleyway. I'll leave that to you.' Amy stuck out her tongue jokingly to prove her point.

Laura didn't take the bait. 'An Audi. That's a bit of a flash motor for somebody working in a factory isn't it? And a plastics factory at that. Not exactly a gusset-wetting kind of job is it? Give me a stuntman or a TV producer or a rock musician any day of the week.'

'That's because you are a fickle fucker,' laughed Amy, her tongue getting looser by the second. Pre-bottled Cosmos were obviously a little stronger than she realised. 'But you're right about the car, I did think it was a touch swanky for somebody who works in a factory. I assume he must have bought it on some kind of buy-now-pay-later deal, or maybe there's more money in his family than I realised. Not that it matters. He could drive a pony and trap for all I care, Riley Hart is a beautiful man and if you must know, the sex is beyond fabulous.'

'You lucky bitch! Here's to you and Riley, I can't wait to meet him,' said Laura, raising her pink glass in mock toast. 'And as for fabulous sex, well let's hope I can say the same after this weekend. The men in the wine bars of Brighton will not know what's hit them when I strut in. I'd like a little more sex than I'm getting right now. Which reminds me ...' Laura skilfully shuffled her way across the bed, pouring herself another glass of Cosmo as she pulled herself along by her feet, dragging her backside. It was girlie multi-tasking at its finest. Not a drop was spilt this time round. 'Pulling outfits for tonight.' She kicked open the lid on her suitcase with her bare foot and stared down at the two dresses lying on the top. 'So do I plump for the mega tight ruby-red body-hugger with the glittery finish or the little black sexy number with the Marilyn-inspired Prom-style skirt? I need to look my best. My future husband could be parking his Porsche on the seafront as we speak!'

Amy scanned her eyes over the two dresses. From where she was sitting they both looked like they would make any potential husband fall to his knees in submission. She had no doubt that Laura could pull in either. 'I thought you were seeing someone at the moment.'

'I kind of am, but he's kind of busy a lot and kind of complicated, so I kind of don't want to talk about him. Let him miss me,' deadpanned Laura. 'And the UK seaside is *always* full of plenty more fish.'

Amy made her decision about Laura's dress. 'Go for the black. It matches your soul. Dark, dirty and perfect for trapping another man. The red one is gorgeous but if we drink any more of this Cosmo then the only thing it will match is your eyes.'

'Decided. Black it is. And as for the Cosmo, sister, I'm afraid the cupboard is bare.' She upturned the empty bottle in her hand to emphasize the point. 'Now let's hit the shower and then hit the town. I'll be damned if the only ride I get this weekend is from a sodding donkey trotting up and down the beach. It's all right for you with Mr Plastic Fantastic and sex on tap but I intend to make hay while the sun shines. And from where I'm stood it's a scorcher out there.' Laura looked out of their bedroom window to check the weather. The sky was azure and cloudless.

An hour later, fuelled by more cocktails, the two young women were enjoying the start of their weekend away in a Brighton seafront bar. A video screen in the corner was playing the latest song by Eminem. Amy stared at the screen from the stool she was perched on by the bar. The song was one of Riley's favourites. It made her smile but with a tinge of sadness. She was missing him. Not that she'd admit that to Laura. She was here for her girlfriend, the last thing she would 'fess up to would be missing her fella. And Laura didn't need to know that she'd already texted Riley a good dozen times since arriving at the bar. He'd only answered once, obviously busy with work.

Where was Laura exactly? Amy swivelled her bar stool around and gazed across the bar. It was pretty full. She spotted Laura in a far corner. She was talking to a heavily muscled man with skin the colour of chocolate. She laughed animatedly as she did so. Amy smiled to herself. Laura was out of the starting trap and obviously in full pulling mode.

Sensing Amy watching her, Laura waved across at her and moved in her direction. She led the man by the hand and introduced him to Amy. 'This is Cain, personal trainer to the stars. He's working with somebody who had bit parts in *Nip/Tuck* and *Peregrine Palace* right now and with some of the celebs from *Ward 44*. How cool is that?'

Amy shook his hand, already knowing where Laura's new rendezvous was heading. Anybody who had any connection to a show that Laura idolised – a worldwide smash soap opera or the UK's top medical drama – was definitely top of her friend's hit list.

It was something Amy was keen to discuss with Laura a cocktail later as Cain headed to the toilets. 'So, I'm guessing that I'll be on my own in the guesthouse tonight then, will I?' It was to be expected.

'Not sure as yet, Amy' stated Laura, her words a little slurred. 'But if his wallet is as big as his biceps then the signs are promising. You'll be okay though won't you? You can spend all night speaking to new beau Riley on the phone. You'd love that.'

From anybody else it may have come across as patronising but not from Laura. There was an honesty about Laura that Amy had always loved, despite the consequences it sometimes meant for her herself on their nights out. Men before mates seemed to be a mantra that Laura had no problem living up to.

'But the jury's out for the moment. It may still be you, me and a kebab on the way home,' laughed Laura.

As Amy suspected, it wasn't. Having discovered that Cain's wallet was indeed as sizable as his muscles and that his car was parked within high-heel tottering distance from the venue, Laura's last words to Amy as she left the bar, waving Cain's car keys in her right hand, were, 'Can you fucking believe it, Amy, he's only driving a freaking Porsche!'

Two hours later when Amy was back in her guesthouse bed snuggled down under the zebra-print reading a Jackie Collins and texting Riley with increased regularity, she finally received another message from Laura. It said she'd be back in the morning and was 'testing Cain's largest muscle' to full capacity. She eventually turned up back at the guesthouse nearly twenty-four hours later, the girls' weekend nearly over. The smudged mascara around Laura's eyes was as black as the dress she'd been wearing.

'I'm exhausted, doll. That man can give any girl a workout I tell you. Do you mind if I crash for a bit? I'm wrecked.'

As it happened, Amy didn't. She'd planned to play text-tennis with Riley on the phone tonight for as long as his busy work schedule would allow and she still had a few chapters of her Jackie Collins to finish. Laura was sleeping like a baby by the time Amy picked up the novel. She was still out for the count as Amy read the final juicy word and texted Riley to say that she imagined that they would both be home a little earlier than planned the next day. Providing Laura didn't hook up again of course.

CHAPTER 7
Now

Having analysed every inch of the letter over and over again, a petrified Amy had tried to relive the last six months. Everything from identifying her husband's body through to organising the small yet intimate cremation service – astonishingly small actually.

Amy had been surprised at how many people had chosen not to come – many of Riley's work colleagues saying that they couldn't bear to see such a great man gunned down so young. For such a seemingly tough bunch, Amy had found their actions rather weak.

Tommy and Jemima Hearn had been there, watching Riley's coffin disappearing behind the crematorium's red curtain. They hadn't shed a tear. It didn't surprise Amy that Jemima hadn't. She seemed grey and harsh, devoid of any warmth and certainly of any love for the man they were cremating. Her tweed jacket and skirt mix and her hair scraped back severely off her face lent her an austere look, her skin pulled so tight that any flow of tears would have been cut off at the source, not allowed to run freely from eyes stretched out of shape. Amy had expected Tommy to show some kind of emotion. He and Riley were good friends, *more* than just colleagues weren't they? But there was nothing. Amy, still frail from the loss of her husband, had been too weak to question it. It had taken all of her strength to force herself out from under her duvet, apply a face of make-up and dress for the service. She had never felt so alone.

The service itself was short yet sweet. Amy had chosen Queen's 'Who Wants To Live Forever?' to be played as Riley's coffin departed. It was one of his favourite tunes and one that he had admittedly 'murdered' many times as he sang it whilst showering. Tears cascading down her face, Amy couldn't help but hear Riley's totally tuneless version playing in her mind as she watched the last corner of his coffin disappear from view. She would have given anything to hear him sing it just once more and for him to appear, dripping wet from the shower, his body glowing from the heat of the power jets and glistening with vitality. But it was not to be. Despite what Amy had always believed, Riley was not to live forever.

The cover of the order of service showed two photos. One of a besuited Riley, handsome and strong, looking as he had done on the night of his death, the ultimate businessman. The other showed a younger Riley alongside his mother, a woman who had died of cancer when Riley was in his teens and never had the chance to see what an upstanding man he had become. His mother, named Bianca, was a woman with kind features and a softness to her face. Amy and Riley had talked about Bianca a lot and Riley had shared his memories of what she was like. She was all about family, caring for her son and husband. The protective arm placed across Riley's teenage shoulders in the photo showed a woman who would do anything to guard her offspring. Amy could feel another onslaught of tears pricking at her eyes as she looked at the photo, wondering if Bianca would have been able to save Riley had she managed to survive the cancer. Would his late father, Cazwell, have been able to save his son either, had he not died? Amy also couldn't help but wonder if there had been more that she herself could have done to protect her husband.

She knew the answer was no but still couldn't stop her imagination from racing into overdrive and mulling over what ifs.

The tears flowed. Amy watched as one of them tumbled from the end of her nose and fell onto the order of service she was holding in her hands. It landed on the poem that Amy had chosen to include. *Death Is Nothing At All* by Henry Scott Holland. The words said everything to Amy and served a dual sentimentality as she knew that Riley had insisted that they used it for Bianca's funeral. It was a poem that she had read many times to a young Riley, during her illness, explaining how death was not to be treated as something so sad, it was merely somebody we loved 'slipping away into the next room'. Amy hadn't heard of it before Riley telling her but she found it beautiful and completely befitting now that he himself had slipped away. It was a shining star of beauty in a blackened sky of woe. But as Amy was taxied away from the funeral, her tears still dampening her face, she knew that death wasn't 'nothing at all'. Death was seeing her husband's body on a mortuary slab with his beautiful features blown off beyond recognition. It was an image that would always haunt her.

Night after night following the funeral Amy hardly slept, images of the carnage at the club suffocating her mind. The Kitty Kat that she knew she would have to reopen and soon if she were to try and keep it at the top of its game. But would people go there now, a place where so much badness had happened? It was supposed to be a place of excitement and happiness, one of carefree elation where all worries could be forgotten to the hardcore beat of a clubland tune, not a place where people would whisper 'that's the corner where so and so had their face blown off' or 'that's where the owner's best friend bled to death'. It would be a destination for the macabre and Amy couldn't bear that. Did anyone ever visit Hollywood's The Viper Room and not still think 'this is where River Phoenix breathed his last', even decades after his untimely death?

Amy had been business-minded enough to keep everybody on the payroll at the Club for the moment. Lily had been brilliant at cancelling all upcoming bookings and DJ residences and generally dealing with everything that needed to be done. There would be a reopening, of that Amy was sure, but that would be a long time into the future. For now, everything was too raw. Amy was too weak. She felt as if she was in the middle of a breakdown, not capable of dealing with the things that life was throwing at her. She'd not even been able to attend Laura's funeral or indeed that of Winston Curtis. She sent flowers but standing at the graveside of her best friend and staring at her beautiful face on an order of service was not something she could face. Not yet … It would tip her over the edge. Laura had been so important to her yet a piece of her own heart still wasn't able to take the pain of seeing her best friend buried.

It was about a week after Riley's funeral that Amy had had to muster up the energy to head to the reading of his will. There was business to be discussed and she needed to be there. Not just for her own interests in the Club but also for the factory. There was nobody to carry on the family business and Amy knew that she would have to step up to the plate to try and make sure that the legacy of Riley, and his father Cazwell before him, lived on.

Tommy and Jemima had been present at the reading of Riley's will too. That was no surprise to Amy as work matters would doubtless be discussed and Tommy's attendance had been expected. But there was something about Jemima being there that really irked Amy. She knew that her own brain was still a scribble of emotions from the loss of Riley and Laura, but something unsettled Amy further from the moment she entered the room where Tommy and Jemima were already seated. Amy was immediately struck by how different Jemima looked, her stony face from the funeral somehow erased. She wasn't exactly cheery but there was definitely an air of smugness about her. As Amy took her seat, she nodded a courteous but automatically cautionary hello to Tommy and his wife. As the reading was about to commence she couldn't help but spot a dry, sardonic pouting of the lips and a raised eyebrow place itself across Jemima's stretched face. At the time she wasn't sure why but as the reading unfurled it became clear. Both Jemima and her husband obviously knew something that Amy didn't. As the last will and testament of Riley Hart was read aloud to the three people gathered, Amy's already crumbled life turned into a pile of powder-fine ashes.

'And to Tommy Hearn and his wife, Jemima, I leave all of my business affairs, including ownership of The Kitty Kat Club.' The voice, devoid of emotion and matter of fact, had belonged to the executor. It had stunned Amy to the core, the word *all* smashing into her brain

Amy leapt to her feet, stumbling slightly on the Gucci heels she had chosen to wear for the reading. Having assumed that there would be business to discuss, she had chosen a killer heels and charcoal Calvin Klein business suit combo to give her an air of gravitas. Even if inside she was marshmallow soft. Judging from what she'd just heard she may as well have worn ripped jeans and a food-stained T-shirt.

'Hang on a minute, The Kitty Kat is my club. Riley and I opened it together. He would never have left it to them.' She turned to face Tommy and Jemima, pointing an accusatory finger as she did so. She spied that a wry smile had now sneaked its way across Jemima's lips. It defined smug. Had the formalities of probate somehow been greased? Was there some kind of underground trickery going on?

'Why would he leave it to you two?' asked Amy. 'Riley always knew that The Kitty Kat was my dream.' Her voice petered out, weakness already taking its toll once again.

Rising to their feet, Tommy and his wife linked their hands, evidently striving for a united front, nodded to the executor and made for the door.

'Well he has, we'll leave it at that, shall we?' was Tommy's parting shot, not a trace of remorse dotting his voice. 'It'll be in good hands, don't worry.' Jemima raised her hand and waved mockingly as they exited.

Amy sank into her chair as she watched them leave the room. Disbelief smothered her. That had been the last time she had seen Tommy and Jemima. Within days they had installed themselves at The Kitty Kat, changed the locks, ripped down the pink neon sign outside and employed a team of builders to turn it into a casino. The Kat had been neutered.

Amy would have fought, but there it was, as plain as day on the will. Riley had left it to Tommy and Jemima, along with his factory building. Within six weeks the Hearns had sold the factory. All that Amy had been left with was the house in Sale. But even that was a poisoned chalice – the mortgage payments were through the roof and with no income coming in, Amy was advised to sell up at a loss and downsize. Her life had gone from flash to trash in just a matter of weeks. Any fight and strength that she had once possessed had been punched from her in the aftermath of Riley's death. With the little money she had that was hers, savings she had managed to build up during her all-too-brief marriage to Riley, she left for London and a new beginning. It may not have been the wisest choice given the cost of living but Amy chose it as she needed to still feel part of something alive when so much around her was dead. London was vibrant and exciting and in the back of her mind she needed to feel that one day maybe she could sample another piece of the action, the glamour that she'd had with the The Kitty Kat Club. There was still a flicker of a dream in the back of her mind. But the dream had become a nightmare. She had rented a small one-bedroom flat and made extra cash by flogging her once prized designer gear on eBay. Needs must when the devil drives and the devil was definitely not driving the kind of car she'd been used to with Riley.

Now the new beginning was looking like it was heading for a U-turn. Riley had mentioned Tommy's name on the letter and it was clear that Tommy and Jemima had definitely had a lot to gain from Riley's death, especially if they'd known that Riley was leaving them pretty much everything in his will. But wouldn't that have been kind of obvious? And *surely* the police would have investigated that?

The police had gone quiet about the whole investigation almost overnight. At the time Amy had thought that their apparent disinterest in following anything up relating to the murders of her husband and best friend was down to a lack of evidence. Who was she to question? If they had no clues, then all they could be was indeed clueless.

For a while she had chased DI Chapman about it, desperate to know the truth but then she'd been told that he'd moved on. The woman on reception she had spoken to on the phone at the station was evidently a fresh rookie and was seemingly more than a little impressed that she was speaking to the former owner of The Kitty Kat Club. It had made her a little bit more talkative than perhaps a police station worker should be. Amy had no sooner introduced herself than … bam, off she flew.

'I loved your club, I tried to buy tickets when Jason Derulo did a PA there. And when you had Scott Disick from the *Kar-*

dashians in town. But I failed miserably both times. Were they nice people? They seem like it?'

Amy was a little bamboozled by the girl's enthusiasm and tried to cast her mind back to when the two stars had appeared. 'Er … yes, they were. Especially Jason,' she fudged.

'That body of his is off the hook insane. I wouldn't mind him being arrested and brought in here, I tell you.' The rookie laughed at her own joke. 'So, you're after DI Chapman. You're out of luck. He's not here. Can anyone else help?'

'When will he be back?' enquired Amy.

There was a pause. And then a hushed reply. 'Well, to be honest he won't be, which is such a shame, as he was always one of the fittest blokes in here.'

'He won't be back? Are you sure?' stumbled Amy.

'He's moved on. Apparently there was talk of some kind of major promotion to a top earning job at the other end of the country somewhere – not sure where. Such a shame. We've all been talking about it.' She stopped in full flow before heading off on a tangent. 'So I assume you won't be opening the club again then? I loved the sound of your theme nights – eighties, gay, hard-house. I wanted to try them all.'

Amy hastily ended the call. She was never told who replaced DI Chapman. At the time she wasn't strong enough to think any more about it and tried to concentrate on her new life. A life without Riley. But now, if he was alive, then she knew that she would have to try and investigate who had attempted to kill him and, more importantly, try to find the man she loved.

She would have to return to Manchester. The letter had come from there. But why would she be able to fare any better than the police? And just six months on from Riley's supposed death was she really yet strong enough to cope with what she might find?

CHAPTER 8
Then, 2001

'If you don't understand something, Amy Barrowman, then you should say so. You'll never amount to anything if you don't start asking questions.'

The voice was angry and belonged to Mr Hawker, Amy's weak-chinned French teacher at the Stephen Hague Comprehensive School in Manchester's Moss Side, a place where Amy begrudgingly found herself Monday to Friday for most of her teenage life. School was not something she enjoyed, to be honest. There were too many things that needed answers, that warranted questions, that required Amy to engage her brain on subjects that didn't really interest her and Mr Hawker was right, fourteen-year-old Amy Barrowman didn't really ask a great deal of questions.

'Stand up, Barrowman.' Mr Hawker was waving Amy's homework at her from the front of the classroom where the rest of the class were eagerly waiting to see what happened next. 'The homework was to write an essay on the delights of French cuisine, as in the marvellous world of French cooking. I was imagining a report on *Flamiche* and *confit de canard*, on *cuisses de grenouilles* and *escargots*, not the fact that your kitchen at home has flowery wallpaper and a tiny breakfast bar that won't fit you and your parents at the same time. What were you thinking?'

Amy watched as a few drops of spittle shot from Mr Hawker's mouth as he reprimanded her. He was not an attractive man and reminded Amy of Mr Garrison from *South Park*, one of her TV guilty pleasures that she loved to watch on her small portable in the privacy of her own bedroom at her parents' council flat back home.

'I just heard you say cuisine, sir, and I thought you wanted a report on our kitchen at home,' offered Amy sheepishly. The sound of giggles erupted from her classmates.

'You thought? You thought? You don't think further than the end of your nose, Barrowman.'

'But I didn't understand what we were supposed to do.' Amy tried to interject.

'So you ask me. I set this homework last week. That's seven days ago, girl. Surely even you might think to ask in that time if you don't understand something. You can redo it for next lesson. And this time I want to know about the fineries of French food, not flaming Formica worktops. *Tu comprends?*'

Amy gave a meek '*oui*' in response and sat down once again as Mr Hawker handed her the essay back, a sea of red pen slashed across it. Her mind drifted off as she stared at the clock at the front of the classroom, willing away the minutes until the end of the lesson and home time.

'I thought you'd already completed that French homework,' said Enid Barrowman, as her daughter bent double over their kitchen breakfast bar writing into her folder, a bank of books and dictionaries spread out either side of her.

'I did, but I misheard the teacher and ended up writing about the wrong thing, so I have to do it again,' said Amy without looking up.

'You never listen, always in a world of your own, aren't you, young lady?' I don't know, what are we going to do with you?' Enid came and stroked her daughter's hair, which was a deep shade of brown streaked with blonde hair dye she had bought Amy from the local market. Enid adored her daughter, who reminded her of herself when she was a young teenager. 'Have you nearly finished? Are you off out tonight? It is Friday so no school tomorrow.' There was genuine interest in her voice.

'Five more minutes and I'll be done.' Again Amy didn't look up. 'Then I'm going to my room. I want to play my music.'

'What are you locking yourself up for yet again? All you do is sit in your room and play your CDs. You should be out with the other girls, having fun and …' Enid hesitated before adding '… meeting boys.' Even without Amy looking up, Enid could see her daughter's cheeks colouring a deep shade of ruby red. The opposite sex was never Amy's favourite topic of conversation.

'Right, I'm done.' Amy slammed her French folder shut before grabbing it with her other books and running off to her room. 'See you later, Mum.' Enid sighed as she watched her daughter's bedroom door slam and heard the first burst of one of Amy's CDs pulsate through the wall.

'What's the racket?' said Ivor Barrowman, walking into the tiny kitchen about thirty seconds later. 'I can hear that in the front room. It's putting me off *Mr Bean*.'

'It's Amy playing her music again. That girls spends too much time in her room.'

It was true. Amy did spend a lot of time in her room. But it was her favourite place. While other girls her age chose to spend their time meeting boys on graffiti-plastered corners of the council estate she and her parents lived on, she would much rather ensconce herself in her bedroom surrounded by the things that made her truly happy. Her CDs and her DVD player that her mum and dad had saved up for months to buy her for her thirteenth birthday.

Who needed the rough boys on the estate offering her cigarettes, a spliff, a love bite or a quick finger behind the wheelie bins when she could surround herself with the much nicer charms of The Backstreet Boys, Usher and Enrique Iglesias as they stared down from the posters that decorated her bedroom walls? They wouldn't let her throw her life away with a teen pregnancy and a lifetime of benefits and trips to the job centre to try and make ends meet. Amy had seen it happen to lots of girls on the estate where she lived. It was a tired old tale. She didn't criticise them, if it made them happy then great, but when she finished her days at school she didn't want to think that life stopped at the corner shop where she did her paper round.

It was that paper round that allowed her to buy her CDs. She'd bought the new one by Britney after seeing her cavort around with a snake on the VMA Awards on TV. What a girl. Amy would love to be like her when she grew up. And she was definitely going to buy the first single by that group put together on the *Popstars* TV show that she tuned into every week. She'd practised being just like them in front of the mirror, singing into her hairbrush and flicking her fringe to the beat.

Music was where Amy could lose herself. It took her to amazing places, to highs that no inner-city estate spliff could ever do. There was such a wealth of fabulous songs out there. She'd bought a *Music Through The Decades* CD set from a local charity shop. It was the best 50p she'd ever spent. Each of the four discs housed a collection from eras before her time. The swingy girliness of the sixties, the glam rock of the seventies, the poppy joy of the eighties and the raving dance of the nineties. Amy loved them all.

Her friends mocked her at school, said that she shouldn't be listening to that 'old shit' when she tried to teach them about it. One or two agreed with her but in general it was a case of 'that's what my granny used to listen to, give me The Chemical Brothers any day of the week.' Couldn't they see that there was so much joyous, awe-inspiring music to choose from? A history of harmonies.

Music was fourteen-year-old Amy's world and even though she didn't have a huge amount of friends, even though she didn't have tastes that everyone agreed with and even though she didn't always get it right in French at school, or in any lesson for that matter, she would show them all.

Amy lay back on her bed and listened to her eighties CD. The Bros tune 'When Will I Be Famous?' came on. Apparently they were like a UK Backstreet Boys back in the day. Great tune. She shut her eyes and imagined herself dancing along to the energising beat.

What was it Mr Hawker had said to her earlier? That she'd never amount to anything. He could shove his French cuisine where *le soleil* didn't shine. She promised herself that the one thing he would be eating in the not too distant future would not be a plate of snails or a portion of frogs' legs, it would be his own words. As would everybody.

CHAPTER 9
Now, 2015

Staring out the train window as it pulled into Manchester's Piccadilly Station Amy felt a canvas of sadness envelop her. She knew it would. It was her first time back since she'd lost Riley and Laura and everything reminded her of them. Things they'd seen. Places they'd been. Moments they'd shared. Bittersweet tears, a fusion of happy laughter-filled memories and sadness about moments never to be repeated.

As Amy descended from the train, her suitcase bumping down the stairs as she pulled it behind her, she took a deep breath and felt the frostiness of the November air hit her face. It stung slightly and parking her case to one side for a few moments she adjusted her scarf and hat, pulling it into place to cover as much exposed skin as possible. The air was biting, a wind blowing down the platform causing the fringed ends of her scarf to ripple in the breeze. It was a Liska scarf that Laura had given her for her last but one birthday. She adored it and just the feel of its fleeciness reminded her of Laura. It comforted her and was one of the few good things about the onslaught of winter; it gave her the chance to wear it again. It was one of her few designer items that she had not attempted to sell in order to pay her rent.

The iciness of the air was a complete contrast to the large blazing globe of deep-orange sunshine that shone out from a poster across the platform from Amy. It advertised a local travel company that specialised in 'wild and wonderful' holidays. Immediately it transported her back. How many years was it? Four? Five? It was the company that she and Riley had used to travel to South Africa with, on one of their glorious holidays together as man and wife.

Just seeing the poster brought it all back. Safari Vacations, for those who like to walk on the wild side …

Then, 2011

'So on behalf of Safari Vacations, may we welcome you to Inverdoorne, one of South Africa's most popular game reserves and a place where today on safari you will be able to see the big five, that's if they're playing ball of course. If we know one thing about animals, it's that they do what they want when they want.'

'What's the big five?' whispered Amy to Riley, her hand in his as they stood listening to the guide currently filling them in about what the day ahead held for them.

'According to the website it's the five animals that were originally said to be the most challenging to hunt in Africa but have now become the most sought after creatures to see on safari. There's the lion, elephant, buffalo, rhino and …' He paused, obviously trying to recollect the fifth which seemed to be escaping him.

'I'll take you as the fifth, especially looking so hot in those shorts,' grinned Amy. 'You suit the camouflage look and you certainly bring out the animal in me, Riley Hart.' She moved her hand from his and placed it across his backside, giving one of his buttocks a playful squeeze, much to the amusement of a middle-aged rotund lady from Bedford who was standing behind them. The woman had been on the same flight as them from Manchester out to South Africa, having booked with the same company.

'Get a room you two,' she joked. 'You're upsetting the wildlife.'

Riley turned to face her and mouthed the word 'sorry'. He wasn't, just the mere touch of Amy's hand turned him on.

But the safari came first. 'Easy, tiger!' he smiled, taking Amy's hand in his once again.

'Is that the fifth of the big five, then ... a tiger?' asked Amy.

'No, it's the leopard,' he said, finally remembering what he'd read on the website. 'And hopefully today we will see them all.'

The voice of the safari guide filled the hot, dusty African air again. 'So if you'd all like to follow me to the jeeps we can start the safari and attempt to find some animals for you.'

'And hopefully some sun too,' said Amy. 'I thought it was going to be blisteringly hot out here.'

'It will be,' replied Riley as they walked towards the fleet of jeeps awaiting them. 'The web said it would be cold in the morning and seeing as it's just a little after 7am it's no surprise really. Give it a couple of hours and the sun will be beating down. In the meantime, I'll just have to warm you up, won't I?' He pulled Amy towards him, wrapping his arms protectively around her. 'And there are blankets in the jeep if you're too cold so we can always spread them over ourselves if need be.'

'As long as I can slip my hand underneath the blanket and play with your "big five" if you get my drift. There must be something about the safari experience that brings out the animal in me. I've been horny ever since waking up.'

'We'll sort that out later, don't you worry,' said Riley, planting a kiss on Amy's forehead as he pulled her even closer. 'Now, *big five* … you cheeky bugger. I think we know I'm a lot bigger than that, don't we? I'm thinking the 'big nine' would be more apt, don't you?' He laughed as they settled into their seats on the jeep.

'Too much info, you two! Keep it in your pants.' It was the rotund lady again who was now seating herself behind them. 'And FYI, I've not been horny ever since I woke up, I've just been ravenous. They do feed us on this trip, don't they?'

Amy and Riley could both feel their cheeks reddening as the jeep's engine burst into life and they headed off to start the safari.

It was hours later that they finally returned to their on-site guesthouse. The day had been an amazing one and there had been food, much to the enjoyment of the lady from Bedford, but not even the delights of a Harrods hamper could have compared with the animals that Amy and Riley had witnessed during the day. They had seen a female rhino enjoying the first drink of the day with her young calf, a herd of zebras excitedly skipping along, their movements almost choreographed with the skill of a professional dancer and even a couple of hippos lazily wallowing in water to try and escape the ferocity of the overhead sun. Add that to the oryx, wildebeest and springbok they had seen and it made for the perfect day.

Amy's favourite had been seeing the lions in the wild. Their proud manes and silky coats entranced her with their deadly beauty. She'd longed to get up close to them but was savvy enough to know that these were no friendly moggies looking for a stroke and a purr-inducing tickle behind the ear. These were killers, beasts who ruled the lands they strolled.

Amy's dreams of touching the wildlife did come true though during a moment that had become the highlight of her day so far, a moment that she was discussing with Riley as they lay on their backs staring up at the night sky behind their Bedrock-style guest-house. It was a luxury chalet that any Fred and Wilma would have been proud to call their home.

'Can you believe we were able to stroke the cheetahs? That was so amazing!' squealed Amy, still high from the experience and the bottle of champagne she and Riley had enjoyed over dinner. 'It was incredible to see them walking so tamely with their handlers. How wonderful of the people here to rescue and rehabilitate cheetahs that might not have lived had they not been saved. What a rewarding job. I couldn't believe we were actually able to stroke them. I could so work here.'

'Not thinking of leaving me, are you?' remarked Riley, his voice traced with a hint of worry.

'They were fabulous but I'd rather stroke you any day of the week. Your bite is pretty sensational.' Amy ran her hand across her T-shirt and let it rest on her right breast. She could feel her nipple stiffening as she rubbed her finger gently across it. It was still a little bit tender from where Riley had been nibbling it with his teeth during an afternoon sex session they had enjoyed the moment they had arrived back at the guesthouse. Given the horniness Amy had been experiencing all day and the flower petals sprinkled liberally across the bed, the mood was one hundred per cent sexual and it had been mere seconds before they had both shed their safari clothes and made love. Their movements were frenzied and urgent, almost animalistic, the subject matter of the day perhaps influencing them sub-consciously. Riley had feasted on her body, allowing his tongue to dive straight into the sugary folds of her wetness, searching to quench his sexual thirst in the same way a parched beast would seek out the nearest watering hole. His own appetite satiated, Riley had moved his mouth to Amy's breasts, feasting on the rosy pink buds he found there. Mixing the ferocity of a lion with the tenderness of a baby kudu, one of the many antelopes that roamed across the plains of Inverdoorn, he had expertly taken her peaks between his teeth as he ploughed the hardness between his legs into her. Their orgasms combined as Amy let out a howl of exultation worthy of a hyena.

'You all right there?' asked Riley, noticing Amy's hand on her breast.

'I was thinking about your bite. My boob is still quite tender, not that I am complaining. That was sensational, you were like a man possessed.'

'Possessed with love for you, yes. Now check out these stars. Have you ever seen anything so crystal clear?'

'Never,' mused Amy. She and Riley had spent the last half hour lying on a towel on the floor outside the back of their guesthouse, as suggested by Inverdoorn's staff. The night sky was pitch black but the stars and constellations dotted across the sky were sparkling unlike anything Amy had ever seen. Like rhinestones placed upon a sheet of the most luxurious black velvet. It was magnificent.

'They're not like this over Manchester, are they?' questioned Riley.

'Nothing could outshine you, my love,' said Amy, her voice purring with suggestion.

Riley spotted it straight away. 'What are you after, Amy Hart? Are you trying to butter me up, young lady?'

'I was just thinking about those cheetahs again. How do you think they'd look at the house in Sale?' Amy smirked to show that she was joking.

'I'll buy you a concrete one to put by the front gates, all right?'

'But I want a kitty cat,' mocked Amy. 'A nice big one.'

'Then that's what you shall have, my angel. The biggest kitty cat in Britain,' replied Riley, rolling over to plant a kiss upon her lips. 'I promise.'

As Amy walked away from the travel poster and out of Manchester's Piccadilly Station to the nearest taxi rank, she let herself smile. Riley had given her the biggest kitty cat of all, The Kitty Kat Club. He'd kept his promise. But now it was gone, taken from her, as was he. And she needed to see whether that was about to change.

CHAPTER 10
Now, 2015

'Well, there's a face I thought I'd never fucking see round here again. What the frig do you want?'

The blunt, joyless churlish welcome wasn't entirely unexpected by Amy. Considering the last time she'd seen Tommy Hearn had been at the reading of Riley's will, she had not exactly envisaged being greeted with open arms and the offer of a cosy catch-up. Not that she had ever really planned to see Tommy again to be honest ... not until that letter and her need to track down the truth behind it. Being with Riley again was all she could think about and if that meant having to share airspace with Tommy then so be it.

'I need to talk, can I come in?' said Amy matter-of-factly.

'Be my guest.' His intonation was not exactly inviting.

Tommy ushered Amy into his office at the Dirty Cash Casino, as the Kitty Kat club was now known. Amy had made a calculated guess that she'd find him there now that his work with Riley at the plastics factory no longer existed. On lonely nights at the flat in London she'd often found herself idly looking at the internet and out of curiosity she'd once googled Tommy Hearn. The 'success story' of Manchester's latest casino had popped up on a website about northern businesses. Unable to stop herself from reading it she'd immediately felt the hair on the back of her neck standing to irate attention at the man who had so easily filled her dancing shoes and stolen her life.

As she walked into the space that had once been hers, had once pulsated with music and been the scene of so much happiness and jubilance, at least before *that* night, she again had the same feeling of contempt wash over her. Every corner held a memory. Instead of the raging buoyant beat of the music, the space now resonated with the soundtrack of endless *kerchings* from the rows of slot machines spaced sentinel-like from wall to wall. Amy had nothing against gambling, far from it, but somehow the scene disgusted her. A hatred of it that stemmed from the loss of what had gone before.

'Welcome to The Dirty Cash Casino, it's your first visit I guess. Looking good, eh?' There was ridicule in Tommy's words, a bragging that pricked at Amy's skin. Added to the almost cataclysmic pounding of her heart within her rib cage, the atmosphere in the room made Amy feel deeply uncomfortable. But she needed to be strong. To conquer her fear.

She sat herself at his desk as Tommy eased into his chair opposite her and lit a fat, stubby cigar. No cigarette ban would ever stop him. He was king of this empire and he made the rules. He ran his hand through his thick mane of black, slicked-back, wavy hair as he reclined back into his chair, blowing smoke into the air. His demeanour was one of pure arrogance. The fat cat who had not just tasted the cream, but made his enemies choke on it.

'I guessed you'd be here ... where else would you be?' she sniped. 'Dirty Cash? It's dirty all right ... the cash that funded this place was my cash and you know it, Tommy. This was my club. You left me with nothing. How can you live with yourself?' A tear started to form at the corner of Amy's eye as she spoke.

It annoyed her. This was not how she was supposed to be. She planned to be forceful, take no shit … tears were not an option. After everything she had gone through she was not going to give this man the satisfaction of seeing her blub like she was watching some emotion-drenched Jennifer Aniston rom-com.

'Come for a handout, have you? Times are hard? I'd heard on the grapevine that you're not exactly doing so well. You're down in London now, aren't you? Streets not paved with gold, eh? There's nothing here for you, Amy …' Tommy left a slight pause before adding '… not anymore.'

Amy needed to be strong. Trying to ignore the ever-increasing volume of her own heartbeat, she spoke. 'I need answers, Tommy, not money. You were a friend to me and Riley. Or at least I thought you were. You came to our wedding. You were there when my parents died. You've been part of my life with Riley for as long as I can remember, so what happened? How can you sit here, somewhere that was once mine and know that you're making a living in the place where my husband … your friend, died? I don't understand … I never had you down as such a callous bastard.'

Tommy stared at Amy, his gaze like that of a feline ready to apply a fatal blow to a passing nuisance of a rodent. 'You never did understand, love. You were never the sharpest tool in the box from the moment Riley met you, were you? I never really understood what he saw in you, but I suppose you must make up for your lack of brains in other departments.' His eyes narrowed and his glance descended down Amy's body as he spoke, his meaning evident.

Amy had never been Tommy's biggest fan but even for him this was nastiness on a scale she'd never experienced before.

'Screw you, Tommy!'

Amy was on the verge of standing up and leaving but she hadn't come all this way to quit so soon. She was stronger than that, despite what Tommy may think. It was her strength that had managed to help her survive the last six months. She needed answers and she needed to find her husband. If Tommy had anything to do with Riley's 'death' then she had to fathom a way to find out about it. For a moment her mind clouded, the thought of being with Riley once more distorting her vision. For them to potentially be together she needed to calm her rage and focus. Not let her armour be penetrated.

'Riley was a good man, a wonderful husband. He was honest and decent. He didn't deserve to die. You came to his funeral. You liked him ... you were sad he'd died ... weren't you?' Amy could hear the uncertainty in her own voice. So much now seemed in doubt.

'I had my reasons for being there. That's all.' He blew another thick plume of smoke into the air from his cigar and stubbed it out into an already-full ashtray on the office desk. A few stray flakes of ash dropped over the edge. 'Now, I assume you're not here to just take a trip down Memory Lane and reminisce happy days, so what the fuck do you really want, Amy? I've got a business to run. In fact I've got quite a few. Selling that factory was a nice little earner for me. It was about time Riley came up trumps.'

'What do you mean, "came up trumps"? You worked with Riley at that factory. You talked plastics with him all the time. Dinner parties with you and Jemima were always a *delight*.' Amy smothered the word with irony. 'You and him would disappear off to discuss work and I'd be left with dull-as-ditchwater Jemima.' Amy saw no point in mincing her words given the attitude Tommy was dishing out to her.

Tommy leapt from his chair in anger. His frame, wide and foreboding, seemed to fill the room as he stared down threateningly at Amy. A curl of hair escaped downwards across his forehead as he spoke. It looked out of place on the normally immaculate Tommy. 'You stupid girl, you truly believe your husband was merely a boss for some bleeding plastics factory? You brain must be as fucking hollow as the pipes Riley was supposedly selling. You never went to the factory, did you?'

The comment floored Amy. It was true, she hadn't. 'Er ... no, why would I? It was Riley's work, I had no need to ... never wanted to.'

'Because if you had, you'd have seen that the whole thing was just a façade. A front. A cover. A sham. Your husband was no more a plastics salesman than you are a bloody *University Challenge* contestant. He was a fucking criminal with ideas above his station and a spending habit that sped way out of control. He'd have been dead long ago if I hadn't helped him out on countless occasions.'

Confusion gripped Amy. It was then that the first tear started to fall. Inhaling deeply, Amy wiped it away, determined not to crumble. She thought of Laura and how she would have coped with the situation she was in. She'd have been ballsy, strong, known what to say and how to react. Amy owed it to her to be the same.

'Criminal? No, not my Riley. Not a chance. That factory was a family business. He cared about it. He took it over from his dad.'

'Don't you get it? There never was a business. That factory was the HQ for all of Riley's underhand activity. You might think that Riley was whiter-than-white but tell that to some of the people he'd bumped off along the way. Your late hubby was one of the most feared underground gangland criminals in

Manchester and much further afield too. As was his dad, Ca-zwell Hart, before him. Except his father was a true gent who earned his reputation and wasn't idiotic enough to blow shit-loads of cash and get into debt up to his eyeballs.'

Gangland criminals? What Tommy was saying was alien to her. That was something she'd seen watching Tom Hardy play-ing the notorious Krays in *Legend*, in a violence-soaked Taran-tino flick late at night when she'd been unable to sleep, or read about in one of her explosive novels. It was somebody else's life, not hers. The lack of understanding floored her. She was silent.

There was nothing Amy could say. It was true that she had never involved herself in Riley's business. Never paid any ma-jor interest or really asked any deeply probing questions. She was not the questioning type, she'd always been told that. She'd enjoyed the riches of designer clothes, exotic holidays and ex-pensive jewellery but had never asked where the money came from. She always thought she'd known. But the thought of Riley being a criminal ... a murderer ... no, not the man she knew. He couldn't have been. Not the man who had made love to her countless times in such a tender and gentle fashion, some-times in the very office where her world was now unravelling like a ball of wool in the clutches of a mischievous kitten. Amy could only helplessly listen as Tommy continued with his verbal shower of destruction.

'That's where I came in, Amy. Always happy to bail Riley out when he bit off more than he could chew. The overheads on the "factory", the cost of this place when it was The Kitty Kat, the monies owed to others. Riley was a headstrong bloke who didn't know when to stop. That's why people went to him when they needed a job doing. He was fearless. But he was reckless too. He'd happily push some poor bastard into the Manchester Ship Canal wearing concrete boots for being a grass or shoot some lowlife scum between the eyes in a Parisian back alley but ask him to balance his books and he was a waste of bloody space. Your late hubby was a bad egg and I was his human cash point. And it turned out he was a pretty good investment as it happens ... or at least now he's dead.'

'So you think he is dead ...?' Amy had spoken before she'd had time to think. The barrage of information ramming into her brain was pulverising her already destroyed senses. Her mind shot back to those evenings when Riley was busy 'at work', that night she'd been left alone in Paris, glances from shifty strangers in chi-chi bars he'd taken her to on nights out, excuses he had made to disappear from a romantic restaurant dinner table to 'take an important call'. There were countless occasions and now they all seemed to stack in line with Tommy's ruinous accusations.

Tommy's reasons for wanting Riley out of the picture were clear – pure and simple monetary gain. Amy wasn't sure that letting him even consider the possibility that she thought Riley could still be alive was a wise move. The man had just admitted to being a huge and heartless piece of Manchester's crime scene, so violence was obviously part of his DNA. If he was behind Riley's demise and was now considering the possibility of having failed in his quest to bump him off then he was evidently capable of sparking into brutality at any second. And as she was sitting across the desk from him, it was Amy who was the closest to potential harm. The thought froze inside her.

'Of course he's fucking dead. What kind of stupid fucking notion is that? He had his face shot off and you sat there, crying into your handbag, at his funeral. Your husband wasn't a liked man. There were a lot of people around here who breathed a sigh of relief when he met his maker. He's dead. What the fuck makes you think otherwise?'

Tommy sounded convinced but he could be bluffing. Amy wasn't sure. This was a Tommy she'd never seen before, more brutal than she'd ever realised. Unable to formulate what to say, her mind a riot of emotion, she remained silent. It seemed the best option.

'Riley made countless enemies over the years. He was ruthless when it came to making people pay if they double-crossed him and he was able to charge a hefty price tag for snuffing someone out. His problem was spending too much cash on needless shit ... like this place before I got my hands on it. If he was still alive, doubtless he'd still be spunking heaps of cash into all sorts of useless ventures to try and make some dough. And doubtless I would still be bankrolling him. No, he's six feet under, definitely. The police gave up on the case for good reason, they didn't want to ruffle too many criminal feathers.'

Amy's bottom lip trembled as she spoke. She was beginning to realise why Riley had been so apologetic to her in his letter. What had he said? 'I have to say sorry. A million times over. Sorry for the misery you've suffered, sorry for the confusion I'm about to cause, sorry for the heartache.'

Yes, this was heartache all right. She'd headed back to Manchester from London thinking that her husband had been a good man to her in life, a true son to his father, someone who had just had his beautifully bright flame extinguished too soon. But now she was being told different. Tommy had spelt it out to her. Riley was a criminal, a hit man, someone who took lives like a beast would lick the last drop of water from the bottom of a trough – with an insatiable thirst and with no thought for those who were to follow. Including Amy. She'd been lied to all her life with Riley. About his dad, about his business, about his relationship with Tommy ...

She could feel her heart snapping in two. 'So, you were Riley's loan shark? The man who bled him dry and constantly made sure you had your pound of flesh to chew on. I thought you were his friend …' Her voice was branded with despair, the fight within her not so much ebbing out of her bones but now seemingly free flowing.

'I loved Riley's father.' It was the first softening in Tommy's voice. 'Cazwell was a good man, a major player. I worked with him as his equal. He treated me well and made sure that I was always on my feet financially. When he was on his deathbed, one of his wishes was that I looked after Riley, made sure that his prized son came to no harm. But the boy was a fool. No-where near as clever as his father. As soon as he took over the business he had no idea about what it took to keep all of the plates spinning. He would try and finance everything by the seat of his pants. Do anything that that bumbling fuckwit, Winston Curtis, told him to. As soon as Riley employed him things went downhill quicker than a fucking ski jumper at the Sochi Olympics. Good job he copped it too. There was no point Riley ploughing money into clubs, flashy cars, houses and a stupid wife who was more than happy to spend his cash if he didn't keep funding the pot. Riley could make a killing, no pun intended, with his work but if you earn less than you spend then you're dead in the water. He was nowhere near the man his father was and he never would have been.'

Tommy was enjoying his revelations. It was as if he had waited for the right moment to come along and suddenly the planets had aligned. The moment he could finally destroy Riley's perfect-husband image for good. Amy found his performance almost demonic in its drama.

'Cazwell had old school values and knew the art of survival. I had happy times with him.' Tommy lit another cigar. The deep pungent odour stung against Amy's eyes as the smoke looped into the air.

A pause. It allowed Amy to speak. 'How can anyone who made a living killing people or feeding off others' misery have any kind of values? And what makes you any better? You're feeding off the carcass of my dead husband and sitting pretty on his hard-earned cash.'

'Wrong again, Amy.' Tommy's voice rose to booming level, his anger mounting again. 'Riley Hart was *never* profitable. I kept him afloat with money I'd earned with his dad. I did it for his dad. A few thousand here and there, it soon snowballed into seven figures. So I had him sign everything over to me, everything. I closed the business, no-one could hold a candle to Riley's father so I was buggered if I was going to try. I didn't want any further fucking damage to his reputation than had already been done by his cretin of a son. This is much more me.' He circled his hands around the room to convey his meaning.

A smile, heavy with spite, opened across Tommy's face. Whatever he was about to say, Amy knew that it would be pure venom. 'Hate to say it, Amy, but Riley's life with you was a complete sham. Remember any paperwork you signed for him? What did Riley say it was for – business deals, money making schemes? That was the contract signing away any rights you had to any of his interests.'

A killer blow but a true one. One that hit hard. Tommy was right, Amy had signed countless forms during her time with Riley. She had never questioned any of them. No wonder it had all been so easy for Tommy to swipe everything away from her. It was all legal and binding. As tight as the ever fastening noose Amy felt wrapping itself around her neck. She'd heard more than she cared to. The truth was choking her.

But what was the truth? Tommy was ruthless and calculating but was he a killer? Would he kill the son of the man he'd obviously adored? He was never a fan of either Riley or Winston, that was for sure, but could he be a cold-blooded murderer? The thought of sharing a room with him any longer repulsed Amy. For her own sanity, she needed to leave and structure her thoughts. Work out what to do next.

She stood to go, tears threatening to fall again. As she turned to exit the office, the door opened and the stick-like frame of Jemima Hearn tottered in. Her skeletal cheeks were sunken and stained with rouge. Her entire face was caked in make-up. She stopped dead in her tracks on seeing Amy.

'What in God's name is she doing here, Tommy?' Her lips, pinched and thin, hardly moved as she spoke.

'She's come to see if I really believe that waste of space husband of hers is pushing up the daisies because she's not convinced,' snapped Tommy. 'But we're done.'

'She thinks he *might* be alive, then? What a ridiculous notion. No, he's dead ... best place for him in my opinion. Can't do any more harm. Now, why don't you sling your hook?'

Amy couldn't take it any longer. She pushed past Jemima and ran out of the office, through the casino and into the biting Manchester air.

CHAPTER 11
Then. 2009

'Well I can now add wild boar to the list of things that I absolutely adore,' smiled Amy, wiping a chunk of bread around the rim of her bowl, mopping up the last meaty traces of the stew she had just devoured. 'That was beyond gorgeous.' She reached out and touched Riley's hand across their restaurant table to show her appreciation.

'On par with "Mucky" Maxwells, then? I thought their chips, cheese and gravy was the way to your heart. Don't I bring you to the best places?' asked Riley.

Amy laughed at the reference to the tiny chip shop that she loved in the backstreets of Manchester's gay Village. She couldn't count the number of times she and Laura, or indeed she and Riley had ended up in there, ordering the calorific trio of treats at the end of a boozy night out. It could be the swankiest of clubs or the most celeb-filled of VIP areas but no night would be complete without a final visit to the best fish'n'chip shop that Manchester had to offer.

'I think the oldest restaurant in … where was it?' She picked up the menu on the table and stared at the wording across the top of it. '… in Catalonia, is a cut above that, don't you? This place is amazing. Wine, food, the sexiest husband on the planet. What more could a girl ask for? Except for a dessert of course. I'm thinking cinnamon ice cream may be on the cards although doubtless it will head straight to my hips. I might force you into working off those extra pounds for me later if you don't mind.' Amy's voice was steeped in sexy suggestion, a fact not lost on Riley as he felt his cock stirring between his legs.

'Not a problem, I'll give you a workout that will see those pounds dropping off faster than the speed of a charging bull. Not that you have any to lose, you're in perfect shape,' winked Riley.

'Right answer,' said Amy, squeezing his hand once more.

'So, coming to Barcelona with me is agreeing with you then?'

'Si, Señor ... me encanta.' Amy's pronunciation of the Spanish tongue for 'I love it' may not have been spot on but Riley didn't seem to care.

'Now that's sexy. When did you start speaking Spanish?'

'Ever since you left me alone all afternoon with a guide book on La Rambla and told me to amuse myself while you dealt with your business. I thought I'd better learn a few phrases in case a handsome passing Spaniard decided to ask what a beautiful young girl was doing by herself in one of the prettiest cities in Europe.'

Riley punched his hand to his chest in jest and took a loud and deep intake of breath. 'Dagger to the heart! Husband scolded and out of action. Mayday, mayday!'

Amy couldn't stop herself laughing at her husband's display of mock injury. 'Well, that's what you deserve for leaving me on my lonesome. You missed a treat, though. The credit cards have taken a serious bruising and I made a visit to the Parque Güell, which you would have loved. It's beautiful up there overlooking the city, you can see for miles.'

'Yeah, I'm sorry work duties got in the way. I would have loved to have seen it with you. Mum and Dad saved up to go there years ago, it was somewhere they had always wanted to go and one of their few foreign holidays, and I remember seeing photos of them in albums sat amongst the colourful broken stones and the ceramic pots. Was it the architect Gaudi who influenced it all?'

'Now who's impressed?' said Amy. 'It sure was. You're not just a chiselled face and a heaving six pack are you, Riley Hart? Under that matador façade there's a pretty smart brain going on too isn't there?'

'One tries,' mocked Riley. 'I am sorry about leaving you though, but you knew this had to be a business trip. I just wanted you here with me. Work is always more pleasurable with you by my side.'

'So how was the world of plastics compared to my visit to the broken tiles and mosaics? Riveting as ever?'

'Deathly dull, but business is business and it looks like I might have won a lucrative contract. I just need to sign some papers and the gig is ours. Which reminds me …'

Riley reached down into the black nubuck leather messenger bag that was placed alongside his feet at the restaurant table. 'I need to have these witnessed and given back to my contact here before we fly back home in the morning. It's just terms of business for the contract about supplying pipes and fittings for local hotels and shops here. Could you sign them for me?'

Riley pushed two folded sheets of paper across the table towards Amy. The section showing had a few words visible and space for a signature. 'Could you just sign it here?' He pointed to one sheet before lifting it up and revealing another identical folded sheet. 'And here.' He pointed to the second.

'Am I allowed to, being your wife? Shouldn't it be an independent witness?' Amy went to unfold the papers but Riley grabbed them before she could. The action was pretty forceful but after a few glasses of red wine Amy didn't really pay much attention.

'That's what I thought but apparently Spanish laws are different. It seems they are perfectly happy for you to sign it. It makes sense to do it now and then I can deliver it while you pack your things in the morning.' There was a slight fluster in Riley's voice. 'Sooner it's done, the quicker the money rolls in. More cash to spend on the latest Prada or Gaultier.'

'Now you're talking. Pass me a pen.'

Riley did so and watched as Amy signed her name across the two sheets. There was a sadness in his eyes.

Having signed, Amy rose to her feet. 'Now, I just need to head to the little girl's room. If the waiter comes over I'd like the ice cream and the largest glass of Spanish liqueur this restaurant has to offer.' She bent down to kiss Riley on the lips and wandered off across the restaurant. '*Te quiero, Señor!*'

'And I love you too, Amy Hart. I truly do.'

So why had he just made her sign away all rights to any interest in his financial dealings? It was not an act that made him feel good about himself. But it was something he had to do. Just another lie to add to the mix. She didn't need to know why they'd really come to Barcelona. What business really needed to be attended to that afternoon while she played happy tourist.

By the time Amy returned the signed papers were back in the messenger bag and the ice cream ordered. It arrived a few minutes later.

'Ow. Brain freeze. That is so cold,' stated Amy as she took a large mouthful of the dessert.

Riley couldn't help but wonder if the body of the man whose throat he'd slit that afternoon and dumped in a large recycling bin in a secluded backstreet of Barcelona's Gothic Quarter had gone cold yet. What would Amy say if she knew the truth about his reason for coming to the Spanish city? He silently prayed that she would never have to know.

CHAPTER 12
Now, 2015

Amy had never felt more alone. Her parents were dead, her husband apparently so and her memories of him shattering into sharp, painful shards of heartache with every single fact of his deceit she was learning. It was at times like this that Amy had always turned to Laura. She could always be relied on in any crisis to speak sense, see reason and stomp her high-heeled way towards a solution. But, of course, she was dead too ... Amy had felt her best friend's last drop of life taper to nothing as she held her in her arms that night at The Kitty Kat Club.

Lying back on the stained sheets of her Manchester hotel room bed, Amy couldn't help but think of her departed friend. She would have thrown some much-needed light onto the murky depths Amy found herself wallowing in. She'd also have told Amy to check out of the sub-standard hotel she was staying at and book into somewhere half-decent. But with no real income coming in and her money from selling jewellery and clothes dwindling away she knew that economising was the best idea. She didn't intend to stay in Manchester any longer than she needed to, just enough to try and find some clues to lead her to Riley, and she would hardly be at the hotel if she kept herself busy, so splashing out on five star luxury seemed pointless. It wasn't that long ago that Riley would have insisted on her settling for nothing less than the best. For now, being frugal was the sensible option.

The stains on the bed sheets ranged from, as far as Amy could make out, faded blood through to indubitably ancient splashes of tea and coffee. Flea-pit was not even close. In Amy's fuzzy-headed state of mind on her arrival in Manchester she had booked herself into the first hotel she could find. The fa-çade and the Reception area had looked okay – window frames painted, Christmas decorations in place, no smashed bulbs on the illuminated sign – it was only once Amy had let herself into her room that she'd realised just how vile the place actually was. The carpet was a mass of cigarette burns, the edges of the curling wallpaper a distressed brown. It was a million light years away from any of the luxurious places she had ever stayed with Riley. But Riley wasn't here now, was he? She was alone ... with no-one to talk to. God, she missed Laura ...

CHAPTER 13
Then, 2004

Laura Cash and Amy Barrowman had first bumped into each other at a glam rock tribute concert in Manchester's town centre. Literally bumped into each other. Amy had been walking back from the bar with two full glasses of Jägerbombs balanced between her fingers ready to lose herself in yet another slab of the thunderous beats of her favourite glam rock tribute act – Sweet Treat. In an era where dance music from the likes of Gwen Stefani, Beyoncé and Shakira ruled the airwaves, Amy was still proud to love music from days gone by. She was all about the tribute and had often thought that she must have been born in the wrong era. Seventies and eighties tunes were just so cool.

Her fringe, straight, long and teased as far down her face as possible, fell across one of her eyes and momentarily caused her to stumble on her platform heels. Glam nights meant dressing up top to toe. Amy adored a theme and the chance to create an outfit for the night. She would happily sit down with her mother's old Singer sewing machine and work her magic with a stack of fat quarters and cotton jelly rolls until a couture era-befitting creation had been born.

As she tried to regain her footing both drinks went sailing from her clutches, one cascading down her own homemade outfit, while the other landed across the ample cleavage of Laura Cash, poured into the tightest bright purple cat suit Amy had ever seen. A triangular expanse of flesh ran from Laura's neckline, narrowing its way between her large, round breasts and ending at her belly button. The entire area of skin was decorated with glitter, which started to run in rivulets as it mixed with the Jägermeister/Red Bull cocktail hurtling down Laura's curves.

'Oh, for fuck's sake. I spent all evening getting that glitter just right in the hope that the lead singer might cop an eyeful,' screamed Laura. 'And now it's sodding ruined. I was hoping that working these beauties might get me backstage after the gig. It worked for one of the boarders in my school last year. She had a whale of a time. Now I just look like I've wet myself. Thanks a lot, I'll have to dry myself off in the toilets now.'

Amy was mesmerised by the vision of glorious femininity standing in front of her. She had never met anyone like this girl before. There was no chance of any red-blooded rocker not noticing the body Laura possessed. She was perfection. Amy was determined not to let her new discovery disappear just yet.

'I am so sorry, it's these bloody heels. I lost my footing. Please let me buy you a drink to apologise,' she said, calculating just how much money she had on her. 'And for what it's worth, you still look amazing. Seriously, I would kill to look like you.' Amy couldn't divert her gaze from the symphony of colour in front of her.

Laura obviously appreciated the compliment and visibly softened as she answered back. 'I suppose it'll dry out, especially in this place. It's so bloody hot and rammed in here. I've never seen so much eye-shadow and lip-gloss in one place ... and I thought I had most of it on my dressing table.' She paused before adding, 'I'll have a pint of lager, but I'll get it. I have wads of cash with me. The name's Laura, and as it happens, you're rocking that outfit too. I adore your lilac bellbottoms. And it's no wonder you fell over on those heels, they're at least a couple of inches higher than mine. I am beyond deeply jealous.'

'I made the outfit myself,' said Amy, pleased by the compliment from the goddess in front of her. Why weren't there girls like this at Stephen Hague Comp?

'Shut the front door,' squealed Laura. 'It's amazing. And the boots?'

'Charity shop.'

Laura held her hand up to high-five her new fashion icon. 'Respect. You and I need to shop together. I never go in charity shops normally.'

Amy bought the drinks using a twenty pound note Laura had given her and the two girls continued to chat, mainly about their love of music and all things fabulous. 'My friend actually managed to kiss Jake Shears from the Scissor Sisters last year when she saw him at some swanky Manchester hotel. She said his skin felt like the softest leather handbag you've ever touched. She wouldn't wash her face for weeks, silly cow, because she reckoned she could still smell him on her. She's with me tonight but I don't think I'll see her again as she wants to shag the bassist from the group and is probably backstage. Lucky bitch. I hope to join her later. What about you, you here alone? I assume not, unless you were binge drinking when I met you. You had two Jägers, right?'

'Yeah,' smiled Amy. 'One was for my mate's boyfriend. Well, I say mate, she's not really. She's just the only person I know who likes this kind of music and to be honest I don't really know her that well. It was just an excuse not to come on my own. Why don't more people like glam? I was glad to get away from them to be honest as they've spent most of the night with their tongues down each other's throats. It can become a bit off putting when you're trying to sing along. I suppose I should go back, they'll be wondering where I am.'

Laura began to scream at the top of her voice. Virtually all of the bar turned to look at her. 'Oh my God! You hear those sirens? It's fucking "Blockbuster". Only one of the best glam songs ever. Come on, down that drink ... you and I are going to dance. If one of the band doesn't spot me looking like this then there's *sweet* chance for anyone else!' She giggled at her own wordplay. 'Now, move it sister, let's hit the floor.'

The two girls had spent the rest of the gig together, dancing wildly to the band on stage. Amy had never met anyone with such a cocktail of personalities before. Laura was happy, adventurous, fun, wild, and reckless and she made Amy want to feel just like that too. Laura did catch the attention of one of the musicians and before heading off into the night with him, the two young women swapped numbers and arranged to meet again. They did, the following week, on a quest to try and track down Brandon Flowers.

They'd never found The Killers' frontman, but the two girls had found a deep friendship, which saw them share so much – from their taste in music as it twisted its way from glam rock via disco to the edgier sounds of the eighties they'd been listening to on the night Laura died – to their varied experiences with men, even though Laura's experience with the opposite sex eclipsed anything that Amy had ever tried. Most nights out ended up with Laura leaving Amy to her own devices as she headed off after yet another man. But Laura had always been there, the naughty to Amy's nice. And Amy found her thrilling.

But now she was gone. The thrill was over. Someone had made sure of that when they'd fired a bullet into Laura's back at the Kitty Kat Club. And even if Amy wasn't sure about anything to do with her life with Riley anymore, she knew that somebody needed to pay for taking away her perfect existence with her best friend.

CHAPTER 14
Now, 2015

'*Sprechen sie* hi-fashion, darling? It would appear that you don't. I suggest you take your foreign, tawdry little rags and peddle them elsewhere. You're not exactly Germany's equivalent of Victoria Beckham are you? Now, why don't you take your collection and give it to someone who gives a shit about your poorly stitched knick-knacks as they certainly have no place in one of England's finest clothing boutiques ... got it?'

Genevieve Peters hung up the phone. She had never been somebody to dress up her words with pleasantries. She had a tongue sharper than the outfits featured inside the four walls of Eruption, her goldmine of a clothing shop situated in one of the trendier parts of Manchester. In the seven years since she had opened the store she had clothed everyone from up-and-coming Hollywood through to young royalty. Not that any of the fashion was designed by her. No, Genevieve left that to the likes of Tom Ford or Roberto Cavalli. She had the shrewdest fashionista eye for spotting what the next big trend would be. With a hard work ethic of 'nose to the grindstone' and a well-accessorised ear to the floor, Genevieve and her team of contacts polka-dotted around the globe to make sure that any forthcoming trend would feature in Manchester's Eruption before it had even hit UK catwalks. She had played a major part in Fashion Weeks all over the globe from the chaotic drama of New York through to the stylish flair of Milan and Paris. Images of her chatting freely with celebrities such as Cara De- levingne or Harry Styles in the front row of all the big name showcases frequently filled the red tops. At the age of thirty- five, the boutique owner, with her jet-black angularly cropped hair and tight black dress, was as feared as her severe fringe was razor-straight. Mostly by her staff, and rightly so, as it was usually they who bore the brunt of her venom, especially her assistant, Meifeng.

Facing the pint-size Oriental girl stood alongside her behind the counter of Eruption, Genevieve let rip. 'Meifeng, if that ab- horrent little German phones again then tell him he can shove his designs so far up his arse he'll be able to bite down on the cheap fucking fabric they're made from. And never pass him on to me again if you want to keep your job here, okay? You're supposed to be my assistant so please assist me by making the right decisions instead of being a total prick. Now, where's my cup of green tea?'

The young Asian girl scuttled out to the back of the shop as Genevieve dismissed her with a wave of her hand. It was only as she lowered her hand and started to flick through a rath- er thick fashion magazine lying on the shop counter that she spied someone on the other side of the shop. 'Oh hello, I didn't see you there behind that mannequin. May I help?' Her voice trailed off as Amy walked out from behind the dummy. She'd been stood there for a good five minutes or so watching Gen- evieve in action. She was truly a piece of work.

It was clear that Genevieve was not overly thrilled to see her. 'Oh, it's you. The last time I saw you I was nearly getting tram- pled to death in that blessed club of yours. I still bear a few war wounds now.' She raised her hand to her cheek, a faint hairline scar still visible 'What do you want?'

'Hello Genevieve, how nice to see you too. I've come to talk about Riley.' Amy's voice was calm, composed, clear and strong – determined to keep the upper hand.

Genevieve's face creased into worry. It was the first time Amy had seen any kind of weakness since she'd entered the shop. She had obviously hit a raw nerve.

'What about him? You had better come through to the back if we're to talk about the dead, although I don't know what you expect me to say. I'll get my assistant to mind the shop.' Amy followed Genevieve through. The atmosphere between the two women had suddenly become much frostier and Amy didn't need to be a weather girl to know that it wasn't just the season that was to blame.

Having shooed her assistant back out to the shop floor, Genevieve made no attempt to sit down or offer Amy a seat. She crossed her arms and stood facing Amy. Her stance was one hundred per cent defensive and unfriendly. Amy guessed that this was to be a pretty curt conversation.

'Your husband, Riley ... I'm sorry for your loss. Good-looking fellow. I saw him at the club many a time. Shame it's gone, I used to take my clients there. Good for business. You must miss it? Nice little earner I would have thought ...?'

'I miss my husband more ...' Amy replied, thinking it was no wonder Genevieve had made such a killing in the fashion world. She appeared to be as cold-faced and as cold-hearted as they come. Ice maidens would seem volcanic in comparison. She could see why she was a potential suspect. 'But yes, The Kitty Kat Club was popular. You came quite a few times didn't you?'

'As I said ... now, what can I do for you? I'm sure as a fellow ...' she hesitated before adding, '... businesswoman, you realise how busy I am. My assistant and I have to get these unpacked by end of play today.' She indicated a bank of boxes stacked against the wall. 'The A-listers of this country are hardly going to look their best if I can't supply them with cutting edge fashions from Seoul through to San Paulo, are they? We can't all wander around looking like we've just come from the soup kitchen, can we?' Genevieve let her gaze take in Amy's outfit, a simple jeans and tattoo-style emblazoned sweatshirt combo, underneath a deep green parka with a faux-fur trimmed hood. Amy had hoped she was oozing Moschino-esque style with a funky edge. The look on Genevieve's face made it clear that the boutique owner obviously felt her look was sporting something much more end-of-line TK Maxx.

Trying to ignore her burning anger towards Genevieve, Amy knew that she had to cut to the chase. The sooner she had spoken to everyone on Riley's letter then the sooner she could hopefully be back in his arms again, even if Tommy Hearn's revelations about her husband's secret life had knocked her for six. Could she love a man who did what Riley did for a living? Her heart and her head were pulling her in two opposite directions.

Pushing aside all ideas of what the future might hold, Amy continued. 'Then I'll be brief. Did you have any reason to want my husband dead? Somebody killed him and two other people that night and I'm trying to find out who.'

Genevieve was floored for a second before slamming her answer back at Amy with more than a hefty layer of derision. 'I hardly knew your husband, and if you think about it sensibly, I was almost left for dead myself the night he died so unless you're implying that I was both responsible for those deaths and for virtually putting myself in an early grave then I really don't have a clue what on earth you could be getting at. I was merely caught up in the messy crossfire. Now, I'm sorry for your loss, I really am, but I must get on.' She held out her arm, indicating the way back through to the shop. It was obviously Amy's time to leave.

But Amy was resolute. She wasn't quite ready yet. 'All I know is that the police didn't come up with any answers for three people dying that night. I know my husband wasn't whiter than white, Miss Peters. I'm not the naive woman you may think I am. Far from it. I just want some answers. My friend, Laura, was killed that night too. I owe it to her to try and find out.'

'That's all very honourable, but I'm afraid I can't help you. Somebody shot three people but I'm just glad I wasn't number four. Now, if you'll excuse me ...' She ushered Amy towards the door. Amy knew it was now time to depart. The conversation had not so much stopped as crashed head first into the end of the nearest catwalk and fallen into the front row on its towering set of heels. It was going nowhere.

'If you think of anything then please ring me, here's my number. I'm just trying to do the right thing,' said Amy. She wrote her mobile number down on a piece of paper on Genevieve's desk and handed it to her. 'I'm glad you survived that night, Genevieve, but I need to try and unearth some answers for those who didn't. I could do with all of the help I can find.' As she turned to leave the shop Genevieve was still scanning the number.

A short burst of chilly winter air ran through the shop as Amy opened the door and walked out. Genevieve could feel her skin begin to prickle into goose bumps. Her lips, normally moistened to within an inch of their pillar-box-red lives under blankets of lipstick felt dry and her throat tightened as she watched Amy walk out of sight. She needed a drink.

She turned to Meifeng, her meek and mild female assistant who had watched the end of the two women's conversation in total silence. She knew her place. After two years working alongside Genevieve it was clear. She wasn't paid to pass comment. 'I can finish off here, why don't you go home for the day. I'll see you again tomorrow,' snapped Genevieve.

Meifeng, whose name translated from Chinese as 'beautiful wind' was out of there at typhoon speed. If she were to keep her much-prized job then out of sight was definitely out of the firing line. Meifeng had dreams of having her own set of boutiques one day and she was learning from the best, despite her boss's poison.

As soon as Meifeng had gone, Genevieve locked the door and flipped the 'Open' sign to 'Closed'. She was done for the day. Orders could wait. What was the point of being boss if you couldn't bend the rules now and again? Besides, her mind wasn't on the job, Amy had seen to that.

She flicked the light switch and looked around her as the shop descended into darkness, the only light coming from the back room. Even if it had been pitch black she could have still simply wound her way back to the counter and out to the store-room with ease. She knew the layout of the rails and the mannequins like the back of her own hand.

Back in the storeroom she sat herself down at her desk, unlocked the top drawer and pulled it open. A bottle of whisky lay inside, resting on a sea of receipts and invoices. The paperwork could wait, she needed a drink, and she needed it now. Unscrewing its cap, she raised the bottle to her lips and took a good, long slug. The liquid scorched her throat slightly as she swallowed. It felt good. She took another. It felt less harsh but just as pleasing.

Placing the bottle back inside the drawer she closed it and unlocked the one underneath it. A photo frame lay face down, obviously hidden from view. She faltered slightly before lifting it out of the drawer and placing it on the desk to face her. It was another moment before she allowed her eyes to rest upon it. The photo was of two people, a man and a woman, their arms wrapped around each other. They were very intimate, obviously together. The man was kissing the woman firmly on her cheek. Both were smiling. There was something so natural about the photograph. They were united.

Genevieve could feel her blood beginning to boil, but allowed herself to stare at it for a few seconds before anger got the better of her. She snapped and lashed out at the photo, sideswiping it from the desk. It sailed across the room and crashed into one of the cardboard boxes before falling to the floor. As it did a solitary crack slashed its way, top to bottom, through the photo. Even from her desk Genevieve could see that the crack was perfectly placed, separating the two people. On one side she saw her own smiling face, on the other was that of Riley Hart.

'How fucking apt!' she said and began to laugh. Her maniacal laughter soon turned to tears.

CHAPTER 15
Now, 2015

Secrets are rarely beneficial. Most secrets are hidden for a reason. If they were tasty nuggets of information to be feasted on by all for a better life then they wouldn't be secrets in the first place. Secrets are nearly always dangerous.

As Amy walked away from Eruption she couldn't help but feel that Genevieve was definitely hiding something. Wasn't it true that the best way of keeping a secret is to bury it and pretend that it doesn't exist in the first place? There were definitely secrets lurking beneath that woman's stern facade. And Amy was determined to try and get to the bottom of them. But how? Genevieve was being tighter than an oyster housing the most delicious of pearls. She was not letting down her guard for anything or anyone; that was clear.

What was her connection to Riley? There obviously was one or else Riley wouldn't have mentioned her in the letter. *What was Riley hiding?* If he was alive, wouldn't it have been better for him to carry on pretending that he was dead? His letter was causing nothing but constant bubbling angst. In just a few short days Amy had learnt that her husband was really a gangland criminal responsible for countless deaths, a man who lied to her in life and never allowed her to share his deep, dark secrets. Why should she try to unearth the truth now? This was a truth that could only lead to more despair. Why continue? Maybe because in Riley's eyes, the letter from beyond the grave was the first honest thing he'd been able to do in years. Was there a sense of wanting to put things right?

Despite any revelations that the last few days had brought though, Amy knew why she had to carry on. She loved Riley and needed to find him. She always had, and probably always would. If there was a chance that maybe he was alive and wanted to be with her then perhaps she should take it. Did that make her weak? Foolish? A sucker for love? She wasn't sure. Amy knew that now she'd started this journey she couldn't stop until it came to its natural end. Whatever that final destination might hold.

Amy was deep in thought as she reached the corner of the street. She knew that her journey to try and discover the truth had only just begun. She still needed to see the actor Grant Wilson, Riley's school nemesis, to question Riley's associate Adam Rich and to talk to his daughter, Lily, the Kitty Kat Club DJ and drug-pusher. Riley had mentioned all of their names. But what if none of them were involved? Tommy Hearn had said that Riley had loads of enemies – he could have been 'killed' by any of them. For all she knew, every gangland crackpot across the length of Europe could have had a hit out on Riley. Didn't Tommy say that the police had given up the case because they didn't want to 'ruffle any feathers'? There was no way that any of those 'feathers' would now want to be ruffled by Amy. The tornado of thoughts billowing around her head scared her.

It was early evening and fairly dark on the streets. The only light came from the rather pathetic Christmas lights strung up outside the shops. A few shoppers still milled around but Amy guessed that most would be feeling festive at the larger malls such as the Arndale. In this part of town it was mostly trendy boutiques, Eruption being the most heralded.

Amy was tired, her mind constantly ablaze with horrific 'what ifs' and questions that appeared to have no answers. She could feel her stomach twist into a knot of hunger. She needed to eat. Between the appetite-crushing state of the hotel and the constant quest to try and investigate Riley's death she had neglected the necessary things in life like fuelling her own body with food.

She could see a bagel shop on the other side of the road. Smoked salmon, cream cheese ... yes, that would fit the bill. She stepped out into the road, her mind still overcrowded with speculation. She was barely two steps in when she heard the car's engine.

It appeared out of nowhere. Its headlights weren't illuminated, so the first she was aware of it was when she heard the sudden powerful revving of its motor and the squealing of tyres as the rubber burnt along the road. She turned towards it, transfixed, unable to move as it advanced towards her. Amy's brain wasn't quick enough to compute the fact that she needed to get out of its way.

The car couldn't have been more than a couple of metres away when a pair of arms roughly grabbed Amy from behind and pulled her to the side of the road. She stumbled as she hit the curve and fell onto the pavement taking the person who had grabbed her down with her. She watched as the car sped past and then screeched to a halt. Amy was sure she saw the silhouette of the driver turn around to look at her before the car turned on its headlights and shot off around the corner out of sight.

'Jesus, you were fucking lucky. Another second and I'd have been scraping you up as road kill,' said a female voice underneath Amy. Literally underneath, as she'd fallen on top of her. 'Are you okay?'

It was only as the two women turned to face each other that a badly winded Amy recognised the person who had saved her life. It was Lily Rich.

'Christ alive, if I was still working for you I'd ask for a raise right now. What are you doing in Manchester, I thought you'd quit town?' Lily looked totally shocked to see Amy.

'I had … I have. I'm just back to try and sort some things out. Thanks for saving me. My mind was kind of away with the fairies. Guess I should pay more attention. Must have scared the life out of the driver. Out for a Christmas shop and I step out in front of their car. Didn't stick around though did they? They must realise they had a lucky escape.'

'Amy, how fucking deluded are you?' said Lily, standing herself up and wiping down the floor length faux fur coat she was wearing. As ever, she looked the epitome of street cool. 'That car was aiming straight for you. It pulled out, sped up, tried to knock seven shades of shit out of you and didn't stick around because it failed. Did you get to see the driver or the registration? I didn't, because it was all too quick.'

'No, I didn't …' Amy began to shudder, a sense of grim apprehension enveloping her. 'You really think that car was trying to run me down. Why?' Amy didn't have to think too hard if she were honest. She'd probably racked up her own considerable list of enemies over the short period she'd been back in Manchester.

'Have you got some secret assassin after you or something?' challenged Lily. 'Some bastard wants you dead, that's for sure.'

'Secret assassin? Maybe … listen, have you got time for a drink and a bite to eat, Lily? I'd really like to catch up with you and seeing as you've just saved my bacon, now would be the perfect opportunity.'

As Lily and Amy headed off to eat, Lily's father Adam Rich was sitting, head in hands, at his desk in his office at his mock Tudor mansion on the outskirts of Manchester. The house was opulent on a grand scale. For many it would have been grossly grand, a shrine to bad taste, proving that money could definitely make something more brassy than classy.

Two stone bulldogs, both at least a metre high, adorned the pillars either side of the electric gates at the front of the property. The pebbled driveway leading to the equally pillared front door housed a collection of cars. A Range Rover sat alongside an Audi R8, sharing space with a Bentley Continental GT. It would have given the flashiest of trashy footballers a motor-loving hard-on the size of Old Trafford.

Next to the front door another large stone statue, this time of a lion raised on its back legs, took pride of place. The lion, its mouth opened wide, baring a set of long stone teeth, was far from alluring. In fact it would have scared the most macho of visitors. But then the home that Adam Rich shared with his wife Caitlyn and their daughter, Lily, was far from inviting. And it was far from a happy one. Behind the large oak front door was hidden many a secret.

Adam Rich thumped his fist down onto his desk. He was not happy, and it was a niggling secret that was causing his consternation.

He was recollecting a phone call he'd taken in his games room earlier that day. It had been Tommy Hearn on the other end.

Snooker cue in one hand as he held the telephone receiver in the other, he had listened to what Tommy had to say.

'What is it, Tommy?'

'I've had a visit from Riley's missus. She's been sticking her oar in and knows the situation about Riley's lifestyle. Just thought you'd better know,' warned Tommy.

'Amy Hart's back in town. Well, fuck me. You think she'll be trouble?' snarled Adam. 'I thought she was out of the picture. What's she know? Not everything I hope.'

'No, not everything, but she thinks Riley's still alive. Crazy cow. And she came here to see if I knew anything about it. The ramblings of a fuckwit widow if you ask me, but she may try digging up some dirt, so I thought you'd better be kept in the loop.'

'You know where she's staying?' asked Adam.

'I do. I had someone follow her from the casino. A right hole, she's down on her luck all right. If she's after cash, she could be a problem. And if Riley *is* alive, he could squeal about all sorts ... including you know what.'

'Yeah, and you know never to speak about that on the fucking telephone. Walls have ears, Tommy,' shouted Adam, banging the snooker cue on the floor in fury as he did so. 'Give me her address. I'll deal with it. Make sure secrets stay buried. I can't afford any fuck ups, not again ...'

Adam hung up the telephone and turned his attention to the woman stood smoking a cigarette beside the snooker table. She was naked apart from a pair of high heels and the sheerest of panties.

'You got trouble?' she asked.

'I don't pay you or any of the whores from the agency I order you from to ask questions. I pay you for a service so why don't we put this snooker table to good use and you show me why you're worth the money I'm wasting on you.' Adam unbuckled his trousers as he spoke.

It was true. Adam Rich didn't pay Dolly Townsend to talk. Despite having a sizable brain in her head and a tongue in her mouth, Dolly was paid to suck, fuck and shut right up. Her client's business was his own and hers was to just lie back and enjoy the ride. And if he chose to keep it a secret from his daft wife then so be it.

'Fine with me, you're the boss.' Dolly knew what to do and say. She slipped the panties down her legs and lay back on the table, legs splayed. She was still stubbing out her cigarette butt when Adam ploughed his cock into her.

Lily and Amy were just sitting down to eat as back in Eruption, Genevieve Peters returned the photo of herself and Riley into the drawer, streaks of black mascara still caked onto her face from where she'd been crying. She'd finished off the rest of the whisky. Her mind felt drenched with confusion. She hated herself for letting him still get to her. She knew he always would. She had no choice. Reminders would always be there. He wasn't worth her tears. She was too strong for that. Or at least she thought she was. She'd never wanted to share him, but she'd had to. He'd made sure of that. It had to be their secret. And now Amy was back again. The other woman .... That stupid cow had no idea. She would never know. Maybe she should tell her. Let her in on the secret, or maybe make sure that she never found out ...

Secrets. What was that famous phrase she'd once heard? 'Three may keep a secret, if two of them are dead.' Benjamin Franklin or someone. She'd picked it up somewhere. Yes, the dead can't share secrets ... only the living can do that.

As she replaced the photo she reached to the back of the drawer and wrapped her hands around the handle of a gun. She pulled it out and stared at it. Even in her whisky-sodden state, a flash of clarity hit her brain as she wondered when she'd ever use it. Again.

CHAPTER 16
Now, 2015

'It's supposed to be a bloody graceful swan, Jean-Paul, not a deformed flamingo that looks like it's gone three rounds with a sodding pack of hyenas, darling man. Can't you reshape it?'

Caitlyn Rich was not pleased. Her latest mirror covered statue, a swan with open wings and raised into position ready for battle was not exactly as she had envisaged when she'd drawn a rough sketch for Jean-Paul, the Hoxton-based sculptor behind the ever-growing reflective display of statues beginning to fill every corner of her Manchester home.

'I may not be a twitcher or whatever they're called but even I know that a swan's neck should be fluid and curvaceous. This one is all a bit too right-angled.' Caitlyn crooked her neck almost ninety degrees to look at the mirrored monstrosity in front of her. 'It's just not very ornithological is it, dear man. Can we rejig? Snap the neck off and start again.'

The look on Jean-Paul's face as they stared at the creation in his trendy London studio was suddenly painted with horror. The temperamental Belgian was used to awkward clients and had been ever since he'd moved to London from Brussels some years earlier, but Caitlyn Rich definitely took the biscuit when it came to being the dictionary definition of the word 'demanding'. Thank God she paid the big bucks and was regular with her commissions. Jean-Paul's stress levels may have gone up since meeting Caitlyn but thankfully so had his bank balance.

'I think the neck is perfect as it is, Caitlyn. I took it from your drawing, which was somewhat ... *angular* shall we say.' Jean-Paul fiddled with the waxed tips of his moustache as he spoke in an attempt to calm his nerves. Caitlyn was one of the most exasperating people he had ever met.

'Yes, but I'm hardly Da Vinci, dear heart, am I? And you know that. I want curves on this neck to rival those on Jennifer Lopez's ass. Smooth, sleek, fluid.'

'But the neck is so thin and the mosaic tiles are fairly big so trying to make it smooth is not always possible.' Jean-Paul was not backing down.

Caitlyn had heard enough. She was late for her next appointment and she needed to make a move. 'It is rather thin I suppose, isn't it?' She reached her hand up to the neck of the swan and tugged at the neck to see how fragile it actually was. She didn't even notice the look of sheer horror on Jean-Paul's face as the neck snapped in her manicured fingers. The sculptor unsuccessfully tried to stifle a high-pitched yell of annoyance as Caitlyn handed him the neck.

'Well there you go, Jean-Paul, it is *too* thin you see. If it can't survive my delicate hands then how will it cope with my Lily running around the house all the time and the maids giving it a good dusting? I've done you a favour. Now, I'll be back down in London in a fortnight, can you sort it all out for me by then, there's a good chap? And we'll talk about the next piece when I'm back. I'm thinking of a mirrored unicorn ashtray for Adam's games room. He always smokes in there so he might as well have something decent to stub his butts out on. Now, I must fly, I have an appointment with a personal shopper at Harvey Nicks in twenty and an eyebrow thread booked in for this afternoon.

If you can sort out the costings for the unicorn that would be marvellous. I'm thinking about four foot high.'

Jean-Paul whispered '*Mon dieu*' under his breath at the vulgarity of a unicorn ashtray. As Caitlyn hurried from his studio, she felt her iPhone vibrate inside the pocket of her Stella McCartney jacquard trousers. Seeing the name across the screen a huge smile spread across her face. She took the call.

'What is it sexy man, you can't wait until tonight? I trust the offer of oysters at my favourite eatery still stands? I am literally counting the minutes. You know I'm a *sucker* for an aphrodisiac.' Caitlyn emphasised the word sucker to stress her saucy double-entendre.

As she hung up and hailed a London cab to take her to Knightsbridge she noticed that she'd missed a call from Adam. Oh well, she'd speak to him when she returned home. She wasn't bothered about missing him. Funny really, when she was away in London – which was becoming more and more often – she didn't miss her husband at all. Why would you miss somebody who you really didn't have that much reason to speak to anymore? They hadn't really spoken properly for the longest time. And now she had 'other interests' in London she really had even less reason to. No, she didn't miss him at all.

She took a pair of crisp twenty pound notes from her Chloe purse as her taxi pulled up outside Harvey Nichols and scanned the line of credit and debit cards housed within.

'Time to do some serious damage to you babies,' she cooed, the thought of shopping pleasing her enormously. It always did.

'Now which joint account shall I use first?' she mused.

The money. Now that would be something she'd miss dreadfully if her husband walked out of her life.

CHAPTER 17
Now, 2015

'You seriously think Riley might still be alive? You are shitting me, right?'

Lily Rich was finding it hard to believe what Amy was telling her. Even after three courses and as many glasses of wine – Lily may have been small but she had the largest of appetites, especially if someone else was paying – her voice was still stamped with disbelief.

'I was at the club. It was definitely Riley laying there with his face blown off. Winston, him and Laura all copped it. There's no doubt.' Sadness washed across her petite features.

'So, who wrote the letter? It was definitely Riley's handwriting and the postmark was only a few days ago. Why would he say that people were out to get him?'

Amy had chosen to fill Lily in on everything Riley had said in the letter with the exception of his mentioning Lily and her father, Adam, as potential suspects. She's also chosen to fill her in on her discovery that her late husband was, in fact, a criminal. A fact which hadn't shocked Lily nearly half as much as Amy had imagined.

'Forgive me for saying, Amy, but seeing as you're not my boss anymore I might as well tell you straight. Did you honestly believe that The Kitty Kat club and all of the riches you guys enjoyed – cars, a fancy house, holidays – were funded by a plastics corporation? Even I know that pipes aren't that fucking sexy when it comes to making big bucks. I never questioned it but I always knew Riley was more than likely mixed up in something underhand and dodgy. I dare say my dad is too, I've heard all sorts of gossip about criminal dealings over the years. To be honest I don't care. Money is money and as long as I can have everything I need then I'm happy. And let's face facts, hideously tasteless mock Tudor nightmares do not come cheap in the twenty-first century, do they? Plus Dad was forever taking Mum away to Monte Carlo and St Tropez when I was growing up and decking her out in enough jewellery to put Paris Hilton in the shade. I've never seen him do a day's work really, and even when he went 'away on work' for a few years a while back, my guess is that he was a guest of Her Majesty. I never asked. Doubtless he and Riley were mixed up in something together. A bunch of smartass crooks. I don't see that as a problem.'

'Do you really think they might have been?' Amy was beginning to think that she was the only person on earth who didn't have a clue about Riley's real life. How had she been so naive? Had she been too close to see what was really going on under her own nose? Even the strongest of minds could be weak when it came to emotion. She never questioned anything. Why would she have?

'He bought you the club and that was his way of keeping you happy. You loved that place. It's no wonder you're pissed off that Tommy and Jemima have turned it into the fucking Dirty Cash Casino. I would be too. I miss those nights at The Kitty Kat. I felt safer dealing drugs there than any of the places I do it now. I can hardly do it at the Dirty Cash as Tommy and Dad go way back. Which, as it goes, is another pointer to my dad being mixed up in it all. Dad would murder me if he found out I was peddling all that shit.'

'I still can't believe that my Riley would be such an evil person. Tommy said he may have killed people along the way.'

'Christ, you are the innocent one, aren't you?' scoffed Lily. 'Life's always been dog eat dog. You must have heard about gangland criminals ever since the famed ones like Jack 'The Hat' or The Richardsons back in the sixties. It was all smoky jazz clubs and glamorous sex scandals back then. Now I dare say it's clubs like The Kitty Kat and bags full of MDMA. I've heard my dad talking about all sorts of dodgy people over the years. Must have been shitloads of times. People that suddenly disappeared from view and turn up sliced and diced in some back alley. The people doing that are not fairy tale characters from some kiddie storybook. These people exist and are brutal. Seems like Riley was part of Manchester's current version. Perhaps even the leader, the king. Pretty cool throne to be sitting on I imagine ... or at least, it was.'

'It doesn't faze you at all, does it? That your dad might be some mass murderer or hated criminal ... or both.' Amy was trying, but failing miserably, to understand. How could Lily be so matter of fact about it all?

'No, not at all. Why would it? If my dad was a baker or some banking twat he might never have been able to look after me and Mum the way he has. We want for nothing. He has obviously reaped the rewards of whatever crafty line of work he's in. Who am I to judge? I may have sold drugs to people who have then gone off and overdosed. So, indirectly I'm a killer. And you supported it in The Kitty Kat, so deep down, so are you. We're all corrupt in our own way.'

Amy wasn't sure that her day could get any lower. It was true now she thought about it. She was no better than the bunch of scum that Riley had obviously been part of. She'd enjoyed the riches, savoured the holidays, loved the feel of the latest fashions and happily dished out the drugs, diced with danger ... but just because it had all been to the backdrop of a dance floor soundtrack she had chosen to ignore it and not consider the potential side effects. Maybe people who'd taken drugs in her club, supplied by Lily, backed by Amy, had died. Maybe parents had lost a son or a daughter, or a child a parent. That made her just as bad as Riley if he was ruthlessly bumping people off. Maybe it made her worse. At least Riley knew exactly what he was doing and chose to live with it. Maybe his only fault was not sharing what he did with Amy. No, Amy felt low ... maybe she was as much to blame for Riley's supposed death, Winston's death, even Laura's death as anyone ... poor Laura.

'How do you cope? Knowing that you could be a part of something ... something so murderous?' asked Amy.

'Because I don't pretend to be anything otherwise, Amy. Never have, never will.' Her words were slightly slurred, the effects of the wine obviously taking hold. 'I know I'm not a good person, Amy, and neither was Riley, however he earned his dough. I may have saved your life today but I just happened to be in the right place at the right time. If I hadn't been on my way to Eruption to pick up some clothes then maybe you'd be on some mortuary slab by now. I don't believe in God, but I do think that maybe somebody wanted me to do something right for you today. To make up for what I've done.'

'Done what? You've always been a good friend to me. I trust you, and I'm rapidly finding out that there is a list as long as my arm of people I can't.'

Amy's words made something inside Lily snap. Something that had been bubbling at the back of her mind spewed forth. Her ex-boss had always been good to her ... maybe too good. Before she could reconsider, she said it. There was no more than a trace of remorse as she spoke. 'A good friend wouldn't have been fucking your husband behind your back, Amy. And a good husband wouldn't have been doing it either. I think you should know that putting Riley on a pedestal is not the wisest of ideas. If he is alive, not that I believe it for one second, then your husband owes you some decent explanations as to why he was shagging me. I'm sorry, really I am, but now you're back I'd rather you know ... you can't trust anyone.'

Amy's day had just reached rock bottom ...

CHAPTER 18
Then, 1988

Jemima Hearn couldn't help but smile as her new husband, Tommy, picked one of the bright pink bougainvillea flowers and placed it gently in the flowing blonde tresses of her hair. Hair that had become increasingly blonde ever since her arrival on the tiny Greek island of Antiparos a week earlier. The golden richness of her locks contrasted beautifully with the honey-glazed tan she'd been developing ever since her honeymoon had begun. And her smile had never left her. It was as bright and as dazzling as the sun overhead, one that reflected across the silky smooth calmness of the Aegean Sea as they had first disembarked from the rickety antiquated ferry boat that had deposited them on one of the smallest and most forgotten islands situated among the Cyclades Islands off the coast of mainland Greece.

For a girl like Jemima it was a beauty that she had never seen before. At the age of nineteen she was seeing places and experiencing riches that she had never imagined. And that was all down to Tommy. A man a few years her senior but a man who had chosen her to be his wife. A man that she knew she was destined to be with from the first time they had laid eyes upon each other at a wine bar a mere twelve months earlier. He was strong, proud and possessed an air of danger that a naïve Jemima found intoxicating. There was a swagger to him and a cocky edge that the young woman couldn't resist. Jemima, who had never even dated a boy before Tommy, was lost in desire as soon as he winked at her across the wine bar and left his friends to come and talk to her. As he greeted her with a kiss, the feel of his skin against hers, the brush of his stubble across her soft round cheek, she could feel a sexuality bubbling within her that had never surfaced before. Hadn't she always been the boring one among her friends? That was how she had always felt. Not the fashionable one, not the intelligent one, certainly not the most beautiful one. Despite her pretty looks, Jemima had never seen herself as anything other than the boring one. That changed when she met Tommy.

The first time she surrendered herself to him sexually was an amazing experience. For the first few months she had abstained, allowing him no more than a feel of her breasts or a rub of her panties. Tommy had tried, he was obviously experienced, being senior to her, but he seemed happy to wait, slowly but gently lowering any barriers that the anxious Jemima may have been putting up.

On the night they had first made love, he had asked her to marry him. Jemima had said yes straight away. In her mind, opportunities like this didn't come the way of girls like her. Strong handsome men, protective and loving, ready to look after her and treat her to the riches of life. She knew from the start that Tommy was professionally involved in something that wasn't exactly as it seemed. She'd met Cazwell Hart and his wife, Bianca, and really liked both of them and it was Bianca who had first told her to 'turn a blind eye' to what 'the boys did in their professional life'. She asked once and Tommy was honest. She never asked again.

They were married and headed to the Greek island of Antiparos for their honeymoon. It was paid for by Cazwell and Bianca, their gift to the newlyweds.

Jemima could see the crystalline emerald waters of the sea through her guesthouse bedroom window as she relaxed back onto the bed, her body naked and glowing from a day's sunshine as she felt the coolness of the bed sheets spread across her skin and watched long panels of warm yellow light cast their way across the floorboards and walls. The flower that Tommy had placed in her hair earlier that day lay on the bedside table, where she'd placed it after removing it from her hair before showering on the return to the hotel.

She stared down at her body. Her small breasts rose up and down, an excited anticipation gripping her about what would doubtless happen when Tommy had finished his own shower. Jemima was looking down at the neat triangle of hair between her legs as she heard the shower turn off and Tommy came back into the room, naked apart from a towel wrapped around his waist. His skin, a hard, muscled, hair-covered shell of desire, glistened with the remaining drops of moisture that still rested on his flesh.

As soon as Tommy saw his naked wife, his erection grew within his towel, distending the fabric. Jemima could see the effect she was having and ran her hands down her own body, allowing the fingers on one hand to part the lips of her pussy as the she dipped two fingers from her other hand into the soft wet folds. It was a confident action that a year before she would have never have dreamt of doing in front of someone. Back then her body was alien to her, something that she wanted to like but wasn't sure how. Now she felt beautiful, like her body was a Disneyland for Tommy's dick to explore and enjoy the rides.

She brought her fingers from her sex and raised them to her mouth, sucking eagerly at the juices coated upon them. It was a lascivious action for such an innocent being and one that

Tommy loved. He ripped his towel off, releasing his proud erect member and moved towards the bed.

He took Jemima's fingers from her mouth and placed them in his, savouring any remnants of the moisture that remained there. It evidently wasn't enough to satisfy his desire and he moved his head between her legs, at first dotting light kisses around the edges of the heat that generated there and taking in the scent of her femininity before placing his hand on the mound between her legs. Parting the outer lips to expose the pinkness of the flower inside, Tommy let his tongue dip into his wife's eager pussy, hearing her emit a groan of pleasure as he did so. Jemima placed her own hands back between her legs and held herself open allowing her lover's tongue to probe deeper, tasting her honey.

His hands freed, Tommy used one of his fingers to work Jemima's pussy at the same time as his tongue, alternating between them as he lapped, nibbled and stroked against her clitoris. She arched her back in euphoria as Tommy let his teeth bite a little harder on her love button. She knew that she would need him inside her soon. As he swapped his tongue for his fingers and pushed circular motions around the edge of her clitoris she knew that the time had come. She could feel her orgasm mounting.

Grabbing Tommy's rich black hair in her hand she pulled him away from her pussy so that he was staring up at her. Her juices still glistened upon his face from where he'd been buried inside her.

'Fuck me,' she said.

It was all the invitation his straining cock needed. Without saying a word, Tommy moved into position and allowed his thick cock to slide into her. There was a slight blurring in her vision as he did so, the joyful feeling of his strength within her causing a momentary blissful giddiness.

Tommy moved his face to her breasts and nibbled at the excited peaks he found there as he thrust into her, clearly lost in the moment. A slick of sweat wrapped itself around Jemima's body, the frenzy of his actions rocking her body. As she looked into his eyes, a lock of Tommy's hair tumbled down across his forehead and a bead of moisture dripped from it onto Jemima's cheek as Tommy allowed his strokes to become quicker.

Jemima's breathing intensified as Tommy let his young muscular body slap against hers, the hardness of his stomach and the covering of hair that rested there pushing against her delicate flesh. Tommy could feel his seed rising within his member. Kissing his wife fully upon the lips, his teeth almost latching onto her lower lip with a tiny bite, Tommy unleashed his sexual flow into her. As he did so, Jemima too let the first waves of orgasm wash over her. She could hear the waves of the sea outside their window harmonious with her own. A feverish electricity ran over her body as she gave herself over to lust. She pulled Tommy close to her as the last drops of his pleasure drained inside her, her body becoming limp as every last drop of sexual energy exited her own core.

As Tommy withdrew his cock and went to lay down beside her he made one final action, pulling back the fleshy folds of her sex, exposing the clitoris once more. It was raised and proud, a glorious tribute to her intense orgasm. He kissed it, the flavour a fusion of his wife's juices and the aftertaste of his own masculine desire.

As they lay together Jemima allowed Tommy to wrap his arm around her and hold her close, resting her head on the swirls of damp, dark chest hair that decorated his strong pecs. Her energy erased, she fell asleep in his arms.

The soft tender glow of their love-making was still there when Jemima woke up. Unlike Tommy. She was alone in the bed. The air in the room was no longer yellow and was tinged with the first murmurings of dark. She guessed she had been sleeping for quite a while, a fact confirmed when she looked at her watch next to the now wilting bougainvillea on the bedside table. How quickly it had turned from a joyous thriving bloom picked from the beauty of one of Antiparos's narrow cobbled streets just a few hours ago to something that now looked a touch sad and in need of some loving to save it.

Jemima called Tommy's name. There was no answer. Rising from the bed she wrapped a brightly coloured sarong around herself and slipped a pair of flip-flops onto her feet. She wandered out onto the balcony that joined their room and looked down onto the beach below. A few people ambled up and down it watching the sun slowly descend over the horizon but there was no sign of Tommy.

A rumble of hunger came from her stomach as she contemplated where he could be. Love-making was hungry work. Maybe Tommy had gone downstairs to fetch some food. The guesthouse they were staying in was small, almost boutique, and the owners, a middle-aged Greek couple and their twenty-something daughter, had informed the Hearns that they could order food any time they liked. Maybe Tommy had a surprise in mind. She'd head downstairs to find out.

Replacing her sarong with a Karl Lagerfeld dress that hung loosely across her frame, Jemima grabbed the spare room key – Tommy obviously had the other – and headed down to the ground floor of the guesthouse. There was no sign of any of the other guests who occupied the three other rooms alongside Tommy and Jemima's on the first floor.

She looked into the dining area to see if Tommy was there. He wasn't. It was empty. She'd ask at Reception.

When she arrived there the desk was empty too but she could hear a faint noise coming from the small office behind the Reception area. She strained her ears to hear a little clearer. The noise was a series of moans, and despite her tender years and somewhat naïve character, Jemima knew exactly what they were. Somebody was having sex.

She smiled to herself, eager to find Tommy and tell him what she'd heard. But as she started to move away curiosity took hold of her. Moving behind the Reception area she tip-toed closer to the origin of the sound. The small office door was slightly ajar. Unable to stop herself, she peered inside.

The guesthouse owners' daughter was bent over a table, her naked ass cheeks exposed as a man, his trousers and underpants around his ankles, stood behind her sliding his cock into her from behind. He slapped her backside lightly as he fucked her. It was Tommy.

Placing her hand over her mouth to silence a horrified scream that wanted to burst forth, Jemima said nothing and ran back to her room. She sat on the bed and cried. She saw the flower again, wilted, a little ugly and now somewhat pathetic on the table. She couldn't help but feel the same.

By the time Tommy returned to their room twenty minutes later the flower was thrown in the bin, out of sight, and Jemima was pretending to be asleep on the bed once more.

When Tommy woke her up he made no mention of his visit downstairs. Jemima made no mention of her sordid discovery. For the moment, just like the wilted flower, that ugly episode would stay hidden away from view.

CHAPTER 19
Now, 2015

Amy's journey back to London after her visit to Manchester was a bittersweet one. She was glad to be heading back to the sanctuary and solitude of her own flat, even if she hadn't yet found her husband. To be momentarily away from all of the reminders of her past life. Of things she'd thought she'd understood and loved. She wasn't sure about anything anymore. If the last few days had taught her anything it was that her life with Riley had not just been a tissue of lies but a huge paper ream of dishonesty.

Her conversation with Lily Rich had left her broken and deeply angry, stripping her of her strength to continue with her search in the northern city. She needed to regroup her thoughts before deciding on her next move in Manchester. Riley making a living behind her back was one thing but making whoopee behind it was a whole different ball game. Finding solace in the arms of another woman. Especially one whom she'd trusted. For a day Amy had just lay on the bed at her hotel and cried, angry at Riley, angry at Lily ... angry at herself. *How had she let that happen? Her husband crawl between the sheets with another woman. Had she not been enough to satisfy him?* A thousand questions had flooded Amy's thoughts as she journeyed back to London. If Riley had written the letter and wanted to be with her then why would he include Lily in his list of suspects? Someone who could blow any chance of a reunion right out of the water? His tryst with her could have remained a secret. Amy would have had no reason to track her down. As it was, her meeting with Lily may have been the result of chance but she would have been compelled to find her eventually as she trawled through Riley's list of suspects.

Lily must have had a reason for wanting Riley dead. Otherwise he wouldn't have listed her. After Lily had confessed to sleeping with Riley, Amy had been unable to think rationally and had left the restaurant they were eating at faster than you could say 'adultery', the destructive force of the revelation finally hitting home. She'd tried phoning Lily afterwards in order to hear her explain further, wanting to know just what had possessed her to sleep with Riley. Why would she do that? Was there more to it than just lust? What self-respecting woman wouldn't want answers about why her husband had strayed? She left a message but Lily never returned her call. But their time would come, Amy knew that.

Amy's thoughts were full of Genevieve too. She was hiding something; that was for sure. Behind that icy cold, hardened exterior, something red hot and dangerous was bubbling away. Amy just had to work out how she was going to get to it.

Back in the comfort of her own London front room, Amy unfurled the letter once more and read it again, trying to comprehend why Riley had written it. It sounded like Riley, it looked like Riley's writing, but the question still remained as to whether it was really from him or not. And if it wasn't then who would write such a thing? And where was her husband?

Did any of it now make any more sense knowing what she'd learnt in Manchester? Amy wasn't sure.

'I'm so sorry. Sorry for it all. Sorry for what will happen. Sorry for making you relive it. Sorry for deceiving you. Someone knows the answer, someone wanted me dead. Tommy, Adam, Lily, Gen-

evieve, Grant ... none of them can be trusted, they all had their reasons for wanting me killed.'

Tommy wanted to recoup the money he'd lent, Adam may have had some gangland involvement, Lily was sleeping with Riley and Genevieve was harbouring some secret. Amy was sure. And she knew that Riley and Grant were not exactly bosom buddies.

'Someone's in the know. There's more I could say, but can't ... it's so weak. So pathetic. So many secrets and lies. God, I hate myself for doing this to you, Amy. I should leave you alone, but I can't.'

Amy didn't know what to believe any more. But she knew she couldn't stop until the truth was hers – whatever it turned out to be. But Amy, for the first time ever, was flying solo. Those she cared about were no longer by her side. Her very being was like a cobweb eager to trap the truth. But any web, no matter how mighty, was only as strong as its weakest strand. Amy just prayed that hers was strong enough.

CHAPTER 20
Then, 2007

A blanket of sadness smothered itself across the Manchester church.

'And so it is that we lay the bodies of both Ivor and Enid Barrowman to rest. May their souls be forever united in the love they shared on Earth. We ask you, Lord, to give your strength to their only daughter, Amy, and to see that she may follow in the rightful path and journey that Ivor and Enid took while they walked among us.'

Amy was aware that the words were being spoken. She could hear them clearly and understand every syllable but yet each and every one of them failed to register in her brain. *How had it come to this?* Just a few short days ago she had been joking with her father that he spent too much time at work with his undertaker colleagues and not enough time with his ever-loving wife. The same colleagues who were now laying her father to rest for the final time. Alongside his wife; Amy's mother. At least now they would be able to spend an eternity together. Amy's world had changed irrevocably in the blink of an eye. Her parents were gone, wiped out in just a few short seconds by a reckless out-all-Saturday-night driver speeding at nearly twice the legal limit and awash with enough alcohol to stock a student union as her parents took a leisurely Sunday morning stroll not far from the estate where they lived. Mercifully they had both died together and almost instantly.

As the daughter of an undertaker, Amy had lived around death her entire life, but the finality of watching her parents being laid to rest was the hardest thing she had ever had to cope with. Thank God she had her rocks, Laura and Riley, with her. Without them she could have willingly easily joined her parents in the afterlife. It was only them who made her realise that she had something to live for.

It had been Laura she had first turned to when the news had come. A slip of a policeman turned up at Amy's door just before noon on the Sunday informing her that he had 'some terrible news'. It had all seemed such a blur but Amy remembered thinking that Laura was there, by her side, exactly when she needed her, dishing out words of comfort and sweet, hot tea.

She'd helped her arrange the funeral too, organising flowers, cars, hymns. She even told her own parents to send some money to her to help pay for the costs. They didn't know Enid and Ivor, but were persuaded by their daughter's kind-hearted motives. She didn't want Amy to worry about cash.

It had been made easier as the firm Amy was dealing with was the one that her father had worked for, but still, if it hadn't been for Laura, Amy was certain that she would have broken down once and for all. It was her best friend who had helped her walk down the aisle behind the coffin, supporting her with her firm grasp of undying friendship. Amy was determined to not let her parents down and to give them the funeral their beautiful loving lives deserved and Laura had helped so much with that. She had to remain strong for them and with Laura by her side she knew she could.

Riley was a pillar of strength too. He and Amy had only met two years before but she was pleased that she had been able to introduce him to her parents. Enid and Ivor had adored him, Enid loving his roguish good looks and cheeky boy-next-door charm while Ivor thought he looked like 'a proper film star from one of those action movies off the telly'. They loved the fact that he made their only daughter incredibly happy. They knew that Amy Barrowman had met her soul mate in Riley Hart.

The Barrowmans had not been rich when they died and it was left to Amy to sort out their estate. Again she had relied heavily on Laura and Riley to help her out. Often she would take herself to bed, tired from the rigours of her life and leave the two of them sorting through mounds of crockery, clothing, documents and photographs they had removed from the flat she grew up in – sifting them into 'to keep' or 'charity shop' piles. Riley would later join her in bed and she would wake to find him cradling her in his arms while Laura slept downstairs on the sofa.

The months that followed her parents' deaths would have been beyond unbearable without Laura and Riley. They both gave her love, but in different, equally necessary, measures. With both of them she could see a lifetime of forever. She had no idea what she would do if she ever had to be without them.

If she had known then that she would lose them both in the space of one short evening a few years later then Amy might not have been able to come through the ordeal of her parents' death in one piece.

CHAPTER 21
Now, 2015

Actor Grant Wilson had always enjoyed being top dog. At school he had always wanted to be the first to touch the sides at the end of the annual swimming races, or be the one who could clear the loftiest of bars in the high jump. He was always striving to be the first to be picked for any team and would do whatever it took to make sure he was. He would even manage to convince the teachers to let him off handing in his homework on time if he hadn't yet cajoled one of the smart kids into writing it for him. Second best was never an option.

Grant Wilson had one of those faces you couldn't say no to. It was a face was which was frequently splashed across the national TV magazines decorating the shelves of the UK's newsagents. Grant sold copies. Women wanted to bed him, men wanted to be him. Thanks to his role as Dr Eamonn Samms on British hit medical drama, *Ward 44*, Grant was one of the highest paid actors on UK telly. It would only be a matter of time before the glamour and megabuck allure of Hollywood came calling. The world was at his feet. But at the moment his feet were chilled to the core ...

Grant Wilson was sitting on the cordoned-off hard shoulder of the far from glamorous M23 motorway. Rodeo Drive it was not. Freezing cold it was. Grant was there filming a scene in which Dr Samms was driving to his latest girlfriend's house when he witnesses a road accident. Being the dashing doctor he sweeps in to save as many lives as possible, women and children first.

'I was told I'd find you here. So this is the joy of an actor's life, eh?' Amy, her teeth chattering with the cold, had just arrived on the makeshift set and been advised of Grant's whereabouts by one of the show's runners.

'Amy, I've been expecting you,' smiled Grant. Amy couldn't help but notice yet again just how handsome he was. 'My agent said that you'd been in touch and that she'd told you where to find me. I don't normally have visitors on set but I thought I'd make an exception for you, seeing as we've been through the same experience ... that night at The Kitty Kat was a fucking nightmare. Like some fucking *Godfather* bloodbath.'

Amy shivered. 'I appreciate you seeing me, although I will admit I had hoped it would be at some cosy studio location or at least within the confines of a centrally-heated Winnebago. And yes, I'm here about that night ...'

'I guessed as much. Listen, we can't really talk here, can we? Dragging up all that death will only put me off this scene. I'm only here shooting for one more night and then I'm finished until the New Year. Why don't we meet up at my hotel tonight? We can talk there – that's best.' It was more of an order than a question.

'It's not just about that night. There have been complications since I received ...' Amy was just about to tell Grant about the letter when a voice boomed across the hard shoulder.

'Dr Samms – back on set! We need to film the rescue of the first child from the car.' The voice belonged to a rather officious looking, clipboard-wielding TV type. Amy guessed she was the assistant producer or someone along those lines. She was grateful for the interruption. Maybe she shouldn't just

divulge her news straight away. After all, Grant was listed as
one of the suspects. According to Riley, Grant had reason to
want him dead, and Amy knew there was no love lost between
the two men ever since they'd been at school together. It just
so happened that Grant had one of those faces that any woman
immediately felt compelled to trust. It was a notion she would
have to shift.

'That's my call. I have to go, but here's where I'm staying. I
should be finished here by about six thirty-ish – if you want to
stay down, book a room and charge it to me. It's the least I can
do for you after you sorted me out with that pixie-looking deal-
er girl at the Kitty Kat. Your discretion was much appreciated.'

A feeling of deep anger passed through Amy at the mention
of Lily. No matter how she tried she couldn't stop the image of
Lily and Riley together from scorching itself painfully onto her
brain.

Grant handed Amy a business card with the name of a hotel
on it. 'If you're not there by half eight then I'll assume you're not
coming. We can talk properly then. See you later.'

As Amy walked away from the actor, she knew that she'd be
there. She had too many questions that needed answering ... and
maybe Grant could be the man to supply them. Maybe he could
be the one to help her find Riley.

Grant knew she'd be there too. No woman had ever said no
to him. Well, not recently anyway ...

Lily wandered into the study at her parents' house and dumped
her small black, furry rucksack onto the mahogany desk where
her father, Adam, sat staring at a bunch of papers. The bag was
still wet from where she'd been rained on during her journey
home from sourcing more drugs. It was a typical winter's day

outside – wet, windy and wildly cold. A few drops of water fell and pooled onto the table.

'Will you fucking get that off there, please?' barked Adam. 'This is a place of business, Lily. The last thing I need is everything getting soaked by you and your stupid bag. It's bad enough in this house with your mother erecting her fucking mirrored monstrosities everywhere. This place is looking like a fucking season ticket to the Tower Ballroom in Blackpool.'

'All right, keep your hair on, Dad. Well, that would only apply if you had some I suppose,' she sneered, pointing to his bald dome. 'I wanted to tell you something.'

'Can't it wait, I'm busy. If I don't work bloody hard to earn a crust then who do you think pays for this bloody house and your mother's extravagant tastes? It's not her, that's for sure. Caitlyn's never done a day's work in her life.'

Lily raised her eyebrows skywards. 'Apart from raising me, that is. Being a mother is a skilled job you know. If she hadn't raised me so well, I'd never have turned out the fine figure of moralistic purity I am today.' There was more than a dollop of sarcasm running through her words. 'Where is the old diva anyway, I haven't seen her for days?'

'She's visiting her sister Lolly in London, bleeding my bank account dry at Harrods no doubt. She spends it quicker than I can fucking earn it that's for sure. Mind you, it leaves me in peace.' Adam's salacious mind immediately raced to the 'peace' he'd enjoyed with Dolly the day before. He may have been paying for it but she was worth every penny and allowed him to enjoy carnal pleasures that Caitlyn had given up on years ago.

'How exactly do you earn your money, anyway?' Lily parked herself on the edge of the desk, much to her father's annoyance. Her clothes were just as sodden as her bag, not that the free-spirited Lily gave two hoots. She wanted to speak to her father and now was as good a time as any. 'Are you involved in anything dodgy? I assume this house wasn't bought with the profit from the purest of professions. There can't be many daughters who don't know what their daddy actually does for a living?'

'What the fuck, Lily? Does it matter what I do for a living? All you need to know is that I work hard and it pays to keep a roof over your head and those increasingly-outlandish clothes on your back.' He scanned the black chunky plastic jacket, sweater dress and orange fishnet tights she was wearing. 'Your taste is weirder than that Grace Jones bird I saw on TV. Strange piece, she is. Flapping around on stage with her tits out.'

'It was just something Amy Hart said, that's all ...' She guessed that she would have Adam's full attention as soon as she mentioned Amy's name. She was right.

'When did you see her?' snarled Adam. 'What are you sniffing around her for? She's trouble.'

'Hardly. The woman's as innocent as Snow White considering she used to run a banging nightclub. It was yesterday. She nearly got herself knocked down and luckily for her I was there to pull her out of the road. I swear the car was actually gunning for her. She's obviously been treading on some toes.' Lily was sure her father seemed to fidget awkwardly in his seat at the mention of the near accident. Did a crumb of a smile just ripple across his face?

'Where was this? And why were you with her, more to the point?'

'I was just passing, out shopping and saw her walk into the road. Didn't even know it was her at first. Anyway, she took me for a meal to say thanks for saving her sorry little ass and told me that Tommy Hearn filled her in about Riley being some sort of big cheese criminal who ended up surrounded by more corpses than an episode of *CSI*. Quite a little killer by all accounts. Sure makes him a whole lot sexier than as head of a plastics business, eh?'

'What was her reaction?' Adam was trying rather unsuccessfully to keep his cool in front of his daughter.

'I think she knows it's true but she's finding it hard to believe. She also thinks that maybe he's alive. Dumb bitch. How can he be? He had his face shot off. That makes for a whole lotta dead in my books.'

Adam could feel a bead of sweat forming in the bulldog folds of flesh at the back of his neck. 'He can't be alive. He can't be,' he stated. Lily wasn't sure whether it was a fact or more of a wish judging from the tone in her father's voice.

For a moment there was contemplative silence. It was Lily who broke it. 'So, is my daddy dearest a hardened criminal too, then? Have you bludgeoned, stabbed and shot your way through life to pay for all of this? I don't mind if you have. You've got the ugly face of a gangland desperado so you might as well have the lifestyle too.'

'Why don't you just go away, Lily? There is no point in worrying your miniscule fucking little brain with more than it can cope with. I earn good money and that's all you need to know.' Adam was beyond dismissive. As far as he was concerned the conversation was over. Lily didn't need to dig any more.

'Your lack of denial speaks volumes. I'll take that as a yes. It's kinda cool – gives you an edge that most fathers can only dream of. Beats being a geography teacher or a traffic warden anyway. My dad, the modern-day mobster. Smart ...'

'Goodbye Lily.' His words were blunt. It was her cue to leave.

Lily walked upstairs to her room.

Once inside she emptied the contents of her bag onto her bed and fished around for a bag of weed and some cigarette papers. Lily was in the mood to get a little high. In fact, as she contemplated the fact that Riley was ... hell, maybe is ... a criminal, she let her mind wander freely, thinking back to the sex they'd enjoyed together. It had been good, toe-curlingly so. God, if he was alive, she'd have adored a repeat performance. Rolling the cigarette papers, Lily decided that she wanted to get so high she'd be risking vertigo.

Having booked into the hotel for the night, as she knew she would, Amy was annoyed with the fact that she took a little bit longer getting ready than she really needed to. She was miffed with herself for having spent the afternoon finding a decent clothes shop to buy a new outfit from and a department store as well for a touch of pampering. When she'd left her flat that morning she hadn't expected to be staying overnight anywhere so luxuries such as a change of outfit and some decent toiletries were not considered. *Why was she bothering?* All she wanted was information.

The truth of the matter was that she was definitely bewitched by Grant Wilson. She couldn't help it. Since Riley had died there had been no male attention in her life. She'd not looked for it, she didn't need it and she certainly didn't want it. So why did she suddenly feel a rippling of desire the moment she'd come face to face with Grant? Simple – the man was hypnotically gorgeous. Despite a clash of conflicting emotions coursing rapids-like through her, she couldn't help but feel that she wanted to look her best. Guilt fused with forbidden attraction. Lustrous blond hair curved back in waves across his head, deep blue eyes that any woman could dive into, immersing herself in lustful longing, and an ice-white smile that screamed 'toothpaste ad', Grant was the peak of masculinity. With a hardened body that was shown to great effect on countless *Ward 44* bedroom scenes, he was the complete package.

But Amy wasn't here on a date and attempted to park any lascivious thoughts at the back of her mind. She may have been living like a widow for the last six months but she was still a woman, and she missed the love-making she'd shared with Riley. There had been no-one sharing her bed since Riley and attractive though Grant was, this was neither the time nor the place. For all she knew, Grant could be the one responsible for her husband's death, or at least a failed attempt on it if he were still alive. But somehow she was still taking longer than normal to make sure she looked as hot as she possibly could ...

It obviously worked. 'Wow, you look bloody amazing,' were the first words from Grant's lips as Amy walked into the hotel bar. She could feel her heart beating inside her chest. *Was it just fear and nerves or a cocktail of trepidation and unnecessary excitement?* Amy wasn't sure.

'Thank you.' It was all that she could think of to say. Anything else would have seemed too awkward. She added 'you too', feeling compelled to repay the compliment.

The first twenty minutes of their conversation, aided by two glasses of rich red wine, were nothing more than basic niceties. Grant asked Amy how she was, how she'd coped since that night at The Kitty Kat, how hard it must have been losing both a husband and a best friend, what life was like for her away from Manchester and indeed whether she ever intended to return to her home city.

It wasn't until they'd sat down in the hotel restaurant and ordered a meal that the conversation turned to the real crux of the matter. It was Grant who shifted the discussion out of first gear, sensing Amy's struggle.

'You know your late husband and I never really liked each other, don't you? In fact I hated him. Always did. We were what you'd call rivals when we were younger.' Grant flashed a hint of a smile to try and ease the complicated nature of their conversation.

'Yeah, I know ... why was that? I would have thought you and Riley would have been mates. You are kind of similar ... I mean, *were* kind of ...' Amy's voice petered out, not knowing how to continue.

'It all stemmed from our schooldays. When you're in the same year together and you meet someone who is just as good as you are at sports and academics and is popular with the teachers and even more so with the girls then it tends to grate slightly. I guess I was jealous.' Grant shrugged his shoulders and flashed a smile.

'But you were what ... eleven years old when you first met? That's pretty mad to dislike someone at such a tender age.'

'Hey. I'm an actor. Vanity is my middle name. I guess it started at an early age. Your husband was always a popular guy, especially with the ladies ... I needed to know I could beat him, compete with him.'

The mention of Riley's popularity with women pinched at Amy's skin. A vision of her husband and Lily together in bed scratched itself across her mind. As her one true love, even the thought of him with another woman brought a nasty taste to her mouth. For the briefest moment a thunderclap of emotion hurtled across Amy's mind. If Riley was alive then giving herself to Grant would be the ultimate revenge for his betrayal with Lily.

She let the thought disappear as soon as it had come, as if too wicked to contemplate. 'I wouldn't have thought you'd have any trouble pulling.'

'Let me tell you something. My mum and dad brought me up to believe that I would never amount to much. Even now, as a successful actor, they don't really give me any praise. It was the same at school. If I wasn't made captain of the rugby team, given the best marks for a project or first in line for a date at the school disco then I wasn't happy. I felt a failure. Dominant parents can do that to even the strongest of lads. I was determined to succeed in everything I did. I had to be number one so that my parents couldn't constantly say I'd failed. Anything less than top of the heap wasn't good enough for them, or for me. If life was to be bearable every time I went home then I had to be able to hold my head up high and be the best. Riley was the sodding thorn in my side.'

It was the first sign of vulnerability that Amy had seen in Grant. It was instantly endearing, despite the evident anger seething beneath the surface.

'I would always try to work harder than any other classmate doing whatever it took to be number one. I studied for hours for tests, revised for weeks for exams just to make sure that I could do my best. It was the same with sports. I had to be the team captain, because vice-captain meant only one thing in my head and that was second best. It was like an addiction. For a while I was top dog. For the first two or three years of school I excelled in cricket, rugby, swimming ... you name it. The same with all of my school subjects. Then all of a sudden one name kept popping up and beating me to captain of such and such a team or top marks in one subject or another. It was always Riley Hart. It seems pathetic I know. I should have thrived on competition, but I didn't. I hated your husband throughout my entire school career and the feeling was pretty much mutual. He hated the occasions when I was number one and vice versa.'

'And you've carried that all of your life. That's ridiculous,' scoffed Amy. 'You and Riley didn't see each other for years after leaving school did you? Surely that rivalry was all behind you, just a boyish thing of the past.'

There was a moment's silence, Grant somehow searching for the right words. 'Blokes are blokes. We let things fester and rot. I hadn't seen your husband for years before that night at the Kitty Kat and God knows that I wouldn't wish what happened on my worst enemy. Nobody deserves to die like that. I thought I was a goner that night too – bullets seemed to be flying everywhere, but I never liked Riley. I make no bones about it. I didn't want him to succeed when he left school and it pissed me off that he got everything passed on to him from his dad. He wanted me to fail too. Call it jealousy. My parents gave me nothing, still haven't. I've earned everything I have, had to overcome every obstacle. I don't think Riley had to fucking work for anything. I'm sorry if that's harsh but you came here for the truth, didn't you?'

Amy was keen to defend Riley – he was the man she'd married after all. Despite everything. 'Yes, I did, but you can't choose your parents. It wasn't Riley's fault that his dad ran a successful business. No more than the fact that yours aren't as supportive as you'd like them to be. You've had the last laugh though, haven't you? You're the biggest thing on UK television. That's rubbing a rather large barrel of salt into the wounds if you ask me.'

'I'll tell you something about your late husband, shall I Amy? He went out of his way to humiliate me many times and that's something that has scarred me for life.' Grant was shaking as he spoke. It was uncomfortable for Amy to watch.

'In our final term – we both must have been about seventeen – we were having an end of year ball. Great big thing – marquee, hog roast, New Orleans jazz band ... the works. It was going to be awesome. Every bloke wanted to be there with the fittest girl on his arm. I had my eyes on a girl called Lottie Webber. I had done for most of my final year. Captain of the netball team, best voice in the school choir, played opposite me in the school production of *Whistle Down The Wind*. There was a real spark between us. She was everything I saw in myself. She epitomised success. And she was drop dead gorgeous to boot. I wooed her, I took her out on dates, and I lost my virginity to her. She was the girl I definitely wanted to be with for that ball. Hell, she was the girl I wanted to be with, full stop.'

'So what happened?' Amy had a feeling of foreboding that she knew where the story was headed.

'Well, the one thing I didn't have at school was money. My parents didn't give me much in the way of pocket money so I couldn't wine and dine Lottie as she deserved. We had nights out underage drinking down the pub and we'd hang out in town but I wanted to give her more. She said she didn't mind. We planned our outfits for the ball. I borrowed a suit, Lottie bought a fancy dress – not the one she really wanted, that was way too expensive, but nice nevertheless. Everything was good. I was ready to be cock of the walk for our end of year bash.

'Then it happened. I turned up at Lottie's house to pick her up and her folks tell me she's not there. The front room looked like a fucking florists, bunches of roses everywhere, but no sign of Lottie. Her mum told me she'd be at the ball. Too fucking right she was.' There was more than a sliver of anger creeping into Grant's voice now. Amy could only sit and listen to the inevitable conclusion.

'I rock up at the ball, all dressed up in my borrowed finery and there she is, hanging off Riley's arm, in the dress that she'd really wanted. She couldn't even look me in the eye, but I knew what had happened. Riley had bought her with fancy flowers and the dress. I wasn't wrong. He strolls over like the big I-Am and just grins. The most idiotic, supercilious grin I'd ever seen. He didn't even really like her – he dumped her after the ball. He just wanted to beat me, to take something away from me and to stick two fingers up. I hated him ... hated him with a passion. He'd made me look a fool and that's the one thing I can't bear. My parents had made me feel like that far too often and I swore nobody else would. Riley did, so yeah, I hated him ... he was pathetic.'

'Enough to kill him?' The words had tumbled from Amy's lips before she'd had a chance to consider them. If she could have swallowed them back then she would have.

'Is that what you've come here to ask me? You think I might have killed your precious husband? I hated the man at school but look who's doing all right now ... despite everything.' There was a swagger in Grant's voice as he spluttered the sentence, his tone rising with his anger. 'You honestly think I'm capable of that. For fuck's sake, Amy ...'

Amy tried to backtrack with an apology. 'No, it's not that, it's just that some things have happened and ...' but her words were drowned out by the scraping of Grant's chair as he pushed it away from the table and stood up.

'Just forget it ... your husband's dead, but it was fuck all to do with me, all right! He was the bane of my life in my teenage years but I've grown up since then. I'm the one on the front of the magazines, no thanks to him. I'm the one with Hollywood knocking at my door. So screw you, Amy Hart ...'

Grant stormed from the restaurant leaving an awkward Amy sitting there alone, a roomful of eyes upon her.

CHAPTER 22
Now, 2015

Dolly Townsend was sitting in a back room at the escort agency she worked for busy talking to one of the girls who had just signed onto the agency's books. The girl, a wispy slip of a thing fresh out of school reminded Dolly of herself nearly two decades ago, full of dreams, aspirations and hopes about the future.

But at the age of thirty-five Dolly was rapidly learning that her once perfectly rounded breasts, cellulite-free thighs and peachy pert butt cheeks were not exactly as rounded, cellulite-free and peachy as they once had been. Not that Dolly was bitter, far from it, she loved her life, but something was missing ...

'I've always thought of my body as a building. One that's a multi-storey. This bit up here ...' Dolly pointed to her head. 'That's the office. That's where all of my thinking and calculating gets done. My brain takes care of all the financial business. But down here ...' She was now pointing between her legs. 'This bit is the nightclub built for fun in the basement. This is where the action happens, and it's up to me who I bring to my club if you get my drift. Always remember that you're the boss. You act as your own bouncer.'

She crossed her legs, both of them still incredibly defined and shapely. 'When I was a new kid like you, I thought life on my back would get me everything I wanted too, darling. I thought I'd be as rich and famous as Cindy Crawford or Linda Evangelista ...' The girl stared blankly at Dolly from underneath her poker-straight fringe, her ignorance of the names glaringly apparent.

'I dreamed of meeting a good man, one to take care of me and keep me on the straight and narrow. Act as landlord to my *building* if you like, to treat me good. Sadly, life doesn't always give you want you want.' She sucked on her cigarette as she talked. If there was one thing Dolly loved doing it was sharing her knowledge and experience with the younger girls. It made her feel good about the fact she sold her body for cash. 'This game can be a good one. Just don't expect it to give you everything you want overnight and always remember that you're the one in control, despite what some of the blokes you meet with might think. You are number one. It's the most important lesson I can give you, that is. Some of the blokes you meet are right arses, they think they can treat you like a piece of shit, but always remember they can't. They're the ones paying, you're the one earning. Prostitution may be a bed of depravity, and it's certainly not always a bed of roses, but it can see you good if you let it. You understand?'

'What's depravity mean?' asked the girl.

Oh dear, thought Dolly. Not the sharpest tool, but at least she was pretty. She'd do all right.

No, Dolly was actually very proud of her longevity in her job. She'd been selling her money-maker since the age of sixteen. With no real qualifications to her name when she'd left school, she quickly learnt that in order to bring home the bacon she was going to have to use what God had physically given her below the neckline as opposed to above it. She had her brain, maybe not one that could balance equations and work out the logic of a split infinitive but her grey matter was sharp enough to know that her tight body and womanly curves were to be her path to a road of financial success.

No, Dolly didn't do badly at all. In fact she was one of the most respected girls on the books of the escort agency she worked for. No, who was she trying to kid? One of the most respected *women*. If a client wanted a versatile, seductive and elite experience with a *girl* then he would definitely be ordering the frothy young thing she'd just been talking to. Dolly had been there, done that, got the bruises, servicing more men than she cared to remember in her time. But she still had *it*, that was for sure ... her regulars told her so.

She was discreet, accommodating and would consider any sexual desire. Which was why at times she'd gained the bruises. Some clients could be a little heavy-handed, but those were the risks. If she'd wanted a safe life then Dolly would have led a simple existence as a shop assistant or a dinner lady like her elder sisters. Both three years older than her, but they looked thirty years her senior, stagnating in a sea of suburban hand-to-mouth existence with their two-point-four kids and husbands who lived to prop up the local bar and deliver a once-monthly shag. Welcome to Dullsville. That was definitely not for Dolly. She had always had ambition.

No, Dolly was happy with her lot ... well, she *had been*, more or less. Maybe a little less lately if she was honest as she'd been feeling that maybe there was a little more to life than opening her legs. A lot more in fact. Other avenues to explore rather than just trying to be consistently sexy and pleasuring men for a handful of bank notes. Dolly thought that maybe it was about time she started to really use what God had given her above the neckline too. She knew she could be savvy. She wouldn't have survived so long without learning a few vital life-lessons along the way. Yes, it was time to ramp her life up a notch. She just needed to fathom out exactly how to do it ...

CHAPTER 23
Then, 2009

The ricochet of the throbbing dance beat burst from the speakers as Amy and Laura writhed their bodies together on the dance floor to the feel-good lyrics of 'When Love Takes Over' by David Guetta and Kelly Rowland. It was a joyous anthem about living life to the max and the two girls were determined to do just that. It was something that Amy had resolved to do ever since the cruel death of her parents two years before. If she'd learnt one lesson the year she'd buried her mum and dad it was that life was all too fleeting and could be taken away at any second. Life was to be celebrated. And on the dance floor of Decoupage, the girls' favourite Manchester nightspot, amongst a writhing mass of hot sweaty bodies, they were going to make sure that everybody could see just how much they wanted to celebrate.

It was a Saturday night and the girls had undertaken their usual weekend routine. Laura had driven from the Northern Quarter to Riley and Amy's house in Sale, where Riley had left them to go out to yet another business meeting. Even a weekend wasn't sacred in Riley's world. The girls had cracked open bottles of spirits to get the party started – gin and tonics and rum and cokes, making them tipsy as they applied their make-up and slipped into their skin-skimming jumpsuits and ordered a taxi to take them to Decoupage, one of Manchester's trendiest clubs. By the time the girls arrived, they would always be half-cut and fully revved up to hit the dance floor. It was Saturday night perfection and it was their time.

Despite missing Riley like crazy, Saturday night was often ladies night for the two women and Amy wouldn't have swapped the time she managed to spend with Laura for anything. They laughed, they loved and they lived. Their smiles were as bright as the laser-beams of light that shot around the club, turning the space into a riot of kaleidoscopic shades.

In between tunes the girls would head to the bar and order more drinks, the brightly coloured delights of Bacardi Breezers or fizzy apple cocktails fuelling them to sashay back onto the dance floor once more.

Laura was as keen to impress the men around her as ever. 'Have you seen the DJ tonight? He is just delicious. Come on, we need to ramp up the sexy and dance in front of him right now. According to the posters he's a hot-shot American who's played some of New York's biggest clubs. He's doing a tour over here right now and knows people like Akon and Calvin Harris apparently. The man is a musical god and he shall be mine.'

It was true, when Laura had her sights set on a member of the opposite sex then there was nothing her poor unsuspecting prey could do to fend off her amorous Venus Flytrap ways. Not that any of them fought too hard to resist. She was a beautiful prize.

'You are incorrigible,' teased Amy. 'But come on then, let's sex it up on the dance floor. No man can say no to that. And for the record, do we know this DJ's name or not?'

'Not!' deadpanned Laura. 'And I don't care. If he's played NYC then he's big. Huger than big and I won't be satisfied until I'm rifling through his twelve inches in the DJ booth, okay!'

'Fair enough' laughed Amy.

As ever, Laura was victorious. As she returned to Amy and Riley's house around midday on the Sunday wearing the same jumpsuit as the night before – it was the usual routine for Laura most Sundays after their girlie nights out – she sported a smile that stretched from one hooped earring to the other. She didn't have a care in the world.

Riley and Amy were sat at the kitchen table drinking coffee. Amy's was black to try and fend off the clouding grogginess of her hangover.

'Well ...?' enquired Amy.

'His name is Blair Lonergan, he's as American as apple pie and just as tasty and he says we're welcome in the clubs of the Big Apple any time we might be Stateside,' beamed Laura.

'And ...?' Amy knew she had to ask.

'Yes we did, in his VIP dressing room at Decoupage. Let's just say I was granted Access All Areas and I repaid the compliment in the best way possible. And that he spun me right round like a record, baby ... in every direction! The DJ one isn't the only box he can work incredibly well, put it that way! Now, I'm off for a shower.'

Riley and Amy could still hear Laura laughing raucously as the water started running.

CHAPTER 24
Now, 2015

Amy hadn't seen Grant Wilson after he'd stormed out of the restaurant at the hotel. She had waited for him the next morning to see if he passed through reception but there was no sign. Amy enquired with the concierge as to his whereabouts but was informed that Grant had checked out with the rest of the TV crew at the crack of dawn that morning. He'd obviously headed off for filming.

For a while Amy considered trying to get back onto the set. She needed to speak to Grant, to tell him about the letter. The rendezvous the night before had not gone at all to plan. The only thing that was clear was that she could now add Grant to the ever-lengthening list of people who would lose no sleep at the thought of Riley meeting his maker. Boyhood rivalries had obviously run scarily deep between the two men.

Unable to fathom her next move, Amy had returned to her London flat. She needed to clear her head. It was staring her in the face that she would have to return to the increasingly complex world of Manchester as soon as possible to try and talk to Adam Rich. There was also unfinished business with Genevieve too. Call it a woman's intuition but she was hiding something from Amy.

Sinking into the comfort of her front room sofa, Amy looked at the photo of herself and Riley staring out at her from the opposite wall. It had been taken at the club. His face was a picture of boyish innocence, but now Amy knew differently. How could one man hide so many secrets? Conceal so many lies? She had discovered so many in such a short space of time. If he was capable of that, then how many more were to come?

Lily had spent a good few hours in her room smoking weed. She'd needed it. The last few days had been a mind-fuck as far as she was concerned. Seeing Amy again had stirred up all sorts of thoughts about Riley. She'd never loved him, so why had she just spent the last half an hour sobbing pitiful tears into her pillow, which was now covered in a swirly rainbow mess of different make-up hues all smudged together. She'd been upset when Riley had died, of course she had. He was her boss and her lover. Good bosses were hard to find and skilled lovers even harder. She'd never felt sorry for Amy. She'd obviously not satisfied him sexually so it was down to Lily to fill in the gaps. He'd satisfied her everywhere. On the desk in Amy's office, in the DJ booth, even on the fire escape during a busy club night.

Getting up from the bed, Lily walked across to her full-length mirror and stared into it. Her eyes were red and glassy. She rubbed them, hoping to make the redness disappear. It made them worse.

She felt tired, really tired and contemplated going to bed. It was only early evening but she could feel her eyes dragging against her face, heavy and craving slumber. Lily was due to head out. She had supplies to collect and places to deal at. But that could wait. She needed to be alone with her thoughts about Riley. About a dead man. A dead man she loved. Or maybe she didn't. Maybe he was alive. And maybe he wasn't. Yes, no, yes, no ... Lily broke out into hysterical laughter and shouted across the room, not caring who heard, 'I'm in love with a dead man!' Her mind felt clouded and mixed. Shaken like a mental snow globe. Her thoughts blended by the weed.

Her bedroom door opened and Adam walked in. The room stank of drugs, a fact not lost on him. His face was ominous like thunder. 'Jesus wept, Lily, what the hell are you screaming about? You're in love with which dead man?'

Lily's mind raced. She was in love with Riley. And didn't little girls always tell their daddies about their crushes? It was time to share. 'I'm in love with Riley Hart. I loved him and he loved me too. At least that's what he said before he dumped me.'

'Dumped you, what are you talking about, you stupid girl? It's the drugs talking. Why do you smoke that stuff?' Adam was more than incensed.

'I was having an affair with him, or at least I was until he told me to fuck off. He didn't want me anymore, Daddy. He broke my heart.'

The crestfallen look on Adam's face told even a drug-addled Lily that her admission had just broken her father's too.

If there was one condition that Amy had permanently suffered over the last six months it was a broken heart. The loss of both her husband and her best friend would have been enough to crush even the strongest of hearts and there were times when Amy herself doubted how she'd found the inner strength to deal with it all. She liked to think it was the guidance of her guardian angel parents looking down on her from above. At least she'd always been able to rely on them. They had never let her down.

Picking up their photo from a small table alongside the sofa, Amy clutched it to her chest. If she held them close to her heart she could pretend that they could still hear its beating. To know that she had survived everything that life had hurled at her. It gave her comfort. It gave her a new burst of strength to carry on fighting. Even though she was so tired. More tired than she had ever been ...

Still clutching the photo to her chest, Amy drifted off into a deep sleep ...

She was awoken by a loud rap at her front door. She'd been immersed in a vivid dream about her and Laura – the pair of them dancing wildly underneath the stars. It had been an idyllic and beautiful image, transporting her away from the harsh reality of life. And it had obviously been a much-needed rest. It was almost dark around her and Amy guessed that she had been asleep for a while. Placing the photo of her parents back on the table Amy reached for the clock – it read 7.24pm. She had been asleep for the best part of five hours. The knock at the door sounded again.

'I'm coming. Hang on a moment.' Amy checked her reflection in the mirror and ran her hands through her hair to make herself feel a little more presentable. She still felt she looked like shit.

Running to the door she reached down to pick up a pile of mail that was lying on the front door mat. Five or six envelopes, mostly junk mail. Clutching them in her hand she opened the door. She was greeted by a body, the face of which was hidden behind a mass of flowers. The flowers moved to one side revealing the smiling face of Grant Wilson.

'I think I owe you a massive apology, don't you?' he offered. 'Can I come in? I hope you don't mind but I grabbed your address from the hotel. You left it to secure the room. I had to do some serious flirting to persuade the woman behind Reception to give it to me but she was a fan of the show so to be honest it was pretty easy. An autograph and a quick selfie on her iPhone and she was happy. I hope you don't mind. '

Astounded, Amy opened the door wide to let him in. He stretched out his arms to give her the flowers. 'I thought this was the least I could do after the utter idiot I made of myself last night.'

'Um ... thanks. I'll just stick them in some water. As Amy walked to the kitchen she threw the pile of mail onto the work surface. It fanned out before her.

In the space of less than a second, she spotted the envelope hidden among the mail, recognised the handwriting and felt her legs buckle underneath her, sending the bouquet crashing to the floor.

It was from Riley.

CHAPTER 25
Now, 2015

'I might be used to women falling at my feet but not normally with quite such gusto.'

Grant attempted a laugh as he handed Amy a glass of brandy. It shook in her trembling hand as she tried to control her nerves. 'I don't normally make a habit of hitting the deck in front of strange men.'

'How are you feeling? That should help,' he said, as Amy started to sip at the drink. 'I still can't believe what you've told me. You really think Riley might be alive?' The evidence at the club that night seemed pretty fucking conclusive to me. You saw Riley. His face had been blown to bits ...' Grant stopped, unsure how to continue, worried his words were coming across as heartless.

'That's the whole point, I can't be sure now. He was unrecognisable, I was out of my mind with panic and I just assumed ... it looked like him. I can see it now ...' Amy shuddered at the thought obviously running through her brain and took a heftier slug of the brandy. 'But the more I think about it, the more blurred it all becomes. I was certain about things until that letter, now nothing makes sense anymore.'

Amy had spent the last half an hour telling Grant about the letter. She didn't know whether spilling the beans to him was a wise move but she needed to share her thoughts with someone and Grant seemed to be her best option. His face had drained of colour when Amy told him that he was one of the 'suspects' listed in Riley's letter. His first reaction had been to tell Amy to go to the police, despite what Riley had requested. She had refused point blank. 'That is not what Riley wanted,' she stated. Wherever the letter had come from, if there was a chance that Riley was alive then Amy had to find out the truth for herself. Finding him was first and foremost in her mind.

'So, what are you going to do about *that*?' asked Grant, indicating the still unopened letter that lay ominously on the coffee table in front of Amy. 'Are you sure it's from him?'

'It's his writing. I know it is,' she said, staring at the handwritten name and address on the front. 'I have enough cards and love letters from Riley to recognise it. I'm just not sure if I can cope with what might be in there.'

Grant seated himself alongside Amy and took her hand in his. It was a comforting gesture, almost intimate, and Amy was glad to have him there. If she had been on her own she was sure she would have been a gibbering wreck. He squeezed her hand and smiled at her. She reciprocated without thinking, letting his hand stay there.

'If you want me to stay with you while you open it then I'm more than happy to ... I am a doctor after all, even if it is a pretend one,' he offered, allowing a slight cheeky grin to paint his face.

Amy heard herself laugh. It was the first time she could remember doing so in months. She drained the brandy from the glass, placed it on the table and picked up the letter. 'Okay, here goes ...' She began to tear at the envelope ...

When Adam Rich was angry there was only one person he would call. When he was horny he would call the same person.

When his angriness and his horniness collided then that one person knew that she would have to be primed to embark on a sexually interesting if somewhat body bruising adventure. But thankfully it would also be a financially lucrative one. That person was, of course, Dolly Townsend.

Dolly could tell from the tone of his voice when he'd summoned her that he was majorly narked about something. 'I need you now, get over here,' he'd barked. 'And bring your toys.'

She'd seen him angry on countless occasions over the years she'd been 'employed' by him, but there was something about his current state that definitely suggested a red mist unlike ones she'd encountered before. And when he demanded the toys then Dolly knew that Adam needed to offload some rage. And she would definitely be on the receiving end. But as long as she was on the receiving end of a tidy wad of notes as well then a little pain was worth a lot of gain.

Dolly was thinking of the money as she bit down on the silicone ball wedged in between her teeth. It was one of the many 'toys' she possessed. Nearly two decades of satisfying every kind of sexual kink had taught her to always be prepared. And if that meant spending some of her hard-earned cash on some tricks for her trade then so be it. The ball was attached by a thick leather strap on either side which wrapped itself right around her head. Dolly winced at the slight discomfort as the hard strap and metal buckles fixed to the ball rubbed against the soft skin on her cheeks. Unable to speak, she tried to swallow slightly to stop her mouth from drying out. It was not a sensation she overly enjoyed but when Adam wanted to play master to her slave then it was a role she would readily undertake if it meant being able to pay a few extra bills and purchase a new outfit or two.

There was no way she could attempt to remove the gag as her wrists and ankles were also housed in restraints, the Velcro cuffs held tightly, their connecting straps stretched and tied securely to the corners of the four poster bed she was recumbent across. It was the usual bed, the usual hotel room, the usual knowing glances from the Reception staff as she had arrived to meet Adam. When Adam wanted to 'role play' then he would always choose to play away from home. He would never run the risk of one of his more vigorous and vocal sexual sessions being interrupted by a nosy daughter or, heaven forbid, the diva Caitlyn herself. No, Adam would always book the same place, a hotel where nobody would dare to interrupt or question him.

Dolly was unable to move her head more than a few inches due to the gag but she could just see Adam's bald dome located between her spread-eagled legs. She flinched as she felt the rough stubble of his chin grate against her pussy lips. It was one of his favourite tricks. He would rub against it, watching her thrash around in discomfort before burying his face in her mound, allowing his tongue to explore deeply inside her, grazing her fleshy walls to soreness before lifting his head triumphantly to grin at her, his face streaked with her wetness. Dolly actually enjoyed the sensation more than she revealed to Adam. After years of sexual experimentation, there wasn't much she hadn't succumbed to or enjoyed within the walls of a client's bedroom. She'd often joked to herself that she could write a book on pleasing men.

Adam reached up and placed his hands on her breasts, kneading them as he buried his head once more between her thighs. His position – leaning forward, arms outstretched, legs bent beneath his body as he feasted between her thighs – gave the impression he was worshipping some unknown deity. A goddess of sexual gratification. In Dolly's mind, that goddess was her. Despite her physical restrictions she still felt in control. She would always agree a 'stop-signal' with Adam before their sessions, even if it amounted to no more than the flick of a finger or the somewhat stifled cry. She knew he respected her, but hell, hadn't she earned it?

She had never seen Adam so transfixed. He had been 'in the zone' from the moment she had arrived. His orders to her were clipped and brusque. Telling her where to lie, what to wear, to say nothing. He had gagged her straight away and tied her limbs. It was then that Dolly had realised that this was to be one of those sessions that only occurred once in a while. Adam was angry, preoccupied and tense. He needed pleasing and Dolly was the sexual slave to do so. When Adam was in this kind of mood, the last thing he would want was chit-chat or pleasant-ries.

Having satisfied his oral banquet of her pussy Adam reached across the bed and rooted through the toys Dolly had bought with her. A row of Venus Balls, a dildo the thickness of a coke can and the length of two and an anal probe. His erect penis bounced in front of him as he did so. He pulled them all out and lay them all on the bed beside him. Dolly knew that he was laying out his choices like a customer browsing a restaurant menu. And given Adam's mood she guessed that there could well be a starter, a main course and a dessert to deal with. And that meant a hefty pay out at the end of it. The idea made her smile inwardly, a vision of a trip to House Of Fraser already flashing through her thoughts.

More money to build a new life with, maybe? Dolly's mind continued to drift, contemplating the things she'd like to buy as Adam picked up the first of the toys and brought it towards her skin. Enough for a decent holiday or a car ...?

All thoughts of shift dresses, sandy beaches and leather inte-riors were suddenly erased as Adam stopped with the toy he was holding, a quizzical look spreading over his face.

It was clear to Dolly that he wanted something else. Adam moved off the bed and walked to the other side of the hotel room. Dolly's gaze followed him as much as the gag and the restraints would allow. *What was he up to?* Usually her toys were sufficient.

He opened a small leather case he had with him and delved into it, pulling out a small black tube of meshed material no longer than his finger. The end of it appeared to glisten in the half light of the hotel bedroom. At first Dolly was unsure what is was, doubtless some new toy Adam wanted to try, but it was unlike anything she'd ever seen before and Dolly thought that she had seen everything fetish there was. It was only when he presented it in front of her that she was able to see exactly how it was formed.

'This is my new toy, Dolly. You're going to love it. It's my finger pin wheel.' Dolly watched uncomfortably as Adam slipped the mesh tube over his finger. The reason for the glistening became apparent. At one end of the sleeve was a small movable wheel of sharp metallic spikes. Tiny pin-prick needles which Adam rotated with his finger. Adam's cock twitched as he did so, the sensation obviously a turn on to himself as he felt the spikes against his skin.

He moved the wheel down and rolled it, gently at first, across her stomach. The sensation, a sweet cocktail of sharp pain and euphoric pleasure, caused Dolly to arch her back. The melange of sensations was better than Dolly had expected. She felt a ripple of desire wash through her pussy as Adam ran the wheel across her skin.

He moved the finger across her breasts, circling her nipples with the wheel. Adam was lost, deep in the sensuality of the situation, marvelling at the tiny red dots that formed across Dolly's skin. Not enough to break the flesh, he had no desire to do that, but he was pleased that his new toy appeared to have struck that beautiful fine line between inflicting harm and heightening pleasure. Dolly had experienced nothing like it before. The stabs against her skin were minute and rapid, one ending and the next beginning before her brain allowed her to rationalise just how it felt. All she knew was that it felt intoxicating. She longed for more.

Adam ran the wheel down her body, taking in every curve he could as he did so. The expectation of what was to come was ripe inside Dolly's mind. She knew where the wheel was heading. How would it feel? If her excitement so far was any indication, then she couldn't wait to find out.

Adam looped the wheel around Dolly's navel and started its descent towards the neat bush between Dolly's legs. The pricking felt exquisite against her skin.

If it hadn't been for the gag in her mouth, Dolly was sure that the cocktail of screaming pleasure and pain she attempted to release as Adam parted her pussy lips and rolled the wheel across the tender pink flesh he revealed there, would have been heard not just in the adjacent hotel room but also in the adjacent county.

Amy couldn't make a sound as she stared at the words on the page of the letter. Why would Riley write to her again? Surely it wouldn't achieve anything but to force her mind to spiral off into yet another tempest of confusion.

Amy read the words laid out in front of her. There weren't many and they were brief and to the point, the handwriting frenzied and somewhat scratchy on the page.

'Dear Amy. You're doing so well. Sorry for everything you've found out so far. Keep at it, as that's the only way we stand any hope of being together. You know that's what I want deep down. I hope you do too. So sorry again. Sorry a million times. I long to be with you. When you were there at Dirty Cash I wanted to reach out. I had to stop myself from running to you when that car nearly hit you near Eruption. It was more than I could bear. Stay strong. Stay safe. Stay mine. Riley x'

Amy could feel herself starting to shake again as she read the words for a second time and then a third. Riley knew where she'd been, he'd seen what had happened to her. He must be following her. He must be close. He'd been there when Lily had rescued her, he'd seen Amy head to the casino to see Tommy. He could be outside now for all she knew, watching her every move. He may have seen Grant arrive at her flat. What would he think? And why, if he was so close to her, did he not make contact? Use a mobile, email or a private app? There were so many choices but none were forthcoming.

Amy wasn't sure what any of it meant or how she felt about it. Confusion clouded her brain. *How could somebody who had once been so close now feel so far away?* She turned to face Grant who was sitting silently alongside her. It was only then that she realised that she was holding his hand again.

CHAPTER 26
Now, 2015

On the surface Genevieve Peters was the embodiment of everything that was smart, hip, happening and bang on trend. Eruption was more successful than ever, her name was hotter than a mouthful of jalapenos, and her rise-to-the-top story was being given more column inches than ever before. So why the hell did she feel so goddamn miserable?

Shutting the door behind her as she left Eruption at the end of yet another money-making few hours, Genevieve reflected on her day. It had been business as usual. Record companies wanting styling for video shoots and press appearances – she'd already kitted out Rita Ora and Demi Lovato in the last week alone – offers of nights out and Eruption's PR begging Genevieve to permit more one-to-one interviews. It was the same old same old. As far as life within the four walls of the shop was concerned everything was decidedly rosy.

But once the lights were off and the door was locked up for the night, Genevieve's life felt as bitter and as icy as the Manchester winter's night she stepped out into as she took the key from the lock and slipped it into her pocket. Something was horribly missing from her life and she knew what it was ... love.

She'd loved before. Just the once. Not that she hadn't had her fair share of offers, or lustful infatuations for that matter. There was the six-month affair with the sculpted dancer with the most Herculean of ebony bodies from the TV dance troupe, the Olympic athlete who could win gold medals for his performances both on the track and in the sack, and the red-hot sheet-scorching sessions with the famous TV actor, but none of them had led to anything more than a string of break-ups, make-ups and then break-ups again.

No, only one man had really managed to get under her skin and make her realise what she wanted when it came to affairs of the heart and that was Riley. She had tasted the forbidden fruit and fallen for a married man. A man that had satisfied her for so long, but like all good things it had come to an end. The fruit had turned sour. And there hadn't been a day since when she hadn't thought about or been reminded of it. As she walked away from the shop in search of a taxi, Genevieve cast her mind back to her first meeting with Riley ...

It had been at a press launch for a new brand of tequila. The brand was being endorsed by one of the models Genevieve used regularly to promote the clothes at Eruption. Normally she would give any kind of launch a wide berth as being seen at the wrong place could be translated as social suicide but she'd decided to go as, firstly, it was at her model friend's request and secondly, it was being held in the coolest of Manchester warehouse venues. With a nose for success, Genevieve had sensed that it would be a night to remember and definitely one worth being seen at. As ever, her razor-sharp instincts had been spot on.

She had noticed Riley as soon as she had walked in. He had his head tipped back and was having tequila poured into his mouth by a woman dressed as the sexiest of Carmen Mirandas, a riot of burlesque fabric and plastic fruit. His suit was fitted and seemed to cling to the obviously rather perfectly-honed body housed within it. His hair, thick and black, fell casually yet somehow perfectly into place around his face. She had the impression straight away that he was a man who could never look anything less than incredible. Or at least she'd thought so until he'd run his fingers through his hair and she'd spotted a wedding ring on the third finger of his left hand. Another one bites the dust. Not that it had stopped him smiling rather suggestively at Genevieve when he'd squeezed by her to reach the free bar a few minutes later.

'Hello, are you one of the few women around here without a bowl of fruit or a pineapple on your head?' As opening gambits went it was certainly novel and caused a smile to flow across Genevieve's face. He was even more attractive close up than he had been from across the space of the warehouse.

'I tend to find that pineapples don't make a good accessory unless they're in a deeply alcoholic cocktail, don't you?' she smirked.

'I don't think I've ever worn one. I don't like to wear anything with a darker skin than me. It makes me look pasty. Unlike you, I don't really suit the pale and interesting look,' he answered.

His skin was flawless and definitely a deep shade of brown. It contrasted with the fresh whiteness of his movie-perfect teeth. 'Somebody's been on their holidays I see. That tan didn't come from walking along the banks of a Manchester canal, did it?' There was a challenging air to Genevieve's voice. If the married man in front of her was flirting then she wouldn't make things too easy for him. Not yet anyway. 'Maybe you and your wife have been somewhere exotic lately.' She stared down at the ring on his hand.

'I love a few weeks in the sun, I'll give you that, but it's been a while so just between you and me, it's mostly fake. The tan, not the marriage that is. She's not here tonight. I'm here alone

... and you?' There was definitely more than a peppering of suggestion mixed in with the flirtation in his voice.

The game was on. He was flirting and she was sure of it. Within a matter of minutes they were downing tequila shots together. For the next hour they had talked about everything from Genevieve's store to Riley's line of work – he had made no attempt to hide the fact that he was involved in dodgy dealings. If anything he seemed proud of the fact. If a man said to a woman that he was involved in 'this and that' and 'made a good living' then it didn't take the sharpest of tools to work out that he was a little underhand in his profession. The only thing that wasn't mentioned again was his wife.

As Genevieve left the party an hour or so later, the taste of tequila still heating her lips, Riley Hart's telephone number was nestling invitingly on her mobile contacts list, as was hers on his.

As she climbed into her cab to head back to her apartment Genevieve couldn't stop thinking about Riley; handsome, mysterious, somewhat dangerous. So what if he had a wife and a career that might not be strictly kosher? She didn't care. He'd won her over at 'pineapple'.

She knew she'd see him again as the cab pulled away. She was right. Within a week he was sharing her bed.

But nothing was made to last any more. Riley hadn't been the man she had hoped. Nothing had turned out to plan. That was then and this was now. Riley was gone. As she watched Eruption disappear out of sight through the taxi window Genevieve knew that there was something she needed to do. Something she didn't do often enough. Driving off into the late November night air she barked an address at the cab driver.

It was forty minutes before she arrived at her destination, an ivy-covered Edwardian block of flats on the outskirts of the city. She paid the driver and jogged to the front door of the flats as fast as her Ballin ankle boots would allow. It had started to rain and she didn't want to risk getting wet. She pressed the intercom for flat four and waited somewhat impatiently as she began to feel the rain becoming heavier on her hair. 'Come on, answer the door ....'

A few moments later the intercom crackled into life. 'Hello, who is it?' The voice was that of an elderly female.

'It's me. I thought I'd better come round. Can I come in?' said Genevieve.

'It's been a while hasn't it, but yes, of course, come on up now you're here.' The tone was clipped. 'I'll buzz you up.'

Genevieve drew a deep breath. She hadn't expected anything less than a lukewarm reception. It was the same every time she could conjure up the courage to visit.

Having scaled the flights of stairs to the flat, she knocked on the door. A woman, aged in her sixties with pure silver hair tied back into a tight bun, appeared at the door. She would have looked like the typical classic cosy little grandmother had it not been for the derisory sneer painted across her face. 'So you thought you could be bothered, eh? To what do I owe this pleasure, Genevieve?'

'I needed to come, Mother, isn't that enough?'

There was obviously no love lost between the two women. Genevieve leant forward to kiss her mother on the cheek. A small gesture, but countermanded as the elderly woman turned away before contact could really be made.

Genevieve walked into the flat. The decor was dark and somewhat stuffy. An episode of *Coronation Street* played on the TV screen in the corner of the living room. Genevieve's mother parked herself back in front of the TV and carried on staring at the programme. She deliberately made as little eye contact with her daughter as possible.

'She's in there if you want to see her, but she's asleep so don't wake her up. The help has only just left.' The remark was dismissive.

Genevieve took off her coat, still slightly damp from the rain outside, and threw it across the arm of a chair. 'Thank you, I won't.'

Walking into the bedroom she stared down into the cot placed in the corner of the room. A small pink bundle of skin, eyes open, showed from underneath the whitest of blankets.

The sight immediately bought a smile to Genevieve's face and the faintest of tears to the corners of her eyes. 'So, you're not asleep after all.'

Reaching down into the cot she wrapped the blanket tightly around the baby and lifted her into her arms. She kissed the baby on her forehead.

'Hello there sweetheart, don't you worry. Mummy's here now ...'

CHAPTER 27
Then, 2013

Tickets for the opening night of The Kitty Kat Club were like gold dust. With a capacity of just over five hundred, the kitty-shaped embossed tickets were in hotter demand than any club outside London had known for years. Word of mouth had spread. Nobody knew what to expect from the music, nobody knew what it would look like inside, but everybody knew that they had to be there. If you weren't in possession of an invitation then indeed you were nobody.

For Amy it had been the day she had waited a lifetime for. This was her moment. The day when the neon-lit hopes of all of her dreams came to fruition. She knew the club would work, it had to ... and her team of 'Party Pussycats' were going to make sure that nobody wanted for anything.

The 'Pussycats' were Lily's idea. Riley had employed Lily as PR for the club and Amy loved her gung-ho nature. Nothing was unachievable. She was determined that people would re-member the opening night of the Kitty Kat for years to come. Tonight had to go down in history as beyond elite. Nothing would be too much trouble for the privileged gathered.

'Nobody will be without a beer, a cocktail or anything else that their hedonistic hearts desire all night,' snapped Lily at the twenty plus women stood before her on the unlit dance floor of the Kitty Kat. 'In less than two hours this place will be heaving with more money and success than you can shake your fur-covered asses at and if I hear so much as a whisper of a complaint from any of them then you'll be out the door faster than you can say *kitty litter*.'

Lily was loving the power. Amy smiled proudly as she watched Lily in action from the comfort of a club booth. She'd been on her feet all day making sure nothing was left to chance but she knew she could leave the 'Pussycats' to Lily. A five-minute sit down before the madness commenced was much needed.

Lily had hand-picked the girls who would be pussycats for the opening night. Weeks of castings had culminated with a troop of girls who were beautiful, buxom and beyond willing to make sure they bagged the chance to be part of nightlife history. They all towered above six feet in their killer heels, and their bodies were ripe, firm and shapely enough to fill every hair of the tight fur Kitty outfits Lily had sourced specially. The fur-bra/fur-shorts combo with kitty ears and whiskers accessories had been found and provided by Genevieve Peters. Lily was insistent that the current talk of the fashion world had to be the talent behind the feline look and Amy had to admit that Lily had played a blinder. The end result was sexy, sultry and powerful, whereas it could have easily strayed into slutty. Amy was resolute that everything about the evening would be class not brass.

'We have more stars coming here tonight than you'd find in a fucking Planetarium. And not just from the UK. You will recognise some major players from Hollywood too. If any of the guests ask you anything that you don't know the answer to then you pretend you do and then find me. The crowd tonight will be expecting a fucking good time, a party atmosphere and a shitload of fun, whatever that entails. We're here to make sure that that happens. Or you'll have me and *her* to answer to.' Lily pointed over at Amy, indicating the 'her' in her order. 'Now, get yourselves ready and organised and do me proud, pussies ... or else.'

As the girls dispersed from the dance floor, Lily walked over to join Amy in the booth. 'Dizzy bitches the lot of them, but they look amazing and they will do exactly what we need, boss, so don't you worry your pretty little head. Everything is under control.'

'Everything?' questioned Amy. 'Nothing can go wrong to-night. Riley's reputation is on the line here too. He's got such gravitas around here and this could be the first of a whole chain of Kitty Kat clubs if it's a success. Are you sure people will come? Oh, and drop the 'boss' ... I hate that. This club may be mine but I can't do the hierarchy thing. It freaks me out.'

'The guests here tonight will be so euphoric they're at the opening night of the best club in Britain that they'll be quivering like a shitting dog with excitement! And if they're not euphoric enough then I will be sure to give them a helping hand with all these babies.' Lily grabbed her breasts and hoiked them up-wards. 'There's enough stash in my bra to blast all of our guests into a fucking narcotic stratosphere if that's what they want.'

Graphic as ever, mused Amy. After weeks of preparation for the opening of the club, Amy was finally becoming immune to Lily's filthy mouth and her talk of drugs. Amy had been against it at first. She and Laura had spent many happy nights out clubbing with nothing more mind-altering than bottles of fizz to sustain their joy, but Riley was adamant that Lily and her pharmacy were a necessary addition to the Kitty Kat experience. Doubtless he was right. He always was.

Her mind lingered on Riley for a moment. 'Have you seen my husband? I thought he would be here by now making sure that everything is ready to go. How come he's not as nervous as I am?' asked Amy.

'Because your husband knows that this place is in very safe hands ... namely mine,' stated Lily, holding up her palms and waggling her fingers. 'He employed me for a reason, you know. And anyway, he'll be back in a bit, he told me he's gone off to get done up to the fucking nines. Hasn't he splashed out on some new Hugo Boss suit for tonight? Doubtless he'll look sharper than vampire fangs. Talking of which, shouldn't you be thinking about getting the war paint on and slipping into something a little more night-time? It's not long till this place will be a sea of silks, sequins, singers and soap stars and that dance floor will be more buzzing than a freaking hive. You can't afford to be seen in anything less than fucking perfection. What are you wearing?'

'Laura's bringing the outfits here. The look for the night is her baby. She should be here any moment now ...' Amy checked her watch. Laura was coming to the club so that they could both get ready together. Both Riley and numerous fashion PRs had offered the girls professional hair and make-up and their own stylist for the night as the opening would doubtless court countless column inches across magazines, blogs and websites, but both of them were insistent that they dolled themselves up together. It's how they had always started girlie nights out. It felt right. And tonight, albeit super special, was to start the same way. For Amy it felt almost like a lucky talisman, auguring a night to remember.

'Right on time, did somebody call?' It was Laura, marching into the club with bags of clothes draped over one arm and her car-size make-up bag clutched in her hand. 'Are you ready for the night of your life, Amy Hart? I know I am. And a sneaky peek to get us in the mood is definitely in order.' She held aloft a huge bottle of champagne. 'Three glasses, Lily, if you please.'

'I'll grab you two. I'll leave you girls to it. I'm off to make this beautiful,' said Lily, circling her hand around her face. 'I'll

see you later ...' Lily started to walk off, before stopping, turning
her head back towards Amy and adding '... boss!' She smirked
and stuck her tongue out. 'Tonight will be the most awesome
fucking night ever, a real night to remember, I promise you.'

Lily had been spot on. It had been the most amazing night. The
Kitty Kat club had caused a media splash like no other club
of recent times. Top US DJ, Blair Lonergan, his career having
ascended into the stratosphere on a worldwide scale since Laura
had first 'sampled his set' flew in specially to play the club, some
of Hollywood's finest were in attendance and there wasn't a reality show either side of the Atlantic that didn't seem to have
at least one of their stars strutting their way around the dance
floor.

   The evening had been a joyous blur for Amy. One minute
she had been applying her make-up and giggling nervously with
Laura, the next she had been schmoozing the who's who of the
media world and the suited sycophants and yes-men who flitted
around Riley basking in his every word.

   It was all she had ever dreamt of and a warm glow of satisfaction and pride had spread through her as she watched those
gathered enjoying her newly created world. As DJ Blair eased
smoothly from one throbbing beat to another, she couldn't help
but marvel to see Laura chatting to Hollywood actress Evie
Merchant, both throwing their hands in the air in blissful high
spirits as they danced, tabloid gossip queen Nush Silvers spinning alongside them, all lost to the beat. To their left, Aussie
drag superstar Latreena Occupado – whom Lily had flown in
from Sydney to perform at the opening night because she was
'the best fucking drag superstar you will ever see' – held a cocktail in the air and closed her glitter-lashed eyes, loving the party

vibe. Her cabaret earlier in the evening had been a huge success, even with the stuffier guests gathered. Amy had been surprised to see even Jemima Hearn crack a smile as Latreena took to the Kitty Kat stage and bitched about the world at large.

Amy wasn't quite sure that some of Riley's colleagues – men who would much rather be propping up the bar at the nearest backstreet boozer than rubbing shoulders with a man in a frock and the media world's up-and-comings – had totally appreciated the designer drag's act but they had all certainly perked up and appeared decidedly hot under their white starched suit collars when UK burlesque star Immodesty Blaize took to the floor. Tommy Hearn's eyes had been on stalks as he watched the temptress of tease slink across the club in a vision of feathers and fabulousness. As were Caitlyn Rich's. It was the first time Amy had met Lily's mum and she had found her beyond cool with a zest for life that she had obviously passed on to her daughter. Caitlyn had charged over to Amy like a heat-seeking missile in heels, gushing about the club opening and her joy that she could be a part of it. 'Oh my goodness, dear girl, this is amazing, just what this dreary little city needs, a touch of London gloss. I'm adoring it. I had a lovely chat with Evie Merchant earlier, just a great actress, and that lady-man was just sensational. So cheeky. Lily's dad would have hated it. He's not one for enjoying himself. Thank you so much for making Lily part of all this, you've made a woman of her, darling. Now, must fly, I want to share some fashion tips with Immodesty and ask her if she'd pose for me. I'd love a mirrored bust of … well, her *bust* for my conservatoire!' Caitlyn had disappeared back across The Kitty Kat in search of the burlesque star, leaving Amy wondering if fashion tips from a woman wearing a frock with some of the most misplaced nude panelling Amy had ever seen would really be appreciated by the international showgirl. But it was clear that just like her daughter, Caitlyn was a woman who believed in what she said, although thankfully her language was far less blue.

Switching the main club lights off at the end of the opening night as Lily ushered the final club-goer out into the early morning light, Riley and a smiling Amy made their way to the Kitty Kat office. Once inside, Riley opened a fridge in the corner of the room and pulled out a bottle of champagne and two glasses.

'I think it's time for us to celebrate, don't you?' whispered Riley, pulling his wife towards him. 'You were amazing tonight, the perfect hostess, everybody loved it. I am so proud of you.'

Pulling Amy even closer he let his lips find hers, his kiss somehow urgent yet tender at the same time. Amy couldn't help but respond, his touch lighting her senses, a warm ripple of desire spreading through her body. A tear formed itself at the corner of her eye. It was one of happiness. She was proud of herself too, this evening had been a long time coming, the seed from which it had grown first planted years ago when she and Laura had first shared their love of music and the joy it could bring.

Tonight had been beyond joyful. Not one person had left the club unhappy and as the first critics and journalists began to file their reviews for the newspapers, magazines and websites, Riley placed the champagne and glasses to one side, momentarily forgotten, as he moved his hand down to one of his wife's breasts.

Riley gave it a gentle squeeze, his fingertips brushing against the hardening of Amy's nipple through the fabric of the LBD Laura had chosen for her for the night. With its crossover straps and plunging neckline, it oozed glamour and was just the style-savvy look that Amy had desired. It also revealed a fair amount of skin thanks to the cut out panel between Amy's breasts and small triangular cut outs on the hips.

Amy let out a gasp of desire as she allowed Riley's hand to travel inside the cut out panel across her chest and find her breast.

His other hand travelled down her body, skimming across the elegant fabric that clung to Amy's curves in all the right places, and reached its destination just below the knee where the fabric ended.

Amy let her tongue explore further into Riley's mouth, loving the feel of her husband's evident desire, as his hand moved under the fabric of her dress and towards the heat that was now almost burning between her legs. It was only a matter of seconds before his fingers moved the lace of her panties to one side and entered into her, her wetness allowing for the easiest of access. She bit down on his lip as he did so.

Unable to control their need for each other to be joined in sexual nirvana, Riley withdrew his fingers, hitched up the bottom of Amy's dress and swept his arm across the office desk, a pile of papers flying to the floor as he did so. The area now clear, he lifted Amy onto the desk and lay her back against the table top. He pulled at her panties, yanking them off with one hand as he undid his suit trousers with the other. His erection sprang free from the confines of his clothes, proud and ready to reach its desired destination.

It wasn't long before it did so. As Riley slid his cock into his wife, the first review of The Kitty Kat went online. It was the first of many.

The reviews were excellent and those lucky enough to have been there that first night spread the word that The Kitty Kat was *the* club to be seen at.

CHAPTER 28
Now, 2015

As Amy stood across the street from the club once more, that opening night seemed such a hazy memory. So much had happened since then to turn her world upside down. The club was no longer a club, which was clear as she stared at the sign for the Dirty Cash Casino that hung outside. But that was just the bricks and mortar. It was the memories the four walls contained, the happy times, the joy and the laughter that had changed. Riley gone, Laura gunned down, so many of the people she had trusted and enjoyed spending time with now lining up as suspects in a whodunit game she wasn't sure how she was supposed to play. Her memories shattered, warped out of all recognisable shape, the red roses of romance and love tarred black with destruction. Life at The Kitty Kat was over for good and Amy's own existence would never be the same again.

Amy had headed back to Manchester after the arrival of the second letter. If the letter was to be believed then Riley was closer than she realised. She'd been unable to stop herself from turning and constantly glancing over her shoulders on leaving her London home ever since she'd read it. Had Riley followed her to London? Was he still based in Manchester? Was he still based anywhere?

That had been the major change in her return journey to Manchester. Her paranoia had escalated through the roof. Before, she'd assumed that if Riley was alive then he would be in hiding, fearful for his life as stated in his first letter. But now things had changed. She found herself staring at people in cars speeding past, those in the queue behind her at the train station, the stranger lurking on the corner of the street where she walked. What if Riley had changed his appearance? His long thick black locks could now be cropped, blond, shaved. His über-sharp fashion sense could be camouflaged with baggy anoraks and heavy winter clothes.

The other change had been that she had not returned to Manchester alone. This time Grant had accompanied her. Now work had finished on *Ward 44* for the Christmas break, Grant had insisted that he tag along. The two of them had shared something at Amy's apartment. There had been a comfort in him being there. Just his mere presence made Amy feel stronger. She hadn't hesitated when he'd offered his company. It wasn't trust. She still trusted nobody, but just having someone experience the jagged life journey she was currently on alongside her seemed strangely beneficial. He listened, he offered advice, he was simply there. He may have abhorred her husband, but he could see that the mystery surrounding his death was eating Amy alive. He seemed willing to do whatever he could to make things easier and that was something Amy appreciated. Nothing was simple any more. She doubted whether it ever would be again.

Grant had left Amy once they had arrived in Manchester and booked into a hotel. Grant had paid for both rooms, a gesture Amy was unable to turn down. Her supply of money was dwindling fast and at least this hotel's sheets would be fresher than the last.

Grant's reasons for heading to Manchester were not entirely unselfish. He'd informed Amy that a casting director for a potential forthcoming American project was currently based in the city and Grant wanted to see him as soon as possible. As he explained to Amy on the train, 'Me going to him as opposed to him tracking me down will give me considerable kudos when it comes to deciding on leading roles. A casting director will always love you more if they know you're keen from the off.' Amy couldn't fault his logic.

While Grant headed off to try and advance his acting career across international boundaries, Amy knew where she had to go. She needed to see Tommy Hearn again. Their last meeting had been a merciless one for Amy. She had learnt the truth about Riley and about how Tommy had callously masterminded her losing everything. It would have been his idea to instruct Riley into gaining her signature, handing everything over to Tommy and his hatchet-faced wife Jemima. Everything she cared about, everything she had dreamt of. Everything that was rightfully hers. Amy needed to fight back, needed to be strong. She would not let the likes of Tommy and Jemima destroy her. She had unfinished business with the Hearns and she needed to confront them again. To readjust the balance of power.

Taking a deep breath, Amy took a pace into the road and headed towards the casino. As she did, a sleek black car screeched to a halt outside it. Instinctively Amy ducked down behind a vehicle on her side of the road. Something was telling her to be careful. An inner sixth sense.

She was glad she had. She watched as a figure vacated the car, brutally slammed the door and marched into the building. It was Adam Rich and he had a face that was far from happy. In fact, he looked ready to kill.

CHAPTER 29
Now, 2015

Jemima Hearn had always been a 'plus one'. She had never really achieved her own identity, she was just the woman who had put up with Tommy's thuggish, philandering ways, ever since she had caught him cheating on their honeymoon in Greece. Deep down she knew she deserved better, but a vulnerability at her core, something that had always been there since her formative years, made her turn a blind eye. Give up the fight.

Women in the world she frequented often didn't seem to have their own identity. They were happy for their 'men' to play Mr Big and bring home the bacon. For as long as she had been Mrs Tommy Hearn that was exactly what she was ... just the wife of Tommy Hearn. Not 'Tommy's charming wife, Jemima' with her own interests and friends. People didn't say of her 'you'll never guess what that wonderful Jemima is up to now,' or 'isn't Jemima the most fantastic hostess?' No, she was just plain old 'Jemima ... is that her name? ... You know the one, Tommy Hearn's missus'. The eternal 'plus one'. If Tommy was invited somewhere then she would be too. But purely as a matter of course. Was she ever invited anywhere due to her own personal popularity? The answer was no. Did people clamour for her sparkling wit and repartee? Equally, no. Jemima was perceived as deeply dull, somewhat wearisome and with the excitement factor of a wet camping weekend.

How had she let it all change? When she and Tommy had first married she was ecstatic. Her husband was her man, her rock, her better half. But now? To be honest, Jemima wasn't even sure if she felt vaguely excited by her husband any more. Tommy had become little more than her 'other half'. The man who had always been there, providing for her so that she could shop when necessary, holiday when necessary, pamper when necessary. Even all of that had become horribly routine. She was supposed to have provided Tommy with children. Wasn't that what the dutiful wife ought to achieve at least at some point during a marriage? Shouldn't that have been her end of the matrimonial bargain? But for the Hearns it hadn't happened. Their sex life was plentiful to begin with. She had loved Tommy with a passion and that passion was ignited nightly between the sheets. But as the years progressed and no offspring appeared, Tommy appeared to lose interest in her. She'd always known he was sewing his oats elsewhere, ever since that first fateful night. Most of the people around him were so who was she to judge? It was part of the machismo world of skulduggery her husband belonged to and something that had always been present in their married life.

At least Tommy had never kept anything about his professional life from her. She had always known about Riley's line of business and his father's before him. They were corrupt, as was Tommy. She had no worries about that, it provided her with the money she needed and meant she never had to work. Quite why Riley had deemed it necessary to keep the truth from Amy was beyond Jemima. She was happy enough to spend his money and reap the rewards, so sheltering her from the truth seemed ridiculous. She found the girl naive and beyond stupid. She was never cut out to be a gangster's wife. Believing the cover of the plastics factory – how bloody idiotic was she? Still, she'd paid the price for her own stupidity. She'd lost her business, lost her home and lost her husband. The first two she deserved. She'd come from nothing, she could go back there as far as Jemima was concerned. But losing the man you loved, that was tough. Nothing prepared you for the heartache of that. That moment when the man you shared so much with is taken from you, so heartlessly and abruptly. No, nobody deserved hearing the sound of their own heart shatter into a million fragments of misery. Jemima knew that, because it had happened to her.

People thought Jemima was a hard bitch. She could understand why. Her lack of confidence in her own self-worth had often translated into an icy silence that many took for rudeness. The deep, carved wrinkles on her aging face gave her an acidic, pinched look. Her grey hair, harshly scraped back off her face into a bun, aged her before her time. Tommy moaned at her all the time to dye it, or have it styled at one of Manchester's top salons. Occasionally she did and Tommy would momentarily reward her with a 'you look nice, dear' but a few weeks later and the grey was back with gusto. She didn't really blame Tommy if he was fucking around elsewhere. She didn't particularly find herself sexy so why should he? Tommy didn't make her feel sexy anymore. That part of her life was over, or at least she had thought it was. Which is why she'd been so surprised when someone had come along to fan the inner flames of her sexual desire once again.

She hadn't meant it to happen. Never thought it could. Things like that didn't happen to women like her. But it had. From the moment Jemima had laid eyes on him something inside her had burst into spontaneous, glorious flames. Her heart seemed to beat stronger within the confines of her own rib cage. Her mind seemed to spiral with the delight of dark, lascivious thoughts and suddenly, more importantly, she felt as if she were more than just 'somebody else's wife'. Tommy was still good for the money, for the kudos, for the companionship, but any spark of love between them had certainly died for good the moment Jemima set eyes on Winston Curtis. And more to the point, the moment he had laid eyes on her. The attraction was mutual and the timing had been perfect. Jemima was looking the best she had in ages thanks to a salon visit and a pampering session that had been forced upon her by Caitlyn Rich. Caitlyn had been offered two complimentary passes for a new treatment spa that had popped up just outside Manchester and as she was one of the few people who actually had any time for Jemima, invited her along.

When Jemima Hearn met Winston Curtis for the first time, her hair was slick, her skin was freshly buffed and her confidence was higher than it had ever been, even if that was just above zero. For the first time ever Jemima embarked on an affair.

Their tryst had continued right up until that awful night he had died alongside Riley in The Kitty Kat. Jemima had been there to witness it – her beautiful lover's body lifeless and bloodied in front of her eyes. Never again would she feel the fullness of his lips against hers or the hardness of his body during their love-making.

She had watched Winston die. The man who had made her feel so much more than a 'plus one'. Sometimes she wondered if Tommy had been behind Winston's death. Maybe he had found out about their love. It was a frightening thought. The murky truth in life sometimes had a strange way of rising to the surface without any definite reason. Jemima had told no-one, maybe Winston had ... she would never know. She could hardly ask Tommy. She would just carry on playing the dutiful wife, maybe until the end of her days. It was what she did. Her role in life.

But it was so hard. It's hard to pretend you love somebody when you don't, but it is even harder to pretend that you don't love someone when you really do. She had loved Winston Curtis, right up until the moment his life was snuffed out. She had no doubt that Amy Hart had loved Riley and that the agony of watching him die was just as horrific. She could respect her for that. But at least she was able to openly mourn him. Tell the world about what a supposedly great man he was. She had that luxury. Jemima had been forced to mourn in silence. She hadn't even attended Winston's funeral because Tommy didn't want to go. What was it he said? 'He was nothing more than a bloody right-hand-Johnny for Riley and he's no loss.' To Jemima he was so much more, he was the man who had made her feel alive again. And now he was dead.

Amy Hart could tell everyone on the planet how much she loved her man. Amy Hart didn't know how lucky she was. And that was something that Jemima hated her for.

CHAPTER 30
Now, 2015

Adam angrily pushed his way through the gaggle of gamblers playing the machines at the Dirty Cash and headed straight to Tommy's office. The door was closed but Adam didn't bother knocking and marched directly in.

'We need to fucking talk. This could get out of hand if we don't put a stop to it now.' The veins on his temples were raised and pulsating with blood as he spoke. 'I won't let anything come back to bite me on the backside, especially not some two-bit wisp of a widow, you hear me ...?'

Tommy Hearn stopped what he was doing, placed his pen on the desk in front of him and leant back in his leather chair to look at Adam. He was not smiling.

'Do you have to come charging in here like some rabid dog from the streets of New Delhi? Christ, man, I could have been having an important meeting in here or something.'

Adam moved close to the desk and forcefully banged one of his fists down on the wood surface. 'So fucking what, Tommy? Nothing's more important than this. Lily tells me Amy Hart is sniffing around and to add insult to injury I now find out my own daughter was getting a good rogering from Riley. If the bastard wasn't already dead, I'd be tempted to kill the randy little fucker myself!'

'Oh that,' Tommy was nonplussed. 'None of us are exactly famed for keeping our dicks in our pants, are we? Jemima's good for many things but sex isn't one of them anymore.'

Tommy continued. 'Surely even a meathead like you knows that Riley Hart was a man pretty much governed by his cock. Your daughter's no angel, so what ... she didn't get up the duff did she, so what's the problem?'

'The problem is that little cunt could cause me all sorts of trouble from beyond the grave if he isn't dead. And yes, I know that's a contradiction in terms before you get smart with me. Some things need to stay hidden. She can't find out anything. Even if he is actually dead but Amy gets wind of what went on I could be history around here. You and I may not see eye to eye on a lot of things, Hearn, but you have to agree with me on this. Our secret can't get out. If I go down I swear I'll take you with me.'

'Care for a drink?' Tommy calmly pulled open one of his desk drawers and reached inside for a bottle of brandy and two glasses. 'It sounds like you could do with de-stressing a bit. You'll be sending your blood pressure through the roof and at your age that's never wise.' He didn't wait for an answer before starting to pour.

'Don't be smart with me, Hearn. This was your mess, you owe me ... you need to make sure this stays buried.'

'It'll stay ... er, *buried*. And that's the operative word, is it not ...? Now, cheers.'

CHAPTER 31
Then, 1980s

Tommy Hearn had adored Riley's father, Cazwell Hart. Working for him was the ultimate dream. Growing up as a lad in one of Manchester's roughest areas, a young Tommy had spent his youth constantly breaking the law. Mugging, shoplifting, nicking cars ... if there was a petty crime that he could attempt then he would. He thrived on the danger, he loved the feeling of power it gave him and he filled with joy at the thought of getting away with whatever he could. School was pointless, a place for wankers interested in test tubes and equations. Tommy wanted his education on the streets and that was indeed where he and his group of sorry-assed, raggy-clothed mates learnt about life.

Kids at the time idolised the likes of Prince, George Michael and Sting, but Tommy had no interest in the hip-thrusting, girl-pleasing ways of the musical stars. His heroes were the darker, more sinister names he heard whispered on the street. The ones people feared, the ones linked to fights and urban rivalries across the city, the ones said to be responsible for people disappearing for good. One of those names was Cazwell Hart. He was spoken of like an enigma, someone whom people had heard of but nobody really knew. Talked of but never seen. Like the Santa Claus of the gangster world. But this 'Santa' was not about giving ... far from it ... Cazwell was said to be all about taking ... taking lives. If someone stepped out of line and needed sorting, then rumour had it that Cazwell was the man sealing the deal. If a gangster could be placed on a pedestal then Cazwell Hart was the man who seemed permanently rooted to it.

Tommy would spend hours every day running the streets with his mates, avoiding the long arm of the law, lapping up tales of how Cazwell and his team of henchmen had successfully undertaken another job. Bodies were found in rivers, offices were mysteriously burnt to the ground, people beaten up to within an inch of their lives ... shit happened but it never stuck to Cazwell. If his name was linked to a crime, somehow he always managed to prevent that connection going any further. Links would be made verbally but hard evidence would be impossible to detect. Cazwell and those around him were obviously masters of their own universe. A universe where there were no laws, no authority and no comebacks. Tommy dreamt of being part of it.

His chance came when he was the tender age of sixteen. Underage drinking in his local boozer, he'd been rolling a cigarette in the beer garden when a man approached him asking him if he knew anywhere he could lay his hands on 'a decent weapon to do a touch of business'. Without batting an eyelid, Tommy had told the man to come back an hour later. Sixty minutes passed and Tommy handed over a gun, wrapped inside a rag cloth 'so there's none of my fingerprints on it' and demanded a 'good rate' for supplying the stranger with a dangerous weapon. He'd asked no questions as to why the man wanted the gun and no mention was made of where it had come from. Tommy had stolen it when he'd broken into someone's house a few months earlier. His sense of survival had told him that one day it would come in useful. The man, part of Cazwell's gang, was impressed. Word had travelled that there was a young, eager to please upstart on the streets, and Cazwell Hart was keen to take him into his fold. Tommy was elated and by his seventeenth birthday he was working full-time for Cazwell, one of the gang, ready to learn the ropes and if instructed wrap them around somebody's neck until the colour drained from their cheeks. The enigma had become a reality. Cazwell Hart was his boss and Tommy would be loyal to him forever.

He was, until the day Cazwell died. By that time Tommy was his number two and proud to be the sidekick of his very own gangster god. He had cried for days when Cazwell died, for once allowing his softer side to flow freely. There was a part of him that had expected to take the reins of Cazwell's empire, but of course, it was not to be. Cazwell's only child, Riley, stepped up to the mark and Tommy stayed as number two. Tommy had made a great living through Cazwell and had been left a considerable chunk of money in his will. It was this money that had allowed Tommy to bail out Riley every time he made a wrong decision.

Tommy had never been a Riley fan from the start and was happy to watch him make mistakes, even knowingly encouraging them on occasion. *Why shouldn't he?* Riley wasn't a patch on his father and in Tommy's eyes he was never worthy to take on the mantle of Cazwell's corrupt empire in the first place. Blood related he may have been but that was all that connected him with the late, great Cazwell. Not that those looking on agreed. Riley was seen as a worthy successor, a modern day equal to his father, which was something that galled Tommy terribly. But some strong-bonded sense of loyalty to Cazwell kicked in when Riley finally bit off more than he could chew, which is where Adam Rich came into the equation. And what a complete car-crash of a fuck-up that had turned out to be ...

CHAPTER 32
Then, 2012

It was mid 2012 when Riley first mooted the idea of opening a nightclub to Tommy.

'Imagine it, Tommy. A place where people could meet, deals could be arranged, jobs could be organised. It would look a lot more legit than people coming to "the factory" all the time. Dad was always saying we should have an incognito HQ for our business.'

Despite Riley having a point, Tommy's first reaction had been to scoff in his face. Riley may have been more than capable of finding his way around a firearm but when it came to monetary affairs he was beyond useless at times, and Tommy knew better than anyone that creating a club, especially one that could become a trusted base for the criminals of northern England to frequent, would cost major money. There was no way Riley could fund it.

It was then that the seeds had begun to germinate in Tommy's mind once again. Riley was right, Cazwell had always said that a base away from the factory would be a good idea. It had been one of the things he'd been contemplating before his death. A club would have made Cazwell proud. *But could Riley be trusted to make it work?* Knowing him, he would probably have bankrupted the place before the first punter walked through the door.

Tommy had money. He could invest in Riley's idea and safe-guard his own capital by making sure Riley signed a few more dotted lines here and there ensuring that everything came back to him. Yes, maybe a club was good idea. A respected venue could be a nice little earner and equally act as a cover-up for any jobs that needed to be sorted.

Despite still being desperate to play the Big I-Am, Riley knew that borrowing the money from Tommy would be his only chance to make it work. As Tommy said, 'Make it a suc-cess, you pay me back ... you fuck it up, I take charge.' Riley was certain that the result would be the former and not the latter.

Tommy lent the money happily, considering it a win-win investment and left it to Riley to find a venue. It was once he had that things started to unravel.

The space was a derelict old office block. Unused, in a good area of Manchester and considering its immense size, the price was incredibly low. It ticked all the boxes. At least that's what the weasel of an estate agent who was flogging the property kept saying anyway. When Riley had taken his name and number from the sign hanging on the front door and phoned him, the agent was insistent that they should move fast. Other parties were interested in buying it too and the early bird was definitely going to be the lucky buyer to get the worm.

Riley could see its potential, as could Amy when he took her to see it. She couldn't wait to get her hands on the property and pushed Riley to do everything he could to make sure it was theirs before somebody else pulled it from under their feet. Riley, keen to please, arranged a cash deal for the venue and planned to meet the estate agent as soon as possible, something that the overly exuberant and somewhat childishly excited agent couldn't wait to do.

It had been a dark, damp morning in January 2013 when Riley had headed to the property to hand over the cash. His appointment was scheduled for 11am. He'd turned up an hour early in eagerness and found the office door open. When he'd ventured inside he'd found the agent discussing a deal with another man. A man Riley instantly recognised as Adam Rich. Adam, the only man with the same kind of feared notoriety in Manchester as Riley's father had possessed and the man who had constantly been Cazwell's arch rival back in the day. The enmity had been passed on to Riley. Adam and Cazwell had clashed over jobs, fought over women and squared up over their competitive gangland manors. Neither wanted to be number two.

Adam was handing over a case full of cash to the agent. Riley had hung back in the shadows cast by the pillars within the office, not letting either man know of his arrival. Automatically he placed his hand on his overcoat and traced the outline of the gun housed inside his pocket. He never went anywhere without it and if he and Adam were inside the same room together then he had a strong suspicion that he might need to reach for it.

Riley listened in to the men's conversation. It was the whiny agent who spoke first, his voice snivelling, his actions shifty. His eyes darted around the room as if looking for someone. 'Right, this place is yours, the paperwork is all here ...' He handed Adam a brown padded envelope in exchange for the briefcase. 'Enjoy it, whatever you decide to do with it.'

Adam, a man who had thrived on his sharp business sense to shape his criminal empire, was not convinced. He could smell a rat. 'Do you not want to count the cash? £250K ... It's all there ... and surely you need me to sign something.' The agent tugged at the case, trying to free it from Adam's knuckle-bound grip.

'No need, you can take the paperwork away with you to read and then sign it when you're happy. Drop it into my office when you can. The address is in there.' He indicated the envelope.

Riley shifted position behind the pillar, trying hard to hear every word. As he did so his foot kicked a stray piece of rubble. The noise was sufficient for the two men to hear. Adam turned to face him and his concentration lapsed as he recognised Riley Hart, causing him to let go of the case. The agent, realising that this was not what he had planned, turned to run from the room, case in hand. Riley, with lightning speed, pulled the gun from his overcoat pocket and fired a bullet into the concrete floor in front of the agent causing him to stop dead in his tracks. He dropped to his knees and cowered with his hands above his head.

'I think you should give the man his money back, don't you?' stated Riley. 'You'd have been wanting mine in an hour ...' Riley held up the case towards Adam. The look on his face told Riley that his nemesis understood his meaning.

'Another buyer ... and you, of all fucking people,' said Adam. An incredulous grin opened across his face. 'Looks like this little twat was trying to take us both for a ride.' He pointed at the agent crouched on the floor.

Riley walked towards the agent and pointed his gun directly at the man on his knees.

'Right, you blubbering little cunt, care to tell me what the fuck's going on here ... trying to sell this place twice over?'

Riley never received a reply. The agent reached into his own pocket as deftly and as inconspicuously as he could and pulled out his own concealed gun. In less than the time it took to draw breath he pointed it towards Riley and the sound of a shot rang out.

The shot hadn't been from the agent's gun. Riley watched as the agent slumped backwards, his face shot away, a pool of deep red blood puddling across the floor. Riley, not even shaken by the close proximity of death, turned to face Adam. The gun in Adam's hand was still smoking.

'I wasn't sure you'd seen him go for the gun ...' said Adam. 'Seeing as we're on the same side for once I thought it was the least I could do ...'

The agent had turned out to be anything but legitimate. The name and address on the door were fake. His real name was Weston Smith, a two-bit con artist who had apparently made a habit of targeting derelict buildings across the country, posing as an estate agent and then proceeding to try and sell the same property to as many different people as possible, pocketing the cash-only deals all the way.

Adam and Riley worked together to dispose of the body, burying it in scrubland at the back of the derelict building. The story would have ended there had it not been for the fact that a few days later word swept through the criminal world that London's most feared tough guy, Jarrett Smith, was asking questions about the mysterious disappearance of his only son. Last seen in Manchester, Jarrett and his team of henchmen had travelled to the city in order to try and find Weston. Jarrett was determined that if his son had met a grisly end then the person or persons behind it would pay an equally fatal forfeit.

Adam was paranoid that Jarrett, one of the few men in life he truly feared, would find out that he was the man who pulled the trigger and that his rival, Riley, would be the one to let the murderous cat out of the bag. Riley played the situation to perfection. He insisted that Adam find out who really owned the building, offer a price nobody could refuse for it and then sign it over to him. In Riley's mind, winning one over on Adam and gaining a club for his own business was the ultimate way to make his dead father proud. The fact that the club would still be signed over to Tommy Hearn was beside the point. Riley had one over on Adam. And Adam could rest easy as his secret was safe from Jarrett Smith and nobody would ever find out about him killing the gangster's son.

When building work started on the club, Adam was emphatic that Weston's body was moved from the scrubland where it risked potential discovery and buried within the foundations of the fresh concrete poured into place to resurface the club floors. His rotting carcass was buried deep beneath The Kitty Kat Club dance floor where Adam knew it would never be found again. The only people who shared his secret were Riley and Tommy.

Adam had been elated that his secret had died when Riley lost his life at the club. Jarrett Smith, a cut-throat of a man who was more than capable of holding a grudge for forever, would never know the truth. Tommy would never say, not wanting any association between the two rival gangland families. That was a feud that could only end in major bloodshed.

But what if Riley wasn't dead? And with the arrival of Amy Hart there was a risk that her snooping around could uncover the truth about the body that lay beneath the floor of what was now the casino.

That was definitely something that Adam couldn't risk ...

CHAPTER 33
Now, 2015

'You know that this hotel has an in-house tailor who will make you a tuxedo if you don't have one. I am not heading to a *soirée* on the rooftop terrace, dear man, if you are not dressed appropriately. I cannot be seen overlooking Times Square clutching a martini in my hand wearing a Joseph Ribkoff leopard print with you looking anything less than Daniel Craig divine.'

'Caitlyn, we're in New York City. They do have shops here if I needed to buy a tuxedo, my sweet, and for your information I did pack two before we boarded the jet in London.'

Caitlyn Rich placed the hotel brochure she was reading from on the bedside table and lay back across the king-sized bed, loving the fresh feel of the cotton sheets against her naked skin. She was in great shape for a woman of her age – forty-seven in reality but thirty-nine to those who dared to ask – and the sexual workout she had just enjoyed with her lover, the man stood equally naked at the end of the bed, would certainly help keep the inches trimmed in all the right places. Her breasts stood proud, even when she lay on her back, but then they would. They were the handiwork of Jona Fleet, the famed Harley Street cosmetic surgeon to the stars, who had made sure that Caitlyn's considerable breasts, not glamour-model over-large but still sizable enough to give good cleavage, did not stray into different time zones from each other and head under her armpits when she lay on her back. Caitlyn had used one of her joint accounts with Adam to pay for the surgery eighteen months ago. Along with a tummy tuck and a chin dimple operation. The results had been so good that Jona didn't just ask her for a reference, he asked for a date, and despite being married to one of the most hardened men in the UK, Caitlyn had been glad to oblige. She and Jona, the man now sharing her hotel suite at Manhattan's reopened famous Knickerbocker Hotel, had been lovers for the past fourteen months.

Caitlyn's sex life had never been better. There was still the odd drunken fumble from Adam when he came in smelling of cigar smoke and whisky on one of his nights out with the boys but to be honest, Adam hadn't really bothered her sexually for years and that was just how she liked it. Adam was her cash cow, her pay cheque, her security. He wasn't her fun, her freedom, her fantasy. He had his lovers, Caitlyn knew that, and she had hers. And Jona was her latest, and with a nine inch erection bobbing between his legs, he was certainly her greatest too.

It was his huge erect phallus that caught her attention again as she stared at him from the bed. 'Well, we need to get rid of that before you go slipping into any clothing as you'd see that delightful monster distending a tuxedo made from the thickest of materials. I love the fact it's ready for action so soon after its last workout.'

'Can you blame it, Caitlyn? Look at you. You could turn any man on with a body like that. Even if I say so myself,' said the surgeon, his cock throbbing with anticipatory delight.

'Well, it's your doing, Jona. Now fix me a Martini and come back to bed. We didn't fly across the Atlantic in your jet for a romantic weekend to not make use of every delightful moment.'

'I'll phone down and order room service. They supposedly invented the Martini in this hotel back in 1912 so nobody is going to make it better than them.' Jona moved to the bedside table and stared down at Caitlyn's curves and the soft, downy patch of hair between her legs as he picked up the phone to order the Martini. His cock, still hard and proud, stood out in front of him. As he spoke on the phone, Caitlyn moved into position at the side of the bed and took his hardness into her mouth, working the shaft expertly with her tongue and lips as he placed the order for two Martinis. Caitlyn nibbled gently on the tip of his erection with her teeth causing her lover to flinch slightly as he hung up the phone.

'Now now, you can stop that right away,' he joked. 'If you're hungry I'll treat you to dinner in one of the sky pods at the St Cloud over Times Square. And yes, I'll be wearing a tuxedo.' Jona climbed onto the bed as he spoke and moved Caitlyn into position, lying her on her back once more underneath him.

'This is no time to talk about restaurants. And what's with all this Amerifying everything … if that's a word. We're both British, for heaven's sake, it's a dinner jacket, not a tuxedo.'

'Well, you started it, my angel. Now. Talking of dinner, I seem to have quite an appetite.' Jona placed his hands between Caitlyn's legs and opened the folds of her pussy to reveal the juicy pink core within. He buried his face deep inside and began licking at the flower within.

Caitlyn threw her head back in delight at the pleasure she was experiencing from his tongue. Neither Caitlyn nor Jona heard the knock of the door from room service as, unable to wait any longer, she moved Jona's mouth from her sex and eagerly slid his nine inches into her. The Martinis would still be on the menu later on.

CHAPTER 34
Now, 2015

Amy's visit to the casino had not gone as planned. She had followed Adam into the building and watched as he marched into Tommy's office. Whatever he wished to discuss, it was clear that he meant business. Determined not to be spotted, Amy had closeted herself as closely as possible, attempting to remain as hidden as she could. Screened behind a fruit machine, she angled herself to try and eavesdrop on the clandestine conversation between Adam and Tommy. It was futile – all she could hear was the constant noise of the gambling machines surrounding her.

She watched through the open door of the office as Adam banged his fist on the table, then stabbed his finger towards Tommy and threw his hands to his head. It was clear he was agitated. She was surprised the door had been left open but even though it was she still struggled to hear. She was sure she could read the words 'Riley' and 'Amy' on his lips. *Was she imagining it?* She had to try and move closer without the risk of being seen. She was just about to try when a voice sounded ...

'Can I help you? Are you looking for someone?' It was a man, early twenties, good looking. From his black waistcoat and crisp white shirt combo Amy guessed that he worked at the casino. 'If you're looking for the cash booth, it's over there.' He pointed towards the far side of the room.

'No, I was after a job.' It was the first thing Amy could think of to say and she was sure the lie was visible on her face as she felt her cheeks begin to redden with embarrassment. 'I was wondering if I could pick up an application form if you have any positions vacant, especially over the Christmas and New Year period. I'm looking to make a bit of money ... I'd be good at it ...' Amy drew her ramblings to an end, aware of just how unconvincing she could hear herself being.

The man, however, obviously as naive as he was handsome, seemed to believe her. 'Oh right, I'll go and find you a form. I'm sure I heard the boss say he was looking for more people.'

The boss. Tommy. Amy looked back towards the office where Tommy and Adam's little one-to-one was still in full, furious flow. She had to try and hear what they were saying. Determined to get rid of the man who was stopping her from doing so, Amy fired off her reply. 'Yeah, that's great, if you could I'd be really grateful.'

'I hope it works out for you,' replied the man with more than a measure of flirtation in his voice. 'We could do with some fit girls working here. I've only been here a few weeks. Used to live in north Wales, thought I'd come to a big city to earn some dough. This is my first job. It's all right, the boss is a bit of a git but he's okay. I'm Jimmy by the way ...'

'Er, hi ... nice to meet you' said Amy, half-listening. Her eyes were still fixed on the office. She could see that Jimmy had his hand outstretched towards her out of the corner of her eye. *God, this was all she needed ...*

'Hi Jimmy, cheers ... yeah, if you could ... er ... get me ... a form that would be excellent,' she faltered, shaking his hand and smiling weakly.

'Sure thing, I'll be right back.' He winked cheekily at her before turning and wandering off.

The conversation, short though it was, was long enough to ruin Amy's chances of attempting to decipher any more of the exchange between Adam and Tommy. When she stared back towards the office, the door was now wide open and only Tommy was inside. Where had Adam gone?

Frenziedly scanning her eyes around the casino, Amy tried to locate him. His bald head, the scrunched up skin on his neck and his broad back were not hard to spot as he pounded his way towards the exit. Whatever he had been saying to Tommy, it was clear that it was both over and had done nothing to appease his tantrum. Amy wanted to speak to Adam, maybe she should follow him. If she did maybe some clue about Riley's 'death' would come to light. She was certain that she'd lip-read his name. But she was here to see Tommy. He was still in his office, his mood not exactly jubilant either from the look of deep worry etched across his features. Amy was unsure what to do. Should she follow Adam or do what she'd come to do and see Tommy?

The decision was made for her.

'I couldn't find a form ...' The male voice came from behind and Amy felt a hand on her shoulder. It was an animated Jimmy. She turned to face him. 'But I've brought the lady who does the interviews here with me, as she said she'd see you now if you fancy ... is that a bit of luck, or what?'

The lady in question was Jemima Hearn and she was standing next to Jimmy. She was the last person Amy wanted to see. She knew she'd been caught, as did a grinning Jemima.

It was Jemima who spoke. 'That's right. Jimmy tells me you want a job at Dirty Cash. I think you should follow me to the office don't you?. Let's see what the owner thinks of your *suitability*.'

Amy felt her heart sink as Jemima Hearn grabbed her roughly by the arm and frog-marched her towards Tommy's office.

CHAPTER 35
Now, 2015

As Amy steeled herself to be grilled by the Hearns in the casino office, Grant Wilson was walking down a street on the other side of Manchester without a care in the world.

It was a crisp, fresh winter's day. The sky was blue with a snap of frost running through it, leaving him with a feeling of invigoration. There was a spring in Grant's step. It felt good to be at the top of his game. His work diary was full and he was a man in demand. The last year had been a major one for Grant. He had seen his star rise into orbit. He was on the verge of breaking through on an international scale. The right part, a well-timed meeting and he could be hanging with the Hollywood hot-shots like Cruise and Clooney by the time the next series of *Ward 44* had aired. He was in control. Just how he liked it, just as he'd always craved. All of the plates he'd attempted to spin over the past twelve months had paid off. They were all still spinning in joyous harmony. And he was their master. No, Grant felt invincible and the visit to Manchester was adding to that. Nobody could topple him.

He liked spending time with Amy. It pleased him. She'd been spat out by life over the last year. But as far as Grant was concerned she was better off without that wanker of a husband of hers, whatever the circumstances. Dead or otherwise.

Grant liked being back in Manchester. His old stomping ground. It gave him the chance to reminisce, to recollect. There was an air of cool about it that the rat race lifestyle of London couldn't always achieve and Grant was determined to try and re-tread an old path while he was in the neighbourhood.

Walking up to his destination he stared at the door in front of him and placed his face against the window framed within it. He placed his hands either side of his face to blinker the reflection of the blue sky on the glass. He let out a smile and attempted to push the door. It opened and he walked inside ...

It broke Genevieve's heart every time she saw her daughter. The relationship between the style icon and her own mother was far from rosy and Genevieve was determined that her bond with her own offspring would be as strong as it possibly could be. At least that had been the original idea when baby Emily came into the world.

Growing up, Genevieve had often dreamt of what it would be like to become a mother. She remembered how, as a child, she would scan the romance books sitting on her mother's book-shelf and pore over the words. She would imagine that one day a dashing, Herculean hero would sweep her into his arms and state his adoring love to her. That she would wear a huge fluffy dress of white on their wedding day and that nine months later she would give birth to the first of many beautiful children. But that was just fiction.

As Genevieve became older, her grasp on the harsh realities of life made her once pure and hopeful mind cloud into a mi-asma of putrid awakening that life was not as black and white as the pages of her mother's escapist reads. Of all of the boyfriends she'd had since first sharing a date outside her local chip shop at the age of fourteen, none had measured up. All of them had been dashing, a few could have been considered Herculean, but how many of them had stated their adoring love? In her teenage years the L-word had been liberally used by her admirers, mostly as a way of trying to crawl inside her knickers. But as Genevieve became a success in her own right, achievement and an ever-growing personal fortune had made her paranoid about what people wanted from her. Her twenties had been a period where, as the walls of her own fashion empire grew, so did the barriers of protection placed around her heart. A healthy bank balance and an unhealthy dose of doubt had come hand in hand. She was afraid to let herself be loved.

As for her youthful flashes of marrying in a huge white fluffy dress ... well, thankfully her drum-tight grip on the fashion world had knocked any such delusions out of the window quicker than you could say 'meringue'. If Genevieve was ever to marry, it would certainly not be in some fairy-tale monstrosity housing metres of shiny, pearlescent fabric.

Not that any man had ever made her entertain thoughts of being betrothed. Well, at least not until Riley had come into her life. She may have known that he was married from their first meeting, but the love-making she shared with him was something that even the idyllic romance tales in the pages of her mother's bedtime reading would have been hard-pushed to describe.

The sex was electric. Genevieve had been able to feel every nerve-ending tingle with a heightened desire as he'd made love to her. There was a connection as she had looked into his eyes. She could feel it – deep, dark and delicious, a carnal fusion of adventure, danger, power, respect and love. It was a provocative mix. The adventure and danger came from knowing that Riley was cheating behind his wife's back. The power and respect came from knowing that he was a man who lived life to the full. Like her, he was unafraid to take risks, to achieve what he desired, even if it meant bending a rule or two. She worshipped him.

The love however, was one-sided. That was something that had become clear on the day Genevieve announced to Riley the ill-timed news that she was carrying his baby.

His face had drained of all colour as she'd informed him, his usual healthy complexion turning ashen and ghostly white. His horror had been impossible to camouflage and with a crushing brutality he had told her to abort the baby. He would take care of it. There was no asking, it was telling. Riley was prepared to murder their baby in the same calculated, cold-hearted manner he organised a criminal hit on one of his enemies. It was at that moment that Genevieve had made up her mind. She was keeping the baby, no matter what Riley wanted. It was at that moment that she'd fallen out of love.

This was not how it was supposed to be. A baby was the last thing she needed at such an early, crucial time in her career. Research trips abroad, front rows at London Fashion Weeks and fashionista lunches were never going to be possible with a mood board under one arm and a bag of nappies under the other. The perfect accessory it was not. But Genevieve had recognised how her heart had skipped a beat and danced with delight when her doctor had confirmed that she was expecting. What she *hadn't* been expecting was such a harsh reaction from Riley. After the initial soul-crushing shock of being told that he didn't have a single trace of desire in him with regards to impending fatherhood, Genevieve had asked him to leave.

Part of her had wanted him to stay, to sweep her into his arms and tell her that he was leaving Amy. That he was ready to be with Genevieve and their child. That part was stamped underfoot immediately, crushed into a mass of miserable specks of heartache. Riley had trampled on her hopes and dreams.

His parting shot had been the worst, his words virulent and unthinking. 'Just get rid of it. Do whatever it takes. And don't let anyone know.' As he barked his demands he had thrown a wad of notes onto the table, freshly pulled from his wallet. Genevieve's eyes, glazed with tears, stared at the notes as Riley walked away from her and out of sight. Their relationship was over, the cost of her silence the final nail in its coffin. She knew it would be the last time they saw each other as lovers.

Genevieve had been thinking about Riley's poisonous words ever since she had arrived back at the shop after seeing Emily. Riley's daughter. He had never even met her, a fact she had hated him for. Now he never would. Emily would grow up fatherless, just as Genevieve had – her own father had left her mother to run off with another woman while Genevieve was still at junior school. Another man who thought with his cock and not with his head. He'd tried to contact Genevieve once after she'd first become successful, looking at her as some kind of family cash machine. He needed money. She had refused to see him.

It had been her father's infidelity that had caused Genevieve's mother to turn to drink. For years Genevieve would return home from school to find her mother slurring words of hatred into a half-empty whisky bottle. It had driven a wedge between them, but Genevieve would always understand her mother's reasons for drinking and would forever blame her father for causing it. She was a broken woman, broken by an unloving man.

At first Genevieve had threatened to place her baby with a foster family. Maybe that would be for the best. But there had been such a fear in her mother's eyes when Genevieve had revealed her plans. Deep within her Genevieve knew that she never had any intention of doing so, but she needed to use shock tactics on her mother if she was to be part of her grand-daughter's life. Genevieve needed her help, having a baby was not something she was prepared to do alone. The baby needed to be surrounded by what family it had. Her mother may have been a liability but she was all Genevieve had. She needed her, as would her baby – as a carer, as a grandmother, even acting as a mother when Genevieve couldn't be there.

The birth had to remain a secret and Genevieve needed all possible blood-ties helping her. She didn't need a baby ruining her reputation. It had only been through clever dressing and a minimum of socialising that Genevieve had hidden the pregnancy from her work contacts during the months before the birth.

Her mother, horrified at the thought of losing her first grandchild to a foster home, had offered to look after the baby. Genevieve turned the offer down, citing her mother's drinking. Her mother swore to never touch another drop. And in all fairness she didn't. When baby Emily was born, Genevieve passed her over to her grandma. A sitter-come-help was hired to help out and it was an arrangement that seemed to work.

'Mind you, like mother, like daughter ... maybe drinking's one of the traits she's passed onto me,' thought Genevieve as she poured herself a glass of neat vodka. She had been wallowing in her own misery ever since arriving back at the shop. She had drowned herself in booze into the wee small hours of the morning, eventually passing out on the office table.

Waking up the next day, she had decided to leave the shop closed. It was her assistant, Meifeng's, day off and Genevieve had little to no desire to deal with the outside world. What was the point of being boss if you couldn't make the odd rash decision every now and again? Despite the banging of her brain, Genevieve reached for the bottle and poured herself a mind-numbing dose of alcohol. She was just about to down the liquid when a figure appeared across the room.

'The door was open. I thought this was a shop, not some morning boozer ...' he said, indicating the bottle. 'What the fuck's happened to you?'

It was Grant.

'What the fuck do you want? Shouldn't you be performing open heart surgery on some poor bastard on TV or shagging some buxom young nurse up against a locker?' spat Genevieve.

'Oh dear, somebody's definitely had a bowl of bitch for breakfast haven't they?' deadpanned Grant. 'I thought you'd be pleased to see me. Hell, I assumed a so-called hot-shot like you would be busy dishing up your next slice of fashion pie to the world. Nobody need dressing today, then? Everyone going *au naturel*? You're obviously fit for nothing,' he stated, noting the full glass in her hand and the slur in her voice.

'Don't come the smug preacher man with me, Grant Wilson. Since when did your sorry arse gain the right to dictate to me about my life? You gave up that privilege the moment you climbed out of my bed and parked yourself between the legs of your next dumbass conquest,' she hissed.

All traces of jest disappeared from Grant's face. 'Oh here we go ... that took ... oh, three minutes by my reckoning,' said Grant, glancing at his Rolex. 'Poor hard-done-by Genevieve is still playing the woman scorned.'

His words were almost mocking, causing Genevieve to snap. Contemplating the failings of her short-lived affair with Grant was the last thing she needed bouncing around her mind when it was already soaked with misery reminiscing about her time with Riley.

'Men are just put on this earth to make women's lives unbearably hard. To make us suffer. Just piss off back to the TV, will you, Grant. Just get out ...' Genevieve's voice became more animated with every word, her anger mounting. 'I should have listened to my head when I first set eyes on your simpering little face ... if I'd have gone home alone that night things would have been a lot better.'

Not that Genevieve really meant that. Despite his indifference towards her, their time together had not been without its pleasures. They had first met a few years earlier when Genevieve had presented Grant with an acting newcomer's award at a London ceremony. The chemistry had been instant. An explosion of lust. They'd left together and screwed the night away at his hotel. It had continued at irregular intervals, the bodies coming together as their paths crossed. What Grant hadn't realised was that Genevieve was making sure that their paths crossed as often as possible. If there was a gala opening, press night or ceremony where she guessed Grant would be then she would make sure that she possessed a VIP ticket. But whereas their bouts of bedroom athletics had become sensual episodes of love-making in her mind, to Grant it was nothing more than a desire to get his rocks off. Grant had no qualms about telling her of other women he'd been shagging as he rode the fame train. An ever-hopeful Genevieve was convinced that maybe she could be the woman to change his bed-hopping ways, needing him in her life. She wasn't in love with him, but he certainly became an unhealthy obsession to her.

The sex was explosive but his interest in her was flickering no brighter than the weakest of flames. It was only when she'd met Riley that her longing for Grant finally died too. But her turn-around of interest seemed to fan the flames of desire within the actor. The power shift had changed. Suddenly Grant thought that maybe he was second best, a feeling he couldn't bear.

Genevieve couldn't face Grant right now. 'You're just a typical fucking bloke, Grant. Take your pretty boy ways and fuck off. I don't want to see you. Not now, not ever ...' There was disgust in her voice.

'So, a drunken bunk-up for old time's sake is out of the question, then ...' Grant had barely finished his egotistical request before Genevieve leapt unsteadily to her feet and attempted to throw the glass in her hand towards him. Unable to keep her balance, she fell to the floor behind the desk, the glass hurtling in completely the wrong direction, missing any chance of contact with Grant and instead smashing against a filing cabinet with a somewhat tragic shatter.

'Woah, somebody's in even more of a state than I realised,' said Grant, a vague trace of concern entering his voice. He rushed around the desk and lifted Genevieve from the floor. She was out cold.

Best thing for her, he thought.

He sat her back at her desk and rested her head on the table. If things had gone to plan they'd have been fucking on it by now, but yet again Genevieve had turned him down. Her loss, he mused.

Grant grabbed her keys from the desk and went to leave the office. The least he could do was lock the shop and post the keys back through the letter box. Genevieve would be asleep for hours and she wouldn't want to wake up to find Eruption looted.

As he was leaving he felt the crunch of broken glass underneath his shoes. Maybe he should clean up. He knelt down to pick up the shards and carefully wrapped them in a scrap of fabric from the desk. As he went to dispose of them Grant noticed more broken glass and a picture frame lying at the bottom of the bin. His curiosity piqued, he picked the frame up, careful not to come into contact with the glass. The tell-tale image of Genevieve and Riley together stared back at him. He felt almost winded by what he saw. Suddenly it all fell into place. No wonder Genevieve had had no sexual interest in him for ages, she was evidently getting her kicks elsewhere. Being rebuffed was bad enough, but the fact that the cause was obviously his archenemy, Riley Hart ... well, that was something else. Grant could feel his hackles rising.

As he left the office he couldn't help but wonder if Amy knew about the apparent affair between Genevieve and Riley ... and whether he should be the one to tell her. That would definitely stir things up ...

CHAPTER 36
Now, 2015

As Amy felt herself being rough-housed into Tommy's office at Dirty Cash by the pinching grip of Jemima, she couldn't help but feel that her attempt to eavesdrop on the conversation between Tommy and Adam had maybe not been such a good idea. In fact it had been a seriously bad one.

Tommy was more than a little surprised to see Amy and his wife standing before him. He raised his eyebrows, waiting for an explanation.

'She was sniffing around Jimmy asking about jobs, believe it or not ... thought I'd bring her in for *an interview*,' sneered Jemima.

Tommy laughed, his lips looping themselves into a decidedly evil grin. 'A job? Is that the best you could come up with? Even if I was the last employer on earth we know that isn't going to happen.' His tone was sneery and mocking.

A pause followed. 'I think we can cut the crap, can't we ...'

Amy let rip. 'You and Adam are up to something bad. I know it. I could tell from your conversation. You know more about Riley's supposed death than you're letting on.'

Any traces of devilish mirth vanished in a flash from Tommy's face.

'And can you make your lobster-clawed shrew of a wife get off my arm please! She's beginning to bruise me.' Amy attempted to wriggle free of Jemima's grip, which was becoming much more vice-like.

Tommy signalled to Jemima to let go. Reluctantly she did so. She'd been enjoying inflicting a harsher pain than was required. She was thinking about Winston. In her mind, Amy deserved to suffer.

'Any more accusations like that, young lady, and you'll end up in deep water,' snapped Tommy.

'Yes, I know, with concrete boots around my ankles. Heard it all before. I'm becoming used to how you all work now. You don't scare me Tommy ...' Amy was determined to show some bravado and stand firm, despite the nervous rhythmic beating of her heart banging within her. She couldn't fear Tommy, she couldn't. She wouldn't allow it. Men like him were fuelled by brutish power and bully tactics.

She continued. 'I know you're hiding something. I could hear you and Adam talking about Riley. I heard a lot before this bitch of a viper took hold of me.'

'There was nothing to hear ... so I find that very hard to believe.' Tommy didn't sound quite so confident. Something in Amy's mind made her think that maybe she had hit a little bit closer to home than Tommy desired. She was determined to try and roll with it. She was beyond fear. If Tommy was involved in Riley's disappearance ... in Laura's death ... then she was determined to try and call his bluff. She owed it to Laura and if Riley was still alive then she owed it to herself to find out the truth.

'I heard you and Adam plotting. You don't like me being back and asking questions about Riley. My best friend is dead, my husband too apparently and I think you're up to your neck in it. You two had so much to gain from Riley's death. I wouldn't be surprised if you had blood on your hands. What are you going to do, Tommy, have me killed too ...?'

'It was three people who died, you giddy bitch ...' Jemima couldn't help herself from speaking. How dare she forget about Winston?

Amy ignored her and stared at Tommy, trying to work out what was happening behind his eyes. Was that a crease of vulnerability she could see there? A reddening of his cheeks? She thought so. She continued to stare, determined not to break his gaze.

'You know nothing, you silly cow. Riley was a criminal, a convict, a killer, a monster, a liar. He got what he deserved. Whoever killed him had their reasons. Your stupid friend and that useless sidekick just got in the way. If anyone's to blame for their deaths it's Riley. So take your stupid, unfounded accusations and lay them to rest because if you don't then somebody might have to lay you to rest with them ... for good.' Tommy flicked his fingers dismissively at Jemima, indicating that he was done with Amy.

Despite the fact that she was sure she could hear her own fear in her voice as she spoke, Amy was determined to have the last word. 'The truth will out, Tommy. Somebody was responsible for Laura's death, and Riley's, if it was him who died ... if it's you, then there's not a person in the land who can stop me from making sure that you fucking burn in hell.'

Jemima grabbed Amy's arm and dragged her from Tommy's office. Amy could see a totally bemused Jimmy staring at her as she was frog-marched towards the casino exit. He attempted a smile, wondering just what type of interview answers Amy had given to be ejected out of the casino with such speed. He guessed she wouldn't be joining the workforce.

As they reached the door, Jemima swung Amy around to face her. Venom was plastered across her face. 'Your late husband had a lot to answer for. People are dead because of him. Good, warm people put into an early cold grave. Riley deserved his own death. The others didn't ...' Amy was sure that a pool of tears had begun to form in the corners of Jemima's eyes. 'Now get out ...'

Jemima swung her arm in fury, the palm of her hand contacting with a full-sounding crack across Amy's face. As she did so, she pushed Amy out into the street through the open door of the casino. Despite her insubstantial frame there was a sheer force behind both the slap and the push, causing Amy to fall to the kerb.

Holding her hand to her cheek, Amy stared up at Jemima. Tears had started to streak down Jemima's face.

'What was that for?' asked Amy, her cheek becoming sorer.

'That was ...' Jemima's voice faltered, her breathing random. 'That was ... that was ... for calling me a viper.'

As Jemima ran off, her sobs audible, Amy couldn't help but feel that there was more to Jemima Hearn than just being Tommy's simpering wife. She hated Riley, and obviously Amy herself by association. Her brutal outburst had definitely just put her well and truly onto Amy's list of suspects.

CHAPTER 37
Now, 2015

Tommy was worried. He had been ever since Amy had been taken from his office. In his heart he knew that Amy was bluffing, but why did his head keep telling him that maybe she had heard more than she was ever supposed to. It was a dilemma that he had been worrying over all day.

Amy had become a hindrance of major proportions. Before she'd been no more than a mosquito to him, buzzing around with no sense of direction, but now, he wasn't so sure. She was becoming smart. More like a bird of prey with a target in mind, ready to strike. And he couldn't risk that target having anything to do with the body of Weston Smith buried beneath the casino. Not even track-proven hard men like Tommy and Adam messed with the London East End boys like Jarrett Smith. Not without brutal payback.

Today had not been a good day for Tommy. Adam's visit and then the face-off with Amy had left him more than unsettled. He needed to do something. It was time for action. But what? Tommy wished that Cazwell was still alive. He would have known what to do. Adam was his arch enemy, but Cazwell would have pulled together with him for the sake of family, for honour, and to keep Jarrett Smith away from his turf. Fuck, who was Tommy trying to kid? If Riley's dad had still been alive he wouldn't have let the situation become such a fuck-up in the first place. But Cazwell was gone ... safe in his grave. Tommy would take the fall-out with Adam if Jarrett Smith ever found out the truth. They'd be the ones choking on their own blood or feeling the force of a crowbar on their skulls.

No, Tommy had to act and he had to act now. If there was any chance that Amy did know any finger-pointing facts then she needed to be stopped. Tommy picked up his car keys and marched out of the casino, a man on a mission ...

Dolly Townsend hated it when the sex she experienced with Adam Rich was interrupted. It was always good. Varied but good. She pleased him, she knew that. She was master of her trade and that, as ever, pleased her.

But interruptions were never welcome, especially when she had literally been a breath away from what had promised to be a rather nerve-fizzing orgasm. Adam gave her the kind of sex that she liked, the kind that she needed. Especially as it paid handsomely. And she gave it back to him in unadulterated layers of pleasure.

Thank Christ his wife was away from home most of the time – in London he said, staying with her sister – as Adam loved calling on Dolly whenever he had a chance. If he was angry she'd play slave to his master, submissive to his needs. Thinking of the extra cash she'd earn was always a soothing mental lotion for any momentary pain she suffered. If he was just back from a job he would often be more caring in his love-making, spending time cuddling and spooning, the warmth between their two bodies seemingly the antithesis of whatever brutal act he had doubtless been undertaking. And then there were the times when he simply wanted to fuck. Hard, deep, fast. They were all panels forming the patchwork of Dolly's professional life.

Today, Adam had been in the mood for the last of those options. She was to go to Adam's house, ready to fuck. Whatever plans she had for the evening were put on hold. When her number one client phoned, then she came running ... all the way to the bedroom and straight onto her back. She had been thinking non-stop about Adam since their last meeting. He was good to her, maybe he could be in more ways than he realised.

Adam had just been ploughing into Dolly from behind – his favourite position for deeper penetration – when the banging at the front door had started. At first they had both ignored it. The house was quiet, apart from the moans of ecstasy emanating from the bedroom, as Adam wanted to listen out for either Lily, who was out working, or Caitlyn returning home. Not that either was likely to. Caitlyn had been away for days and as far as he knew was still in London, even though any attempt to ring her had gone straight to answerphone. She normally phoned before returning home. As for his daughter, Lily, she'd said she wouldn't be back until tomorrow when she'd hurriedly left the house earlier that evening.

But as the banging on the door continued, it had put Adam off his stroke and Dolly could feel his erection wilt within her. Pulling out of her, Adam had grabbed a dressing gown and angrily marched off to answer the door, leaving a totally frustrated Dolly wondering if she should finish herself off. Assuming that Adam would be back as soon as he had dismissed the ill-timed caller, Dolly lay back on the bed and lit up a cigarette.

When she was stubbing it out some five minutes later and there was still no sign of Adam, she decided to try and see what was happening. If play-time was over then she needed to know about it. She'd still want her full fee though.

Slipping on a silk kimono, Dolly looked around the room. She longed to live in such luxury. Dolly dreamt of being surrounded by beautiful handmade rugs, ornaments that probably cost more than Dolly's entire flat and with chandeliers hanging from every ceiling. One day, she said to herself, *one day ...* in fact, maybe one day soon.

Dolly could hear voices coming from downstairs. They were raised and angry. At first she thought it may have been Adam's lucky bitch of a wife coming home from yet another shopping trip, doubtless with another over the top mirrored statue – the house was becoming overrun with them – but as she strained to hear, she could tell that both voices were male. Moving to the door, she opened it as quietly as she could and sneaked out onto the landing. The voices were coming from a room off the main hallway at the bottom of the house's sweeping staircase.

She could hear Adam and the man he was talking to – Adam called him Tommy – quite clearly. It was apparent that both of them were worried about something, and that it was pretty major whatever it was. Seating herself at the top of the staircase, she lit another cigarette, listening to every word and soaking up the information like a sponge.

Eavesdropping had never been so interesting, or as potentially rewarding. As Dolly tip-toed back into the bedroom when the men brought their heated interaction to a close, she couldn't help but smile to herself. She realised that this was the moment she had been waiting for. The moment when maybe the luxuries she'd dreamt of so many times in the past could finally be within her expertly manicured reach.

Slipping off the kimono, she stubbed out the cigarette and lay back on the bed, awaiting Adam's return and looking forward to what she knew would be a rather jaw-droppingly wondrous orgasm.

CHAPTER 38
Then, 2008

'That is some fucking rock, Amy! Russian cosmonauts could land on that and be exploring for days. I am seriously jealous.'

Laura hadn't been able to take her eyes off Amy's diamond wedding ring ever since Riley had slipped it onto his new wife's finger earlier that day. The ring was obscenely large and even Amy had been taken aback by its sheer size when her husband had first showed it to her. Riley had picked it himself and was determined that Amy shouldn't see it until the big day. Big being the operative word. It swamped her finger and rested on her hand alongside her equally blinged-up engagement ring like a massive sparkling Frisbee, causing light to bounce off its every facet like a Las Vegas night skyline. Amy adored it, partly because it was larger than she had ever imagined but also because of the oversize smile that spread itself across her husband's face every time he looked at it. Lord only knows what it had cost but if the illustrious world of plastics was doing so well then who was Amy to question the cost? It made her dreamy with the euphoria of romance.

'You are now officially my wife. That slab of beauty proves it. Together forever, till death do us part and all that,' said Riley, taking his wife's hand in his and whisking her off for yet another dance at their evening wedding reception. 'If you will excuse us, Laura, my gorgeous new wife and I would like to strut our funky stuff.'

Laura pointed at a smirking Riley as he waltzed Amy off to the dance floor. 'He is such a keeper. If you ever grow tired of him then send him my way and get him to bring the ring too.'

Riley winked at Laura as Amy raised her eyebrows jokingly and stated, 'Not a chance, sister!'

Amy was the happiest woman alive. The day had been everything she had been planning for months. The beautiful rural church in a tiny village just outside Manchester had been picture postcard perfect. The summer roses growing around the lych gate were in full bloom, the weather was hot enough to warm the skin but still a cooling breeze stopped the humidity from straying into the uncomfortable, and her best friend, Laura, had looked every inch the perfect bridesmaid. The only cause of misery to the new Mr and Mrs Hart was the absence of their parents, all of them taken before their time.

The ceremony had definitely been a meeting of two different worlds. Amy's friends and what family she had left were low-key, from a world where wedding costs would normally be kept to a minimum and the evening reception would amount to a local pub band and a basic spread of sandwiches and finger food.

So the marriage of Amy Barrowman, one of their own, to the successful, ruggedly handsome and undoubtedly loaded businessman, Riley Hart, was a real show-stopper.

Riley's side of the church was rammed with suited and booted, dressed to impress with diamonds and pearls. The right/left rich/poor divide in the church was wider than the age gap between Madonna and some of her beaus, but neither bride nor groom cared. They only had eyes for each other and as long as everyone seemed to be enjoying themselves, which they did, then how could the day be anything other than the most wonderfully romantic success?

The evening reception was held at one of the most expensive hotels in Lancashire, last seen within the pages of *Hello* magazine as the wedding venue of a Formula 1 racing car driving and his pit-stop girl turned *Big Brother* star girlfriend. Amy and Riley made sure that caterers had been called in to see that nobody was ever hungry, a never-ending supply of starters, mains, desserts and various *amuse-bouches* arriving at the tables with appetising regularity.

Then there was the music. One of Manchester's trendiest club names spun the tunes, his set a heady mix of mainstream pop, Motown magic and US soul. Riley and Amy's first dance was to a retro delight of a tune they both adored, 'Together We Are Beautiful' by Fern Kinney. It had been playing on a radio station in the car on one of their first dates together and both of them had instantly made it 'their tune'.

Laura had been a torrent of tears as she watched Riley move her best friend around the dance floor. She'd originally planned to film the first dance and upload it onto You Tube but not being able to focus through her waterfall of tears blitzed the idea. Not that the tears had stayed for long. In true Laura fashion, she had made a beeline for one of the guitarists in the Indie group Riley had hired for the night. She'd seen them a few times on *MTV* and guessed that they would be well connected. A smiling Laura had last been seen heading off with the baggy-haired musician to make a few connections of her own in the privacy of her hotel room.

The band hadn't gone down so well with everyone. Jemima had looked on as they swayed their way around the specially built reception stage and looked down her nose in disgust at what she saw as their 'grubby outfits' and 'hair that looked like it needed a damned good wash'. Staring at them as if they were as welcome as an oil slick at a bird sanctuary Jemima turned to her husband and asked, 'Why are they wearing trousers that don't bloody fit?'

Tommy huffed. 'They look like a bunch of fucking students ...' Unsurprisingly, the Hearns had not stayed the entire evening.

Amy wouldn't have cared if all of her guests had disappeared. As she moved around the dance floor she only had eyes for one person and that was the hunk of a man wrapping her in his arms, stroking his fingers through her hair, allowing his lips to gently nuzzle against her forehead and whispering words of love in her ears. It meant the world to Amy to feel the safety of his arms encircling her. It was a feeling that she hoped would never leave her.

CHAPTER 39
Now, 2015

'I thought we'd always be together,' said Amy, staring into the bottom of her empty red wine glass. 'I just find it so hard to contemplate the fact that Riley's not around anymore.'

'So, have you convinced yourself that Riley's really dead, then?' said Grant, refilling her glass from the other side of their Manchester hotel restaurant table.

'I think I didn't really know my husband when he was alive, so how the hell am I supposed to know what's going on now he's supposedly dead? Dead men don't write letters and somebody did, and it was his handwriting. I can't deny that. So he must be alive, but as he's not contacted me in person, how can I tell?'

'And what about Tommy Hearn and Adam Rich? Are you sure they're involved?' Amy had filled Grant in on her run-in with the two men at Dirty Cash, and on her encounter with Jemima. After Grant had questioned her about the ever-darkening stain of a bruise on her cheek Amy could see no reason not to share what had happened with him. His company was proving invaluable as a way of sharing the burden of her ever-mystifying life.

'I'm not sure about anything, but I would put money on them knowing something about what happened that night. Neither of them liked Riley, that's for certain, but whether

Tommy is a cold-hearted killer ... I don't know. Adam kills for a living according to Lily, so anything's possible with him, but what does he have to gain? Other than his gangland rival being out of action for good. Christ, and to think I used to lie awake at night worrying that I wouldn't know the finer details of the plastics trade and would be an embarrassment to Riley. I didn't think for one second it was all a cover up for something so ...' She searched for the right word, her mind lost in thought, before deciding on '... diseased'.

'I have to ask you a question, Amy,' said Grant.

'Fire away ...' said Amy, glad of the momentary distraction.

'I was mentioned in that letter. You let slip that Riley listed me as a suspect. You know there was no love lost between us and yet we're sitting here in a hotel sharing a bottle of wine, having dinner and you're telling me your suspicions about his potential killer. Does that not strike you as more than a bloody bit odd?'

'Shouldn't I trust you, then?' It was a genuine question.

'You know you can trust me. I wouldn't be following you up here to Manchester if you couldn't, would I? For what it's worth, I think Riley is dead. I think you're much better off without him too as the fact that he lied constantly to you when he was alive is despicable. But I understand that you loved him ... still do. If you can forgive him for his lies about his job and his indiscretions then who am I to judge him? I just hope you find peace in all this, whatever the outcome. But I can't see this having a happy ending, can you?' Grant's words were bluntly matter of fact but still carried an air of compassion.

'I may be naive, but even I'm not stupid enough to think that this particular story can have a happy ever after. Even if Riley is alive, and of course I hope he is, I don't think I can forgive him for what he's putting me through. And as for you ... Well, I'm kind of hoping that my judgement in trusting you is a wise one. Like you say, you don't have any real reason to be here with me. You've had your film meeting in the hope of being the next Channing Tatum and you could disappear any time you like. I'd be lying if I didn't say that having you here is making things slightly more bearable.'

'Actually, about that...'

Amy could tell that Grant was on the verge of some kind of admission. She could feel an all-too-familiar stone of disappointment fall into the pit of her stomach. 'Go on ...'

'The meeting wasn't the only reason I came to Manchester. I needed to see someone else, someone involved with Riley's letter.'

The stone in Amy's stomach seemed to instantly grow into a boulder as Grant continued.

'I came to see Genevieve Peters. I've known her quite a long time. We were ... er ... involved, once. Not any more though. There wasn't any real commitment, we were just mutually incompatible, shall we say? We ...'

'You were sleeping together.' Amy cut him short, straight to the point. 'And that affects me how, exactly?' Amy didn't want to admit that an unexpected and not altogether welcome pang of jealousy had fired through her as she said it. A momentary suggestive flash of what Grant would be like between the sheets flickered across her mind. She rapidly tried to push it away.

'Yes, I'm no angel. She's a good-looking woman, I'm a typical man ...'

'You don't have to explain yourself to anyone, least of all me, Grant. You can sleep with who you like.' There was an uncharacteristic harshness in Amy's voice, perhaps betraying her disappointment. 'So, did you see her ...?'

'Yes, and that's why I figure there's something you ought to know. She was drunk and had been crying.'

'Ice maiden Genevieve. There's a turn-up for the books ...' Amy was monotone in her delivery. 'I didn't think she had any form of emotion or weakness in her.'

'Yeah, well I think someone has defrosted her heart at some point in the past.' He faltered for a moment. 'That's what I need to tell you about.'

Amy sat in silence waiting for Grant to continue. He did.

'Genevieve likes to drink, she did even back when I was with her. I think it all stems from her mum, as she liked to hit the bottle when Genevieve was younger.'

'So?' Amy was trying not to sound harsh and uncaring. And failing badly.

'When I went to Eruption I found Genevieve in the back of the shop, in her office.'

'I know it,' stated Amy, recalling her catch-up with the boutique owner in the very same room.

'She became a bit lairy when she saw me and to cut a long story short, tried to throw a glass at me which smashed everywhere and she passed out.'

Amy just raised her eyebrows, her lack of emotion showing once more. 'And ...?'

'I checked she was okay and decided to leave but before I did I went to clear up the glass all over the floor. I went to put it in the bin but when I did I found a framed photo in there. It had obviously been thrown in, as it was cracked.'

With a sense of dread, Amy knew she had to ask. 'Of what?'

'Genevieve and Riley. Together.'

'So what?'

Amy tried to explain that it could have been innocent, since Genevieve and Riley knew each other from the Kitty Kat, but she could tell that Grant thought there was much more to their relationship than a passing acquaintance. In her heart, where

the ball of angst from her stomach had now migrated, spreading
yet more despair, Amy knew that there was too.

But she needed a second opinion. Needed to hear someone
else say it out loud.

'What, you think they were having an affair?' After the revelation about Lily and Riley sleeping together, the idea didn't
seem so unlikely.

Grant was stony-faced as he answered. 'Judging from the
photo, I'm certain of it.'

CHAPTER 40
Now, 2015

Lily's night out was heading from depressing to beyond cataclysmic. Even in her blurred state of mind as she stumbled her way across the beer-soaked dance floor of The Black Hart, she knew that her life was definitely suffering from what even the most upbeat of people would call a downward slump.

How had it come to this? It didn't seem that long ago that she was the one at the shining musical heartbeat of Manchester's most talked-about scene. The girl who could turn up the volume all over town. Back in the Kitty Kat days she was one of the key figures organising who came in, who got smashed, how people looked, how head-fucked they wanted to be. She was even experiencing some of the best sex ever thanks to her affair with Riley. She was in control.

But now ..? Bouncing drunkenly into the leather clad, patchouli-smelling clients of The Black Hart, one of Manchester's lower than low-rent dives, Lily was beginning to question where it had all gone wrong. And the excess of drugs and drink she'd taken throughout the evening was not aiding her thought process.

Lily had been doing a lot of thinking about Riley. Of all the men she'd ever been to bed with, it was Riley who had really managed to worm his way underneath her skin and burrow his way into her heart. She'd loved him. She could pretend all she liked that it had been just a meaningless shag fest but it hadn't. Not to her anyway. There was so much more to it than sex. It was only now that she could see that.

So why had he dumped her? It had to be because of that stupid wife of his, surely? She liked Amy as a boss at the club, she even liked her as a person, if she was honest. Totally harmless, completely naive, she was everything that Lily considered herself not to be, but as a love rival – that was something else, a whole different ball game. No, Riley had broken her heart into a million jagged edged scraps and even though Lily had spent months thinking that she could handle it, she was beginning to realise that now she couldn't. The fucker had turned her world upside down. She could have killed him herself when he tossed her aside. It was a moment that Lily Rich would never forget.

There was something feral about sex with Riley Hart. Almost as if it was extra deliciously dirty because it was behind his wife's back, escaping the confines of his everyday union with Amy.

That was half the attraction for Lily. She liked the danger of it. The animalistic nature of it. Sex with Riley was hard, urgent, forceful and powerful. He was a big man, the complete opposite of Lily's petite frame.

Riley would carry her around, lifting her into the air, her legs wrapped either side of him as he ploughed his cock into her. He would grab her hair and bend her ninety degrees over his desk, or a chair or the DJ booth if he found her alone at the club, yanking her knickers to one side before slamming his rod into her. Often he would force her to her knees and make her hold her hands behind her back, face-fucking her with his dick until she swallowed his seed.

And Lily loved every downright dirty moment of it. Lily had never been a 'love me tender' kind of girl, she liked to please a man, whether she was giving or she was taking. She loved what he made her do, loved how it made her feel, and she had started to love Riley himself.

But Riley had obviously become bored by it. One day at the club as she had tried to blow him in his office, Riley's cock had wilted at her touch, his lack of interest limply evident.

It had never happened to Lily before and she needed to know why it had occurred.

'Not in the mood, then?' Her tone was jocular but she was far from joking.

'Look Lily, you're a great girl ...' It was clear to Lily straight away where the conversation was going.

She stood up as Riley spoke. He did his trousers back up.

'But?' she asked. There was always a but.

'I'm a married man.'

'You were married when you first stuck your cock in my pussy.'

Riley, never one to mince his words or waste any more time on something he didn't deem important than need be, finished the conversation.

'It was good while it lasted Lily, but it's over. I don't think we should do this anymore.'

'Why not? I thought we got on really well. Knew where we're coming from?'

'Which is?'

'That you and I are alike. Both free-spirited, strong, fierce people, who like to shag like rabbits.'

'But it was just a bit of fun, Lily. Nothing more.'

It was the first comment that had really stung Lily. 'A bit of fun? Is that all I am to you?'

'Well, it's not like you're falling for me, is it? I'm with Amy. She's my wife. This is just ...' Riley struggled to complete the sentence. '... well, this.'

Lily, normally so strong, could feel the quivering of tears growing inside her.

'And if I was falling for you?'

His answer was quick, clear and destructive. 'Then I'd say fuck off, we're never going to be together, are we?'

Suddenly it was clear to Lily. The reason why their sex was so brutal, lacking in pillow talk or sweet nothings. Because there was nothing behind it. She was merely a receptacle for his sexual relief. Their relationship had been nothing but a vacuum of lust. How had she been stupid enough to think otherwise?

She wouldn't let him see that she was hurt. Forcing her voice to be as upbeat as possible she stared Riley right in the eye. 'Be together? No fucking way. You're right, it was good, but enough is enough, eh? No more tears.' She was quoting one of her mum's favourite songs. 'Right, I'll crack on. I've got some shit to sort out in the cloakroom. If you ever change your mind about ...' She pointed to Riley's groin. 'Then, just let me know. We're sexually good, you and I.'

'I won't change my mind.' His words could not have been more dismissive.

'Laters.' It was all Lily could say before quitting Riley's office. She walked straight past the Kitty Kat Club's cloakroom and into the ladies toilet. She walked into a cubicle and shut the door behind her. Sitting on the toilet, she started to cry. Her heart broken.

No more tears? What a crock.

Lily thought that she had managed to rid any feelings she had for Riley from her heart. That all of her emotions were long gone. So what had changed? It was simple. All of a sudden there was a chance that maybe Riley was alive. If Amy thought so then why shouldn't she? Stranger things had happened in the murky world Riley had frequented. She'd spent years hearing snippets of people disappearing, being erased, moved elsewhere for their own good through her father's work. She'd not really paid any interest to the hows, whys and wherefores. But maybe something like that had happened to Riley? Maybe one of his jobs had plunged him deeper into some dangerous gangland-infested waters and he had to scarper before it was too late. Stage his own death maybe. Yeah, she wouldn't put that past him. He was always a cunning sod.

But if he didn't die then who had their face shot off in The Kitty Kat? In all the melee of that evening maybe bodies were swapped? Without a face, one suited, muscled chunk of bloke could look pretty much like another. The criminal world was always full of cover-ups and backhanders. Yeah, it could happen, Lily decided, as if willing it to be true.

She tried to steady herself against the wall of the pub as the drugs rushed through her again. It felt clammy against her skin. Why had she come here? It had never been near the top of her list when it came to dealing drugs and it was the kind of bar where someone puking up their gut lining in the corner would improve the look of the place. It was the complete opposite of everything she'd loved about The Kitty Kat. Her father would die if he could see Lily now, peddling shit in some Manchester backstreet crap hole. Especially given the fact that Lily was more off her head than most of the scraggy, hairy-faced blokes and tattooed, scrawny-arsed women surrounding her. She needed to get out, to escape.

But it wasn't just The Black Hart she needed to escape, she needed to put all of this shit behind her. She was taking more drugs than ever before. But they were necessary. She needed them to cope. That's what she told herself. She'd put them all behind her one day. She needed a springboard to another life. One with a man she could love and persuade to love her back. Maybe that way she could love herself a bit more too. And maybe, just maybe, that man could still be Riley ...

Despite the cocktail of booze and narcotics clouding her mind as Lily carelessly zigzagged her way towards the exit of The Black Hart, she had already decided that it was high time to try and meet up with Amy again. She'd know more about the truth behind's Riley's 'death' than anyone. If there was information to share, then Amy Hart would have it. She looked at the sign above the bar with the name of the pub on it. The Black Hart. She giggled to herself ... The Black Hart ... Amy Hart ... Riley Hart ... she'd never really thought about it before. All these fucking hearts and here she was with a broken one. But she'd soon sort that.

Before leaving she headed off to the toilets for another thick white line of cocaine. One for the road.

CHAPTER 41
Now, 2015

Amy needed time out. She was more scared than she'd ever been in her life. More scared than she could ever imagine being again. Scared of the future and what it might hold.

Having woken up in a blind panic in her hotel bed that morning after experiencing the most lucid of nightmares, Amy definitely needed to take a step back. Even in her sleep, her brain was awash with images of Laura dying in her arms, Riley's exploded face and a whirlwind of maniacal grins all boring into her. Genevieve, Grant, Adam, Tommy, Jemima, Winston, Lily ... they were all there. She'd woken up bolt upright, a waterfall of sweat staining the sheets beneath her.

All she'd thought about lately were the what-ifs of that night at The Kitty Kat. Would she ever find peace? There were times when she questioned just why she was chasing the truth. The police had let the entire episode slip through their fingers. Where were the dental records? Why hadn't she looked for a distinguishing mark, something that would have convinced her above everything that the body in front of her at the mortuary was Riley's? Then all of this doubt she now felt would be clarified. Riley was dead, end of. If she could bring his killer to justice then great. But the cop in charge had moved 'overnight'. Everything had been conveniently hushed-up. Tommy had said as much. If the boys in blue had chosen not to know, then did she really want to?

Riley's letter had brought nothing but extra torture into her life. His affairs with Lily and Genevieve, his duplicity about his job, his allowing Tommy and Jemima to take everything that should so rightly be hers had all done nothing but cause her pain.

Where would it all end? For her own sanity, Amy needed to stop. Just for a while. To stop chasing. Stop risking the chance of unearthing yet another body blow from beyond the grave.

Staring out of the window of her Manchester hotel room she looked at the winter's sky. It was full of dark snow clouds, a contrast to the crisp, blue air of the day before. As she watched, a light dusting of snowflakes began to tumble Earthwards from the clouds.

Growing up, Amy had been taught that the clouds were the edge of heaven where the angels sat, looking down to Earth making sure that all of those people they cared about were healthy and well. Her mum and dad had been religious people who had instilled in her the values of being good in life in order to gain entry through the Pearly Gates and into heaven.

Back then she had believed it. Do unto others as you would have done unto yourself and come the day of reckoning then eternal joy would be yours. Amy could feel a pinprick of tears starting to form in the corners of her eyes as she thought about it.

What would her parents have thought about all this now? Riley's criminal connections and his infidelity? They'd never have believed it. Not of the man their daughter had fallen in love with. Was there still a miniscule corner of her soul that could still love Riley after everything that had occurred? Amy wasn't sure that any love within her would be able to survive in the quagmire of blackness painting her inner emotions.

Before she could control it, the tears started to fall. Deep, desperate sobs forced themselves from her throat. Days of pent-up emotion flowed from her body. Sinking to her knees, Amy let her body succumb to the emotion, allowing her entire being to surrender to her apparent weakness. She needed to cry, to let the tears of her own misery wash over her. She placed her hands across her face and felt the rivulets of moisture run between her fingers and drip down onto her bare legs. She cried, on and on until no more tears cascaded forth.

It felt strangely satisfying. She felt somehow stronger, as if the expulsion of woe had been a mental boot camp for her soul, something that her body had needed to do, regardless of whether she had chosen to or not. Wiping the last teardrops away from her cheeks, Amy looked skywards again, as if to heaven beyond the clouds. Today she knew exactly what she needed to do. It didn't include any of the players from the production she was currently starring in – the tragic tale of Riley Hart. No, today Amy needed to walk away.

Walking into the bathroom, she turned the shower dial on the wall and watched as the jets of water burst into life. She let her nightdress, still sweat-soaked, fall to the floor and stepped into the water, ready to cleanse herself of all potential bleakness, if only for a few hours.

Having left a note for Grant at the hotel Reception, Amy hailed a cab and told the driver her desired destination. As the taxi pulled away from the kerb Amy looked through the window, slightly dirty from the polluted city air, at the snowflakes tumbling past. The snow was getting heavier. The TV report that morning had suggested that it wouldn't last for long and would be unlikely to settle, but Amy enjoyed watching the flakes. It gave an added festive air to the many Christmas decorations already dressing the city.

She focussed on the medley of people she could already see enjoying the early morning weather. Mothers, gloved hand in hand with their children, no doubt heading off to department stores in search of yet another Christmas gift, suited business-men striding to their meetings, shop owners brushing away the flakes of would-be-mushy snow from outside their premises. The normality of it all was somewhat comforting and Amy let herself relax back into the softness of the back seat of the cab as she watched the outline of the city disappear behind her. Her eyelids felt heavy and she allowed them to close, the consistent hum of the motor acting as a lullaby in her ears.

Amy must have dropped off, her fatigue taking her over. The next thing she heard was the voice of the cab driver informing her that they had reached her destination. She paid the man and asked if he could come back for her in two hours. She wanted some time to herself but she was aware that her destination was remote enough that she could not necessarily be guaranteed to find a cab later, especially given the time of year. The driver said he would be back at midday and she watched as he headed off.

Amy had come to the village where her parents were buried. It was a place that she used to come to regularly but it was the first time she had been back since moving to London. It was a rundown yet peaceful spot not far from where her parents had raised her. There was something about it that seemed almost joyful to her.

The cemetery surrounding the church was iced with a dusty frosting of snowfall, and it crunched ever so lightly underfoot as she walked to the plot where Enid and Ivor were buried. Her mind filled with happy memories of days gone by with her parents. Learning to ride her first bicycle, crying onstage when she'd played Mary in the nativity because she wanted to be one of the wise men as she liked their outfits more, country dancing for them at her school fete. Those days seemed to belong to another era now, one she could hardly relate to anymore. Yet a smile of happy reflection still spread itself across Amy's face.

Standing in front of their gravestones, Amy took off her gloves, placed her fingers to her mouth, kissed them and touched the two marble headstones, once for her mum and once for her dad. Her warm breath swirled in the cold air as she spoke, a simple, 'Hello, it's me'. No more was needed.

Amy ran her hand across the top of the headstones, brushing away the small depth of snow that had gathered there. Kneeling down, she traced her fingers across the words engraved onto the front of the stones. 'Forever In Our Thoughts, Joined In Peace'. For Ivor it read 'Loving Husband and Father', for Enid 'Loving Wife and Mother'. Amy remembered how when the stones had first been placed, she and Riley had said that maybe one day they would be able to say that Enid and Ivor would have been loving grandparents too. It was such a shame that that would never happen. In her mind's eye Amy could easily picture a baby boy, the image of his dad, bouncing on his grandfather's knee, or a cherubic girl, ringletted and freckled, gazing into her grandmother's eyes. Picture perfect but now a pipe dream. Three pieces of the family jigsaw were gone for good.

Amy spent the next ninety minutes in quiet contemplation, tidying up the area around the graves as best she could, pushing away leaves and stray twigs. She ventured into the church, firstly to escape the bitter winter's air for a few warming minutes – the snow may have stopped but the air was still icy – secondly, because she wanted to offer up a prayer. To pray for a solution to her woes, to give her the inner strength to find justice, at least for Laura if for nobody else. She was alone in the church. It felt light years away from the mayhem and the madness of all that had surrounded her over the past few months. The club, the casino, the arguments, the revelations – everything seemed to fade into the background. Albeit momentary, it was hugely welcome. Amy lost herself in its tranquillity.

Amy checked her watch. It read ten to twelve. She needed to head back to the front of the church. The taxi would be here soon. She couldn't risk missing it. She'd barely heard any kind of transport drive by since she'd first arrived.

Pulling her coat tight around her, Amy walked through the gate at the front of the church and sat on a bench situated on the pavement. It had done her good to visit her parents' graves. There was a calm weaving its way through her body that she hadn't experienced for some time. Whatever the days ahead were going to throw at her, she was sure that it wouldn't break her. She wouldn't let it.

The roads were eerily quiet, the only sound around coming from the flittering and tweeting of a robin redbreast, dancing its way around the graveyard, no doubt in search of a much-needed winter's meal.

Amy looked at her watch again. Five to twelve. As she stared at the face, a loud crack of noise filled the air. She jumped, startled. What was it? A car exhaust perhaps? Kids messing around with a new toy? But there was no-one in sight. There was something about it that sent a horribly familiar chilled ripple of fear through her veins.

Again the noise sounded, this time a corner of the wooden bench she was seated on splintered as something impacted with it. There was no doubt in Amy's mind as to what it was. Somebody was shooting a gun and unless she was very much mistaken, they were shooting it right at her. A third shot and another splintering of wood no more than six inches from her leg proved the point.

Despite a stupefied feeling of momentary paralysis, Amy knew that she was a sitting duck and needed to run. To hide. This was no random teenager with an air pistol firing off a few arbitrary rounds. This was someone who wanted her blood.

Or maybe they didn't. Three shots and not one had hit her. Maybe they were a warning, a sign to back off. Either way, Amy wasn't sitting there waiting for shot number four.

Running as fast as her legs would carry her she sprinted from the bench, back through the gate and into the church. As she did so, she could hear the sound of a motorbike starting behind her. Looking around as she moved into the sanctuary of the building, Amy saw a leather-clad biker disappearing off out of sight. Amy was sure that whoever it was had been responsible for the gunshots. Had they followed her here, to the place where her parents were buried? To somewhere so private and personal to her? The thought made her see red. She could feel her skin prickle with rage. Somehow this had to end, but she couldn't walk away now. If she did, then whoever was behind all of this would win. And that was something she couldn't allow.

Amy was still sheltered in the doorway of the church when her taxi driver turned up some fifteen minutes later. He wound the window down as she approached the car. 'Sorry I'm late, love, there was some sort of roadblock on the main road getting out of town. I bet you've been bored stupid waiting. It's as dead as a doornail round here.'

Amy climbed into the back seat, her eyes still scanning in all directions. 'You have no idea,' she said ...

CHAPTER 42
Now, 2015

Genevieve Peters had managed to do a lot of things in her relatively short life, but she could count the things that she was embarrassed about on one hand. And there was only really one of them that shamed her to her very core.

Her one continual grown-up pitfall of shame. The one embarrassment that kept raising its ugly head, Kraken-like from the deep on a never-ending roundabout, was her drinking. Every now and again it would spiral out of control. And here it was again. For such a strong woman, how could Genevieve allow herself to be so pathetic time and time again?

Shame gripped her as she stumbled into the front of her shop and picked up the keys that had been posted back through the letter box by Grant because she'd been too pissed to even stand. She nearly threw up as she bent to retrieve them.

To the outside world she was supposedly the mean super bitch, dressed immaculately with a poison-dart sharpness and a business sense which had catapulted her to the top of her game. A woman who could be seated alongside Anna Wintour, Naomi Campbell and Alexa Chung during Fashion Weeks in Milan, New York, London, and do it with pride. But she knew the truth. Underneath it all, she was a mess. A drunken mess. It wasn't a wagon that she chose to fall off very often but when she did, Genevieve could fall faster than a gangly-legged newborn deer. That did not make her proud. And the last few times she had fallen had all been caused by one thing. Or more to the point, one person, Riley Hart. He was behind her latest dive into insobriety. She knew that, even if he was seemingly pushing up the daisies.

He'd been at the epicentre of her last major drunken incident too. God, incident, that underplayed it somewhat. If that *incident* had ended as Genevieve had originally planned then baby Emily may have ended up without a mother as well as a father. At least for a couple of decades while mother dearest resided at Her Majesty's pleasure ...

Emily Peters was eight months old and had many of the things that any child could want from life. A beautiful crib, soft blankets, regular feeds. What she didn't have was the love of a father figure, or, of course, the extra cash flow that a second parent could bring into any family.

Sure, Genevieve had managed to keep her fashion business going more than successfully, even while she'd been secretly pregnant and if anything, business was better than ever, but she couldn't help but smart every time she saw or heard or read about how well Riley Hart was doing. He was the father of her child, yet he wanted nothing to do with her and was determined that the world shouldn't know.

At first he had paid Genevieve for her silence, splashing out on rather beautiful if somewhat useless gifts like a rocking horse, a star in the night sky and a jewelled jack-in-the-box. Totally pleasant but equally pointless. Genevieve's mum called it 'fatherhood from afar'. Riley never called round to visit. At first Genevieve had been happy with the arrangement, determined to show Riley, as she could any man, that she was a survivor, a strong-minded female who was in control of everything in her life, including the unexpected and the unplanned. But rocking horses and stubborn feminism did not pay care assistant bills or buy never-ending supplies of nappies and baby food. Genevieve needed cold, hard cash.

She'd tried asking for it on many occasions, turning up where she knew Riley would be – whether it be at work or play. Monthly child support payments weren't too much to ask. Not from a man who was at the forefront of his chosen industry, even if that industry was snuffing out the lives of all those who put themselves in his way. He could afford to pay, that was for sure, but the more Genevieve asked, the more belligerent Riley appeared to become. He would not be held to ransom. That was clear. Any payments would be on his terms, as and when he chose. As the months went by his choice was swinging from once in a blue moon to not at all.

A few weeks before the shootings at the Kitty Kat Club, Genevieve decided to take matters into her own hands. She'd been drinking in her office at the back of Eruption again, alone and brooding over the fact that she was desperate for Riley's cash. His financial input would make motherhood, even her warped left-of-centre style of it, so much easier.

The answer, as it often did, seemed to be sitting so clearly at the bottom of her whisky glass. She would fight Riley in the only way he would understand – with the threat of violence. Chancing her luck that Riley would more than likely be at the club given the early evening hour, Genevieve rooted around in her drawer, pulled out her gun and hailed a cab to the Kitty Kat. She'd heard from Lily Rich that Amy was enjoying a holiday with her friend Laura, so now was the perfect time to find Riley on his own. In her mind it was a case of do or die. Either he'd pay the cash or he'd pay with his life. Any consideration of the consequences of Emily growing up fatherless should Genevieve succeed with her plan was drowned in an ocean of alcohol.

She arrived at the club to find Riley in his office. The timing was indeed perfect. He was alone, the cleaners clearing away the stains from the night before already gone and the staff for the night ahead's entertainment still hours away. Riley was never pleased to see Genevieve lately as her arrival would always signify one of two things – she was either here to discuss all things fashion with Lily, or she was here to see him. From the stagger of her drunken walk and the sneer on her face, Riley guessed she was not in the mood for discussing oversize hats and sky-high heels.

'I need to talk to you, Riley. You need to hear what I have to say,' slurred Genevieve, trying to steady herself in the office doorway. 'You and I need to talk ...'

'Come back and see me when you're sober, Genevieve,' said Riley, barely looking up at the work from his desk. 'But I've already said everything that I need to. I've made that clear.'

His nonchalance and disregard towards her incensed her inwardly. She could feel her fingers twitching towards the gun housed in her trouser pocket.

'What's clear is that you and I have a daughter and that you don't give me any money to help raise her. I want cash, Riley. You pay me regularly or I tell the world it's your baby. And I know you don't want that. So we do this my way or you get what's coming to you. The law is on my side. Legally you owe me. Plus it's the principal of you owning up to being a father.' Her voice was loud yet trembling, a lethal mixture of anger and fear. She knew what Riley was capable of. Who was to say that he wouldn't turn on her?

'Since when have I have ever done anything legally? And keep your fucking voice down,' barked Riley, his eyes looking beyond

Genevieve, fearful that someone might hear. 'If Amy or any-body finds out then you'll never get a penny. I swear, Genevieve, don't fucking push me ... you're more than capable of bringing up that child on what you earn. Plus you really wouldn't want to piss me off, would you? It would be so awful if something unforeseen happened to your home, your business, or if some accident was to tragically befall someone close to you. If your poor assistant suddenly lost an argument with a passing car, for example.'

Genevieve had guessed that Riley would resort to making threats. 'You don't scare me,' said Genevieve, her wobbling voice suggesting otherwise. 'And besides, that's not the point.' It wasn't all about cash for Genevieve. Sure, the money would make things easier, but making Riley cough up was more about gaining his respect. Making him learn that he had to take re-sponsibility for his actions, listen to her demands. And gaining some self-respect as well.

'Amy. *That* woman,' scoffed Genevieve. 'It's all right for her, she's been handed all of this thanks to you. Obedient little wife, playing with the musical toy given to her by her oh-so-rich hus-band.' She circled her hands, indicating the club around them. 'She's never had to do a day's work since meeting you. She just takes the money, organises her little dance nights and lets you fuck her when you've got time. She's not got a clue has she? About what you do? Who you are? Who you've been shagging? What made all of this? Silly little bitch.'

'You still here?' Riley's tone was deliberately dismissive. The last thing he needed was some kind of lecture about how his marriage worked. One of the main plus points about his love for Amy was the fact that she just saw him as a human being, not some monstrous gangster. The divide between his personal and his professional life was something that Riley had always strived to keep as wide as possible. Besides, he wasn't sure that Amy would have been able to handle it. She wasn't like Genevieve – his former lover was an armour-plated piece of work. Strong. At this precise moment, far too strong and gobby for her own good.

'I'm going nowhere, Riley, not until we sort this out.' Her voice began to crack, emotion rising to the surface like oil on water. 'You need to listen to me. You need to look at me. We're equals you and I, Riley. We know how life works. You don't piss me off. You can't afford to. I mean it ... you don't fuck with me.'

It wasn't until the word 'fuck' that Riley finally looked up from his desk again at the woman stood in front of him. He was a feared criminal for Christ's sake. Nobody messed with him, not even the mother of his unwanted child. She needed telling. 'Look, I've had enough of—' His voice stopped suddenly as Genevieve pulled the gun from her pocket and aimed it no more than two feet away from his head. 'What the fuck are you doing?' he asked slowly.

'You need telling, Riley. I've tried to be nice. I've asked time and time again. I want you to support Emily. Not with gifts like some sporadic drop-in dad. Not that you ever have dropped in. I want regular money. Decent pay outs. She's not going away and neither am I. She's your daughter. You need to start paying a lot more or ... or else ...' The wobbling of the gun clutched in Genevieve's sweating hand escalated as she spoke. She could feel herself spiralling out of control.

As could Riley. He'd stared down the barrel of a gun on countless occasions, but never for such a personal reason. Stubble-faced hoodlums and gap-toothed crooks he could handle but a protective mother wanting more for her baby was another matter altogether. A much looser cannon. He knew he would have to act quickly.

In Genevieve's mind, all she wanted was an end to her trauma. Either Riley was going to pay or he wasn't. She needed to show him how serious she was, one way or another.

'You don't want to do that. Honestly, Genevieve, you don't. What good would firing that at me do? Kill me for not supporting you? Oh, that'd be a difficult one to explain to our daughter in a few years' time wouldn't it? *Why don't I have a daddy, Mummy? Because Mummy murdered him, darling.* Yeah, I can't see you winning any prizes for best mother that year, can you?'

Riley's tone, albeit derisory, had the desired effect. He could sense what he'd said circling around Genevieve's brain, the potential consequences of her actions taking shape within her mind. Tears streamed down her face. For such a strong woman, Genevieve suddenly looked pitifully weak. But Riley was more than aware that it was at a rock bottom moment of fragility that a person could snap.

'I'll always be more of a mother to her than you could be a father. You don't even want to know her. It's like you're ashamed of her, of us ... of me.' Genevieve's finger quivered alongside the gun's trigger as she spoke. She was finding it hard to see it clearly through her tears. 'Do the right thing, Riley ... for her. Give the girl a father. Every girl deserves that.'

She let out a desperate sob, her mind transporting her back to her own childhood, growing up without a father. Watching as her own dad walked out on both her and her mum to live a life with another woman. She'd never forgiven him for that. She'd erased him out of her life. Maybe she'd have to do the same to Riley. If he didn't care about her and Emily then he wasn't worthy of being a father in the first place.

Her finger started to squeeze on the trigger, stroking its curve. Her ever-increasing trembling made it difficult to take a firm hold but Genevieve knew that she could do this. Riley was becoming more and more blurred, barely more than a shape through the curtain of tears coating her eyes. Emily would never need to know that her dad was a waste of time who didn't want to know her. A criminal who dispensed of people as if they were spent matches.

'This is for her, Riley ...' Genevieve squeezed the trigger.

Riley knew that this was his one moment to react. And it needed to be lightning-quick. He could see how distressed Genevieve was. Her anger and the alcohol made for a lethal concoction. He threw himself to the floor as Genevieve fired the gun. The bullet missed Riley and embedded itself in the office wall behind him. Before Genevieve even had time to consider firing a second bullet, Riley threw himself towards her, grabbing her in his arms and twisting hers in an attempt to make her drop the gun. It fell to the floor.

For a man of his size it was easy to overpower her. She crumpled under his force, her legs buckling as she too fell to the floor. She hit the side of her head on the office desk as she fell. A stab of pain, mercifully numbed by the drink, shot through Genevieve's mind. Unable to take any more and not really sure about what had happened, she lost control. Her tears, copious and flowing, raced down her cheeks.

Riley felt a need to comfort her, somewhat alien considering what she'd just tried to do to him. He put his arms around her, making sure that the gun was well out of her reach. Her sobs magnified as she let her body fold into his. Despite her situation, she knew deep down that his death would not be the right answer.

'Why am I doing this?' she said, her voice a pitiful whisper.

'Because you care about your child, as any mum would do,' answered Riley. For a moment his mind cast back to his own mother, Bianca, when she was alive. How she would have done anything to protect her child. The thought softened any feelings of anger he housed towards Genevieve.

'So why don't you? Why don't you care about our child? About Emily?'

'Because it shouldn't have happened,' said Riley. Blunt words, but said with regret and some compassion. 'I don't want to ruin what I have with Amy. I know that's not what you want to hear but it's the truth.'

It wasn't what she wanted to hear. Genevieve may have disliked Amy's existence but at that moment the person she disliked most was herself. For letting herself get into this position, for letting Riley do it to her.

'Can't we just push all of this to one side and start again?' said Riley. 'This never happened. You won't go to court about Emily. Amy will never find out. And I'll never tell anyone that you just tried to kill me. You're better than all this.'

Riley placed his hand underneath Genevieve's chin and raised it up towards his face. He could smell the whisky on her breath as he leant down to kiss her. He opened his mouth and ran his tongue against her lips. Genevieve didn't respond. Something inside her told her not to.

She pushed Riley away. 'You're right, I am better than this. I'm better than you. Kissing you and letting you make love to me again would be the easiest thing in the world, but I can't. How can I love a man I can't respect?'

Riley loosened his grip on her as she staggered to her feet. He made sure that the gun was still way beyond her reach. 'You pay me what I need, Riley Hart, or it won't just be your wife who hears about Emily. It will be the world.'

As she stumbled from the office, Genevieve could feel a strip of self-respect running back through her, despite having nearly put her own daughter in a position where her mother would be locked up for murder. She had told Riley what she wanted and shown she was serious. She wasn't sure what was to come next, but whatever it was she would make sure it was to Emily's advantage.

Riley would not get away with neglecting his child.

As Genevieve placed the keys in her pocket and stumbled to the back of the shop again, this time to try and tidy up before heading home, she placed her fingers to her face and traced along the tiny scar that still remained from where she'd hit her head on the desk. It was almost a perfect match for the one on her cheek she'd gained in the shootings at The Kitty Kat.

She'd never imagined what had happened next. Who could?

CHAPTER 43
Then, 2014

'Well, if this doesn't take away the stresses and strains of running one of the most talked about clubs in the UK then I don't know what will,' said Laura as another cool stone was applied to her body in order to rub in the most delicious flow of Manuka honey.

'And the aloe gel and aloe-based wrap comes next,' purred Amy as she lay face down alongside her best friend in one of the seventeenth century treatment rooms at the Monestero Santa Rosa spa on a clifftop in Italy's Amalfi Coast. 'This is sheer bliss. I feel like my body has just melted into one big pool of honey. I didn't realise how stressed I was about getting the club off the ground.'

'You deserve this,' sighed Laura, shutting her eyes as another viscous pouring of honey was drizzled onto her skin by one of the spa staff. 'That opening night was wild and every night you have organised since has been a huge success. And fair play to Lily because she has been fending off the Z-listers outside the club who want to come and sit their sorry little asses in our VIP areas like nobody's business. Who the hell wants some skank from a TV show about girls getting pissed, shagged and wetting themselves rubbing shoulders with a bona fide Hollywood superstar.'

'Yeah, because you've never gone out on the piss, pulled some minger and then wet yourself in the cab on the way home, have you?' deadpanned Amy.

Laura chose to ignore her. 'They shouldn't turn up unless they're on the guest list. Anyhow, why didn't Lily get invited along to this girlie weekend of ours then? She does more at that club than I do, to be honest.'

'I did suggest it to Riley, but he was adamant that it was to be just you and me. And to be honest, I agree. Lily works for me and Riley, you happen to be my best friend. And always will be. You deserve the success of The Kitty Kat just as much as I do. You've lived this dream with me, ever since we first met at Decoupage. Riley and I could not have opened The Kitty Kat without you. You've always been there for me, no matter what, and seen me through some major upsets.'

'That's what friends are for.' Laura reached out and grabbed Amy's hand, giving it a squeeze of support. 'Now, I was thinking about some more theme nights at the club seeing as the eighties and gay ones have become pretty legendary. How about a 'Single Ladies' night? Or a fetish night? You know, all Beyoncé-fied Sasha Fierceness at the first one and all Gaga extreme outfits on the second. Hashtag strong, hashtag unique!'

Amy wasn't sure that either was such a good idea and was about to say so when one of the spa staff interrupted. 'Okay, ladies, it is time for your wrap. If you would both like to turn over onto your backs we can wrap you both.' The masseur's accent was as rich as Italian chocolate.

'With an accent like that, you can turn me anyway you like,' grinned Laura. 'It's hot. You'll be making me very hot under the collar. Not that I'm wearing one of course.' Laura shifted her body, somewhat coquettishly towards the man.

The masseur smiled, but with no hint of flirtation. It was obviously something he had heard and experienced a million times before. He was a total professional. Besides, he knew that both Laura and Amy would be cooling off any overheating after the treatment by visiting the spa's famed ice fountain.

When his back was turned preparing the wrap, Laura turned to Amy and mouthed the words, 'How can he resist this? He must be gay'. She jiggled her boobs to emphasise her point. Amy was still giggling as the first layer of wrap was applied to her body.

The ice fountain had indeed cooled the girls down and had revitalised and refreshed them after the intense relaxation of the wrap. It was great to be away from Manchester and just chill for a few days. Later that evening, as they wandered around the rosemary and lemon scented tiered gardens housed within the spa's building, a former monastery, both women were in a reflective and relaxed mood.

'I'm not used to seeing you this chilled out, Laura. No bottle of Prosecco, no man chasing, no reaching for your latest Viva Glam MAC lipstick, no Twitter, no Facebook, no mobile glued to your face. It's nice to see.' Laura had always been much more a social media, tap-the-app kind of girl than Amy, but it was lovely to see her friend not Instagramming or the like.

'I know, get me! But it's this place, it's just so beautiful, isn't it? Staring out across the azure of that sea you can't help but feel that it's nice to just totally relax and forget about any stresses back in the UK. Not that I really have any to be honest, well, maybe one or two that I should deal with.' There was a definite sense of contemplation behind Laura's gaze and a softening of her voice. Amy was used to her friend hurtling through life at the speed of a car chase from *The Fast And The Furious* so the difference in her demeanour was clear to see.

'I'm so lucky to have you in my life, Laura. I've always said that. You and Riley were the only people who helped me cope when Mum and Dad died. You are my strength.'

'Well, the feeling is mutual, sister. One hundred per cent. And as for men, well they ruin everything sometimes, don't they? Why do we let them, eh?'

Amy reached out to take her friend's hand again. Something was obviously irking Laura, she never slated men. Maybe Amy would try to delve a little deeper into what was making her think that way. When the time was right. The serenity of their surrounding did not lend itself to further investigation.

'It was the sisters here who first made the concoctions for the treatments,' said Laura. 'I read that on this place's website before we came.'

'Oh I read that too,' agreed Amy. 'And the fact they used to bake delicious filled pastries too called *sfogliatelle*. Very "Patisserie Week" on *Bake Off*. They were shell-shaped and apparently quite delicious.'

'So was that masseur today,' said Laura. 'Delicious, I mean. Do you think he does private sessions?'

Amy couldn't help but raise her eyebrows and smile. So much for the calm. The moment for serious talk had just left the building.

CHAPTER 44
Now, 2015

Despite everything, Tommy Hearn loved his wife. He may have had a funny way of showing it throughout their married life together but underneath it all he loved her. Jemima was the wife he needed as she let him do exactly what he wanted.

Sure she wasn't as glamorous as Bianca Hart, Riley's mother, had been. She had had that retro sixties glamour when it was all beehive hairdos and mini-skirts, but Jemima was a pretty woman. He'd been bewitched by her when they'd first met. Her prettiness was striking, but she was meeker than any young woman he'd ever met. That was one of the things that drew him to her. Tommy was a wide boy, someone who wanted to rule the streets in the same way Cazwell Hart did and the thought of having a girlfriend who was pretty enough to be admired but quiet enough to let him puff his chest out and play hard man was just what he wanted. She didn't even have to be the sexiest of women in the bedroom department as he could obtain that wherever he liked. If Tommy had learnt one thing at an early age it was that his rugged good looks could definitely bring women to their knees. Literally. Jemima was good in the bedroom though, he'd give her that. There had been a time when their sex life was electric. But things had changed, life had moved on and the pair of them had become a sexless yet understanding couple.

How it had happened was something Tommy was ruminating on as Jemima served him a glass of whiskey in the front room of their five bedroom house in Wilmslow, Cheshire. If you had money in Manchester, it was where many of the rich and famous chose to live.

He watched her as she served him the tumbler of liquid. She barely looked him in the eyes as she did so. Her hair was grey and scraped back as per normal. Why didn't she dye it? Style it? Frame her face in a better way? Occasionally she did, normally on the insistence of Caitlyn Rich, one of the few women in their world who paid any attention to Jemima. Caitlyn was hard to say no to. Tommy wouldn't want a wife like that.

Jemima had made an effort for a while. When was it? About up until the time of the shootings at The Kitty Kat? Yes, probably about then, thought Tommy. But lately she'd made no effort at all. But there was still a prettiness there, hidden away, Tommy could see that. Just that lately it was buried deeper and deeper behind a façade of misery and harshness.

Tommy watched his wife sit down opposite him and open a book to read. It was a trashy love story no doubt, a tale of some lonely female tourist being whisked off to paradise by a dashing Sheikh or a muscle-bound prince. His wife definitely had a style when it came to her choice of escapist read and it was always the more romantic the better.

Was he to blame for her being the way she was? Had he made her the woman he saw before him? Deep down he thought that maybe he had. But he'd always been honest with her, always provided for her, always stayed by her side when yes, there were more exciting, sexual, fire cracking females out there. But that wasn't what Tommy wanted, at least not in a wife. He wanted someone he could rely on. Someone who would live his life alongside him. Someone who would see him as number one.

Yes, Tommy Hearn could see that his wife had changed over the years, he could see that he had probably created the bitter and sad woman he was staring at right now, and he could see that she had let herself go. He could also see that she was easy to love, because she let him be exactly what he wanted, a man who answered to no-one. She always had done, and that pleased him greatly. Tommy Hearn had always walked with a swagger and he was changing for nobody. He just couldn't see how arrogant that made him.

CHAPTER 45
Now, 2015

Caitlyn Rich adored New York. She always did on her numerous visits to the Big Apple – the bright, dazzling, enticing lights of Times Square, the lightly-cooked, beautifully fresh seafood at Midtown's Le Bernardin, the erotic luxury of shopping for lingerie at Kiki De Montparnasse. Every sidewalk turn and every countless corner housed a delight that only New York could offer.

But her now regular trips there with her cosmetic surgeon lover, Jona Fleet, were proving to be the best moments she had ever experienced in the city. Waking up alongside a man who truly cared for her was a joyous intimacy, especially one who could fix both her looks if need be and also fix the aching she now often experienced for a nerve stimulating bout of love-making. And Jona's nine inches never disappointed. Which was something she hadn't been able to say about her husband, Adam, for the longest time.

It was becoming apparent to Caitlyn that she was seeing less and less of her thuggish husband and that neither he nor she seemed to care about it. It was a fact that was brutally obvious as Adam walked into the entrance hall of their Manchester home to find Caitlyn directing two poor workmen in no uncertain terms where to place her newly finished mirror-mosaic swan.

'Oh, you're back then? How was your sister?' barked Adam as he elbowed his way through the front door of their home, a cloud of cigar smoke accompanying him. It was clear form his frown that he was not in the best of moods.

'Yes, darling, I'm back and she's fine,' she lied. She'd not seen her sister Lolly for six months, but she was a fabulous cover for Caitlyn's affair with Jona. 'Which is more than can be said for you. You have an expression painted across that aging face of yours that could curdle the thickest *crème fraîche*. Did you miss me, darling?' There was more than a spoonful of irony in Caitlyn's tone. She didn't actually believe Adam had missed her since the late nineties. He certainly showed no interest in where she was most of the time. If he'd looked at her passport lately he would have seen the visas proving that she and Jona had taken a bite of the Big Apple no less than four times in the last twelve months and also two trips to LA, where Jona was attending a cosmetic surgery show as an international speaker.

'Miss you?' grunted Adam. 'The only bloody thing I miss is the masses of cash you keep spunking up the wall while you're away. How much did you spend this time?' And what the fuck is that?' he said, pointing at the swan being carried by the two workmen. 'Haven't we got enough of those bloody things around here now? It's looking like some bloody Arab palace in here.'

As had become customary, Caitlyn ignored him. 'Check our credit cards, darling, I withdrew a few hundred and used it wisely.' Caitlyn had learnt long ago that Adam never really paid much attention to the money she spent. He moaned about it, that was for sure, but he had bigger fish to fry than sitting down and balancing the pounds and pennies. And Caitlyn always used the joint accounts wisely and only in the UK. For her 'lay-cations' as she liked to call them with Jona she would only ever use cash or transfer money from a joint account into her own solo one. She and Adam may have had

complete understanding that each of them had their 'own interests' when it came to their marriage but a sassy lady like
Caitlyn knew that the last thing a woman should do to a man,
especially one who waved a weapon at people as a profession,
is rub the fact she had a lover in his face. Did he know? Maybe?
Did he care? Definitely not. As long as it was out of sight, it
was out of mind, and as long as Caitlyn was still happy to play
the trophy wife when required, then Adam was content with
his marital life.

'What have you bought this sodding flamingo for?' he
snapped, pointing to the statue again. He tilted his head in an
attempt to try and see it from a different vantage point. 'It looks
deformed. Bloody rubbish.'

Caitlyn watched as Adam marched across the hall and into
his office. 'Yes, dear, I missed you too,' she said between gritted
teeth as he disappeared out of sight.

But for once, maybe Caitlyn was in agreement with Adam.
She tilted her head too to look at the statue. He was right, it did
still look like a deformed flamingo.

Turning to the workmen, Caitlyn clapped her hands twice
and placed her fingertips to her lips in consternation. 'Right,
you two, put this thing back onto your van and hotfoot it
back down to London tout de suite. I shall be phoning Jean-
Paul immediately to tell him that his swan will not be swimming its way into my luxury abode until it's had a complete
makeover.'

As the two workmen picked up the statue and shuffled their
way back to the front door, one of them turned to Caitlyn and
said. 'For what it's worth, I thought it was a flamingo as well.'

Caitlyn shooed them out and shut the door behind them.

'Dear man, your opinion is worth nothing,' she snipped, before rushing off to phone Jean-Paul. It may have been Adam

who used guns for a living but the Belgian sculptor would be getting a verbal 'Force Caitlyn' with both barrels.

'You've bought a swan for the entrance hall as well?' asked Lily. 'How many statues does that make now? We've already got David and his mirrored cock in there, Immodesty Blaize's rack in the greenhouse and enough shiny skulls, French bulldogs, doves and glitterballs to give Europe a mirror shortage. You're becoming obsessed, Mother.'

'Well, excuse me for wanting to make our home a little more glamorous,' answers Caitlyn. 'And do you have to be so coarse? The statue of David has a penis, not a cock, and the greenhouse, as you call it, is a *conservatoire*, Lily.'

'Tom-ay-to, tom-ar-to' smiled Lily. 'So I'm a little rough around the edges, it must be the way you and Dad have raised me.'

'Well, dear girl,' said Caitlyn, taking her daughter's face in her hands and staring deep into her eyes. 'You do a look a little rough, it has to be said. What have you been doing to yourself?' Lily had only just surfaced from her bed where she had spent most of the day and had come to join her mother in the Rich sitting room. 'I turn my back for two seconds ...'

'Two seconds,' scoffed Lily. 'You're hardly ever here these days. You talk about making it a home. It's hardly yours anymore. You're always down at your sister's.' Lily stuck her fingers in the air and double-quote-marked the words 'your sister's' to make her meaning clear.

Caitlyn shifted awkwardly in her seat. 'Your auntie likes company, what can I say?'

'And you must love looking after her because you always come back with a spring in your step and a smile across your face.'

'When did you get so smart?' asked Caitlyn.

'When I grew up. I've been around long enough to know exactly what goes on underneath this roof and more to the point, outside of it. You and Dad aren't the cosiest of couples at the best of times and I can understand why, especially now I know what Dad does for a job.'

Lily explained to her mother about the conversation she had had with Adam and also about her recent catch-up with Amy Hart.

'Amy Hart is back in town, is she? Well I never. I bet that pleased your father hugely.' The sarcasm was clear. As was the reason that Adam had possessed a face of thunder when he'd arrived home earlier.

'I know what Daddy does. He's a gangster, isn't he?'

Caitlyn stayed silent, unsure what to say.

'I'm fine with it. None of us are virginal pure, are we?' stated Lily.

'Your father is a good provider, Lily. That is all you need to worry about.'

'Believe you me, I know that, and I'm more than happy to lap up the maids, personal chefs, posh cars and riches of the Rich household when need be. Why do you think I still live here? I'm lazy and can't be arsed to move out. Who needs responsibility? But are you okay with what Daddy does? Have you always known?'

Caitlyn took hold of Lily's hand. 'I have known what your father does ever since we first met each other and I fell in love. I gave my heart to the man I wanted to be with, and it just so happened that he doesn't have the most honourable of jobs. Not everyone can marry a charity worker or a Nobel Prize winner, darling. But your father's job has bought this house and everything in it. It's put clothes on our back and food on our table. Given us a lifestyle that is pretty darned good. You are definitely my daughter, Lily Rich. You love the finer things as much as I do. My feelings for your father may have changed over the years and maybe we're not as *cosy* – as you put it – as we once were, but I will always be grateful for the opportunities he has put my way. If I hadn't have met him I might have ended up a secretary or a hairdresser or something, but really, darling, you know me. I don't have a perfect manicure just to go chipping it on a PC keyboard and I certainly don't want to go around smelling of bleach and perming solution. That's not very me, is it?'

'So you turn a blind eye to it all?'

'Your father and I turn a blind eye to a lot of things. But the one thing that we both truly care about is you. So tell me, what's been going on in your life to make you look like you should still be celebrating Halloween, when in reality we're skidding towards Christmas? Those dark circles under your eyes are not an attractive look for one so young.'

Lily knew she looked rough. Her drug taking had been getting a little too out of hand and she had begun to question everything in her life. When she worked at The Kitty Kat Club she possessed a *raison d'être* but now she was without purpose. She sold the drugs to make some money, but that wasn't why she did it. She could have blagged money from her parents, but after the independence of working the club so well she did not want to revert to handouts. The drug-dealing gave her something that was hers, but what it also gave her was the opportunity to take more herself, and that was spiralling out of control, especially now that it was Riley Hart who was filling her thoughts.

'I'm just tired,' lied Lily. The last thing she wanted to confess to her mother was her increasing reliance on narcotics. 'It's just that Amy Hart coming back has given me a lot to think about. She thinks Riley might still be alive and that it wasn't him who was killed at the club.'

'Now there's a stupid bombshell if ever I heard one. Don't the police do all sorts of records and checks, dentistry and things like that, to make sure a corpse is who they say it is? Who the hell did she bury or cremate or whatever she did, for God's sake?' A streak of major panic flashed across Caitlyn's face. If Riley was alive, not that she could see how he could be, then Adam could be in serious danger. She was fully aware of the Weston Smith business. Blind eye and all that.

'I thought the same, but apparently the police have washed their hands of the whole thing. But Amy thinks Riley still might be hiding somewhere.'

'Has she tried his mobile?'

'Er, yeah … I think she's tried most things, Mother. He seems to be incommunicado.'

'So why is all this giving you something to think about and turning your beautiful face into something from a zombie comic? I need to get you some pampering, dear girl. Freshen up that skin a little.'

'It's the talk of Riley being alive. I'm hoping it's true. When he was alive …' She hesitated, wondering if she should carry on, but doubtless Adam would tell her mother if she didn't. 'We were having an affair. It ended because he dumped me, but I loved him, Mum. I think I still do.'

Caitlyn's mouth dropped open. 'You were having an affair with Riley Hart? You stupid girl, how could you?'

'Er, hello? Kettle, pot, black. You just said you can't choose the profession of the man you fall in love with. And as for affairs, isn't your hypocrisy a bit rich coming from someone who spends half their time at their *sister's*?' Again Lily double-quote-marked the air as she said the word.

Caitlyn knew she was right. Lily was a smart cookie. She pulled her close and hugged her. 'Oh you poor girl, you really are your mother's daughter, aren't you?'

CHAPTER 46
Now, 2015

The first ever photograph of people was Boulevard Du Temple, taken by Louis Daguerre back in the 1830s. It was an image of a busy street but because the exposure time was over ten minutes, the city traffic was moving too much to appear.

It was one of the strange facts that Jemima Hearn could remember from her school days. Along with the largest volcano in space being on the surface of Mars and US President George Washington not possessing a middle name. She found it odd the things you remembered in life. But at least these were things that would always be documented in history. They would eternally be talked about. Not like her love for Winston Curtis. That was something that had died the moment his life was extinguished that night at The Kitty Kat.

Jemima was sitting in the driving seat of one of the Hearns' collection of motors, a beautiful Aston Martin V8 Vantage. It was her favourite to take out on the road and she had spent the last two hours driving herself to a peaceful lakeside spot in the Peak District, south of Manchester from their home in Wilmslow. It was a place she often came when she needed to clear her head and escape the tedium her life had become.

The reason Jemima had been thinking about the first ever photograph was that she was staring down at the one photo she had of her and Winston together. Lily Rich had been taking Polaroids at the club one night, as part of some kind of retro promotion to drum up publicity for the Kitty Kat, taking pictures of the various models and actresses and dreadful people off the TV who seemed to migrate there and giving them out. As ever, Jemima had been there to play loyal 'plus one' to Tommy, who was there to keep his eye on Riley, who was keeping his eye on everyone. The same old monotonous story. The only ray of light had come from Winston being there supporting his employer and unbeknown to anyone else, supporting Jemima. Allowing some love to finally shine brightly in her heart.

Lily had been running around with her camera, aiming it at everyone. Every time she even so much as pointed it in Jemima's direction, the sneer of disdain Jemima had given had been enough to send Lily scurrying off in search of some insipid glamour girl with a vacuous grin wider than her breasts. Jemima hated having her photo taken, she always had. It was a confidence thing. Even if she was looking pretty good after a makeover at the hands of Caitlyn Rich. But there was one moment when she'd been talking to Winston. He'd made time to find her, to melt her heart with that exquisitely cheeky, full-lipped smile of his, as he always did, and plan for their next rendezvous. Planning moments when she could get away from Tommy, from his constant absorption of the world he lived in. His world alongside Riley. His one before that, alongside Cazwell. Neither of them seemed to feature Jemima anymore. She was more like his employee than his wife.

There had been that moment when the madcap Lily had shoved the camera in her face yet again and she had been talking to Winston. Happy to seize the opportunity, Winston had wrapped his arm around her and pulled her towards him, his bear grip making it impossible for her to resist, not that she'd wanted to. Unable to stop herself, she smiled, a smile that lit up her entire face. Jemima had what people called 'one of those faces that never looked happy', but the beam on both her and the face of her delicious ebony lover as they stared out of the photo was immeasurable.

It was one of the last times she remembered being truly joyous. She couldn't even begin to think of the last time Tommy had made her feel like that.

No, staring at the picture of Winston, the man who could no longer light up her world, she knew that her one chance of true happiness had passed her by and that she desperately needed to do something about it.

Jarrett Smith had carried a photo of Weston in his wallet ever since his only son had first gone missing. Okay, so the lad could be a waste of space but he was still his lad, part of the Smith dynasty who had been ruling the grimy streets of London for the best part of forty years. His name, and his father's before him, had become one of the most feared within the confines of a London postcode. If you messed with Jarrett Smith, then there was only one possible outcome and that was game over. The three strike rule never applied. You fucked Jarrett over once, then it was always a case of taking the fast route to six feet under.

But Jarrett's notoriety was spreading. He'd been aware of that ever since he'd made his first 'business trip' to Manchester following Weston's disappearance a few years earlier. The entire city had clammed up, people were afraid to talk to him, word reached him that even the so-called big players in Manchester were running scared. Every avenue of exploration had become a dead end, a cul-de-sac of nothingness. Nobody knew what had happened to his son, Weston. He'd been seen, he'd been doing his usual ducking and diving, trying to avoid the law, but nobody seemed to know who with and why. Lips had been sealed as if by superglue. Mouths tighter than oysters, petrified of spilling a pearl of knowledge that could land somebody in Jarrett's blood-splattered bad books.

But as the months and years went by, people would become careless. Jarrett knew that. This was a marathon, not a sprint. The truth about Weston's disappearance would come to light sooner or later and Jarrett would be there to deal with those to blame.

His first suspect had been Riley Hart, the newest upstart on the northern block, pussy-assed son of Cazwell. Manchester's number one? Tell that to his widow. He'd obviously been slack. Barrel-load of bullets straight into his skull. No, if he was to blame, then he'd already paid the price.

But what if it wasn't him? Jarrett still needed revenge. If his son was as dead as Jarrett reckoned he was deep inside – he'd have been back sponging for money if he still had breath in his body no doubt – then someone would have to pay. And it was an eye for an eye, a death for a death. Revenge would come, it always did in the end.

It was being served right now for someone else. Another person who had dared to cross Jarrett. Three months after being swindled out of £300K by his apparent friend and co-owner of his prize racehorse, Jarrett was finally getting payback. With a gun lodged tightly against his back, Jarrett roughly pushed the son of his former mate out of the back of his own Mercedes. The car smelt of piss where the terrified teenager had wet himself with fear as one of Jarrett's men had driven the Mercedes to their current destination, a construction site in south east London.

It was just before midnight and the place was clear of workmen. He'd have to get the car valeted tomorrow now. Fucking little prick. Still, what was a bit of piss on your leather uphol-stery when revenge was about to be dished up?

The construction site was being used during the day to build an extension onto one of London's exit roads. The site was a mass of cranes, machinery and deep, half-dug holes ready for the insertion of huge concrete pillars to act as foundations for the new road. Well, Jarrett was about to add a unique insertion of his own.

'So, where's your fucking dad gone with my money, then? Why would he fuck off with Jarrett Smith's hard earned dosh, sunshine?' He rammed the weapon into the lad's spine, forcing him to let out a pathetic whimper between pitiful sobs.

'I've told you, I don't know. Please Mr Smith. I've not seen him since he ran off. Please just let me go … please …'

Mr Smith … a nice touch, Jarrett liked that. A bit of respect. He had an idea his former mate had fled to the other side of the world. Australia or New Zealand. No matter. Wherever he was word would reach him. Word that you don't fuck with Jarrett Smith. Not even friendship bought you that liberty. No-one was worthy of absolution. No-one.

'I think Daddy's down under. Headed south. You can fuck-ing join him,' snarled Jarrett.

'Please … I swear I don't know where …'

The young man could say no more. With one swift push, Jar-rett forced him brutally over the edge of one of the deeply dug shaft holes. It was deep – deep enough for what a demonically smiling Jarrett wanted. He knew that from having one of his men stake the site out during daylight.

The lad's screams filled the air for a split second as he plum-meted downwards before coming to a final, dramatic silent crunch as his body hit the bottom. Jarrett's work was done. The arousal of revenge ran through his veins.

As Jarrett sat back in the car, this time up front to try and avoid the young man's piss, he reached into his wallet and pulled out the photo of Weston. 'I'll find the culprit, son. I'll unearth the truth, don't you worry. Revenge will come, sooner or later ...'

As Jarrett was driven back to London, he knew that his next move might have to be a return trip to Manchester.

Jemima wound down the windows of the Aston Martin, the cold winter air hitting her as she did so, and stared out at the scenery around her. The trees, devoid of leaves at this time of year, seemed to have a sinister life all of their own, each branch and twig twisting and turning its way like the gnarled fingers of a storybook witch. The surface of the lake in front of her appeared dark and brooding, almost ashen in its stillness. She looked around. There was no-one else to be seen. It was pure serenity.

Winston would have liked it here. He liked the open air. They could have come here for picnics, for endless bottles of champagne, laughing together and talking about how life could have been had they met at a different time. They could have stayed, staring out onto the lake on a balmy summer's night, waiting for the sun to fade to a dusky light before making love in one of the many hidden lanes not far from the water's edge. Winston would have adored that too. He could have told her that he loved her, protectively placed his arms around her and told her that the world could be a perfect place. Winston might not have been perfect, but he could have been perfect for her.

Jemima smiled to herself. It wasn't too late. They could still be together. Winston was waiting for her. She'd be better off with him. She knew that now. What had Tommy called him?

'That useless sidekick'? How fucking dare he? She'd show him exactly who 'that useless sidekick' was. Taking a pen from the glove compartment she turned over the photo of her and Winston and wrote on the back. 'To Winston, the only man who truly made me happy. Forever yours, Jemima x.' Her body shivered in the cold air as she wrote. She underlined the word 'only' and placed the photo in her winter coat pocket, zipping it in so that it would rest in place. She smiled, a feeling of total readiness passing through her. Her work was done.

Memories of her last weekend with Winston flooded through her mind. Visions of him turning to her as they picnicked, wiping a smudge of cream from her lips where they had been eating strawberries, the taste of champagne on his lips as he kissed her and held her in his arms. The sound of his voice as he told her 'I love you, Jemima Hearn, both inside and out'. When had Tommy last said he loved her? Thoughts of Winston brought a smile to her face again. A smile of happiness, of knowing what was right, of knowing what she wanted.

Her next action was to unlock the hand brake of the Aston and let the car roll down the slight incline that ran into the lake. She was still smiling as the freezing cold water poured into the car through the open windows. A huge shock to her system. But this was what she wanted. To be with Winston again. Jemima was already dead by the time the car disappeared below the surface of the water.

CHAPTER 47
Now, 2015

Amy decided not to tell anyone about the shooting incident at the church. Not even Grant. Somebody was trying to warn her off, she was convinced of it. If they had wanted to kill her, then surely one of the three bullets would have done so. To miss once was unlucky, but to miss three times was almost definitely deliberate.

Amy had made another decision when she was on the way back in the taxi. She needed to start fighting fire with fire. So far she had constantly felt back footed, always playing catch-up in a rather sinister voyage of discovery. If she was to find Riley then she needed to try and take what little control she could, and that meant doing whatever it required to try and garner the right information to lead her to her husband.

Telling the taxi driver that she'd had a change of plan, she asked him to drop her at Dirty Cash. Once there she ventured cautiously back inside – the last thing she wanted was another run-in with Tommy and/or Jemima – she only had one cheek left unbruised. No, she wasn't there to see them, she wanted to speak to Jimmy, the handsome and eager-to-please employee who had last seen her being marched off the premises the day before. Luckily for Amy he was working.

'Back for a second interview? I wasn't sure the first one had gone particularly well given the rate of knots at which you left here yesterday,' he winked, more than a hint of suggestion in his eyes.

He was flirting. Perfect. Amy wouldn't need to work this too hard. 'Hi Jimmy, yeah it didn't go too well, and I didn't get a chance to see you afterwards either which was another downer.' His face lit up. 'Look I can't really talk here. I think the bosses didn't take to me. Can you take a lunch break? I'd love to speak to you about something. There are a few things that you could help me with.' Amy angled her head coquettishly to one side and chewed slightly at her bottom lip. It was a pure prick-tease manoeuvre.

There was no way Jimmy was going to say no. 'Er ... sure. I'm off for an hour in about twenty minutes. There's a great sandwich place on the corner of the next street. We could meet there. My treat.'

Amy could feel herself blushing slightly. The poor boy was definitely thinking he was onto a winner. 'No, I need to ask a favour so lunch is on me. Just don't have anything too exotic and expensive in your sandwich, okay?'

'Cheese and pickle it is! Can I ask you one thing though? The bruise on your cheek. You didn't have it yesterday. What happened? Were you hit?'

Amy had to think quickly. 'Oh that ... no, I whacked it on a taxi door. I wasn't looking what I was doing,' she fibbed. What was another lie to add to the mix? It wasn't like she'd been honest with him about anything so far.

Amy breathed a sigh of relief as she walked back into the cold afternoon air outside Dirty Cash. She'd been dreading bumping into Jemima or Tommy again. Luckily neither had been there.

Amy stared across the road searching for the sandwich shop. A warm drink would do her good. If they'd been meeting in a bar she would have definitely ordered something a little stronger. After the episode at the church her nerves were in tatters.

Amy located the shop and started to walk across the road. Some inner sense of paranoia made her feel like she was being watched. *Was it Riley again?* She scanned around, letting her eyes dart in all directions. She was right. A lone figure, deep in thought, his gaze penetrative, stood on the other side of the road from her. She could feel his eyes burning into her. *She didn't know him, did she?* She stared directly back at him, searching for recognition. Suddenly aware that he was being watched too, the man ducked his head and walked off down the street. Maybe she was paranoid? Manchester was full of all sorts of weirdoes and loonies. Or maybe he was staring at her bruise. Or maybe he fancied her? Or recognised her from the club? There could be a hundred different reasons. He was gone now, but even his absence made her feel a tad uneasy.

A shiver seared through her veins. Deciding she was just being paranoid, Amy hurried to the sandwich shop to wait for Jimmy.

Amy and Jimmy were finishing off the food they had ordered. Jimmy seemed fidgety and awkward as he pushed the last few crumbs of bread around his plate. They had volleyed flirtatious pleasantries back and forth between them whilst eating but he knew that he'd been asked there for a reason. Jimmy may have been a fairly naive young man from Llandudno but he knew that he'd been treated to lunch for more than just his company. He guessed he would have to take the bull by the horns.

'You're a nice woman. I'm not normally chatted up by ladies like you, and certainly not treated to the dizzy heights of cappuccino and wholemeal butties by them, either.' He laughed, a mixture of nerves and irony as he spoke. 'I'm more of a bag of chips down by the pier kind of guy. Why did you ask me here?'

'You're a really nice guy, Jimmy ...' Amy could hear how lame she sounded already.

'But ...?' he asked.

Amy opened the floodgates and told Jimmy as much as she needed him to hear. About Riley's letter and Laura's death, her hatred of Tommy Hearn and Adam Rich, about the Kitty Kat and how it was now Dirty Cash, Riley's lies to her, moving away from Manchester and her current visit there with Grant. Although it felt somewhat cathartic to share her story, Amy felt exhausted by the time she had finished, as well as more than a little wary. She didn't know Jimmy at all and nice though he seemed, she had no idea where his loyalties lay, especially now that she'd more or less confessed that he wasn't going to achieve anything romantically should he decide to help her.

Jimmy sat agog listening to her story, his mouth open, his eyebrows raised.

'So, asking you out on a date right now would be completely the wrong thing to do?' asked Jimmy when she'd finished.

'I come with more baggage than Manchester Airport, so yeah. But I need your help, Jimmy ...'

'I guessed you were telling me all of this for a reason. What can I do?' Jimmy chewed lightly on his fingernail as he wondered what was coming next.

'I need somebody on the inside of Dirty Cash. To be my eyes and ears. You can guess from yesterday's performance that I'm not exactly greeted at the door like a returning Olympic gold medal winner. But I'm sure that Tommy knows something about Riley and Laura's deaths. Or Adam does, or Jemima. There has to be some little nugget that they may let slip when I'm not there which could help me. I need to sort this once and for all. To lay my husband's memory to rest or track him down. You may hear all sorts about him in there but I need you to listen in and let me know what's being said. My husband spent a lot of our life together lying to me, I know that now, but I need to find out the truth.'

A moment's pause. 'Losing your husband and your best friend … that sucks, man. Do you really think he's dead? That's pretty freaky to think he might have been able to fake his own death.'

'So much chaos went on in the club that night, I'm not sure of anything anymore. Is Riley alive? That's the million dollar question, Jimmy.' The mention of money jogged Amy's mind.

'Of course I'll pay you for your trouble, Jimmy. I'll make it worth your while.' Amy wasn't really sure how. Her funds were dwindling, but if need be she still had possessions like her wedding ring back at her house in London. She hadn't worn it for months, the sight of it too much of a gigantic, agonizing reminder of what she once had. She wasn't sure if she'd ever want to wear it again. She'd sell something to pay Jimmy if she had to.

'I'll listen out for you, of course I will. If anyone says anything about that night I'll contact you straight away. Shit, you've been to hell and back …' Jimmy reached across the table to take Amy's hand in his and gave it a gentle squeeze of understanding. 'You don't have to pay me, but there is one condition …'

Amy could feel her heart sinking. There was no such thing as a free lunch. *What did he want?* She needn't have worried.

'When this is all over,' he smiled, 'can you introduce me to Grant Wilson? My mother loves him in that doctor show of his and if anyone can get me connected to some seriously fit women then he can. Although for the record, they'd have to go some to be as beautiful as you.'

Amy caught herself laughing at his cheek. 'It's a promise, you'll have your introduction.'

Jimmy stood from the table and wrapped his coat back around his body. 'Listen I had better go, my break is nearly over and if I'm to start acting like a cop from *Broadchurch* for you then I need to make sure I stay on the right side of the bosses. I can't afford to be late. How do I contact you?'

Amy scribbled her hotel details down on a piece of paper and her telephone number. 'I'll be staying here in Manchester for a while. There's so much I don't know. This is one screwed-up jigsaw and there are still a lot of pieces missing.'

'Well, you can count on me to do what I can.' He took the paper and pushed it into his coat pocket. He was almost at the door when he turned round to face her. 'And for what it's worth, I think Riley Hart was a fool to ever cheat on you. If I was your fella then you'd be treated like a princess.'

Amy admired his charm. 'If you were my fella, then I'm sure I wouldn't be in this bloody mess in the first place. Now go spy …' She waved her hands towards the door.

As Jimmy left the sandwich bar, Amy headed to the counter to pay. She wasn't sure if having Jimmy on her side would prove beneficial, but it certainly couldn't do her any harm. At least it felt like she was doing something, talking control again. Even just sharing her story with him seemed to take a pressure off her shoulders.

What Amy didn't realise as she walked back out into the fresh, wintery Manchester air, was that she'd also been sharing the story with the man sitting on the far side of the sandwich bar. Just far enough away to be able to hide himself behind carefully placed menus and lose himself in a dimly lit corner, he was still close enough to be able to hear the young woman talking about Riley Hart, to hear the words Dirty Cash, Tommy Hearn and Adam Rich form on her lips and to know that maybe one of them, or both, might know something about the disappearance of his only son.

Yes, Jarrett Smith was highly pleased that he'd headed back to Manchester, that he'd gone to Dirty Cash, recognised the woman he'd seen coming out of the casino as the ex-wife of Riley Hart and secretly followed her with the stealth of a lion hunting a gazelle into the sandwich shop. Any potential leads that could help him find out what had happened to Weston definitely had to be investigated.

And they would be.

CHAPTER 48
Now, 2015

Dolly Townsend had already spent the money in her head a million times over. There would be a new house, somewhere posh like Prestbury or Alderley Edge. Somewhere where her sisters could visit, with their stuck-up rods planted firmly up their backsides, and finally realise that Dolly was the one in the family with taste, class and wealth.

She'd see them once every so often, just enough to make them green with envy and always just before jetting off to some sun-drenched holiday hot-spot frequented by film stars and top models. She'd take photos of herself lying on some white sandy beach with a cocktail in one hand and a millionaire tycoon in the other. After flying home on a private jet she'd have an eager to please chauffeur pick her up at the airport, ready to ferry her wherever she required and service her every need. Her life would be like a continual episode of *Keeping Up with the Kardashians*.

Oh, life would be one long diamond-encrusted experience for Dolly ... but only once she had the money. And to gain that she needed to work wisely with the information she'd heard from Adam and Tommy. The news that Weston Smith was buried in the foundations of Dirty Cash was the golden egg she'd been waiting for all of her life. The story had been on constant rotation in her mind ever since she'd overheard it.

She'd written things down at the first opportunity, making sure that all of the details were correct. She couldn't afford to let anything be wrong. Adam had shot Weston. Riley had blackmailed him into buying the building for The Kitty Kat. Weston's body was buried underneath the dance floor, which was now Dirty Cash. Weston was the son of a London mobster called Jarrett Smith. It was like some kind of fucked up Jason Statham movie. And Dolly was sure that she could end up playing the heroine.

Her first instinct had been to try and blackmail Adam. The man was beyond wealthy and he would be the one with most to lose should the information land in the wrong person's lap. But what was there to just stop Adam pumping a bullet into her brain and disposing of her in just the same way as Weston Smith? *How many people would actually miss a middle-aged prostitute?* The same with Tommy, he had obviously been part of the gangland world for decades and would probably think nothing of having Dolly's sorry white ass bumped off. No, Dolly had to play it shrewd and that meant going to Amy.

From what she'd heard, Dolly knew that Amy was the fly in Adam and Tommy's ointment right now. Her reappearance in Manchester had set all of them seriously on edge. She had them flipping like a pair of jumping beans. The ex-Mrs Hart was loaded, surely. You didn't spend years married to Manchester's number one psycho without stashing away a pound or two. Yes, Amy would be a much safer bet and that was why Dolly needed to speak to her. Her money was as good as anybody's and if Dolly had her way then a good chunk of Amy's dosh would soon be hers.

Dolly had heard the men mention where Amy was staying. A fancy hotel ... she knew it well. Dolly had stared at many of the bedroom ceilings there on countless occasions. It had been a favoured haunt of some of her clients over the years. She'd made good money between the crisp cotton sheets there.

But as Dolly closed the door on her own apartment behind her and headed off to the hotel, she was hoping that today's jaunt to try and track down Amy would be her most lucrative visit to date.

Dolly was not the only woman who wanted a one-to-one with Amy. Lily was determined to track down her former employer too.

She needed Amy. She was her passport to Riley, even if she was probably the last person Amy ever wanted to see again. If he was still shuffling his rather impressive body around Planet Earth then Lily needed to find him. If he was alive he'd never get back with Amy. Not now, she knew too much. His secret criminal career, the fact that he'd been shagging Lily ... It was all too much for a poor, foolish naïve woman like Amy Hart.

No, Riley would want somebody strong and independent, a real ball-breaker of a female – somebody just like Lily. What was it he'd once said to her when they'd been shagging in his office? That she fucked like she lived her life – hard and fast and loud. Just how he liked it. Yeah, Lily would always remember that. She was hard. Called a spade a spade. She lived life in the fast lane, and she was as vocal in life as she was in the bedroom, not afraid of confrontation. That's why Riley liked her, that's why he furnished her with gifts. Like the time he'd bought her the most incredible Irregular Choice shoes. What was it he'd said?

'Amy would never wear a pair like these. They're real fuck-me shoes. Such a turn on.'

'And you know you can fuck me in them any time you like, boss,' said Lily, slipping off her own shoes to try them on. They were exquisite. Vintage style with a designer modern edge. The kind of shoes that could only be worn by a true individual. The cream floral textured fabric looked like it had been dipped in glitter and glazed to perfection. Lily loved them. They were unique, stylish, kooky and a total talking point. The one thing they weren't was boring. To Lily, they were the perfect gift. They symbolised her. And to Riley, seeing Lily wearing them with nothing else but her nipple ring as he drove his cock into her as they shagged on his office desk was sheer perfection too.

'Fuck me harder, Riley. Show me who's boss,' she suggested as he withdrew his cock to its very tip before thrusting it back into her on the edge of the desk.

'Fuck, Lily, I love it when you talk dirty,' he cried, holding her shoe-clad feet in his hands as he cannoned into her. Three strokes later he could hold his orgasm no more and they climaxed together.

Yes, what Lily Rich had to say, both in the sack and out of it was always worth saying, and what she needed to say to Amy was that Riley, if he was alive, was hers. And nobody else's. She may have had her heart broken once, but Lily was not going to have it happen again.

As Lily left the Rich family home to head to Amy's hotel, fuelled by another fat line of cocaine she'd just chopped out on her bedroom dressing table, she was feeling good about herself. Feeling one step closer to Riley, wherever he was.

CHAPTER 49
Now, 2015

Grant was worried about Amy's disappearance. After the note she'd left him that morning at the hotel, he'd expected her to be back by now. She'd been gone hours. *Where was she?* He'd tried ringing her but her mobile had headed straight to voicemail.

Not knowing was driving him insane. With the people she was dealing with anything could have happened. There was so much violence. He needed to do something. But what ...? All he could think of was to go after her.

He could try Dirty Cash, or head back to Eruption. Maybe she'd gone there to question a pissed-up Genevieve, who was doubtless still wallowing in her own misery. No, any kind of action was better than nothing when his mind was working overtime. Sitting at the hotel trying to learn lines for his next season of *Ward 44* was not working. His brain was elsewhere, frazzled, his concentration as frenzied as the wings of a hummingbird in flight.

Looking from his hotel window down at the street below, the remnants of snow still visible on the pavements, Grant scanned around and knew that he had to act. Pulling on his coat and a woollen hat to cover his face – he'd been recognised by lots of the hotel staff and customers and now was not the time he wanted to stop for autograph hunters – an apprehensive Grant headed out of his room, down to the lobby and out into the frost-bound air.

Grant kept his head down and walked along the street. He had reached no further than fifty yards from the hotel when he slammed, full pelt, into Amy. The force of their collision knocked her backwards, almost causing her to tumble.

'Oh my God, where have you been? I've been going out of my mind with worry.' His words, apparently a mixture of relief and annoyance, shot from his lips.

'Ease it, mister!' said Amy, steadying herself from where their bodies had clashed. Grant put his arms around her to help her regain her balance. 'I told you I needed to clear my head. I went to see my parents' graves and then, well, I went for a walk around. I needed to try and formulate some kind of perspective on all this. About trying to find Riley.'

'I'm just glad you're all right. I just thought that something might have happened to you, what with the circles you're mixing in.' He pulled her close and hugged her. Amy let herself rest against him for a moment longer than maybe she should have.

'I'm okay ... honest. If there's anything positive that's actually coming out of all of this shit then it's the fact that I'm toughening up more than I ever felt possible.' Her voice seemed weaker than the actual words. Grant wasn't convinced she meant it. 'I'll be challenging the toughest crims in Manchester by the time Christmas arrives,' she said, attempting a feeble joke.

Amy attempted to move away from Grant's embrace, but the force of his arms wouldn't let her. Any kind of intimacy with another man after Riley still felt alien to Amy, but the warmth of Grant's body against hers was a welcome one.

'Don't you two look cosy? Researching a romantic role are you, Grant?' The voice belonged to Lily. The sound of her voice made the actor unleash his grip. Amy could feel her face colour with embarrassment as if she'd been caught out and an ocean of anger at seeing the woman who had been getting her end away with her husband rose to the surface.

'Hello, Lily ... what the hell do you want?' said Amy. It was all she could think of to say. Just looking at Lily still flashed brain-branding, painful images of her and Riley together.

'I need to see you, Amy. Alone, if possible.' She stared at Grant, hoping that he would understand her request for a little privacy. He didn't reply.

'Cat got your tongue, Grant?' said Lily. 'I need some privacy with Amy.'

Amy looked up at Grant too, wondering why he hadn't replied. The look on his face portrayed that something was wrong. Very wrong. It unnerved her. 'What is it, Grant?' His gaze focused straight behind both her and Lily.

'I don't believe it,' he stammered. 'Look ...' He pointed across to the other side of the street. Lily and Amy both followed the direction of his gesture. Both of their faces fell as they realised that standing there across the road was Riley. He was wrapped up against the weather, his body covered in a heavy overcoat and, like Grant, a hat pulled down over his forehead, but all three of them were as sure as they could be about his identity. It was Riley.

'It's Riley,' exhaled Grant, confirming their thoughts.

Amy could feel her legs buckle underneath her. She felt as if she had been punched in the stomach but she was determined to seize the moment. After everything Riley had put her through over the last six months and now given what she knew about his sordid little affairs with Lily and Genevieve, she was certainly going to have her say. A maelstrom of hurt, fear, bitterness and confusion exploded within her. Riley wasn't dead. Finally it had been proven. He was there, no more than a road's width away from her. She tried to focus on his face, to see if a trace of a smile was visible, a symbol of elation at seeing her again. It was hard to keep him in sight, the traffic on the busy road between them consistently blocking her view.

'Fucking hell, he is alive,' said Lily, her mind racing at the vision before her. 'It is him, isn't it ...?

'I'd know that face anywhere,' stated Grant. 'It's him ... What the hell does he think he's doing? He owes you an explanation.'

Grant had no sooner finished his sentence than he started to run in Riley's direction. It wasn't easy, the road between Riley and the trio was busy. Cars screeched a halt as Grant ran out into the street, narrowly avoiding running him down. He turned to shout at Amy and Lily. 'Stay here, I'm going to get him ...'

As he did so, the figure on the far side of the street started to run, away from the group. From the pace he sprinted off at, it was obvious he didn't want to be caught.

Grant weaved his way across the road. Watching him go, Amy began to scream. It was uncontrollable, a feeling of hopelessness gripping her. Why would Riley venture so close and then turn tail and run away from her? Why would he do that to her, to the woman he said he still loved? It was time for Amy to seize the moment. She began to shout. 'Riley Hart, you fucking come back here, you lowlife. You are not leaving me again. You've put me through enough shit once, you are not doing it for a second time. Come and give me some answers you bastard, tell me why you've made me suffer. Come back ...' Her voice trailed away as she watched Riley run off. He wasn't even man enough to answer her screams. She saw red, but her anger turned to misery in a heartbeat.

Amy began to cry, unable to contain her tears, as she watched Grant chase after Riley. A clash of emotions clamoured through her head. Was she pleased to finally see him, to know that he was alive? The thought that he hadn't been blown away so hor-rifically in The Kitty Kat was a welcome one, but immediately questions about who had died, who she had cremated, how she had been deceived and why Riley was running away from her now that he was so close, detonated in her thoughts. Was it see-ing Lily there too? Or Grant? The three of them together?

The figure disappeared into a small side street, turning as he did so to see Grant advancing towards him. Within a couple of seconds both men were out of vision.

'Sod this, he can't get away,' said a determined Lily. 'Not again. You stay here, I'll help catch him.' Lily ran out into the road. A couple of seconds later, she too had disappeared from sight, leaving Amy feeling useless and alone. She could feel a tightening in her chest, her heart beating wildly within her frame. It was as if somebody was squeezing their hands around her heart, draining life from it. More fear gripped her. Finally she had her answer but somehow she felt hollow. She attempted to breathe deeply and rhythmically, to stem the frantic beating inside her.

It must have been five minutes or so before she seemed able to regain any normality in her breathing. The choking on her heart seemed to ease. She was wiping away her tears as a frantic and hysterical Lily came back into view from the small street on the other side of the road. She signalled to Amy and shouted across the traffic.

It sounded like 'Jesus, come quick ... I think he's dying.' Amy had a job to hear exactly what Lily was saying above the noise of the cars rushing by. Finally forcing herself into action, as both Grant and Lily had done before her, she dashed out into the road to join Lily on the other side.

Lily grabbed her hand and pulled her into the side street. 'Come quick ... before it's too late.' The street was almost deserted, just a few people milling around. They watched, confused, as the two women ran past them. Turning to the right, Lily guided Amy into an even smaller avenue, really no more than an alleyway, off the side street. There were thousands of tiny streets just like this dotted all across inner Manchester, all of them virtually identical, with plastic rubbish skips and metal fire escapes lining both sides. But this one housed a horrific addition. Lying at the far end of it was a body, face down, crumpled against the ground.

As they approached, Amy could see a slim trickle of blood running out from underneath it, trickling across the road's surface. A bloodied knife lay alongside the figure. They recognised the body. It was Grant, and he'd been stabbed. Amy turned to Lily. She could feel her lip tremble as she asked the question. 'Is he dead?'

CHAPTER 50
Then, 2004

Death was never easy to deal with. The finality of it never became any easier. Riley Hart had already had to watch his poor mother, Bianca, die in a hospital bed, a victim of a dreaded cancer, and now he was sitting by his father's bedside watching the life slowly ebb from his hero.

Cazwell Hart – a man who had challenged the meanest of men and won, delivered the cruellest of blows and survived and administered the harshest of punishments and always come out on top. But now here he was, in front of his only son and his faithful colleague, Tommy Hearn, being delivered the cruellest blow of all. His own body, once a mass of muscle and male strength, was failing him. A series of strokes had gripped Cazwell over the past twelve months, taking away his force and, in his final days, his dignity too. No longer could he rule those he wished to with an iron fist. His brain, his brawn and his bravado had all fallen by the wayside.

The shell before him was not the man that Riley Hart had always looked up to. That man had died weeks ago. But on the family doctor's instructions, he and Tommy had gathered at Cazwell's bedside to witness his final moments. The light in Cazwell's eyes, one that had once shone so bright, was fading fast.

Cazwell raised his head to look at his son. A line of drool hung from his mouth. For the past week or so, Cazwell's head had hung permanently down, as if his neck could no longer hold it in place. A nurse was there round the clock to feed Cazwell, to clean him and attend to his needs. Tommy himself had taken turns to help the man who, as far as he was concerned, had given him his life, his dreams, his ambitions. There had been talk of placing Cazwell in a home. Tommy and a young Riley wouldn't allow it. The once proud and mighty lion would never be caged anywhere other than his own jungle.

As Riley looked at his father, for a millisecond there was a spark of recognition behind his eyes. Was Cazwell trying to tell him something? Where had the strength come from to look directly at his son for the final time? Cazwell moved his head to look at Tommy. Again, an understanding. Confirmation of what Cazwell had instructed Tommy when he had first been confined to what was to be his death bed. Tommy nodded as he stared into the soul of his boss. Everything would be okay, business as usual, he would make sure of that. Cazwell could die with that knowledge.

Cazwell swung his head round to face his son again. The line of drool that hung from his mouth broke off and fell onto the silk pyjamas he was wearing. There would be nothing less than the best for a man of his greatness. Tommy had made sure of that.

Riley could feel the corners of his eyes pricking with tears as he watched his father take his final breath. As Cazwell Hart, king of the streets, shut his eyes one last time and drifted into eternal slumber, Riley smiled. Not because he was happy, but because he wanted to let his dad know that, just as Tommy had promised, everything was going to be all right.

It wasn't until Riley had left the room that he allowed the tears to come. When they did, for the longest time, he thought they would never cease.

CHAPTER 51
Now, 2015

Jemima Hearn's car was found the next morning. It would have remained underwater for days, maybe longer, had items from inside the Aston Martin not floated to the surface, allowed to escape from their icy, watery grave through the open windows. When a mass of receipts, classical CD covers and a selection of flyers for the Dirty Cash Casino had been found floating like a flotilla of litter on the lake's surface by an early morning dog walker, the alarm was raised. When such a collection gathered in what was normally a tranquil and litter free area, the police were informed. The flyers led them to Tommy, who admitted that he'd been about to call them as his wife and one of his cars had been missing overnight. Within ninety minutes the car had been towed from the murky depths of the lake and the grisly discovery of Jemima's body, still belted into the front seat, had been made.

Tommy had wept uncontrollably when he'd been informed of Jemima's death. His mind, unable to comprehend why his wife would end up at the bottom of the lake, immediately assumed that foul play had been involved. If you lived by the sword, it was likely that those you loved and those around you could die by the sword too. It was a life lesson he'd seen learnt many times in his years alongside Cazwell and subsequently, Riley.

But the police begged to differ. There were no signs of foul play. No stab wounds or bullets or traces of struggle. Nothing that Tommy had expected. He had enemies and maybe revenge was being served to him with his wife's death. But no. It was Jemima who was enacting her revenge. Her revenge for every moment that she'd felt like no more than a plus one, her revenge for those moments Tommy didn't even seem to know she was alive. Her revenge for those moments when maybe he had forgotten that he loved her.

The discovery of the photo in her coat pocket proved that. Through the miracle of a zipped waterproof winter coat pocket and an ink that managed to somehow stay legible, the words were decipherable. The words on the back of them would live on, branded on Tommy's mind until the day he went to meet his maker too. 'Winston, the *only* man who truly made me happy. Forever yours, Jemima x.' 'Only' underlined.

The ultimate payback from beyond the grave. Jemima had been in love with another man. A man who had worked alongside Tommy and Riley for the longest time. A man whom Tommy had never considered anything more than a yes-man, someone of little significance to the life he was such a part of. But for as long as Tommy Hearn lived, Winston Curtis would always be the man who had managed to make his wife feel like a woman again.

It's said that the life of the dead is placed in the memory of the living, and Tommy's memories of Jemima would always be discoloured with the thought that he had been unable to make her happy in her final days. That he had failed as both a husband and perhaps as a man. Maybe he should have shown his love a little more after all.

CHAPTER 52
Now, 2015

Amy had spent the rest of her day at the hospital with Grant. He was lucky to be alive. When she and Lily had found him she was convinced that the actor was dead. Afraid to move him, Amy had called for an ambulance. It had been fifteen minutes before they'd arrived. The paramedics had confirmed that Grant was still alive, but that he was incredibly lucky. The blade had missed penetrating his heart by millimetres.

Amy travelled alone to the hospital with him. The revelation of seeing Riley and the subsequent stabbing of Grant had left Lily both shell-shocked and twitchy. She had no desire to remain around the police, with more than her fair share of narcotics inside her, and it was clear that Amy had no interest in her being there either. She would never forgive Lily for sleeping with Riley, nor he for sleeping with her when she eventually tracked him down.

Lily had convinced Amy not to tell the police about Riley's reappearance, insisting that it was best to keep quiet for now. Riley would only be implicated in the attack and anyway, it was best for Grant to tell them his side of the story when he came round. Only he knew the truth behind the stabbing, even if it seemed obvious to Amy that her brutal criminal of a husband was the man who had tried to end Grant's life.

Maybe it was the extreme situation that the two women had been forced into that, for a brief moment, calmed her anger towards Lily, but Amy had to admit that perhaps she was right. Trying to explain about Riley and the letters would only make for more pressure and she was already at saturation point. No, as far as the police were concerned, she and Lily knew nothing, saying that Grant had run off from them for reasons unknown and when he didn't return they'd gone looking for him.

Grant had stirred into life at regular intervals throughout the afternoon, even opening his eyes on a couple of occasions. But the loss of blood and some rather heavy painkillers ensured that he remained pretty much out of it. Stitches were applied to his wound and the doctors said that he would be kept in at least overnight. Since there was nothing else she could do, Amy decided to return to the hotel.

Walking into the Reception, Amy caught sight of herself in one of the full length mirrors either side of the revolving door. For a woman approaching thirty she felt that she had aged over the last few days, the lines around her eyes and forehead had become deeper and more ingrained. Her mind flashed immediately to Laura. She would have hated to see Amy looking so haggard. She would have had the answers straight away. 'You need a good long soak in the bath, Amy, and one of those fabulous Clinique face masks. Those lines will disappear faster than apple sauce at a hog roast.'

Laura always had the answers. God, she missed her so much. She doubted if she'd ever have another friend like Laura. Somebody so refreshingly vibrant and decisive and with a zest for life more active than the back row of a cinema.

'Right, an early night for you, I think,' she said, staring at her reflection. She really needed to find her husband but she had no idea where to go and she had to face the fact that he had run away. Plus, no man would like to see her looking like this. She pulled at the skin of her cheeks to look at her eyes. God, they were nearly as red as the bruise on the side of her face.

Making her way across the lobby, Amy pressed the lift button, ready to go to her room. As she stood there, one of the hotel staff from the Reception desk called to her and handed her two sheets of paper. 'These two messages came for you today Miss Hart, one on the phone and one was hand-delivered.'

As she stepped into the elevator and the doors closed behind her, Amy unfolded the first sheet. It was from Jimmy telling her that Jemima had killed herself and that Tommy had been crying ever since the police had been to tell him. For a moment Amy felt sorry for Tommy, the two of them united in the loss of a loved one. But it passed as quickly as it came. She didn't wish anyone dead but there was no way she was going to mourn for Jemima.

The second message was from someone called Dolly Townsend. The handwritten note read, 'Hi, you don't know me but I know of you through Adam Rich. I need to see you. It's about your late husband. I have information that I think you'd definitely like to know. If you care to meet me, and I think you should, then come to this address tomorrow at noon. If you can't, then ring my number.' She had added her number and the name of a wine bar on the other side of Manchester at the bottom of the note.

Dolly Townsend? Who the hell's she? thought Amy. And what does she know about Riley? A wave of suspicion that she was yet another of Riley's mistresses flooded her mind. Whoever she was, whatever she was, it would have to wait until tomorrow. All Amy wanted to do right now was tuck herself under her hotel bedspread and sleep for a thousand hours.

CHAPTER 53
Then, 2014

Laura and Amy never really argued but occasionally there would definitely be a difference of opinion. And you could wager money that it would always be about Laura's inability to commit to one man. There were times when Amy thought that Laura actually wanted the kind of stable relationship she had with Riley – and that she desired it more than she actually cared to admit with her happy-go-lucky manner and her fuck-them-and-chuck-them ways. Sensitivity didn't seem to be a word in Laura's vocabulary when it came to the opposite sex.

A point which Laura was keen to lock horns about, albeit in her own facetious way. 'Of course I'm sensitive, Amy. I'm beyond sensitive about guys. I'm the girl who is so allergic to nuts I suffered a severe reaction just from snogging a man who'd had a bag of salteds at a wine bar. That's how sensitive I am.'

For once, Amy was not in the mood to joke. 'I'm not talking about food allergies, Laura, I just meant that maybe sometimes you're not overly sensitive to the needs of men beyond the bedroom and maybe that's why you're still single.'

If there was one thing that nobody, not even her best friend, could criticise her about, it was Laura's treatment of men. She knew how to make them happy and not just between the sheets and one day the whole world would see that.

'Why are we talking about this?' she said, clearly annoyed. 'You may be quite happy to be walking around with a sign saying "meek and mild loyal little wife" hanging around your neck but as you well know I am much more the loving and leaving kind than I am the marrying kind. Now, can we drop the subject? I thought we'd come here to try and relax. You're giving me knots of stress in my shoulder blades that not even the niftiest of boy scouts could untie.' Laura's manner may not have been quite arctic but there was definitely a frostiness in the air.

Amy remained silent. It had always been the difference between them. Whereas Amy had been keen to commit to a lasting relationship straight away, Laura's inability to settle down was something that irked Amy every once in a while. For two women with such similar tastes in so much, this was one subject where they were poles apart.

There were times when she wanted her best mate to experience exactly the kind of happiness she had with Riley. Was that conceited and selfish? Amy hoped not. She just had the impression now and again that perhaps her best friend was not as carefree as she made out.

Laura seemed determined to prove the point about the knots. 'So how is ... er, what did you say your name was again ...? supposed to de-stress me?' She looked up at the man towering over her.

'My name's Wolfgang. From the German, *Wulf* meaning wolf, *gang* meaning path. Second name's Amadeus ... my mother was a huge fan of the composer.'

The man Laura was talking to was her masseur, currently kneading his hands rather deliciously into Laura's naked upper body as she lay face down in the candlelit massage room at

one of Germany's top health, massage and relaxation spas. After
the girls' trip to Italy earlier that year and Riley compliment-
ing them both on how well they looked when they had flown
back to the UK, Amy had been insistent that they should do it
as often as possible. Spas in the UK were great and Laura and
Amy tried to go at least once a month but it was Laura who
had found their current German one online. She was mightily
impressed by the fact that German spas had a very liberal policy
when it came to nudity. Hence why they had flown out for another girlie weekend away. Everything had been *wunderbar* until
they had steered into the conversation about relationships.

Amy was lying on a massage table alongside her friend, naked apart from a towel around her waist, having her stress levels
worked upon by Micha, one of the luxury European health complex's rather skilled and always handsome team of male workers.
It appeared that good looks were a prerequisite to working there.

Rich ladies from across the globe visited the resort to get
away from their overbearing husbands and to be treated to some
'pampering' from the rather adorable male staff, but for Amy it
was simply yet another place to unwind, chill out and spend a
few days relaxing and catching up with Laura.

For Amy, nobody's hands could compare with Riley's when
it came to the feel of them against her skin and for her, the
spa visit was just a perfect way to de-clutter the complexities of
her business life, but Laura's motives were not surprisingly now
somewhat different, her eyes lighting up when she had heard
from other women at the spa that the staff were very attentive
indeed. She was loving the close proximity and, if the ladies
were to be believed, potentially intimate nature of the handsome staff at the German spa, which was why she was in full flirt
mode with Wolfgang.

'If I wasn't sensitive then I wouldn't be able to tell Wolfgang here just how fabulous his expert fingers feel against my tender lily white flesh, would I?' She winked in his direction as she spoke, giving more than a hint that she was enjoying his Teutonic touch on many levels, her vexation with Amy seemingly extinguished.

He smiled back, revealing a set of teeth that most Hollywood actors would pay millions for. Laura could feel her nipples rising to attention.

'You have never been sensitive when it comes to guys, Laura,' continued Amy, *her* annoyance not extinguished, even though she knew her advice was falling on deaf ears. 'You're the one who told one man you went out with that the only reason you were with him is because you were incredibly smart and that opposites attract. And then there was that guy who drunkenly attempted to shag you at a party and couldn't get it up, so what did you say? *Oh look at your cock, it's like a penis but only in miniature.* The poor red-faced bloke ran out of the door faster than Mo Farah.'

'So I shoot my mouth off sometimes. You wouldn't have me any other way, would you? That's why we've been friends for so long. Anyway, what's the latest news with the club?' asked Laura, determined to change the subject away from her lack of desire to commit. One day she would do, to the right man – she knew that, but not just yet.

'Top notch, we're getting bigger all the time. The music websites and bloggers are queuing up to write features about us and the editors of every magazine from *Glamour* through to *Vanity Fair* are asking for a spot on the guest list, plus the number of VIP stars ready to party through our doors is getting longer every day. I've received emails about Robert Pattinson, Greg

Rutherford and Grant Wilson already this week alone. Everyone wants a piece of The Kitty Kat.'

'A stellar cast list,' purred Laura, her voice deepening as Wolfgang manoeuvred a particularly pleasing double circle of thumb pressure across her upper back. 'Make sure I'm there when they pop in, won't you.'

'Like I could keep you away. If star fucking was an Olympic sport you'd win a gold medal every four years, that's for sure.' Amy's annoyance was diffusing as it always did whenever they crossed words. She couldn't help but laugh. 'Now, if you'll excuse me, I think Micha has worked his magic hands with me and I'm ready for a rather soothing session in the Jacuzzi. Are you coming?'

From the look on Laura's face she already knew the answer. 'I think Wolfgang here has a little extra work to do. And besides, the lady at Reception says that he's massaged a few Hollywood starlets and I am dying to pump him for some extra gossip about which rich bitches have had work done. I'm sure he's seen a scar or two.'

'We'll leave you to it then,' smirked Amy, as she and Micha vacated the room. *Hell*, thought Amy, *if I had a pound for every time I've said that to Laura, then I'd be a millionaire.* She enjoyed her times away with Laura, even if sometimes they spent the majority of their stay together in separate rooms while Laura sampled more hands on delights. She'd tried to do it in Italy, and doubtless they'd be coming back to Germany again in the very near future if her forthcoming 'treatment' from Wolfgang was a success. Which, if the smile on his face as Amy said '*auf weidersehen*' was anything to go by, it certainly would be. Laura was wanton, wicked and wild. Amy just wondered whether sometimes Laura was a little bit wanting too.

She just wished that Laura could find the man to make her fully happy like she had with Riley. It took a best friend to know that sometimes Laura, deep-down, perhaps needed something more.

If Amy had known then that this particular spa visit was to be their last together then she would have silenced her thoughts, determined that not one disapproving or contrary word should come between them. She would also have stuck to Laura's side like a limpet, making the most of every treasured moment.

CHAPTER 54
Now, 2015

Dolly was already draining the last few drops from her glass of vodka and tonic and was contemplating a second when Amy walked through the door of the wine bar. Dolly had made sure she arrived in good time and even though it was still early in the day, she figured a little Dutch courage was wise considering what she planned to say.

She could see Amy's gaze oscillate around the bar, which was already full of suited business types entertaining their clients, their secretaries or both. Dolly stood up and beckoned her over. Unsure of how you greet someone you're just about to try and fleece for a large amount of cash, Dolly simply held out her hand and said, 'Hi, I'm Dolly Townsend, thanks for coming to see me.'

Dolly liked the look of Amy. Her thick blonde hair, evidently not natural – she could see that from the half inch or so of dark roots that grew at the base – was swept back behind her pretty face, and secured at the back with a grip. Her skin was clean and fresh, although Dolly was sure that she could make out a hint of a bruise on one of her cheeks, unsuccessfully covered with a layer of make-up. Her clothes, an oversized woollen jumper teamed with a thick belt and a pair of tight stonewashed jeans, looked good on her. She estimated that Amy was in her early twenties, not knowing that she was actually guessing a good five years too young.

'Your note intrigued me. You know something about Riley? There was no way that I couldn't come. So what do I need to know?'

'Why don't we both order some drinks and I'll tell you what I know ...'

Grant winced as he attempted to pull his jumper on over his head at the foot of his hospital bed. One night housed within the white, sterile walls of his private room was more than he could bear. What was it about hospitals? They always seemed to have that inbuilt smell of sickness – a fusion of maxi-strength cleaning agents, body odour and piss. Grant couldn't wait to leave.

After having stitches administered to his stab wound, Grant had spent most of the night out for the count. He had woken up that morning to find two policemen waiting outside his room. They had eventually been let in to see him, and he had told them what he could about the attack. Or at least his version of it ...

'I was in the street, it was no more than an alleyway, to be honest, and somebody jumped me from behind. I guess it was just some chancer hoping to steal a bit of extra cash for some Christmas shopping. I didn't see their face. I just saw the flash of the blade and the next thing I knew I was coming in here.'

One of the policemen scribbled notes onto his pad while the other carried on questioning Grant. His face appeared quizzical and Grant wasn't altogether sure that he believed his story. 'What were you doing on that street, sir? There's not exactly a lot of shops down there and the friend who brought you in here, a Miss Amy Hart, said she wasn't sure why you'd run off away from her. She did seem fairly hysterical and confused though, to be honest.'

Good girl, mused Grant. *So, Amy hadn't said anything about him chasing after Riley.* The last thing a celebrity like Grant needed was to be involved in some kind of seedy back-street stabbing. The producers of *Ward 44* and any would-be Hollywood employers would probably not exactly jump for joy at his wholesome image being soiled with scandal.

'The God's honest truth,' smiled Grant, hoping his famous pearly whites would work their magic as far as his credibility was concerned. 'I nipped in there as I needed a pee. You'd be surprised how many times a star like me gets asked for autographs when I'm stood at a urinal with my old chap in my hand. I hate using public loos. I should have gone to the toilet back at my hotel. I didn't. The cold air kicked my bladder into action, so I thought I'd just nip off and ... er, have a slash. I didn't tell Miss Hart exactly what I was up to, because it's not ... well, it's not exactly the nicest thing to discuss is it? Anyway, I thought I'd only be a couple of minutes. I guess the bloke who stabbed me must have followed me in there thinking it was a nice quiet place to pounce. After my wallet, no doubt.'

Grant continued to smile as the policeman with the notepad continued to write. There was a smirk across his face. Grant was praying that they believed his story. It was all he could think of.

'So it is you, sir,' smirked the questioning cop. 'I thought I recognised the name. The wife's a big fan. In fact, she thinks you're the best thing since sliced bread. She drives me insane with it. She'll be livid when I say I've met you, especially if I told her you've been roaming the streets near where she works. She's the manageress of a shoe shop about ten minutes from where you were stabbed.'

Grant seized the moment. 'Listen, officer, I'm sure you can appreciate that it wouldn't exactly be brilliant for my career for the whole world to find out that I was stabbed whilst attempting to have a piss in a Manchester back street. I don't know who did it, I didn't see the bloke, I was jumped from behind. Nothing was stolen, thank Christ, and I'm still alive and kicking. I know I'm lucky but what are the chances of just sweeping this under the carpet? It's kind of embarrassing for me ... I've got some big deals on the table, especially Stateside, and I really could do without any aggro that might screw them up.'

The copper paused. 'We *should* investigate this, a stabbing has taken place. An attempted murder. GBH. Section 20 and all that. You are seriously lucky to still be able to talk, let alone act ...'

'Maybe an autograph for your wife would help?' interrupted Grant.

A hint of a smile came immediately. 'Well, that would certainly put me in her good books.'

Grant rolled with it. 'I could pop into her shop as well. Buy some shoes. Have a photo taken for the wall. Would that help bury this for me? I know it's a serious offence but I really don't wish to pursue it.'

The officer's grin told Grant that he'd won. 'You'd do that for her? Bloody hell, I'd be the best husband in the world if you did that. You'd mention it was my idea?' It seemed that the policeman was more than happy to put personal before professional.

'I could say we met on the street ... that you asked me especially for your lovely wife. Now, pass me that pad and I'll sign an autograph for her and you can tell me her name and where the shoe shop is.'

'She's never going to believe this. Thanks a lot.' He grabbed the pen and pad from his colleague and handed it to Grant. 'Her name's Yvonne ...Y... V ... O ... N ... N ... E.' Grant signed his name and listened as the police officer told him where he could find the shoe shop, writing down the address. He kept his smile in place until the two officers left the room, relieved to be alone once more.

As they disappeared out of sight, Grant screwed up the piece of paper with the address on it and threw it to the floor. Even if he needed new shoes, which he didn't, he had absolutely no intention of visiting the shop. All he wanted to do was get out the hospital and back to the hotel. He needed to see Amy.

Amy hadn't a clue what to expect from her rendezvous with Dolly, but she certainly hadn't expected the conversation to begin with Dolly's brash admission that she was a prostitute. She'd seen many things at the Kitty Kat Club in her time there but strangely she had never knowingly met somebody who admitted that their job was selling sex. God knows Laura gave enough of it away when she was alive but even she never actually charged for it.

Amy's first thoughts were to ask Dolly a hundred different questions – weirdest sex ever, was it always one-on-one, any famous clients – but all of that initial excitement flushed from her mind when Dolly threw in the name of her most regular client – Adam Rich. She sat back and listened as Dolly told her all about what she had overheard during the conversation between Adam and Tommy, taking in every word as she sipped at her drink.

Yet again, Amy was floored by what she was hearing. She wasn't that surprised to learn that Adam had shot somebody for Riley. She was rapidly becoming used to the fact that her husband was far from pure. What really shocked her was Dolly's tale that a body had been buried underneath the dance floor at the Kitty Kat Club. The idea that every time Amy had been dancing there with Laura or with one of the many happy, party-loving customers they were actually dancing on somebody's grave horrified her. It further sullied her already scarred happy memories of The Kitty Kat and contaminated her recollections.

'Why are you telling me this?' asked Amy. 'I don't own the club any more. There is no club. That body is buried under Dirty Cash now.'

'I know who the body is. If word got out it could cause trouble. Trouble for Adam, and for Tommy, and for your husband if he's still alive ... and I guess for you too.' Dolly took a swig of her vodka, the grouping of tiny lines circling her mouth becoming more pronounced as she did so. There was harshness in her face, but Amy could see that it was definitely underlined with desperation. Whatever Dolly was hinting at, this kind of conversation was definitely out of her comfort zone.

'And why is that?' asked Amy.

'Because he's some fucking mental bigwig criminal's son and that bigwig has been looking to find out what happened to his pride and joy for years.'

'And why exactly could that hurt me, Dolly?' Despite her first impressions, Amy was rapidly going off the woman across the table from her.

'Because if you don't pay me for my silence then I'm going to tell his dad everything I know. And when he finds out then he's going to want revenge. Revenge for the death of his son. He'll want to get even with the people responsible and that's Adam Rich and your husband. And seeing as your husband doesn't seem to be around anymore then surely it stands to reason that he might go after Tommy or his wife or you, the people connected with him. My silence could stop all of that from happening.'

'You might screw other people for a living, Miss Townsend, but there's no fucking way you're screwing me over. You're messing with things that are darker than any murky dealings you might have experienced flat on your back.'

Dolly looked crestfallen. This was not the response she'd wanted. She had automatically assumed, wrongly it would seem, that Amy would immediately crumble and offer to pay up for her silence, scared that she would meet a similar fate to the man under the dance floor.

As Dolly put down her drink, she looked straight across the table at Amy.

'So, what I am supposed to do then? I have all this information and I thought it would help me better myself somehow. Do you think I enjoy getting fucked for a living, Amy? Because even though I'm bloody good at it, I've done it long enough. I'm at an age where I need more. I need cash, more than the likes of Adam Rich pay me. You managed to bag the rich husband. You're one of the lucky ones. You've got money to burn, enough to keep you up to your neckline in designer gear. What have I got? Nothing tangible.'

Amy's fuse was lit. 'Join the club, Dolly,' she snapped. 'You know nothing about me. The reason I don't own the club any more, the reason I don't live in Manchester any more in my great show-off marital home is because nothing's mine. I lost it all when Riley died. The club was signed over to Tommy and his wife, who's been found dead by the way.' As she said it, Amy couldn't help but wonder if Dolly's story and Jemima's sudden death were connected. 'I couldn't keep the house because the payments were too much and Riley's business dealings were a complete mystery to me. I didn't have a clue about anything. So even if I did want to pay for your silence, which I don't, I can't. I barely have any money to my name. Any I do have goes towards the flat in London and my weekly shops. I manage to keep my head above water but I have to be pretty creative. You'd be surprised how much a girl can cobble together from eBay sales if she needs to, not that it has anything to do with you.'

'But I thought ...'

'Well, you thought wrong,' snapped Amy.

'I'm sorry.' Dolly's words were soft and as she began to speak, Amy could see a film of tears glazing across her eyes. 'I didn't know. All I wanted was to better myself, to have enough cash for the future. To move away from here into a nice house with a bit of greenery out the back. A few holidays every year, far flung places. I'd like to find a man who loves me for who I am as opposed to the talents I can demonstrate between the bed sheets. I want to stand on my own two feet as opposed to just lying on my back. I can't blackmail Adam as he'd probably send me to the bottom of the nearest river. I'm fully aware that I'm no more than just a good shag to him, but other girls could take my place quite easily. You were my only hope. I thought telling you about Jarrett Smith would be my ticket to all of that happiness I've been looking for. I guess I was wrong. Look, I'm sorry, I've wasted your time.' Dolly stood to leave, having no more to say.

'Hang on, Jarrett Smith ... I know that name. Riley used to mention him. Some contact from London, something to do with his plastics business down south I thought.'

'Jarrett Smith is the hardest fucking criminal in London,' said Dolly. 'It's his son, Weston, who's buried under the club. He's a nasty piece of work. If he knew what exactly happened with Adam and Riley then he'd be in Manchester, like yesterday, getting his own back. Weston was his only son. I went on the Internet to see if I could find any information about him. There wasn't much but one thing was definitely clear. Jarrett Smith's notorious but somehow the police can't touch him. He seems immune to the ways of justice.' Dolly reached down and delved into the pocket of her coat, hung over the back of her chair. She took out a folded print-out of something she'd found online and handed it to Amy. 'That's him. I hope neither of us ever run into him.'

Amy looked at the cutting. Her body froze. 'I already have. He was watching me outside Dirty Cash yesterday. I can't believe I thought he was something to do with Riley's business ... or at least the business I thought Riley was involved in. Before I found out about all the lies. Before I found out about everything and ended up with nothing.' Amy's voice started to wobble as she amassed all of Riley's lies in her mind. Everything he had told her, the lines she'd believed.

'I'm sorry, Amy, I really am. I've been looking at this from the wrong angle. You and I are more similar than I ever imagined,' stated Dolly. 'We've both been screwed by men all of our lives. We just need to work out how we both end up on top.'

CHAPTER 55
Now, 2013

Lily liked her music loud. That was how she played it at The Kitty Kat when she guest DJ'd. The louder the better. Especially when she had things on her mind. It seemed to help her grasp some form of lucidity about the many fucked-up things that seemed to be writhing across her thoughts. Her father was out, Caitlyn was indulging in retail therapy in Manchester, doing some serious damage to another of the Rich joint accounts, and Lily was alone at home, holed up in her bedroom, her only company a bag full of weed.

She'd spent the last few hours as stoned as she could, the weed acting as a comedown after the plentiful lines of coke she'd been snorting with alarming regularity over the last few days.

She needed to drown out the outside world in order to concentrate on what was formulating inside her mind. Laying back on her bed she knew that she was playing the waiting game. She checked her watch. Give it another twenty minutes.

How long had it been since she'd placed that phone call? Half an hour? Yes, give it another thirty minutes at the most. She'd look out of the window in fifteen to see what was happening. To make sure she was ready. This could be her moment.

Silence. Yet somehow the sound of the cogs whirring in her mind seemed to be deafening. Five minutes passed. Then ten ... she moved to the window and looked outside as five more minutes disappeared, seemingly in an instant. A lone figure approached the door of the house. Lily had given the visitor the code to the iron gates protecting the Rich family home when she'd phoned. She wanted to meet on home turf.

A smile crept across her face as she headed downstairs and opened the front door. 'You came ... I knew you would,' she said. She opened the door wide and motioned for the visitor to come in.

It was early evening when Grant received a knock on his hotel room door. He popped a codeine into his mouth as he climbed off the bed where he'd been relaxing and walked to the door. His shoulder was still throbbing, but the doctors who had discharged him from hospital earlier that day had said that regular painkillers would be necessary for a while.

He opened it to find Amy standing on the other side.

'Evening,' she said. 'I see you've been discharged, then.' She seemed somewhat flat. She was. Her meeting with Dolly had left her fearful of what could be around every corner. If Jarrett Smith was in town then there was not one iota of her that felt at all safe. He knew who she was, that was clear.

'Hey, how are you? Feeling a bit better than me I hope. My shoulder is bloody killing me.' He laughed, somewhat inappropriately. 'Come on in ...'

'I need to talk to you, Grant.' Amy was in full flow before she even stepped one foot into the room. 'That was Riley we saw, wasn't it? He's alive isn't he? You, me and Lily didn't imagine what happened yesterday did we? Why hasn't he come back to see me?' The questions came thick and fast.

In silence, Grant shut the door behind her. It felt somehow strange to them both that it should just be the two of them together within one hotel room. More improper than awkward.

There was an overly long pause before Grant spoke. 'It was him, yes. I'm sure of it.' He sat himself back on the bed and patted for Amy to sit alongside him. She did so.

'What happened, Grant? You and Lily ran off after him and the next thing I know you're bleeding all over the pavement. What have you told the police?'

Grant filled her in on his conversation with the police officers. She was grateful that he'd kept Riley's name out of it. Lily had been right. The situation was enough of a mess as it was without the police becoming involved.

'But who stabbed you? Was it ...' Amy couldn't bring herself to say the word.

But she knew confirmation was coming. 'Riley? What do you think?' Grant held her hand, just as he had done in her London flat when she'd received the second letter. So much had happened since then. Amy found it a comfort.

'I don't know ... why would he?'

'It all happened so quickly, Amy, but one minute I was chasing him, then he'd vanished, and then the next minute somebody tried to skewer me with a knife. I didn't get the clearest of views but if I was a gambling man I would stake my last dollar on it being Riley. I only lied to the police because I didn't want to cause you more pain. Now he's alive, the last thing you want is him disappearing off to jail. He could have killed me. He didn't. I was lucky. But it was definitely him, I know it.'

So did Amy. Riley was alive and she didn't know whether to feel elated or distraught. Or just plain terrified.

CHAPTER 56
Now, 2015

It was a very rare occurrence indeed but for once Caitlyn Rich was not enjoying her shopping trip. And she was woman who could shop with WAG-capabilities; a woman who could run up a bill in dollars, euros, pounds and pence no matter where she was in the world if there was lingerie, perfume, décor and *objets* to be purchased. And Caitlyn was very much of the belief that if you couldn't find what you wanted in the shops then you had what you wanted commissioned, hand-made and hand-delivered.

No, Caitlyn's mind was very much pre-occupied and it wasn't with designer frocks or the latest celebrity perfume – and she was normally a huge sucker for a fancy bottle and a Hollywood name. No, Caitlyn had more pressing issues on her mind as she sat alone in Selfridge's San Carlo Bottega pushing a portion of seafood pasta around her plate. Despite it smelling delicious and indeed tasting so, she had tried it on many occasions, she had no appetite. Her inability to shop and eat were both connected.

She had heard about Jemima Hearn's death. The Manchester grapevine had been working overtime. Why hadn't Adam mentioned it to her? Maybe he didn't know yet. Her first thought, like many who were in the know about the disappearance of Weston Smith, was that perhaps her death was a revenge killing. The grapevine told another story though. That Jemima had killed herself and left a note stating her love for Winston Curtis. Caitlyn found the former option much more credible even if gangland gossip had proven that the last option was in fact true.

Jemima was having an affair? *Good for her*, thought Caitlyn. *I never would have guessed she had it in her.* The last time Caitlyn had sat in Bottega was actually with Jemima herself. She had brought Tommy's wife out for a makeover, as she often did. Jemima wasn't exactly the easiest person to get on with, but Caitlyn saw it her duty as a fellow woman to help her make the most of herself. It had obviously worked if she'd bagged Winston.

Caitlyn couldn't help but wish Jemima had confided in her about the affair. Lord knows she had enough experience in dangerous liaisons behind your other half's back through her affair with Jona. They could have compared notes. Caitlyn's mind drifted to what Winston may have been housing between his legs. She'd never been with a black man and she would have loved to have pumped Jemima for information. Was it true what they said about black guys? How would he have stood up, she wondered, no pun intended, against Jona's nine inches? She was sure she and Jemima might have laughed about it all. Now the poor cow would never laugh again. It made Caitlyn sad.

The other reason that Caitlyn couldn't concentrate on her normal retail revelry was that she had spoken to Adam on the phone earlier too. They had discussed Amy's return and Lily's confession about her affair with Riley. They were two subjects that neither of them liked.

'Amy is convinced Riley is alive, which is why Lily is all over the shop,' said Adam.

'She can't be with him, Adam. It'll be over my dead body.' The irony of what Caitlyn was saying was not lost on Adam.

'If the truth about Weston Smith comes out then it could well be. Jarrett Smith will stop at nothing to gain his revenge, and that could mean you, me, Lily, Amy, anyone connected to his disappearance being in the firing line. We all need to try and lay low for a while and hope to God that the truth doesn't come out.'

'I'll go back to my sister's. Stay there for a while,' said Caitlyn. It seemed like a good idea and obviously meant her being with Jona. 'I can stay there until the coast is clear. What about you?'

'I can look after myself,' stated Adam. 'Amy Hart won't squeal, I won't allow it.'

'I always knew that this would come back to bite you on the behind, you stupid man. The one thing you should never do is put your family in danger.'

'It's that danger that keeps bankrolling you, you silly bitch.'

Caitlyn was in no mood to hear what she already knew. 'I'll see you later,' she said and hung up.

She knew what she needed to do and there was no time like the present to do it. She looked inside her Chloe Paddington bag and scanned the contents. She had her passport, always handy should Jona decide to hire a jet for them and head off somewhere on a whim. She had money and credit cards. What else did she need? Nothing. If Jarrett Smith was about to start hunting down prey, then that included her, if only by association, and she would be better off getting away right now.

She grabbed her phone from her bag. The battery was nearly dead, but she could still make a quick phone call. She made two. The first was to Lily. She didn't pick up so Caitlyn left a message telling her daughter that she was going to London for now and that she too should quit Manchester as soon as possible and maybe join her in London – she didn't explain why, but told her to trust her mother – and one to Jona telling him that she would be with him in a matter of hours. As she ended her second call her phone died, the battery spent. She would have to purchase a charger *en route*. At least she would have finally bought something today.

She headed straight to Manchester's Piccadilly train station contemplating how today had been possibly her least successful shopping trip ever.

CHAPTER 57
Now, 2015

As she lay in bed Amy shivered, the freshness of the night air against her body pricking at her skin, giving her goose bumps.

She stared at the clock on her hotel bedside table. It read 3.24am. The room was in complete darkness apart from the large digital letters displaying the time. She hadn't slept all night. How could she? The husband that she had spent the last six months mourning was alive. She'd seen him with her own eyes.

Images of his face smashed around her head, battering against her skull. Emotions leapt wildly, popping like corn, mental rapid gunfire confusing any semblance of sense she tried to formulate. Six months ago Riley's face was one she had looked at with complete love, total adoration ... but now ... she couldn't be sure. What had he done to her? Why was he doing this?

Their life together had been a sham. As counterfeit as a dodgy bank note. He may have loved her in his own way, but not like she'd loved him, the kind of love where your face hurts from smiling every time you look at the person of your dreams, the kind where your heart skips not just one beat but several every time his arms loop themselves around you.

She missed his caress. Their sex life had been wonderful. For such a big, muscular man, his touch had often been light and gentle, his skin barely tickling hers to new heights of pleasure. His kisses, butterfly-soft, had traced their way across her body, bringing her more blissful gratification than she'd imagined possible.

How could somebody who had served her so much pleasure now be bringing her so much pain? The torture of knowing that he had cheated on her, the pain that his life was secret to her, never to be shared ... *why would he wish that upon the woman he'd married? Professed to love?* Amy couldn't understand, and in her darker, more terrified moments she wasn't sure that she wanted to.

If the revelations about their former life together were to be the price she had to pay to have him back, alive again in her arms, then Amy wasn't sure if she could cope with the price tag.

Here she was, lying alone in a dark hotel room fearful for her life. Her husband a murderer, she herself the target of some crazed gunman. Riley had become the epicentre of a world of crime, horror and brutality which Amy didn't want to frequent anymore. She didn't care about the richer or the poorer, money meant nothing to her compared with true, honest love, but when she'd married Riley, she had believed that it would be for the better ... not for the so much worse.

As she lay there watching the numbers on the clock tick on, minute after minute, her emotions swung fitfully between triumphant joy at knowing that Riley was still alive and a blackened hatred at what he was putting her through. As the minutes advanced, it was the blackness that began to take over. She didn't deserve this. If her only crime was loving Riley so much then why did she feel she was being punished? Punished by his affairs with Genevieve and Lily, punished by his deceit, punished by his ongoing disappearance. All she had ever done was stay true to her one true love. A word scorched itself through her thoughts ... *Why?*

Slipping out of bed, Amy adjusted the T-shirt she was wearing. It had been one of Riley's and she pulled it down below her hips as she moved towards the hotel room door. She didn't turn the light on, knowing the layout of the room in her mind. She placed the key card in the door, opened it and walked out into the lit corridor. The brightness of the light caused her to wince momentarily as her eyes became accustomed to it.

Grant's room was adjacent to hers. It took her no more than half a dozen steps to reach it. She rapped on the door, lightly at first, but when no answer came she tried again, her knocking more urgent.

A dishevelled Grant opened the door. He was wearing only pyjama bottoms. It was clear to see why his body was such a hit with ladies everywhere. A white pad of cloth covered part of his chest where he'd been stabbed. He rubbed his eyes to focus on Amy.

'You okay ...?' he questioned.

'Can I come in, be with you? I need to be held, Grant. I need to feel loved. Just hold me ... please.'

Grant smiled, held out his hand and gently led Amy into his room. He only said two words. 'Of course.'

As Amy lay down on the bed with Grant and felt his arms move around her, enveloping her with his warmth, she felt a needle of guilt pass through her. But before she could even try to fathom its meaning and work out whether she wanted to react to it, she fell into a deep, much-needed blanket of sleep.

CHAPTER 58
Now, 2015

Nothing fazed Adam Rich, not normally. But then today, so far, had not been a day like any other. He'd woken up hung-over, the excess of Jack Daniel's he'd drunk the night before still uncomfortably swallowing the inside of his head.

It wasn't very often that Adam let himself drink too much but when a colleague had asked him to join him for an evening's poker game he'd gladly accepted. His wife was spending his hard-earned cash and moving fucking ridiculous statues into their home, his waste-of-space daughter was playing all sorts of raucous tunes throughout the house, not allowing him to think clearly and all the talk of his killing Weston Smith was really beginning to swamp his every thought.

The evening poker had turned into a late night and it was easily 3am by the time he'd returned home. The house was quiet, Lily obviously out or asleep – the former, knowing her. He fell asleep on the sofa. The only noise when Adam woke up mid-morning the next day was the banging inside his head from the whisky and the ring of his office telephone. At first he ignored it, but when it kept ringing he knew that somebody was desperately trying to get hold of him.

Stomping his way to his office, he snatched up the phone. It was Tommy, telling him about Jemima's death. A boulder of foreboding shattered inside him. Jarrett had killed Jemima, he knew it. He'd found out about Weston's death, that he and Riley were responsible and he was back to kill his way through those nearest and dearest, causing as much horrific misery as possible. He'd have to check on Caitlyn and Lily, make sure they were okay. And watch his every move.

His mood only changed somewhat, disbelief replacing despair, when Tommy informed him that Jemima's death was a suicide and that she'd killed herself over the death of Winston Curtis.

'What, she was shagging the bloke who worked with Riley? Fucking hell, Tommy, right underneath your nose, you poor bastard.' As ever, Adam spoke before he thought. 'She was swallowing a length of black cock and you never even knew?'

'No, I had no idea.' Tommy's voice was weak, uncharacteristically so. 'But that's not why I rang. Can you come over?'

'Are you fucking messing me, Tommy? I was out last night and my head feels like somebody's taken a bleeding dump in it this morning. I'm going back to bed ... I'll swing by later if I—'

Tommy cut Adam off in full flow. 'I've seen Jarrett Smith. He was here this morning. I'm sure it was him. I wasn't going to come in, what with the news about Jemima, but some of the staff haven't turned up – the bunch of lightweights have probably clocked off early for Christmas – so I needed to sort some things out.'

Adam could feel the blood drain from his face, sudden fear and the hangover causing him to stagger on his feet. 'Are you fucking sure?'

'Ninety per cent, yes. I'm sure he was getting into a car outside here. He had someone with him. I don't think he saw me, but he's got to be here for a reason and I don't think it's to open a tab at the casino, do you?'

'I'm coming over. Don't move.' Adam slammed the phone down, chucked on some clothes and was out of the door in minutes. He only stopped on the way out to make sure that the gun in his pocket was loaded with bullets. It was.

Both Amy and Grant had woken up mid-morning too. The air of awkwardness between them as they realised the spooning position they were still in lasted only a few seconds, Grant smiling to break any embarrassment.

'Thank you,' said Amy, her meaning simple and clear. The comfort she had felt from being in his arms was immense. She hadn't realised just how much she had missed the touch of a man's body against hers. The shared experience between them had not been sexual in the slightest, despite Grant's obvious erection, pushing at the material of his pyjama bottoms as he stood up off the bed. Amy couldn't help but smile as it caught her attention.

'Sorry, force of habit ... morning glory and all that,' grinned Grant, moving his hands in front of his crotch. 'I'll go and freshen up in the bathroom and see you later. What are your plans for today?'

Amy hadn't really thought. She had no idea how to get hold of Riley. She did have unfinished business with Dolly but that could wait for now. She needed to see Lily. She had obviously come to the hotel to see her for a reason, but with the appearance of Riley, all of that had gone out of the window.

'I'm going to see Lily. She came here to talk about something. I need to know what it is. Not that I really want to hear anything that she has to say. Plus, if Riley is back I want to make sure she has no plans to reignite their affair.'

'Why? Are you going to take him back?' asked Grant. His question seemed multi-layered, as if his own interest were at stake, but Amy wasn't sure whether she was imagining it.

'To be honest,' said Amy, pulling her knees protectively to her chest as she sat on the bed, 'I don't know if I can. I need to see him I guess, but I've no idea how. He has all the balls in his court. What he's done to me, to you ... to so many people ... is totally foreign to me. All this hurt and suffering. But I need to know what happened at the club, why my best friend died, even if my husband didn't. I have no choice. I'm doing this for Laura.'

A cloud of reflective silence hung between them for a few minutes, neither knowing what to say next. It was Amy who ended it.

She looked at Grant. 'Do you want to come to Lily's with me? I could do with the company.'

Grant hung his head slightly. 'Listen, Amy, do you mind if I don't? I was actually thinking that maybe I should get out of your hair for a bit to be honest. Don't take this the wrong way, but the stabbing has made me realise just how serious this all is. I will do whatever I can for you, but I don't like Riley, I never have. And being stabbed by him, well ... that's not exactly what was planned in my mind when I came here with you. Do you understand?'

'Of course, this is my fight, not yours.' Amy could feel the disappointment in her voice. She had got used to Grant being around.

'I'd be lying if I didn't say that I think you're fucking mad for chasing after him in the first place, after everything he's put you through. You're worth better and he deserves your hatred. But I guess that's not my call is it? I'm going back to London. My agent has set up some meetings and well, I need to make sure this is all healed before I start filming again in the new year,' he said, motioning towards his stab wound. 'I hope you find peace with all this, Amy. Riley owes you an explanation. If somebody tried to kill him, then I think there are more likely candidates, given the somewhat seedy nature of his work, than TV folks like me. This is all getting a little too real for me. I prefer my drama on the pages of a script. But I'd walk away from all of this if I were you.'

'I know ...' whispered Amy, 'But I can't. I'm sorry you became so involved. You've been amazing. When are you going?'

'I'm going to head back this afternoon. You can ring me any time you like. Stay here at the hotel for as long as you want. I'll leave my details at Reception, charge it all to me. Just don't ever let Riley stay here with you, eh? I'm not paying for that little shit, okay?'

Grant's voice had a hairline of jest running through it, but his meaning was clear. His opinion of Riley would never change. Amy could see that their bitter schoolboy rivalry would be something that would run deeply within Grant for a lifetime. Plus there was the somewhat graver matter of the stabbing.

'You'll always hate him, won't you?' It was more of a statement than a question.

'Of course I always will. We'll always clash so I think it's best that we're not in the same city at the same time, especially with all the crap flying around at the moment.'

Grant went to walk away, heading for the bathroom.

Amy knew it was her cue to leave.

'Can we stay in touch?' she said. They had shared so much, after all.

Grant turned towards her, a mask of sadness across his face. 'I'd like that, I really would. You have my numbers. Don't be a stranger.'

'One last thing, then ... I need to know. You could have told the police about Riley stabbing you. You could have had a warrant out for his arrest, had him charged with bodily harm or something. Why didn't you?'

'And cause you more pain? I like you Amy, I've grown fond of you. Really fond.' His meaning was clear. 'But you're so wrapped up with Riley and everything that's going on, and that's totally understandable. There's no room for me, not now, maybe not ever. That's another reason that it's best I'm not around you for a bit. I couldn't tell the police. Not because of him. Just because of you. You look after yourself, you hear ...?'

Grant moved back over to Amy and kissed her gently on her cheek. The one with no trace of bruise. Amy felt a tenderness in his touch. He turned and shut the bathroom door behind him. There was no more to say.

Adam and Tommy had talked themselves around in circles. This was another thing that unsettled Adam. He liked his conversations to have a beginning, a middle and an end. Endings had to be mapped out.

If Jarrett Smith was in town, then Adam wanted to know what they could do about it. *Where* could they find him? How would they deal with him? And more importantly, what exactly did he want? The two men had argued, Adam showing no compassion for Tommy's recent loss.

'For fuck's sake, Jarrett Smith was here and you let him slip through your fingers. What kind of fucking wuss are you, Tommy? We need to finish this.'

Tommy spat back. 'Well, what exactly do *you* think *we* are supposed to do, Adam?'

'We need to sort the fucker. If he's back here seeking revenge for Weston then he's getting a bit too close for comfort. We need to stop it.' Adam pulled the gun out of his pocket to indicate his intention.

'And what good would that do?' barked Tommy. 'We'd have the whole of London gangland after us then, wouldn't we? Dirty Cash sees me well, Adam, I don't want to fuck anything up. This all stays buried with Weston. With Riley out of the way your secret's safe.'

A storm of rage ran across Adam's face. '*My* secret? It's *our* fucking secret, sunshine. If anyone links me to that death, then you're coming with me, all the way to hell if need be.'

'Okay, *our* secret,' rectified Tommy. 'Now, get out of here and take that shooter with you. If Jarrett Smith has anything to say then I'm sure he's going to let us know. There's nothing we can do for the moment. For all we know he might be here on some other kind of business. We've just got to hope that's the case.'

'I don't believe that for a second,' cried Adam. 'And you're not fucking stupid enough to either.'

Adam was right, Tommy wasn't.

Adam felt twitchy driving back to his house, unable to shift his deep seated feeling of uneasiness. He'd just spoken to Caitlyn to tell her about Jarrett and she was sensibly pissing off to London again. Meanwhile, his day was going from bad to worse, and as he turned into his street and saw Amy walking towards his house he knew that it wasn't going to get any better. What did she want?

Pulling alongside her in his car, Adam wound down the window to speak to her. 'What are you doing here? Can't you just let your fucking husband rest in peace?'

'Not when he's still alive, no, I don't need to.' Her words floored Adam.

'He's alive? You're deranged. His face was blown off and he's living it up with Satan. He's probably trying to strike a deal with the devil's helpers to see if they can melt down Beelzebub's trident for drug money for him.'

'Then why did I see him two days ago, here in Manchester?' said Amy. 'And not just me, Lily saw him too. Why don't we go and ask her? Is she home?'

Riley alive? The thought wrapped itself around Adam's throat, squeezing it dry. Who the hell was blown apart at the club then? He tried not to let it show on his face. 'I've no idea, but she's a creature of the night normally so she'll probably be sleeping like a baby right now before heading off to whichever shit-heap she chooses to spend her time at. Jump in.'

Adam pushed open the passenger door of the car, allowing Amy to climb inside. He pointed a remote control at the iron gates protecting the property and keyed in the code to open them. They swung open and the two of them drove up to the house.

'Lily, get down here now.' Adam was shouting up the stairs as loudly as he could as soon as he set foot inside the Rich family home. 'Amy Hart is here to see you. And I bloody want to speak to you and all ...' Amy could see a vein in Adam's forehead throbbing as he spoke. He was a man on the edge.

There was no reply from above. Nothing unusual.

'Stupid girl is probably wearing her bloody earphones or something. She can't hear a damn thing when she's wearing those great big things. Lily!' Adam shouted again, this time a little louder, 'Get your scrawny little ass down here now!'

'Maybe's she's not here. Maybe she's managed to track Riley down before me,' Amy looked worried. 'Just tell her I need to see her ...'

Adam stomped his way up the stairs, shouting Lily's name as he did so. He was used to his daughter not answering back. He turned to face Amy. 'Well, are you coming or what? If you want to see her she'll be stoned off her face on her bed listening to some godforsaken racket. Maybe you can talk some sense into her about your wanker of a husband.'

Amy followed Adam upstairs.

'She'll be in a world of her own with those bloody stupid earphones on her head, you mark my words ... all she does during the day is listen to music and take fuck knows what. It's a pity that club of yours isn't still going, at least you gave her some sort of PR job, even if she was peddling that shit of hers. But I suppose when you're sleeping with the boss you can do whatever you bloody well like. You know about that, I suppose, my Lily sleeping with Riley ...?' Adam didn't really care if she didn't, half of him hopeful that he could be the one to break the news.

Amy was struggling to keep up with Adam as he marched along the landing towards Lily's room. 'Yeah, I know, your skank of a daughter dropped that bombshell on me a while back. Another thing I didn't know about Riley.'

They both reached Lily's bedroom door. Adam pounded his fist against it. 'Lily, are you in there?' Still no answer. He pushed the door open. 'Take those bloody earphones off for Christ's sake ...'

His words petered out to nothing as he looked into the room. Lily was indeed lying on the bed, her earphones placed on her head, but from the look on her face it was clear that she was not listening to any kind of music.

Lily's eyes bulged out of their sockets, her mouth was open, her features contorted into a scream of abject fear. Her skin was almost blue. The spiral cord connected to her headphones was unplugged from her music system and had been wound tightly around her neck, looped around as fiercely as possible, rinsing the life from Lily's slender frame. There were scratch marks across her neck from where she had obviously tried to pull the cord away as it snuffed out her existence, her fingernails digging into her own flesh.

Amy screamed. Adam, a rasp of fury and despair rising in his throat, sank to his knees. For a man who never cried, the tears came easily.

'Not my Lily, no ... not my beautiful daughter. Who would do this to her?'

Adam looked up at Amy. Automatically she reached out to stroke his hand. Nobody deserved to see someone they loved like this. That was a lesson Amy had learnt all too well that night at the Kitty Kat when she'd looked into Laura's face and when she'd been faced with the body she had thought was Riley.

'Who would do this ... who?' he sobbed.

Neither answered, but they both had the same name in mind. Jarrett Smith.

CHAPTER 59
Now, 2015

The murder of Lily Rich sent shockwaves through the seedy underbelly of Manchester. Nobody stepped forward to say that they were behind the slaughter, but nobody needed to. For those connected, even through the most tenuous of links, to Lily and the Rich family business, the word in every gutter, at every after hours gambling den and at every canal side warehouse, was that it was Jarrett Smith's doing. A tsunami of terror seemed to sweep through each and every district of Manchester, causing a battening down of hatches. Nobody spoke Lily's name, scared that word would get back to Jarrett. People linked her death to that of Jemima Hearn's. Even those who had heard that the casino owner's wife had taken her own life were suddenly making up their own minds and deciding that maybe the two deaths were connected.

Lily's funeral was a quiet affair, perhaps ignored by many, people seemingly scared to be seen mourning one of Jarrett's victims. Adam and Caitlyn sat at the front of the crematorium, both stony faced as the coffin containing their daughter disappeared into the furnace. Tommy chose to stay away, saying the death was too soon after that of his own wife, who was only just fresh in the ground herself.

Amy had phoned Grant, who had been stunned at the news. Again he chose to stay away. Being seen at the funeral of such a notorious killing was not deemed good for his image. Instead he sent a huge spray of wild flowers and berries, a riot of rich purples, sunshine yellows and bright whites. 'Lily was such a colourful person in life, it just seemed rather fitting for her funeral.'

Amy would never like Lily after what she had confessed to her about Riley, but the sight of her lying dead was an image that obliterated thoughts of Lily and Riley together. Amy knew it was a callous thought but at least now there was never a chance of reconciliation between them.

One person who did choose to go was Genevieve Peters. She had been fond of Lily and saw a lot of her own feistiness and spunk in the young woman. Genevieve had been lying low for a while, spending time with baby Emily and forcing herself away from the booze. She needed a clear head, especially if what she was hearing on the Manchester grapevine was true, that Riley Hart had been seen alive. If he was then maybe more payments could be coming her daughter's way, feathering her nest for the future, although like everyone else who had heard the rumour about Riley, she couldn't help but wonder who had actually been killed if it wasn't Amy's husband.

Genevieve could only imagine the heartache that losing a daughter would bring. Lily's death made her think about how she would react if Emily was ripped from her. The thought destroyed her. She would go to the funeral to pay her respects. It was the least she could do. Plus, she had a sneaky suspicion that Amy might be there too and she had something she needed to share with her.

After the service, as the few mourners in attendance migrated away from the crematorium, Genevieve made a beeline for Amy as she walked along the pathway to the entrance. Amy had been expecting it ever since she'd spied her underneath her veil of black organza.

Genevieve got straight to the point. 'Is it true, then? Riley's alive?'

Her tone was a clipped hybrid of hope and disbelief.

'This is hardly the time or the place, Genevieve, is it?' snapped Amy.

'I would have thought the timing was perfect. As one life is put to rest, another seems to come back from the dead. Have you seen him?'

Amy sighed. 'Yes, I have. But not to talk to. What's it to you? Think you have a chance with him again, do you? I didn't realise you were as good at undressing people as you are at dressing them.' Amy couldn't hold herself back. She wasn't going to let Genevieve have the pleasure of serving her poisonous affair with Riley to her with the ultimate shock factor. 'I know you two had an affair so if you've come here to try and start a slanging match then it's too late.'

The revelation knocked the wind out of Genevieve. 'That's not why I've come here. I came to pay my respects to Lily. I liked the girl.'

'Even if she was shagging Riley too? Maybe you all had some Kitty Kat three-way behind my back. Or is her tawdry little affair news to you?'

Amy could tell from the wide-eyed shock on Genevieve's face that it was.

'I had no idea, but I suppose if a man strays from his wife in the first place, then there's more than a likely chance that he'll stray from the mistress too. A hiker never walks just one path after all,' vented Genevieve.

'No, but some paths are definitely older and have been trodden more than others!' retorted Amy.

Genevieve could feel little pinpricks of anger rising on the back of her neck. She had not come here for a catfight, even if Amy seemed to be itching for one. 'Look, what happened between me and Riley is history. He went back to you didn't he? That must tell you something. I just want what is rightfully mine.'

'Which is what exactly?' growled Amy.

'Look,' said Genevieve, trying to calm the situation somewhat. She could sense other mourners around them, including Caitlyn Rich, beginning to stare over at their heated exchange. A bitch fest at a funeral would do neither of them any favours. And the last person she would want to upset was Lily's poor mother.

'Can we meet? Away from here? There's a park I know on the other side of Manchester, near my mother's house. Can we meet there? There's a coffee house. I could meet you this afternoon, at say, two o'clock. It's important.' She handed a slip of paper to Amy, the location of the park written upon it.

Amy knew she didn't really have any choice. Genevieve obviously had something to say. 'I haven't spoken to Riley, you know, Genevieve. I don't know where he is. I don't have anything more to say to you.'

'No, but I have something to say to you. Something you need to know. Will you meet me?'

'Okay, I'll be there.'

'Fine ... and thank you.' Amy didn't get the chance to ask what she was being thanked for as Genevieve turned on her heel and disappeared out of view, the sound of her heels clipping against the crematorium pathway tarmac.

CHAPTER 60
Now, 2015

Jarrett Smith loved the fact that people were talking about him. It caused his chest to swell with a sense of pride, his ego to inflate with the joyful knowledge that yet again he was the main man.

What was it that his late mum, Violet, the silver-haired matriarch who had ruled over Jarrett and his dealings with a hard face and an even harder attitude, used to say? 'Jarrett, if someone spends a week talking about you and a week thinking about you then they've done a fortnight's fucking good work.' As far as Mother Smith was concerned all press was good press.

Violet had also instilled in him the belief that no task was beyond completion, that there was no problem that could not be solved. And for the last few years Jarrett had lived with one baffling conundrum that kept rising to the surface of his thoughts like a dead goldfish in a bowl of disease-ridden water. What had happened to his son, Weston? Violet wouldn't have stopped until she'd found out exactly what fate had befallen her grandson, no matter who she had to cross, trample over and snuff out to get there. It was another thing that Jarrett had learnt well. Which is why he'd taken action ...

Standing outside Dirty Cash, Jarrett knew he had to be quick. In, out, in the car and off. That was how it was to be. Two of his most promising specimens, protégés from his team back in London, had joined him and the three of them had headed to the casino together. The two men, eager to please, flanked Jarrett as he walked through Dirty Cash's foyer and into the main gaming area. All three men knew what they were looking for ... or rather, *who*. It was Jarrett who spotted him first.

Jarrett motioned to one of the men to return to the car, while he and the other headed over to their prey. The casino was relatively quiet, just a few die-hards playing at the machines and tables. Jarrett was careful not to draw attention to himself, his movements as stealth-like as possible. He felt for the gun in his pocket and withdrew it, drawing it into his palm, his finger slipping expertly around the trigger. It was loaded, ready to use if need be.

Within seconds, like a trap-door spider springing forth from its burrow ready to devour the most innocent of baby birds, Jarrett was upon his target.

He jammed the gun into the man's ribs and whispered in his ear. 'You make one noise, one false move and this gun blows your insides all over that far wall, you get it?'

The terrified yelp from the man's throat told Jarrett he did.

'Now, just come with me and do as I say if you want to live to see another Christmas, okay?'

Jarrett's henchman pushed the petrified soul towards the door. He knew it was his cue to walk. A tight knot of fear gripped him as the two men, Jarrett's gun still jammed into his side, made sure that there was no way he could stray from their chosen path. He felt like he couldn't breathe, any attempt to fill his lungs with air becoming stuck, as if barbed, within his throat.

Out in the cold open air, his panic rose as the door of a car opened, its engine already purring, a cone of dark grey erupting from the exhaust pipe. His head was pushed down roughly and he was forced into the back seat. The man with the gun joined him, making sure that the weapon never lost contact with the young man's casino uniform.

The other man slammed the door and ran around the car to sit in the front passenger seat. He was barely seated before the word 'go' was bellowed from the man in the back. As the car sped off, a screech filling the air and the rapid movement of the tyres blackening the road, the young man knew that he was in deep trouble. Dread gripped him in every pore of his body as he looked into the eyes of the man alongside him. They were eyes without mercy. Even a naive lad from North Wales whose closest brush to danger before now had been recklessly defying a lifeguard and swimming in stormy Irish seas could see that. They were dark, soulless eyes without any hint of compassion.

Jimmy could feel the coppery, metallic taste of blood running into his mouth as yet again the force of one of Jarrett's henchmen's fists slammed into the side of his face. It diluted with the tears that had been freefalling from his eyes.

Jimmy had no idea how long he'd been tied to the chair he was sitting on, his hands roped behind his back, his legs bound equally tightly at his ankles. It could have been minutes, it could have been hours, it could have been days for all he knew. He'd been drifting in and out of consciousness so often that he barely knew his own name any more.

'I've told you, I don't know anything about your son, I don't.' His pitiful sobs had been on repeat, as had his story, ever since he'd first started being interrogated. He stared around at the brick walls surrounding him. A warehouse, he guessed. The dilapidated walls, a mass of chipped white paint and natural brickwork, reminded him of the municipal swimming baths in Llandudno where he'd grown up. A place where he'd been able to laugh, to splash around, to play with his friends. It was a happy place. How ironic that he should think of that now, when he was sure that the room where he sat was the place where he was certain to die.

'Then I'll ask you again, until you tell me the truth, won't I?' barked Jarrett, walking around Jimmy, circling his victim like a vulture over a rotting carcass. 'My son disappeared in Manchester, I'm sure it had something to do with your employer, Tommy Hearn, and Riley Hart, who just happens to be the man who was married to your lunchtime date, Amy, recently. You can understand why I might think that you know more than you're letting on, Jimmy.' Jarrett's voice became more deafening with every word, his usage of Jimmy's name as he spat his words portraying more than a hint of exasperation.

'We can stay here all day and all night if we have to. You're not going anywhere until you tell me everything you know. As long as there's breath in your body, Jimmy, then there's breath to tell me the truth, isn't there?' He cracked his knuckles as he talked, the noise magnified within the room.

Jarrett stopped directly in front of Jimmy and crouched down onto his heels so that his face was directly in line with his quarry. 'It's such a pity too, isn't it?' Jarrett placed his hand on the boy's bloody chin and rotated his face from side to side. 'Such a handsome lad, I thought that when I followed you from that sandwich shop. You'd have broken a lot of birds' hearts in the future. Pity you became mixed up with the wrong one. Such a fucking shame.' His eyes narrowed in mock pity as he spoke. 'Now, tell me again, what did Amy Hart say to you about my son?'

Jimmy had told Jarrett and his henchmen all that he knew. He had no more to say. 'I don't know her that well. She came into the casino for a job she said, but she was thrown out by the bosses. She came back to see me and asked me to keep an ear to the ground about things that went on there, but honestly I don't know anything. I swear to you. I fancied her, what can I say, she's a good looking girl and I thought I was doing her a favour ...'

Jimmy's words were cut off as another crack landed squarely, this time a punch aimed at his stomach. It was Jarrett who had delivered it, having risen to his feet for maximum force. 'A favour!' Jarrett's face was twisted with rage as he spoke, flecks of spit flying from his lips. 'A favour! She's done you no favours, sunshine. Far from it. She's put you slap bang in the middle of one of the biggest fuck-ups I've ever known. Somebody has taken my son away from me. Somebody connected with the woman doing you a favour. I can't rest until I know exactly what's happened to him, and if you're able to point me in the right direction then I am going to keep torturing you until we've pulled every last detailed piece of info out of you like a winkle from its fucking shell!'

Jarrett stopped. For a moment the only sounds that filled the air were distressed sobs as Jimmy tried to catch his breath again. A viscous line of snot ran down from one of his nostrils. He attempted to sniff it back up. 'I don't know anything.' It was barely more than a whisper. 'I was just listening out for Amy. Just being an ear for her.'

'Just being an ear. That's all you are to her, eh? Well, we'll see, shall we? See if she thinks of you as more than that.'

Jarrett reached inside his jacket and pulled out a penknife from his inside breast pocket. He opened one end to reveal a short, stubby blade. He ran his finger lightly over the edge of it and turned his fingertip towards Jimmy. A thin line of red blood began to appear. A drop formed and started to loop its way down Jarrett's finger. Before it could go too far, Jarrett placed his finger in his mouth and sucked away the blood. 'It's a sharp fucking knife. Goes straight through flesh ... no problem at all.'

Jimmy's eyes opened wider in horror as he contemplated what was about to happen. He shook his bound hands and ankles with as much energy as his tired body could muster, causing the chair he was seated on to move slightly. 'No, please, I beg you ...'

Jarrett signalled to his two henchmen to hold Jimmy still. They did so with ease, their combined force extinguishing any flame of fight left within Jimmy.

'You're Amy Hart's ear? Let's see.' Jarrett moved behind Jimmy and pressed the young man's head firmly against his jacket. He ran the cold blade against Jimmy's cheek, letting its short length rub against the flesh. Jimmy was unable to see what was happening with Jarrett standing behind him but he knew what to expect. Out of the corner of his eye he saw a glint of reflection from the blade of the knife as the light within the room hit it. He heard a swishing sound as the blade passed quickly alongside his face and for a moment there was silence. Nothing but complete and utter silence.

Then the pain began. A searing slash of agony shot through the right side of his face and heavy rivers of blood sped down his cheek. Jimmy screamed, writhing in the worst pain he had ever experienced. He was still screaming when Jarrett reappeared in front of him, a demonic smile plastered across his face. In one hand he held the penknife, in the other was Jimmy's severed ear.

CHAPTER 61
Then, 2013

The sight of Rio de Janeiro's *Christ The Redeemer* through their helicopter window took Amy's breath away. It was a spectacle that she had longed to see ever since she had first heard about the enormous statue as a little girl, and as their transportation flew around the tip of the Art Deco masterpiece she reached out and squeezed Riley's hand in excitement, a tiny squeal of exuberance escaping from her lips.

It was mixed with a tinge of sadness. 'My mum and dad would have loved to have seen this. It's such an amazing sight.' It had been about six years since her parents had died and there still wasn't a day that Amy didn't think about them and about how her life with Riley was all they had ever wanted for her; to find happiness with a good man. She counted her blessings despite everything she had gone through.

Amy had to shout to make herself heard from underneath her helicopter ear protectors and above the sound of the engine. 'How on earth it was built on top of this mountain is beyond me. Viva Brazil for getting it up there, say I!' Amy couldn't quite take in just how massive the statue was.

'Well, it's been up there since 1931,' smiled Riley, his own voice equally loud. 'I don't have a religious bone in my body, but that is one pretty impressive erection.' He smiled, knowing exactly where the quip would take the conversation.

'Just like yours last night,' said Amy, giving Riley's knee a squeeze. The only other person sharing the helicopter they were flying in above the Rio skyline was the pilot and judging from his limited English when they boarded the flight, they were pretty sure he couldn't really tell what they were saying. 'And as for being religious, you were definitely giving me a few "oh my God's" back on the beach last night if I remember rightly.'

'Can you blame me? You were on fire last night,' said Riley.

He was right. Amy didn't know whether it was the tropical, exotic, exciting heat of the Brazilian weather or the sight of Riley wearing a figure hugging wet T-shirt – they had been caught in one of Brazil's intense fifteen minute downpours as they wandered back to their hotel along Ipanema beach, swaying slightly after an evening of *caipirinhas*, Brazil's favoured cocktail, a rather heady blend of sugar, lime and *cachaça*, Brazil's most common distilled alcohol.

The heavens had opened and so, apparently, had the floodgates of Amy's libido.

The sky was already almost black, the virtually pure ebony that only a tropical stormy sky can give and stained with a coating of rain-soaked clouds. The lovers ran along the sidewalk, leaping between the puddles that had already began to form due to the storm. A lightning crack illuminated the air, highlighting the beauty and serenity of the beach and the proud mountains that gazed down across Ipanema. Mountains that just hours before had looked upon a mass of hot, oiled bodies feeling the intensity of the Brazilian sunshine as they lay on the powder fine sand enjoying the rays. Amy and Riley had been two of them, their skin turning a vision of gold with the heat.

Now it was clear that they were both experiencing a heat of a different kind as the once full beach lay empty in the downpour. Despite the rain, the air was still warm and Amy pulled Riley to a halt as they ran, making it clear that she wanted to go no further. She brought her husband towards her and placed her hands against his chest, feeling the swell of his pecs underneath the now sodden T-shirt he was wearing. The outline of his nipples was evident through the thin cotton. Amy let her fingertips skim over them and looked up into Riley's eyes. Without saying a word she said everything that needed to be said. The smile that curved itself across Riley's face showed that he was in total agreement.

Taking him by the hand, the rain still lashing down onto their bodies, Riley and Amy leapt down onto the beach. They immediately jettisoned their Havaianas, enjoying the feel of the moist sand underneath their feet. Neither of them knew where they were going but a sixth sense between them guided them to their destination. They ran together to an area of the beach far enough away from the sidewalk to be out of sight from other tourists crazy enough to be out in the deluge, but close enough to the ocean for them to hear the crashing of the waves as the surf met the sand.

Amy immediately tore at Riley's T-shirt, pulling the material over his head. His hair, thick and black, clung against his face, swirling its way down his forehead. He pushed it back, his bicep flexing as he did so. The mere glimpse of it in the moonlit storm turned Amy on even more then she already was. She undid the buttons on the loose cotton blouse she was wearing and threw it onto the sand. She was already braless and Riley immediately swooped to take her firm young breasts in his hands, raising the peaks of her nipples upwards before taking one of them in his mouth. A thunderclap sounded overhead as Riley bit down gently onto one of her buds. Amy heard nothing but her own ecstasy.

Lowering his wife onto the sand Riley undid the belt on her cut-off denim shorts and manoeuvred the wet material down her legs. Her panties followed. She lay there naked, staring up at her god of a husband as she removed his own shorts and jockey pants. His cock was already standing to attention, as proud and as impressive as the statue staring down at them atop the Rio mountains. A zig-zag of lightning cracked across the sky again, followed shortly by a powerful roar of thunder. The storm was almost directly overhead. There was no way the two of them should have been outside in such weather conditions, but there was something about the storm and the sheer organic feel of the rain against their lustful flesh that both electrified them and magnified their already unstoppable desire. It was as if Amy could feel the thunder moving through her. There was a brutality in her need for Riley to make love to her. For someone who had spent most of her life being Little Miss Perfect, Amy adored those moments when she needed to be Little Miss Perfectly Filthy.

Reaching up to take Riley's girth in her hand, she felt the hard flesh throb. The heat between her legs, already wet from the storm, became even wetter with her own need for her husband. She could feel the sand clinging to her flesh and she guided her man by his cock down onto the sand with her. Another lightning bolt filled the sky. They were alone on the beach, but Amy was oblivious. There could have been a coachload of redneck American tourists looking on at the wonderment of Riley and Amy's bodies as they prepared for unity and Amy wouldn't have been able to stop herself. The mix of *caipirinhas*, the warm rain against her skin and the heat she was feeling from her unquenchable thirst for Riley's cock inside her were a hypnotic fusion.

Amy lay back and raised her hips off the sand and guided Riley's eager flesh into her. A few grains of sand rubbed against the tender skin of her own sex as his member slid inside her sweet folds. She let out a gasp of delight as she felt his satisfaction fill her, the rumble of the storm exciting her further as she took his length. She raised her hips even more, eager to attempt to gain more of him inside her, bucking and whimpering as she did so.

Amy could feel her pussy twitching around his cock as Riley started to pump harder, increasing the speed of his strokes. He brought his lips to hers, planting shallow, gentle, teasing kisses upon her, ones that he knew from experience would arouse her even more than she already was.

The rain fell harder onto her body, no doubt mixed with the sweat from Riley's own muscular core. She lay under him watching her lover savour every moment as he worshipped her body. Just as she felt her own orgasm mounting, a carnival of wondrous explosions igniting between her legs, Riley took one of her ankles and raised it up into the air, resting it at his shoulder level, altering his position about forty-five degrees without withdrawing his cock from her pussy. He was almost sideways to her as he plunged his hardness back into her, her hips askew. Amy let out a scream, masked as another symphony of thunder sounded in her ears. The granules of sand that had worked their way inside her and the hyper-sensitivity of her pussy took her to new heights as Riley's masterful fucking brought her to the edge. She dug her fingers into the wet sand and heard the waves crashing onto the beach as her own sexual waves of desire erupted. As she peaked, Riley's own rapturous orgasm thundered inside her.

Amy felt as if they were at one with the storm. Another thunderclap sounded and a lightning flash decorated the sky again, almost simultaneously. The storm was directly overhead, the thunder and lightning coming together as she and her husband just had. A symmetry of climax and climate.

Riley remained inside her for the longest time as they lay on the beach, holding each other in their arms. It was a moment that neither of them ever wanted to end.

Amy stared up at the outline of *Christ the Redeemer* on the skyline and drew her husband into her, whispering 'I love you' as she did so. She needed him to know. She was so lucky to have him in her life. As they lay there under the Brazilian sky it was a perfect moment.

It was a moment that Amy was thinking about as she walked to meet Genevieve in the cold Manchester air. She would not let what she now knew about the fashionista and her husband, or indeed what she knew about Riley and his sordid affair with the late Lily Rich, stain her memories. People may change, but memories don't.

Memories like the beautiful ones she had shared with Riley in Brazil, South Africa, Spain, France, and every single perfect moment of their married life and home life together were turning into snapshots that she was becoming increasingly unsure how to deal with. Since Riley's letters and especially since his anger-inducing reappearance they were nuggets of beauty that she sometimes dared to reflect upon but at other times would only allow herself a fleeting glimpse at. She was rapidly learning that with each and every day and with each and every revelation that was hurtling her way she was having to find the perfect spirit-strengthening balance between the fondness of the memory and the inner pain that it could produce.

But Amy was now certain of one thing. No matter what was around the corner she wouldn't let anyone trample over memories that she once held so precious.

CHAPTER 62
Now, 2015

'I'm not going to plead for forgiveness, Amy. That's not why we're here. Riley was the married one, I was a free agent when we were together.'

Genevieve ran her manicured finger around the top of her coffee mug as she spoke. There was no remorse in her voice. Her tone was clinical and calculating. It was no more than Amy had expected. She'd never liked the woman and still held the opinion that she would be more than capable of being a top-of-the-list suspect in the mystery of Riley's 'death'.

'You can be sure that I'll be mentioning the fact that my husband couldn't keep his dick in his pants when I eventually get to speak to him.' Amy's tone was equally devoid of emotion as she dropped a lump of sugar into her own drink.

The two women had been involved in a volley of snipped, bitchy conversation ever since they'd seated themselves within the coffee house. Amy had followed Genevieve's instructions and arrived dead on two o'clock. Despite her dislike for the woman, something had told Amy that she needed to meet her.

'I wasn't going to come. But you *were* on Riley's list of people who might have wanted him dead, so I guess I owe it to myself to try and see just how likely it was that you wanted him bumped off.'

'You can't really believe that, can you? I may be many things, Amy, but a killer isn't one of them.' Genevieve felt a sudden chill pass over her as she momentarily thought about how close she'd been to killing when she'd pointed a gun at Riley. Maybe Amy's thought that she could be so capable wasn't that ridiculous after all.

'You weren't my first choice. You'd have so much to lose with your business and everything. But you are a hard bitch, that's for sure, and now I know you were sleeping with Riley ... well, a woman who's been dumped by a man is capable of anything in the way of revenge, is she not?'

'There are a million people out there who had more reason to see Riley dead than me. I may not have been his biggest fan in the end but he's more use to me alive.'

'I only have your word for that, and forgive me if that doesn't exactly count for a lot from where I'm sitting, Genevieve.' Amy could feel her bile rising. 'You've not exactly been the most truthful person.'

'You want more than just my word. You want the truth? Then I think it's about time you found out, don't you?' There was defiance in Genevieve's voice. Whatever she had to say, it was clear that she was not going to take anything lying down. 'I'm not the bad guy in all of this, despite what you think. Riley is. So what if I was having an affair with him? So what if he was quite happy to climb into bed with me because he wasn't satisfied at home? That's not my problem. You told me this morning that he was shagging poor Lily so it's obviously not a one-off.'

Genevieve's words were stinging Amy, scorpion-like, but her inner anger strengthened her fight. For a split second she considered the possibility that if she'd been more of a wife to Riley then maybe he wouldn't have strayed into the open arms of other women. But she rightly pushed the thought away. In an ocean of doubt, the one thing she could be sure of was that she'd always been a good wife to Riley. If he'd chosen to stray it was of his own doing, his own pathetic weakness, not because of any lack of attention in the marital bed. He had never wanted for her love.

'So, what is the truth? Why am I here?' asked Amy.

'Because it's time. Come with me. I'll show you the truth.' Genevieve rose from the table and walked towards the door. Amy knew she had to follow despite the confusion stalling her brain.

Amy followed Genevieve out of the coffee house and along the path that led away from it down a gentle slope to a play area at the bottom. It was empty apart from two small children playing on a see-saw under the watchful eye of their mother and a lady in a heavy overcoat pushing a pram.

Neither of the women uttered a word until Genevieve stopped and sat herself down on a bench in the play area. It was a perplexed Amy who spoke first. 'Just what the hell are we doing here? I think both of us are a little too old for swings and climbing frames, aren't we?'

'I have somebody I want you to meet,' said Genevieve. She beckoned to the woman with the pram who wheeled it over towards where she and Amy were sitting. Amy could see that the woman must have been around retirement age.

Amy stayed silent, uncertain of what to say or how to react.

'Amy, this is my mother. Mum, this is Amy Hart.'

'Hart as in Riley?' The words fell from Genevieve's mother's lips before Amy had even had a chance to exchange pleasantries.

'Yes, I was his wife ... still am. Why, did you know him too?'

Genevieve raised her hands as if to silence the two women. 'She's heard of him, Amy. I've talked about him.' She pointed to the pram. 'This is Emily.'

Amy leant over to look inside the pram. The cutest angelic face gazed at her, wrapped up warmly against the winter air. She couldn't help but smile and wave at the bundle of joy gurgling happily.

'She's my daughter, Amy. She's two years of age.'

'She's adorable, but why are you ...' Suddenly the penny dropped. Actually not so much a penny as a whole bag of loose change. Amy stared down at the child once again. Those eyes, that nose, there were similarities.

'No, you're not telling me she's ...' Amy's words trailed off, afraid to say the words out loud.

Validation. Genevieve completed the sentence. 'She's Riley's.'

'Are you sure?' Amy really didn't need to ask. The roundness of the nose, the dimpling of the chin. The evidence was there.

'I'm sure. Riley was the only man I was sleeping with when I fell pregnant. And Emily does look like him. Plus there's this ...' Genevieve turned to her mother who produced a folded sheet of paper from inside the pram. 'It's the birth certificate.'

Amy unfolded the sheet, a photocopy, and scanned her eyes across the details. Riley's name was listed as Emily's father.

'Did Riley know?' questioned Amy.

'Oh yes, he knew all right. But he didn't care. He wanted nothing to do with her. I wanted money from him to help raise his daughter and all I received was the odd handout or useless present. I was going to take him to court for maintenance payments but I didn't. You may ask why. I think we all know your husband's rogue dealings in life, Amy. He could have been pretty persuasive in making me reconsider. Bricks through windows, friends and loved ones being followed by menacing strangers. You get my drift? Plus, to be honest, I didn't want to put you through it. I'm really not sure why, that's so out of character for me. But then, of course, he died.'

Amy remained silent.

Genevieve's tone, although briefly smudged with caring, became cold and beyond matter of fact as she spoke again. 'Except he didn't, did he? Emily's dad is still alive.'

'No, he ... er, didn't ...' faltered Amy. She was looking directly into Genevieve's eyes as she spoke. There was a love there. Maybe no longer a love for Riley, but there was definitely a mother's love. It was the first time she actually believed that Genevieve had nothing to do with Riley's shooting and the events surrounding Laura's death. No mother would try to kill the father of her own child, surely. Nobody would want their daughter to grow up without a dad. Had she known about Genevieve's attempt to shoot Riley, Amy would have seen the irony in her thoughts.

'I really thought you might have been behind the shootings. You're such a hard woman. Colder than December. But you want him alive, don't you? You couldn't kill him. You haven't got it in you.'

Genevieve turned to her mother. 'Can you take Emily back to the car, Mum.' It was a statement rather than a question. 'I'll be along in a few minutes. I need to speak to Amy.'

Genevieve's mother turned the pram on its wheels and started to push it away from the women.

'There are certain things I do not want my mother to hear, Amy. I didn't try to kill Riley, no. God knows there have been times when I could have done. I wanted him and he went running back to you. I don't know why, I never will. But I'm telling you this. Even if he sees my time with him as no more than some cheap affair like he had with Lily or fuck knows who else, I will not be fobbed off with nothing in return. He left me with a baby. And that means that I'm entitled to money. Money for his daughter, *our* daughter.' She stressed the word *our*, emphasising the one-time bond between her and Riley.

'So why are you telling me this?' asked Amy.

'Because if Riley's back he'll be back for you. That is certain. I don't know why Amy but he saw something in you that no other woman could compare to. I don't know why he'd choose you over me but he did and even though I wouldn't change a thing about having Emily, if Riley is back on the scene and you two end up together then I want the regular payments I'm entitled to. You can tell him that from me. I hope you find out who killed your friend Laura, I do. I hope whichever poor bastard died instead of Riley gets to rest in peace but if I don't start seeing the cash from Riley then I will not hesitate to make both his life and yours a living hell. Now, if you'll excuse me, my mother and daughter are waiting.'

It wasn't until Genevieve walked out of view that the full effect of what she had just said hit Amy. If she and Riley ever were to become as one again, there would always be a third party in their relationship and that would be his daughter from a somewhat squalid and deceitful affair.

CHAPTER 63
Now, 2015

Tommy's mind felt like a *piñata*. One strategically placed hit and all of its contents would come flying out. It was rammed to every last corner with thoughts that just a few short days ago hadn't been there. So much had changed in such a minimal space of time. And there was no doubt in Tommy's mind that he was reaching a volatile breaking point. He was spinning out of control.

What had happened to the glory days where he was proud to stand alongside Cazwell Hart? Everything had seemed so effortless back then. If a problem needed solving, it would be solved. Without question. No fuss, no nonsense, just action. Cazwell was a master of his trade, the king of his locale. Those had been the halcyon days all right. Working alongside his idol. But with his unbecoming weak and feeble death had come change and as Tommy sat in his office at Dirty Cash staring at the calendar on his office wall, all he could think was that Cazwell's death had been where the rot had started to set in. Just a few years earlier.

Riley Hart had caused the rot. Cazwell's once-great empire had begun to crumble under its new owner, foolish decisions had been made and it had been down to Tommy to try and pick up the pieces, both financially and professionally. He'd done it all, as requested, in memory of Cazwell, just so the Hart family name could live on in gangland history. He'd bailed out the errant son time and time again to preserve the dynasty, in order to stop Riley's canker from destroying the strong roots of the Hart family tree.

He'd been glad when Riley had died. There, he'd said it. He hadn't been sorry to see him go. Life was easier. Tommy and Jemima gained everything, Tommy had made sure of that. Tommy would never know what Cazwell would have thought of it all. He hoped he would have understood why he'd done what he needed to do to make sure that he and Jemima were catered for.

Jemima. They'd been so strong, or so Tommy had thought. They'd been able to cope with everything together. The laughter and the tears. It was to have been their names which would be spoken of with respect throughout Manchester. How had he been so blind?

People would say that Cazwell had taught him well. But now, the whole world was probably laughing at him. Word had doubtless spread that the reason behind Jemima's death was because of her love for Winston Curtis; because of Tommy's failure as a husband.

Riley was back. Word had spread about that too. He'd been seen. If it was true, that changed everything for Tommy. Anything he'd been left in the dead man's will would revert back to a very much alive Riley. Tommy would be left with nothing. The loss of Dirty Cash would be added to the loss of Jemima ... what else was there? He'd be left with nothing but memories.

And now Jarrett Smith was in town, seemingly hell-bent on revenge. He'd killed Lily ... Tommy knew it. He could feel it in the pit of his stomach. Maybe he knew about Adam's involvement in Weston's death? Maybe he knew about Riley's. Nobody was safe anymore. They were all guilty by association. Jarrett was getting closer. Too close for comfort. That very morning had proven it. One of his staff had told him. He cast his mind back to the conversation.

'Boss, can I have a word?' It had been Lester, one of his more reliable bar workers.

'Shoot.' Tommy had been in no mood for meaningless chat.

'Jimmy's gone off now. That means we're another pair of hands down.'

'Gone off? Where's he gone? Not another one who's decided to fuck off home early for Christmas? If he has I'll fire the little prick anyway!' Tommy had had enough of his staff disappearing without so much as an explanation.

'I don't think so, some blokes came in here earlier and they seemed to march him off. I can't be sure but I think one of them had a gun. Jimmy looked petrified.'

Tommy froze in horror at the mention of the word gun. 'What did the man with the gun look like? Can you describe him?'

Lester did. There was no doubt, the man was Jarrett Smith. But what the hell did he want with Jimmy? Tommy didn't need to guess. He already knew. Jarrett would be circling around Tommy, killing off those around him. Jimmy was clearly a warning to Tommy that Jarrett was back. The poor boy was probably already dead, his body face-down in a Manchester canal or his head spiked on some inner city railing, displayed as a gangland trophy.

Everything was moving in on Tommy. Jemima's death, Riley's reappearance, Jarrett abducting his staff from under his own roof, Amy's interfering. Tommy felt out of control. What would Cazwell do if he'd still been alive? He wouldn't have let this all get the better of him. No way. He'd react.

Tommy needed to finish the job in hand. To emulate his former employer. Live up to Cazwell's legacy and to end what had already been started. What did he have to lose? If he did nothing, then he could end up losing everything. Slipping on his coat, Tommy grabbed his gun from the top drawer of his desk, checked it was fully loaded with bullets and left Dirty Cash. Some new ideas had just squeezed themselves into his already overloaded brain and he was determined to put them into action.

CHAPTER 64
Now, 2015

'Would you care for another drink while you're waiting, madam?'

Tempting though it was, Dolly had already downed two rather generous gin and tonics and a third would not have been an overly wise idea. She dismissed the waiter with a shake of her head. She needed to keep her thoughts treading the precarious tightrope line between Dutch courage and perfect definition. She had things to say and she was hoping that she'd be able to verbalise them sooner rather than later.

Dolly had spent the last two hours sitting patiently in the lobby of Amy's hotel. Sitting there was alien to her. There had been many occasions when she'd breezed through the very same Reception, heading off to one of the hotel's eight floors in order to satisfy another eager client, but today was different. This wasn't about lying on her back and thinking of England, this was about standing up and being counted. Dolly needed to do everything she could.

It was another twenty minutes before Amy pushed her way through the hotel's revolving door and into the Reception. She was wrapped up against the winter cold but even hidden under her hat and scarf, Dolly could see that she'd been crying.

Dolly rose from her seat and grabbed Amy's arm as she walked past, making sure that she had her attention. The wide-eyed expression on Amy's face portrayed more than a modicum of surprise. After their last meeting she hadn't expected to see the prostitute again. She was not totally displeased to see her.

'Oh, hello ... what are you doing here?' Amy pulled off her hat and unhooked her scarf from around her neck. 'I thought I'd made myself clear. I have nothing to give you, Dolly, even if I wanted to.'

'I know. I'm not here for that,' said Dolly. 'I've been thinking a lot since we met and I figure I have a way that both of us could come out of this with at least some kind of positivity. You've been used as much as I have. I'm sorry I asked you for money. I didn't realise everything that had happened. It just seemed the easiest thing to do. I now know it's not.'

Amy believed her. Despite everything, there was something about Dolly she liked. There was a real air of genuineness about her. She obviously did what she did to make life better for herself and if Amy could help her with that then her own sixth sense and sisterhood spirit told her to listen to what the woman had to say.

Dolly began. 'Can we talk, Amy? I have an idea about what we should do. Why don't we sit down? You look like you could share a few problems yourself. You've obviously not had the best of days.'

'It's not been good, but then none of them are lately, to be honest.' Amy rubbed her eyes. 'Look, why don't you order us both a drink, and I'll just go and tidy up a bit in the bathroom. And tell the waiter to put them on my account, okay. This one's on me,' she said, giving a weak smile.

Dolly sat herself back down and beckoned to one of the hotel staff to order some drinks. She hadn't been sure how Amy would react to seeing her again, but the smile put her at ease. Something inside her, call it female intuition, was sure that she and Amy could make a perfect team.

Flicking through page after page of his script for a forthcoming episode of *Ward 44*, Grant was not exactly learning his lines. In fact, for an actor who prided himself on usually being able to memorise the dialogue of Dr Eamonn Samms with an almost photographic memory, Grant was hardly taking in a word.

He was missing 'the team' he'd inadvertently formed with Amy during their brief time together. His mind was racing with thoughts of how soon it would be before maybe they could be together again.

But Amy had shit to sort out, that was clear. She needed to see Riley, work out what was left of their ghost of a marriage and to see if anything could rise, phoenix-like, from the already lukewarm embers of her trust in her husband. Grant knew that for now he would have to take a back seat. But taking a back seat to that man had always irked him, ever since their schooldays together. The man was bad through and through, he could have told Amy that. Always happy to crush and abuse others. He didn't deserve happiness with anybody.

But now wasn't the time to charge in and say so. He knew what he wanted to say to Amy, how he wanted to hold her, but until the moment was right, there was no point in even considering what might be. For now, Grant would have to wait, to be patient and to not run before he could walk.

Trying to push all thoughts of Riley, and more importantly Amy, from his mind, Grant focused back on the script in his hand. But something told him that the dramatic medical actions of Dr Samms were going to remain a complete mystery to him for a long time yet.

Amy couldn't quite believe what Dolly was suggesting to her.

'You seriously think we should take the information about the body underneath Dirty Cash directly to Jarrett Smith? The man is a crazed criminal.'

'And so are half the people you and I hang out with, including your absent-without-leave husband, Amy. And from where I'm sitting, I'd say you and I are in a pretty strong position to bargain.'

'He'd kill us ... the man is an animal.' Amy wasn't convinced that Dolly had thought the idea through.

'Why would he? We'd be giving him the information he needs about his dead son. All the man would have to do is pay us for it. He may be a psychotic nutcase but he's bound to be a businessman too. We'd be on his side in this, finally laying to rest an emotional struggle he's lived with for years. Solving the mystery of what happened to his son, Weston.'

Amy still wasn't won over, despite Dolly's certainty. 'But we'd be condemning Adam and Riley. I don't give a shit about Adam but Riley is still my husband, the man I loved.' Amy stopped herself, suddenly aware that she'd used the past tense. 'That I love ...' Her words were far from assertive. Her uncertainty made her think. Again the perfect memories of days gone by washed through her mind. But that was another lifetime now, and maybe one with a person she could never relate to again. There could never be a repeat performance, as the channel had changed. Had it changed beyond all hope? She was still unsure.

'So, we play down Riley's part in it all. Stick all the blame on Adam. If Riley is still alive and you want to be with him then that's up to you, only you can decide that, but we walk away with a cash hand out from Jarrett Smith and he gains closure and the chance to wreak punishment on Adam. We both need money, Amy. I want to start a new life. I'm fed up of parting my legs for a living.'

There was more than a ripple of sense in what Dolly was saying. 'And you'd gladly screw Adam over? Jarrett would kill him, you know that.'

Without a hint of remorse, Dolly replied. 'How many people do you think Adam Rich has killed in his life? Dozens of them, hundreds for all I know. An eye for an eye and all that. If that's what it takes for you and me to come out of all this with the chance of a new life, then so be it.'

Amy hated to admit it but Dolly's idea, harsh though it seemed, was winning her over. 'But there's a chance that Jarrett won't pay up and then we're back at square one. He could kill us.'

'I'm willing to take the chance, Amy. My life is pretty fucked up as it is. If this is my one chance to improve myself then, d'you know what, I'm happy to take the risk. You should too. And if Adam goes squealing to Jarrett that Riley was involved then it's just his word against ours. I think we can be more convincing. Act the helpless pair of naïve females.'

'But you like Adam, don't you? You'd be condemning him to almost certain death.'

'I like Adam Rich's cash, but that's all, if I'm honest. He'll be trading me in for a younger model before too long anyway. She'll be the one getting humped to pay her rent. And there is the small matter of Adam's wife. Not that they have much of a relationship, judging by some of his pillow talk with me. A bumper pay out from Jarrett means I don't need the likes of Adam any more. I can put all of that behind me. Adam's spent a lifetime fucking me, so I figure it's time I repaid the favour, don't you?'

Amy sat in silence, her brain fizzing at Dolly's proposal. It could work. She needed money – even if she and Riley became one again there was no guaranteeing what state his finances would be in – and Dolly needed money too. Adam would take the rap for Weston's death, Jarrett Smith would be appeased. Riley could remain disconnected from Weston's shooting.

But could she condemn a man to death? That's what Amy would be doing if she agreed to the plan and it worked. From what she'd heard about Jarrett, he'd hardly let Adam off with a slap across the back of the legs. Would Amy be able to be at peace with herself if she had Adam's blood on her hands? He'd looked so crestfallen when she'd seen him earlier at Lily's funeral. As did Caitlyn. If Adam died, that would be the diva's entire family gone within a few days. And Amy had nothing against Caitlyn.

Amy couldn't do it. Her mind was made up. Taking a life would lower her to the level of those around her. To Adam and Tommy and Riley. No, that couldn't happen. She'd not been raised by Enid and Ivor Barrowman to believe that murder was ever a good thing.

'I can't, Dolly. You do it if you want, but I can't. Leave Riley out of this. He didn't pull the trigger, after all, but I can't be a part of this ... I can't send a man to his grave.'

Dolly was not going to take no for an answer. 'But what if he was the man who tried to have Riley bumped off in the first place? You told me Adam was one of Riley's suspects. I wouldn't put it past him. He had so much to gain by having Riley dead, didn't he? The secret of Jarrett's son died forever with Riley.'

A fog of confusion spread across Amy's mind. If Adam was behind the plot to kill Riley, then he'd had no qualms about seeing her husband dead, seeing her a widow. Or about seeing her without a best friend. Even if Riley hadn't died that night, Laura had. If Adam was behind the shootings then maybe making him pay for his sins was the right thing to do. And even if he wasn't, he had admitted within earshot of Dolly that he was indeed the man who had taken Weston's life. How many others had he taken?

Amy's thoughts swung like a pendulum. Maybe Dolly was right?

'We need to find Jarrett Smith, Amy.' Dolly was resolute. 'He's our chance for survival in all of this. We can do this ... you and I ... together. Sisters united and all that ...' Dolly raised her fist in solidarity. 'We just need to find out where he is.'

Before she had a chance to decide what she wanted to do, Amy's thoughts were interrupted by one of the staff from the hotel Reception. It was a middle-aged man carrying a small brown cardboard package in his hand. 'Excuse me, Miss Hart. This package has been left for you. The man over at Reception who left it said it was quite urgent ...'

He handed her the square shaped box.

'Which man?' Amy quizzed as both she and Dolly stared over towards the Reception desk.

'The one wearing the—' The man turned and pointed as he spoke, but his words cut short. 'Oh, he was just there. He's gone. Quite thickset, your kind of age, I would imagine ...'

It was a fruitless description. It could have been anybody. The messenger returned to his post.

'An early Christmas present, maybe?' smirked Dolly.

'Doubtful,' smirked Amy back. The smirk lasted no longer than the time it took her to open the package. It was replaced by a scream, which Amy tried to suffocate as it escaped from her mouth, aware of fellow guests sitting around her.

'What is it?' asked Dolly.

Silently Amy handed the box to Dolly. Placed inside it, on a sea of red tissue paper, was a human ear. The note alongside it read 'Miss Hart, please find enclosed a piece of your friend Jimmy, who might not be hearing "Jingle Bells" with much clarity this Christmas. If you want to make sure the rest of him doesn't end up the same way then I suggest you come and pay me a visit. And no police. Jarrett Smith.'

Listed underneath was the address of a warehouse in one of the industrial parts of Manchester, and a time. Amy was being summoned.

It was a horrified Dolly who spoke first. 'Well, at least we know where to find Jarrett now.'

Amy had made up her mind.

CHAPTER 65
Then, 2015

Seven days before the shootings at The Kitty Kat Club ...

'She isn't really blind, you know. You can tell from the way that she looks at Lionel. And that sculpture looks no more like him than I do. Hashtag loser.'

Amy was enjoying another somewhat highbrow evening in at home with Laura, slumped in front of the television flicking through the music channels on rotation. Having managed to give herself a well-earned night-off from The Kitty Kat – was there really any point in being the boss if you couldn't? – Amy had left Lily in charge and with Riley meeting a client for work, it was left to the two young women to amuse themselves in their favourite way. And that meant slobbing out in PJs, two delivery pizzas and endless bottles of fizz to keep them giggly as they wallowed in musical heaven.

So far the friends had segued their way from discussing Meghan Trainor's ripe booty in her latest video – 'one hundred per cent pure love' stated Laura – to playing Snog Marry Avoid about the collective members of One Direction, Coldplay and Maroon 5. They had critiqued Annie Lennox's eighties Eurythmics hair, Laura deciding that it would look too severe on her own head as she'd look like she was 'wearing a red swimming cap', discussed how good Bruce Springsteen would have been in bed back in the day – 'sweaty and frenzied' were their chosen adjectives – and how at least four out of the five Spandau Ballet members would be worth climbing under the sheets with.

A rather drunk Laura had also been quick to point out that if she ever turned up at The Kitty Kat with hairy armpits 'like that German Red Balloon woman', namely Nena, then Amy would be 'perfectly justified' in blowing her brains out.

'What is that all about?' sniggered Laura, cramming another slice of pizza into her mouth. 'She looks like she's housing a couple of poodles under each arm. It's rank. Top tune though.'

'And very European, Laura,' slurred Amy, the bubbles from her champagne having risen straight to her brain as well. 'It was all the rage on the continent. It was *trés chic!*'

'WWW dot gross! Well, thank Christ it's changed now. If I'd have seen any Fraus at that German spa we went to sporting a bushy pit I'd have had to have words. In this day and age there's no excuse,' sneered Laura. 'I shall continue to take a razor to mine at every opportunity and I suggest you always do too. Despite our love of all things nostalgic, that is a retro chic we can do without. Even Julia Roberts looked far from her normally beautiful self in my opinion when she turned up at that film premiere years back with enough underarm hair on view to crochet a clutch bag. And she is gorgeous!'

Their latest topic of conversation was dissecting the finest details from Lionel Richie's video for 'Hello'. He was a particular favourite of Amy's, always had been, even if his most famous lovefest had been released three years before she was even born. She and Laura were considering seeing him headline at the famed Glastonbury festival in just a few months' time. Amy adored the song, the sentiment behind it pulled at her heartstrings every time she heard it. It was pure enchantment.

'I don't think for one minute she is blind,' said Amy, referencing the leading lady in the video. 'She's an actress, for God's sake. But he loves her and she loves him and she's made that glorious statue of him because she loves how he makes her feel.' Amy was an eternal romantic, especially after bubbles.

'Well, it makes me feel deeply sick. Schmaltzy bag of nonsense. Like anyone would ever make a clay head for a fella, even if he did sing like that. She'd be better off giving him head, not making him one. That wins a bloke over every time.' As ever, Laura was straight to the point, even more so when fuelled by alcohol.

'So, you're telling me you'd never do anything that romantic for the man in your life … if there was one?' smirked Amy.

'I would if it was, say, someone like Blair Lonergan,' said Laura, referencing the trendy US DJ who had played at the opening night of The Kitty Kat. 'He must be hugely connected after all the shit he's done. His name would open doors at all kinds of bars and clubs. We'd be flying all over the place being internationally glamorous. He could have a statue dipped in diamonds if it meant I'd be living in the lap of luxury between time zones.'

Amy wasn't biting. 'Seriously though, when it comes to men don't you wish there was a certain someone in your life to keep you warm at night? Wouldn't you like …' Amy searched for the right words. 'Well, something like me and Riley?'

That old chestnut. Laura had her responses lined up and ready to go. 'A one man woman? Are you mental? I am out there to have fun while I can. You and Riley may be like peas in a pod but it's all very vanilla. All very hearts and flowers and picking out leather sofas. I need a bit more spice with my romance, and by romance I mean sex life.'

'But even you were moved to tears on our wedding day. Well at least you were until you went off to shag that guitarist. That band might be coming to the club by the way. They were on TV last week with their latest track. I told you they were going places.'

'Well, the guitarist certainly did on your wedding night,' sniggered Laura. 'And yes, your wedding day was lovely, but it was joyous because you loved it and that meant I was loving you loving it. But that degree of commitment and emotion is not for me, not yet anyway. I'm like a bee, flitting from flower bed to flower bed collecting nectar wherever I can, and that works for me. You're kind of Anna from *Frozen* and let's just say that I'm much more Ursula from *The Little Mermaid*, shall we? Except without the timber. Now, pass that bottle ...'

Amy relaxed back into the cool comfort of the leather sofa as she refilled Laura's glass. She giggled silently. Laura was right. They were polar opposites in so many ways yet somehow they had always been there for each other. It was a unique bond. Shared loves, shared thoughts, shared joys.

Laura pointed at the remote control which was lying by Amy's side. 'Now, turn this tune up. Everybody is raving about this group. The drummer is just beautiful. He'd get it if I had my way ...'

Sipping on her own bubbles, Laura contemplated just how good her life was – her marriage to Riley, her beautiful home, the successful club and her best friend, Laura. It made her happy. 'What about the lead singer, does he receive the Laura Cash seal of approval?' she asked, gazing at the rather unkempt guy grabbing the microphone and forcing his somewhat unhealthy looking, crooked-toothed grin into the lens.

'Go with that minger? Over my dead body.'

One week later she was just that.

CHAPTER 66
Now, 2015

One of the many things that Tommy had learnt from his years working alongside Cazwell Hart was that if you asked enough questions, eventually you would unearth the answer you were looking for.

There wasn't a pounding headache that couldn't be cured or a gnat of a problem too frustrating to crush. It was just a case of asking the right people. And after decades of underhand dealings in every dingy, graffiti-covered, piss-soaked back street in Manchester, Tommy knew that there was a network of shady low-lives he could hound in order to discover the whereabouts of Jarrett Smith.

The seedy rumble of gossip on the Manchester grapevine had grown ever louder since Jarrett had first been spotted. His notoriety meant instant recognition and a tidal wave of fearful expectation had flushed into every part of the city. It was amazing what you could learn if you pointed a loaded weapon at the right person, and according to more than one snivelling two-bit gangster determined to try and please the big guns, rumour had it that Jarrett and his henchmen were holed up in a warehouse on the far side of Manchester.

The air was dark and heavy with the dank, cold gloom of winter as Tommy approached the warehouse. He'd parked his car as far away from the building as possible to avoid any fears of his arrival being pre-empted and as he moved towards the building the only light capable of highlighting the beads of nervous sweat that had begun to form around his hairline came from a solitary bulb hanging above the main entrance.

The area, once a hive of activity with its smoke-billowing factories and bustling industry had been derelict for years. Tommy knew it well. He'd been there many times with Cazwell back in the nineties and early noughties.

But the familiarity of his surroundings did nothing to quell Tommy's nerves. When he'd been there with Cazwell, he'd always had a role to play, as directed by his boss. Whether it be money to extort, men to recruit or bodies to lose, Cazwell had guided his team with the expertise of a sergeant major leading his troops into battle. Every move had been calculated so that there was no margin for error. Victory was the only option.

But now Tommy was alone – he was leader, front line and lowly private all rolled into one. This was something he needed to do, needed to see for himself. He couldn't trust anyone else to do his dirty work for him. He owed it to Cazwell to put this to rest. If Riley was back then he'd deal with him face to face come the time. He couldn't think about that now. One thing at a time was all his ever-clouding mind could deal with.

Jarrett Smith had made this personal the moment he had stepped back into Manchester, into Dirty Cash and marched one of his staff away at gunpoint. Tommy didn't give a shit about Jimmy, he was nothing more than some daft lad from a nondescript town who worked for him, but he did give a shit about his own reputation and that of the late, great Cazwell. Nobody could stray onto Tommy Hearn's patrolled turf and get away with it.

The handle of the door was rusty and a low, grinding creak sounded as Tommy pulled the large metal door towards him. It was louder than he'd expected and the sudden noise made his already terrified bones jump.

A set of dimly-lit stairs reached out in front of him. It was too dark to see where they ended but as he stood at the bottom of them, carefully moving the door back into place behind him, Tommy strained his ears to hear a mash of voices sounding from the top of the stairs. He couldn't make out any of the sentences, the words muffled by the walls and the heaviness of the night air, but it was clear from their tone that there was more than a hint of anger and emergency about them. There was definitely more than one person, and he couldn't be sure, but one of them at least seemed to be ... no, surely not ... was it? He needed to know.

Certain that he was in the right place, Tommy moved as quietly as he could up the stairs, being careful not to make a sound. He pulled his gun from his pocket and gripped it tightly in his hand. A film of sweat had formed on his palms. Why was he so nervous? He could handle this. He knew he could. He would succeed like Cazwell, not fail like Riley. He had the element of surprise. If it was Jarrett, and he was sure it would be, then supremacy would be Tommy's. But who did the other voices belong to? As he moved up the stairs he could begin to hear them more clearly and yes, he was right. He hadn't been imagining things, one of the voices was female. And he was certain he recognised it as the voice of Amy Hart. *What the fuck was she doing here?*

Wiping the beads of nervous perspiration from his forehead with the back of his hand, Tommy reached the top of the stairs. He wiped his hand on his trousers as he stared through one of the four small, dirty panes of glass encased in the top half of the door separating him from the cavernous, illuminated room beyond. The door was slightly ajar and allowed him to both hear the voices as well as see the figures beyond.

There were six people in the room, all bunched fairly close together but a good thirty yards or so from where he was standing. It would make being able to do the job Tommy had come for more difficult than he'd hoped. He needed a clear shot.

One of the figures was Jarrett. Two of them, both brandishing guns, were obviously his henchmen, one figure, bloodied and slumped to one side, barely alive it would seem, he recognised as his staff member from Dirty Cash. The other two people present were female. One he vaguely recognised, but he couldn't work out where from. As for the other, it was definitely Amy Hart.

Any doubts Amy had allowed into her brain about how to handle the situation with Jarrett Smith had evaporated the moment she had opened the package containing Jimmy's ear. It had suddenly become her mess to sort out and in some strange way had given her a sense of strength. Everyone else who had become embroiled in the whole sorry saga of life since the shootings was Riley's doing – everyone from Genevieve and Grant through to Adam and even Dolly had been involved because of being named in Riley's letter or of their own choosing.

But not Jimmy. That had been Amy's choice. She'd seen that maybe the young lad, obviously sweet on her, could be advantageous to her needs and had chosen to drag him, albeit not exactly kicking and screaming, into the epicentre of her jeopardous world.

He had nothing to do with Riley, no inkling of the world he'd frequented and certainly knew nothing that would warrant him being a danger to Jarrett. But the London criminal was using Jimmy to get to Amy, and it was down to her to try and salvage what she could, for Jimmy's sake. His life, if he still had one, depended upon it.

Dolly had been insistent that she accompany Amy to see Jarrett, a fact that Amy was secretly grateful for. But as the two women vacated the cab that had dropped them off outside the warehouse, Amy was still unsure whether she was being sensible in allowing Dolly to become involved. If it was just a case of money, she could try and coerce a hefty dose of cash from Jarrett on her own and then split the amount with Dolly afterwards. That way Dolly could safely keep her distance. Enough people had already paid a price for their involvement, some with their lives.

'You don't need to do this, Dolly. I can do this on my own and make sure you're looked after,' said Amy. 'I can handle this.' Her voice was full of a bravado that she didn't feel she possessed. Inside, she had never been more scared ... well, not since the night at the club.

'But the whole point is that you don't have to, Amy. Not alone, anyway.' Dolly reached out and took hold of Amy's hand as she spoke. Her skin was cold but the meaning behind her words was clearly warm. 'This is the first thing I've been able to do in a long time that might actually be doing some kind of good. I've spent years taking money from the likes of Adam Rich, knowing full well what kind of man he is. He takes lives, earns money, which I'm very happy to then pocket for sleeping with him. Doesn't that make me as bad as him deep down? At least if I grass him up to Jarrett Smith I might be doing something to restore the balance. Lily wouldn't be dead if it wasn't for him, and maybe not your friend Laura either. Let's do this ... for them.'

There was no more to be said. Keeping hold of Dolly's hand, the two women walked into the warehouse.

Jarrett had not expected to see two women. He knew Amy would come, but this other woman ... who the fuck was she? It was the first thing he'd asked as Amy and Dolly had walked into the room, his gun pointed firmly in Dolly's direction.

As a horrified Amy looked at the battered body of Jimmy tied to the chair, Dolly had remained as cool as a cucumber. 'So you're Jarrett Smith, I assume. You can put that down, soldier,' she said indicating the gun. 'I'm here to be of use to you. The name's Dolly and I'm a friend of Amy's. Where she goes, so do I. Especially as I know what happened to your son. Weston, wasn't it?'

Her attitude, coupled with the mention of his son, disarmed Jarrett momentarily, especially her use of the past tense. Happened. He lowered the gun.

'You know what happened to Weston? Then you tell me, or I shoot Jimmy here straight through the head.' He raised his weapon again and aimed it at the seated, bruised body. Unable to stop herself, Amy rushed over to wrap her arms around the young man, grateful that he was still breathing. A feeble groan tumbled from his lips, and one of his eyes, swollen and purple from where he'd been beaten, opened slightly. There was the merest trace of recognition registered there as he spied Amy.

It broke Amy's heart. 'You leave him alone – he has nothing to do with this. Nothing at all. I have all of the information you need, not him. Hasn't he suffered enough? Look at him, for Christ's sake. He can barely breathe.'

Amy wiped a few long strands of his blond hair, matted with blood, out of his eyes and back across his forehead. An attempt of a smile formed on his lips.

Jarrett indicated to Amy to move away from Jimmy with a flick of the gun. She did so and stood alongside Dolly. She was both angry and scared. She had no idea what Jarrett's next move would be, but one thing was for sure, Amy was not giving up this battle without a fight.

She was about to speak but Dolly beat her to it. 'We have a trade-off. You pay us a substantial amount of money, enough to set up a new life, and we'll tell you exactly where your son's body is. We know where he's buried and we know who put him there.'

'So, Weston's dead.' Despite having known it in his heart for the longest time already, a desperate note of final realisation sounded in Jarrett's voice. For a second he was no longer the hardened gangland criminal, but merely a father mourning for his son. His hand, brandishing the gun, dropped back down to his side, a collage of recollection washing over his face.

'Yes, he is. And we know the man who shot him. So what's the information worth?' said Dolly. Amy couldn't help thinking that either Dolly was an accomplished actress, had an amazing inner strength or she'd been watching too many episodes of *Mad Men*. She seemed to be almost relishing the danger of the situation.

'It's worth me not blowing your brains out,' stated Jarrett. 'Now speak ...'

'And what would that gain you?' asked Amy, bravery rising within her too. 'I've lost nearly everything I've ever had and she just wants a better life than the one she has now.' She cast an apologetic glance at Dolly as she spoke. 'You kill us and we take your son's resting place to the grave with us. Apart from his killer, we're the only ones who know. Where does that get you? It's hardly vindication, is it?'

Jarrett started to pace from side to side, the mechanics of his mind revving into action. His two henchmen, paid to carry weapons and keep their opinions to themselves, merely watched as their boss circled Jimmy and the women.

After what seemed like an age of silence, Jarrett spoke. 'So, what's it going to cost me?'

Dolly was certain that everyone in the room would have simultaneously been able to hear the internal explosion of elation that thundered inside her. Determined not to be undersold, she seized the opportunity. Maybe Jarrett was coming round to their way of thinking. If he was, this was no time for indecision.

'Two hundred and fifty thousand each. We tell you the location of the body now and when the money is deposited in our accounts we tell you who buried it there. Simple. And before you ask us why you should trust us, ask yourself what we've got to gain from duping you. A man of your considerable criminal connections and obvious lack of pity would have us both tracked down and chopped into mincemeat before getting out of bed in the morning. You find out who killed Weston, and we get to start over again. It's a win-win.' Dolly had dealt with men like Jarrett Smith all of her life, even if it was normally with her legs in the air. In her experience it paid to flatter them as much as possible.

Both women waited with baited breath for his response. Amy was glad she hadn't spoken first as she'd never have had the balls to ask for such a hefty sum.

Sam was still pacing. 'So, your information costs me five hundred thousand and I just let you two walk off down the yellow brick road with my money to your new lives ...' He laughed, emphasizing his apparent disbelief at the suggestion. 'And you let me deal with whoever killed my son ... is that it?'

'More or less,' said Amy. 'And you pay Jimmy fifty thousand, too. It's the least you can do after everything you've done to him.'

'You ladies never know when to fucking stop, do you?'

'Those are the conditions, take them or leave them,' voiced Dolly. 'Otherwise your son lies buried for forever and you don't have a clue where.'

'Five hundred thousand ... with a fifty grand tip for laddo here.' Jarrett spoke the words slowly and staccato as if weighing up whether the bill he was expected to pay would be worthy of the service he'd receive in return.

Thoughts of Weston on his knee as a boy, riding his first bicycle, unwrapping his first Christmas present, invaded his thoughts. He made his decision.

'Okay, you're on. I admire your reasoning, ladies. I have nothing to gain from killing you, and only some cash to lose for keeping you alive. But if you double cross me, be sure that I'll track you down. Wherever you may be in the world, there's no far flung beach resort or remote log cabin where I won't find you. As you so rightly said, I have connections everywhere.' He stared directly into Dolly's eyes as he spoke. 'You appear to know me so well.'

'I know your type. Blood runs thicker than water. It's all about family. What you want is peace about Weston. That's the one thing we can give you.'

A raising of the eyebrows. 'So where is he? You tell me that now. I'll make some phone calls, and I'll have your money here, in cash, first thing tomorrow. Then you give me names.'

'He's buried underneath the old dance floor at the club I used to run, The Kitty Kat. He was there when the club was built,' said Amy.

'But it's not a club any more, it's the casino, Dirty Cash?' questioned Jarrett.

'You know where it is,' said Amy. 'You've obviously been there.' She glanced at Jimmy.

Jarrett was still digesting the information when the loud crack of a bullet sounded from the door on the far side of the room. The crack was followed by one of Jarrett's henchmen dropping dead to the floor, a sunburst of deep red blood spreading wide across his chest signalling his demise.

All eyes turned to face the origin of the bullet. Tommy Hearn, a crazed, demonic look on his sweat-drenched face stood by the door. 'Why the fuck are you telling him that?' he screamed.

As Tommy ran towards the group, two bullets rang out. It was a sound that still haunted Amy every time she heard it, reminding her just how fragile life seemed to be and how easily it could be snuffed out. The two shots had no sooner sounded than a pair of bodies fell to the floor. Death had come once more.

CHAPTER 67
Now, 2015

Careful not to be seen, a lone figure walked into the Reception of the Manchester hotel where Amy had spent the last few days. A huge overcoat wrapped around their frame, and a woollen hat, some would say a little oversized, was pulled down over the person's face. Combined with a scarf pulled dramatically up over the face covering the neck and chin, the resulting strip of flesh left on show would, from a distance, be indistinguishable as either male or female.

Despite the heavy nature of the garments, the figure did not seem out of place. Most people entering through the revolving doors and into the warmth of the lobby were cocooned in a sheath of dense, heavy, woollen fabrics, protecting against the ever-decreasing temperature of the biting December UK weather. To any passing onlooker it would have seemed that the person underneath these layers had just felt the need to be incubated a little bit more.

But comfort was not the reason for the outfit, it was camouflage. This was function, not fashion. Moving to the Reception desk, the figure handed an envelope to the bespectacled lady working behind the counter.

'Could you deliver this to Amy Hart, please?' The voice was almost inaudible, muffled by the scarf.

'I'm sorry, who did you say ...' The woman scanned the name on the envelope and stopped. 'Oh, it's for Miss Hart. I shall make sure she receives it. Who shall I say it's from, er ...?' She was unsure whether to add 'sir' or 'madam'. The figure had already turned and was walking away from the counter towards the exit so a clear look at their face was nigh on impossible.

A one word answer sounded from beneath the woollens. Again it was hard to distinguish. She thought it sounded like Tyler, or Miley ... or maybe it was Riley. She couldn't be sure.

Slipping the envelope into the pigeon hole for Amy's room, the hotel worker moved back to the counter. Turning to her work colleague alongside her, she said 'Blimey, some people need to form their words properly. I've no idea what they said. And as for Miss Hart, I've never known somebody receive so many messages. She's a popular lady.'

Focussing on the Japanese couple standing in front of her, she carried on with her work. Not more bloody tourists flying in for Christmas, she thought to herself. Painting on her best saccharine smile, as fairy-tale-fake as it could be, she asked through gritted teeth, 'Welcome to Manchester, do you have a reservation?'

The first shot had been fired by Jarrett's henchman. The thick-necked thug may not have been much older than most school leavers, but his education alongside Jarrett Smith had meant that he had an A+ when it came to firing guns. His aim was steady, his reflexes quick, his loyalty, as ever, to his boss.

As soon as Tommy had started to run towards the group, the henchman had known that he had to react. He'd just seen his colleague, an equally young and just as delinquent man, have his short life wiped out by Tommy's bullet and he was determined that he would not be dealt the same fate. Neither would Jarrett.

His shot hit Tommy squarely between the eyes, his death instant and painless. His eyes were still open as he landed on the floor. As he did so, the jolt of his body against the hard, dust-strewn concrete caused his fingers to squeeze, as if in spasm, against the trigger of the gun. It was that which caused the second shot.

The bullet flew through the air, its target unknown. But everything has to land somewhere. If Tommy Hearn had somehow managed to cheat death and keep his body alive for another half a second he would have seen the bullet slice through the fabric of Jarrett Smith's trouser leg and land with a satisfying bone-crunching crack within Jarrett's kneecap and watch on as Jarrett fell to the floor in agony. But he didn't. The last thing that went through Tommy's mind was the thought that maybe he would be seeing his wife, Jemima, again very, very soon and that maybe Winston Curtis would be by her side.

CHAPTER 68
Now, 2015

Amy stared at the broad back of the doctor disappearing out of sight from Jimmy's hospital room. It reminded her of Grant and of the countless scenes she'd watched on *Ward 44*, as his character, Dr Eamonn Samms, saved yet another life before strutting heroically from the room and doubtless into the open arms of another more-than-willing-to-please female character. But that was fiction, and this was most definitely real life. Horrifically so.

The doctor in question here – she checked Jimmy's records at the end of his hospital bed for the name – a Dr Aston, had diligently tended to Jimmy's wounds, patching his bruises and cuts, stitching any open wounds and generally, in true Humpty Dumpty style, trying to put the young casino-worker's body back together again. He'd told Amy that Jimmy was indeed lucky to be alive.

In the aftermath of the shooting, it had been Jarrett, writhing in agony from his bullet wound, who had somehow taken control of the situation.

He'd demanded that the henchman still alive take Amy, Dolly and Jimmy away from the premises and drop them, to quote him 'in the middle of nowhere'. He explained, in between his gurning throes of agony, that Dolly and Amy would be furnished with their money the next day, as would Jimmy, but the trade-off was their information about Weston's killer, plus complete secrecy about the death of Tommy Hearn and about how Jimmy had come to end up in such a state.

The henchman grabbed the two women, both in shock at the loss of lives around them, and untied Jimmy. The three of them were driven away from the warehouse and dumped, as instructed. Amy had phoned for an ambulance to take Jimmy to hospital, telling officials that she and Dolly had found him beaten up by the side of the road. It was an easy story to believe as the area of Manchester they'd been dumped in was one of the roughest.

The henchman had then returned to Jarrett at the warehouse, who was still jerking in agony with a handkerchief pressed to his knee, trying to stem the blood flow.

'You take me to the hospital, leave me outside the main entrance and then come back here, making sure no-one follows you. You then dispose of these bodies,' said Jarrett, surveying the two corpses in front of him. An idea came to him. 'In fact, torch this place, with them in it. I want them, especially him ...' He signalled Tommy, '... unrecognisable. Then arrange for the money to be brought to me at the hospital. You do it, or you'll be joining these two in a fiery hell. I'll make the arrangements for the cash, just get back to London and get it to me at the hospital for first thing tomorrow.'

Jarrett was being admitted to the hospital, citing a drive-by shooting – always a convenient story – and the henchman was halfway back to London to fulfil his boss's wishes by the time the fire service turned up at the warehouse to try and fight back the inferno of flames razing the building to the ground. By morning all that remained was a pile of ashes, housing the secret of two lost lives.

Dolly walked back into Jimmy's room carrying two cups of machine tea. She handed one to Amy. 'How's the patient? Poor bastard.' She shivered as she stared at the swollen, distorted face staring back towards her from the bed.

'Dr Aston says he looks worse than he is. A few days and all of the swellings should go down and the marks should start to fade. Apart from his ear, which it's too late for, he should be as good as new. They should be able to do some kind of surgery to make it look as normal as possible though.'

'Has he regained consciousness yet?' asked Dolly.

'He'll be out for a while now as the doctor's sedated him, but he did come round earlier. We had quite a conversation. How do you apologise to someone for nearly getting them killed and ruining their life?'

'And giving him £50,000. That's not exactly a bad pay off. How did he take it? Is he okay with it all?'

'What do you think? He's a normal lad from North Wales who's hardly ever seen a £50 note, let alone £50,000 cash. He's owed every penny after what he's been through.'

'If that shark stumps up the money,' said Dolly. 'I don't believe any man until he delivers exactly what he's promised, especially one who's just been shot in the leg. He could have bled to death for all we know.'

'I have a horrible feeling Jarrett Smith is virtually indestructible, don't you? He's like a cockroach, and just as nasty.'

'But even cockroaches would have a job to survive a raging fire, wouldn't they?' said Dolly, her face suddenly distracted by a TV wall-mounted in the corner of the room. The image on the screen was silent where Amy had muted it earlier but the story was clear to see. A disused warehouse on the outskirts of Manchester had been burnt to the ground. The picture being aired was the location where Tommy had been shot the night before.

'He's torched the place, with Tommy and that other bloke still inside,' stated Amy, contemplating the fact that she was becoming more astute in guessing the moves of hardened criminals with each and every day. 'Jarrett Smith will have been long gone and on his way to safety by the time the match that started it was even ignited.'

A voice sounded from the doorway. 'Yes, all the way to this hospital. And I don't think he'd be overly keen on being called a cockroach, especially when he's gone to all the trouble of calling his banker for you both.' It was Jarrett's henchman, red-eyed and unshaven. The two women could see that he'd been up all night and just like them, was wearing the same clothes as the night before.

'You what?' questioned Amy.

'You two are not overly easy to track down, but I guessed you'd still be at a hospital somewhere with him.' He pointed at Jimmy. 'It was going to take more than a couple of plasters to put him back together.'

'And Jarrett Smith is here?' asked Dolly.

'Two floors up and one bullet lighter. And he said to tell you that he's ready to be more than five hundred grand lighter if you're still prepared to name Weston's killer.'

'Oh, we're prepared,' said Amy, a now ever-present defiance in her voice. 'Just lead the way.'

CHAPTER 69
Now, 2015

In theory, the last twenty-four hours should not have ranked as anything even remotely near a success for Jarrett Smith. His kneecap had been virtually shattered beyond use and he was on the verge of handing over a major chunk of money to people he didn't give a rat's arse about, but as he lay in his hospital bed, his eyes shut, all he felt as he stared at his self-made blackness was happiness. Finally he would be able to take revenge on the person or persons responsible for taking his only child away from him. The thought that he would never see Weston again formed a bolus of misery in the pit of his gut which he knew would never leave him but the idea that finally he, the gangland god Jarrett Smith, would be able to do what every criminal in the land had expected him to do for years, gain his revenge against his son's killer, turned him on immensely.

His eyes automatically opened as the knock on his hospital room door punctured his thoughts. Dolly and Amy were standing there.

'Ladies, please come on in. I can see from your empty hands that you haven't brought me flowers. How heartless.' His welcome to them seemed overly jovial and slightly creepy and immediately put the two women on edge. Gingerly they walked to his bedside. Unsurprisingly it was Dolly who plucked up the courage to speak first.

'Let's just got on with this, shall we? You know we're not here to sign your plaster,' she said, nodding towards the cast encasing virtually the entirety of his leg.

'What a pity. I was just going to ask someone to fetch me some crayons. You could write down the name of my son's killer.'

'The money comes first. We've told you where Weston's buried, so now you need to cough up.' Amy could feel her voice beginning to crack as she spoke, a fusion of tiredness and deep-seated fear.

'All in good time,' sneered Jarrett. 'How do I know you're telling the truth? Weston's underneath the floor at Dirty Cash, you say?'

'Yes.' The two women spoke as one.

'Owned by Tommy Hearn?'

'Yes, until you killed him last night. Unless he's part undead I suspect his days of checking the winnings from the blackjack table are well and truly over. I assume his body was part of the little barbecue you arranged at the warehouse too.'

'What can I say, Amy? If you start playing with the big boys you're bound to get more than just your fingers burnt. It was his doing, not mine. My men were merely defending themselves.'

'Can we have the money now? £250,000 each for us and £50,000 for the poor bugger fighting for his life under this very roof,' interrupted Dolly, her patience running thin. 'He'll live, but no thanks to you. His pay-out will make life a little easier every time he looks in the mirror at his disfigured features though. So we'll just take our money and leave, okay?'

'Fair enough.' Jarrett clicked his fingers and the henchman hovering behind Amy and Dolly pulled out two briefcases from a cupboard placed at the side of the bed. He handed one to Dolly.

'There's two hundred and fifty grand in there. You tell me who killed Weston, you take the money and then you fuck off out of my sight – I never want to see either of you again.'

Dolly opened the case and looked inside. It was packed edge-to-edge with bank notes. For a moment she could feel her nipples harden at the thought of finally having her own substantial mass of money.

'It's all there,' said Jarrett. 'So who killed Weston?' He gazed towards Amy. 'You receive this case when I hear the name. There's £300,000 in here for you and your little boyfriend down the corridor. And just like I said to your mate here, I never want to see you again. If I do, I'll kill you, get it?'

For a moment Amy hesitated. She thought of Riley and the destruction his shooting had caused, his betrayal of her with other women, his lies about his career and his secret love child with Genevieve. She thought about Tommy and Jemima, now both dead, about the duplicitous Lily barely cold in her grave, and about Grant nearly losing his life in some Manchester back-street. She thought about Laura's last breath in her arms. Should she be accepting money to try and improve her own existence as a consequence of all of this misery? Not that long ago she wouldn't have even dreamt of doing so, but now ... The thought disappeared as soon as it had arrived. She was a different woman. She held out her hands for the briefcase.

'You'll never see me again. I've seen more than my fair share of low-lives over the past few weeks.'

'So ... who was it?' asked Jarrett.

Amy suddenly found Caitlyn Rich's face papered across her thoughts. She liked Lily's mum. A final word of bargaining needed to be actioned. She looked straight into Jarrett's eyes. 'You promise me that you'll just do what you need to with the person we mention and nobody connected with them? An eye for an eye, not a matching pair? Just one name and you go after that person only.'

'I promise.' Jarrett's answer was both swift and, Amy thought, believable. She could ask no more.

'Adam Rich,' stated Amy. There wasn't even a heartbeat of regret as she spoke Adam's name. Dolly was right. He'd killed enough people in his time and it was he who'd pulled the trigger on Weston. If Amy had just signed his death warrant then so what? It was no more than he deserved.

Jarrett gave a sharp intake of breath as she spoke the name.

'Thank you Miss Hart. Here's your money.' He nodded for the henchman to hand Amy the other case. She looked inside. Again it was full of bank notes. It was the first time she'd felt financially secure in months. Surely she deserved this money after everything she'd been through.

'What will you do to him?' She spoke out loud before even asking herself if she really wanted to know.

'Have vengeance, Amy, what else is there? Not that you'll ever know. Neither will he. Mr Rich will rue the day he crossed paths with my son. Vengeance should always be unexpected and it should rarely be public. Vengeance is patient. It can wait a lifetime if necessary, but vengeance never dies. But Adam Rich will, of that you can be sure.'

'Let's go, Amy ... we're done.' Dolly was moving towards the door, the case tightly gripped in her fingers.

Amy wasn't quite ready. 'One more thing ... why did you kill Lily Rich? Did you think Adam might be behind Weston's death? She didn't need to die. She was young. She had nothing to do with Weston's death.'

'I don't have to answer that, but seeing as I'm not exactly able to run off given my condition, then I'll tell you.' Jarrett was smiling, but not in an amicable way. 'Everybody has been talking about who killed Lily. How it must have been me. London gangland leader turns up in Manchester and one of the north's biggest criminals finds his daughter dead in his home. Put two and two together and what do you know, Jarrett Smith strikes again ...'

He paused before adding, '... but there's just one problem in all of that. Despite what everyone is saying, I didn't kill her. Hands up, honest guv'nor, it wasn't me.'

Something inside Amy told her that he was once more telling the truth. Which left her with another burning question, one which Jarrett couldn't answer ...

'Then who the hell did?'

CHAPTER 70
Now, 2015

Amy opened her eyes and stared at the ceiling of her hotel room. She knew every inch of it off by heart. It was all becoming far too familiar to her. She longed for her own bedroom again, the warm comfort of her own sheets and pillows and the chance to pick something to wear from a hanger in a wardrobe as opposed to out of a suitcase. It surprised her to realise just how much she was missing her London home. But that would have to wait until she'd found Riley and discovered just who she had cremated.

When she'd moved to London after Riley's death it had been out of necessity. Tommy and Jemima, may they rest in miserable peace, had fleeced her out of nearly all of her assets and left her with no more than the house to sell. With the minimal money she'd gained from the sale, she had quit Manchester and headed to London. It may not have been the perfect bolthole financially, but it was the perfect sized bolthole. Amy saw London as somewhere for her to get lost, to disappear from view and try and piece together the fragments of her tattered life.

But if being back in Manchester had taught Amy one thing about herself it was that she had no real desire to return to the city full-time. There were too many ghosts at every turn.

Running her hands through her hair and yawning, Amy checked the time on her watch. She'd been asleep for the best part of thirteen hours. It didn't surprise her. After she and Dolly had collected their money, she'd spent most of the afternoon with Jimmy at the hospital, watching him regain consciousness and finally able to show him the cash he'd been promised.

She prayed as she looked at the scars and vivid collection of bruises across his face and body, hoping that they would disappear in the not too distant future. The bruise on her own cheek was now almost gone. Jimmy's would surely follow suit. She hadn't left his side until early evening when he'd finally drifted back into a recuperative slumber.

She'd caught a cab back to the hotel and raced across Reception attempting to beat the closing doors of the lift. As far as she was concerned, the sooner she was in bed the better. She just slipped through them before they shut behind her. Within five minutes she was washed, undressed and enveloping herself in a deep, deep sleep.

Her throat felt dry and coarse, as if coated in sandpaper. She needed a drink. Grabbing a glass from the bedside table she stood up and walked towards the bathroom. As she filled the glass at the sink she stared at her own reflection. Her features looked crumpled and squashed, her eyes veined with fatigue.

She glugged back the water and filled the glass back up, this time dipping her fingers into the cold water and running them across her face, attempting to wake herself up. 'God, Amy, you look wrecked, some of that money is definitely being spent on pampering, girl. I think I need to get myself back to one of those spas,' she said to her own face, pinching her cheeks in an attempt to resuscitate some sort of colour back into them.

Her mind cast back to her last pampering session in Germany with Laura. Even though it wasn't that long into the past, it felt like a lost other lifetime looking back now.

All thoughts of massage and seaweed wraps disappeared as a knock on her bedroom door reached her ears. She wasn't expecting anyone and immediately felt on guard. Since Grant had disappeared back to London there was nobody to knock on her door. The thought of it made Amy feel alone and vulnerable. She hesitated a few moments, uncertain what to do.

Composing herself, Amy left the bathroom, moved to the door and put her eye to the peephole hoping to see who was on the other side. Nobody was visible. Her heart skipped a beat, afraid of the sudden mystery. Panic gripped her.

What if it was Adam? Maybe he'd found out that she'd grassed him up to Jarrett. Maybe Jarrett was back with another threat of violence, or maybe Riley was finally ready to meet her face to face. She was still none the wiser about who had tried to kill him. Maybe she'd never know. Amy's mind raced at the possibilities.

'Who is it?' she asked. No reply.

Amy gripped the door knob, ready to twist it open, and took a sharp intake of breath. She couldn't live in constant fear every time she heard an unexpected knock. She wouldn't allow herself to. She'd faced criminals and seen people die, a mysterious knocking was not going to tip her over the edge. Her life had changed beyond all recognition.

As Amy went to open the door she spied an envelope on the floor. Whoever had knocked at the door had obviously slipped it underneath. She was sure it hadn't been there before she'd gone into the bathroom.

A frisson of dread marched across her skin. The stationery was the same and the handwriting was beyond doubt. It was from Riley. He had delivered another letter. Without a moment's thought, Amy yanked at the door handle and twisted it open. Nothing. She took a step forward into the corridor and looked in all directions. There was no-one to be seen. Whoever had delivered the note had gone.

Stooping to pick up the note, Amy rushed back into her room and ran to the telephone on the bedside table. She pressed zero for the Reception desk. If a mystery stranger had just been upstairs with a note for her then maybe they could be spotted trying to leave the hotel.

It picked up after two rings.

'Hello, this is Amy Hart, Room 414. Has somebody just been up to my room to deliver a note? I was wondering if you could tell me who it was.'

The voice at the other end was female. 'That's easy, Miss Hart. It was me.' Her tone was clipped and a touch exasperated. 'When you didn't answer I just slipped it under the door. I meant to give it to you yesterday when it was delivered but we haven't seen much of you so I thought I'd bring it up.'

'Did you see who delivered it? A man, a woman, what did they look like? What time? Somebody must have seen them ... I need to know.'

'Well, I'm afraid you can't.' The receptionist could sense Amy's desperation and to her it was more than peppered with rudeness. 'It was me who took it from them. Funny thing is they were so wrapped up in their clothes I couldn't really tell you who it was, man, woman or Yeti. Will you be needing anything else, Miss Hart?' The receptionist pushed her glasses up her nose, impatient to end the call.

'No ... er, that's all,' Amy hung up.

The receptionist muttered 'rude cow' under her breath and replaced the phone back in its cradle. If customers couldn't be bothered to answer their doors then it was hardly her fault, was it? She turned back to the line of customers forming in front of her and painted on another smile.

In her room, Amy began to open the envelope ...

CHAPTER 71
Now, 2015

'Feed the world, let them know it's Christmas time ...'

If Genevieve had heard the song once, she'd heard it a thousand times already. How many versions had there been now? Four, five, she'd lost count. But sure enough, you could listen to any radio station over the Christmas period from now until the end of time and it would be a festive, bauble-decked mass of Band Aid, Mariah Carey, Slade, Wizzard and The Pogues.

But as she cradled little Emily in her arms, she turned up the volume on the radio and bounced her arms to the rhythm of the song. It was as ridiculously festive and as incredibly catchy as ever and was definitely putting her in the mood for Christmas. Only a few days and it would be upon them.

This year she would try and spend it differently. Previous ones had been passed in a blur of industry parties – schmoozing buyers, press and fashion houses with a bottomless supply of Moët & Chandon.

Christmas was all about giving in the fashion world and it had always been a time when Genevieve had been sure to try and impress those around her, sowing the seeds for the working deals of the future with gifts. But gold, frankincense and myrrh were replaced by the fashion world's equivalent of designer accessories, brand names and booze.

But this year there had been none of that. Genevieve's personal life had taken over. Work, for once, had been pushed to the back of her very fashionable wardrobe.

Emily's features were becoming more and more strikingly beautiful with every month. She was stunning. But every time Genevieve looked at her daughter she was reminded of Riley.

The year had started with Genevieve trying desperately to winkle-pick some semblance of child support from him, her attempts sometimes hostile, sometimes met with threats, and always fruitless. Then Riley had been 'killed', leaving Genevieve to contemplate the fact that her daughter would never see her real father. For over six months she had had to live with that. But then Amy had come back to Manchester and things had changed. Her life and Emily's had suddenly experienced a state of inversion. Riley wasn't dead. And that meant money for his daughter. There was nothing to hide and everything to gain. Amy knew the truth.

This Christmas would be different. Riley would be made to pay. Genevieve would make sure of that. And after everything that Amy had been put through, she was certain that Riley's wife wouldn't want to know him anymore. A woman, even one as weak as Amy, would never forgive all that. And maybe, just maybe, there was a slim chance that that would leave the door open for Riley's love affair with Genevieve to re-blossom.

All Genevieve needed was for Amy to be out of the way. Preferably for good. If Riley was back, then didn't little Emily deserve a chance of really getting to know her father and to be part of a proper family?

As the final rousing choruses of 'Do They Know It's Christmas?' faded from the radio, Genevieve looked into her daughter's eyes. They were a carbon copy of Riley's. 'Would you like your daddy back and that nasty Amy lady out of the way?' cooed

Genevieve. 'Well, maybe Santa Claus has listened to mummy's wishes, little Emily. Wouldn't that be the perfect Christmas?'

Caitlyn Rich's Christmas would be far from perfect.

She was more distant from Adam than ever before and that was saying something. They had not been singing from the same carol sheet for years if she was honest, and if Lily's death had taught her one thing it was that life was too short to settle for second best. Despite being supposedly united in grief by the death of their only daughter, Caitlyn knew what she had to do, and the thought of her Jona – because that was how she was thinking of the cosmetic surgeon these days, as hers – made the decision so much easier.

Caitlyn knew that she would never be able to hold her own baby girl in her arms again. Somebody had made sure of that when they'd wrapped an earphone cord around her neck and pulled it tight. In the same way that somebody had squeezed the last drops of life from Lily's body, life had seemingly squeezed the last drops of joy from Caitlyn's marriage to Adam. Not that there were really any to squeeze. It was all so clear now. She'd only stayed with Adam for the longest time because of Lily. The money was beneficial, but Jona's income was probably greater than Adam's, and certainly much more honest, and again the harsh reality of Lily's death had taught the frivolous Caitlyn that money could not buy happiness. She doubted if she'd ever be fully happy again. Not without her Lily. No amount of mirrored statues, New York fashions and age-defying cosmetic procedures could ever bring her back.

It was par for the course for marriage to a mobster. A felon would always be more married to his job and his underhand lifestyle than he would to his wife. She'd seen it happen with so many of her friends. Isn't that what had happened with poor Jemima Hearn? Once the novelty of the blinding dazzle of riches beyond your wildest dreams and endless security boxes full of jewellery wore off, then life suddenly became as dull and as lifeless as a bag of uncut diamonds. And just as rough. Life with a con bored her. You were never their equal, you were just their other half. Now she needed a relationship that was fifty-fifty and had satisfaction that reached further than the clasp on her Michael Kors purse, and that meant being with Jona, being with somebody who made her feel as happy as she could possibly be given what life had dealt her of late.

Pulling up outside the Rich family home in her car, Caitlyn switched off the engine and lifted the urn containing Lily's remains from the passenger seat. 'My broken Lily, welcome home, my poor fallen angel.' Caitlyn was aware that her daughter had been far from a saint when she was alive.

Caitlyn clutched the urn to her chest and walked to her front door. She looked around at the house as she did so, taking in every inch of the brickwork. It stirred no emotion inside her.

Opening the door, she called to her husband inside. She was greeted by silence. The only movement came from the gentle swaying of a few Christmas baubles, blown by the winter's wind, on a small festive tree near the front door. Doubtless the maid had erected it. Caitlyn hadn't been back to the house since shortly after Lily's funeral, preferring to do her grieving with Jona in London. Pretty as the tree was, Caitlyn had nothing to celebrate.

'Your father's not home.' Caitlyn was speaking to the urn. 'And neither I am, Lily, frankly neither am I.' She looked around at the statues she'd placed in the entrance, the huge mirrored David and the swan she had commissioned. It still didn't look right if she was honest. She didn't care. Now that Lily was dead, she didn't care about anything in the house anymore. And she didn't care if Adam never walked through the front door again.

Dolly Townsend was looking forward to Christmas. More so than ever before. She couldn't open the doors on her advent calendar quick enough. The sooner she could open the presents she'd treated herself to the better. She had money to burn and it was burning brighter than a cathedral full of candles on Christmas Eve.

Dolly had shopped constantly since she'd taken Jarrett's money. Any images that had threatened to linger in her thoughts of dead carcasses, Jimmy's battered body or the potential of what might happen to Adam Rich had been instantly gift-wrapped and disposed of courtesy of her own festive excitement. Dolly may have stared into the faces of hardened outlaws and lifeless corpses over the last few days but it was certainly worth it now that she could stare into the countless faces of the Queen on each and every banknote she possessed.

This would be her last Christmas in this apartment, maybe in Manchester. By Christmas next year she'd have a much bigger place, a huge garden out the back with nodding, illuminated mechanical reindeer across the lawn. Hell, what was she saying, she'd buy a real reindeer and pay a handsome young man to look after it for her. From now on Dolly's life would be all about Santa emptying his sack and making her life complete with all of the lovely gifts she could afford to buy herself, and not having to rely on scum like Adam Rich emptying the sack between his legs into her in order to earn enough money to buy a decent turkey.

Dolly flicked on the TV and sat down on her sofa with a huge tin of chocolates she'd just bought. As she started to unwrap the first one, a clip of Kylie Minogue singing 'Santa Baby' came on the screen. As she hummed along, a melting chunk of chocolate inside her mouth, Dolly couldn't help but think that Santa had finally hurried down her chimney with just the sort of gifts she's always longed for. That would show her stuck-up sisters. She'd have the happiest Christmas of them all.

CHAPTER 72
Now, 2015

The handwriting was just as distinctive as ever. The swirling of the y's, the scratchiness of the t's, the looping of the s's. It was unmistakably Riley.

Amy started to read the letter. His third to her. She was shaking much less than she had been with the previous two, a fact that didn't go unnoticed by her. Quite what it meant, as yet she wasn't sure.

This time Riley's words weren't rambling and as random as they had been in the previous two letters. She began to read.

'Dear Amy,

There are still things I have to tell you. Bad things. But I can't be away from you anymore. We must meet. Can we? Is there a chance? I hope so, pray so. All I want is you. I think I know who wants me dead. They can't win. We can beat them. You and I together.

Meet me at the cottage. Remember, where we stayed? Just you and I. Our place. Log fire burning. I'll be there, Amy, waiting for you. I've rented it again. The key is there. Usual place. I'll join you. We can put this behind us. The start of something new.

I want to see you. I want to see you so much. I'll meet you at the waterfall. Our place, our truly special place, I remember it so well. I love you. Truly. This is our time, our place.

Love Riley x'

* * *

So, this was it. Riley finally wanted to meet. There was no doubt in Amy's mind that her husband was alive. That phrase 'our place' – he'd used it three times.

That was what Riley called the cottage. 'Our place.' Outside Manchester, it was no more than a quaint pile of stones housing a small living room and kitchen and the tiniest of bedrooms.

Amy could hear Riley's voice in her head 'This is our place, away from the world. Just you and me.'

He'd left the key there already. He'd been there. No wonder she'd not seen or heard from him for a few days. The key was in the usual place. Underneath the flowerpot with a painted yellow sunflower on it just outside the front door. It was where they always left it when they went exploring. They had been exploring when they'd found the waterfall. Again Riley had called it 'our place'. It was like a fairy glade from a children's book, hidden and secret, enchanting and magical. She and Riley had spent hours there, looking into the clear ripples of the river and throwing stones into the water or watching them bounce off the rocks and fly over the fall's edge to the perfect dell below. They had always been the only people there, lost in their love and in the comforting rush of the flowing waters.

They had spent many weekends there, the owners always giving them priority over other potential occupants. It was an oasis of calm away from the madness of their Manchester lives.

Amy folded the letter back up and placed it in the envelope. She would go to the cottage, to the waterfall. To meet her husband. To hopefully put all of the heartache she was suffering to rest.

Maybe this was the beginning of the end? Or maybe it was the beginning of the next chapter? Amy couldn't be sure of anything anymore.

But whereas the cottage and falls had always been a haven of love before for her, she was now sure of one thing alone; that her visit there would finally give her the chance to work out exactly how she now felt about Riley. And hopefully that she might find out who was behind the shootings that caused the death of her best friend, Laura.

Hopefully ...

CHAPTER 73
Now, 2015

Deduction. It can mean drawing a logical conclusion, or taking something away ...

It was the word 'deduction' that was stomping its way through Amy's head as she stepped off a train at the sleepy little village about ninety minutes outside of Manchester. The last time she had been there was hand in hand with Riley. There were moments when she could still feel his touch if she closed her eyes and thought back. Now all that she could feel was the biting cold seeping through her gloves as she took hold of her suitcase and pulled it behind her in search of a cab.

The train journey had given Amy time to ruminate, her mind becoming more and more overgrown with tangled thoughts as the world zooming past the train window turned from urban decay into sparse, wintery countryside. Her natural logical deduction told her that Riley would be waiting and that he would be able to explain and justify his actions to her. She would find out the answers to her questions. Why had he faked his own death? What had he hoped to gain from it? Who had she mourned? And who was behind everything? Only deductive reasoning based on these facts could lead her to her own conclusion of whether their love could be salvaged.

The other 'deduction' running through her mind was the deduction of vital things in her life since Riley's shooting. The things that had been taken from her, subtracted from her existence. Things she had once held so precious, such as trust, unity and harmony, had now all been destroyed. Maybe even love.

And then there were the people. Three people had died at the Kitty Kat back in May. Laura, Winston and Mr A N Other. Jemima, Tommy and Lily were now all dead, all united in their hatred of Riley and the things he had put them through. Poor Jimmy was still bandaged and bruised in his hospital bed. So many things had been deducted. *Had it all been worth it?* Amy didn't think she'd ever know the answer to that.

The truth of the matter was that Amy didn't know if she loved Riley any more. Breaking hearts never make a noise. How could she tell? But she knew that truth was a transitory, flexible concept and maybe the truth was that her heart was no longer capable of giving love to a man she had once believed to be the perfect husband. Sometimes imperfections were just too strong.

Hailing a taxi at the rank outside the station, Amy welcomed the rush of warm air as she opened the back door and allowed her body to sink into the sanctuary of the interior. The taxi driver, a smiley-faced lad in his late teens with skin the colour of coffee, turned to face her and let his eyes linger on her just a little longer than necessary as he asked 'where to, love?'

She handed the driver the address of the cottage without saying a word. She was in no mood for chat, but her brain was dashing from thought to thought. This journey would be life-changing, one way or another – yet again her world was about to spin dangerously off its axis. She was heading back to the cottage where she and Riley had spent so many glorious times together as man and wife. 'Our place.' Amy began to reflect …

Then, 2012

The cork popped and flew across the room, bouncing off the row of polished stones topping the fireplace and propelling itself onto the white furry rug lying in front of the hearth.

'No, don't let it go to waste,' giggled Amy, pushing the two champagne glasses in her hand underneath the jet spray of golden liquid spouting forth from the bottle in Riley's hands. She squealed as a mist of sweet-tasting bubbles landed on her skin.

'Don't worry, there are plenty more bottles in the fridge,' laughed Riley. 'I always persuade the owners to stock up when they know we're coming to stay. Now come here, Mrs Hart, and let me toast your good health in the very best way.'

Riley pulled Amy towards him, the glasses spilling slightly as he did so. He was bare-chested and had been ever since they'd returned from swimming near the waterfall that afternoon. It had been yet another idyllic day at the cottage. The late August weather was perfect, the sun high in the sky with shafts of glimmering sunlight forcing their way through the lush green forest surrounding the glen. It had been their own perfect world, just the two of them, lost in the dappled waters as they splashed around, laughing, watching birds flit from tree to tree or an occasional inquisitive squirrel venture forth to come and see what humans dared to disturb the woodland peace.

The visit had featured, as it always did, a session of tender love-making, Amy arching her back in pleasure and enjoying the cool, smooth feel of the waterside rocks against her skin as she savoured the feel of Riley rocking to climax inside her. Somehow their moments of alfresco love-making on their visits to the cottage seemed even more intense and magical than the love they shared together back in Manchester. Every nerve-ending seemed to pop with an even more gratifying intensity.

It was obvious from the hardness between Riley's legs as he pulled Amy's body towards him that he was in the mood once again for enjoying his wife. His lips, full and eager, crushed against hers and letting the bottle in his hand drop to the floor, he placed his palm against the back of her head and drew her excitedly into him. Their teeth buffeted together as their tongues explored each other's mouths and Amy's nipples rose to stiff pointed peaks underneath her bikini top.

'Hang on there, cowboy!' said Amy, as best she could through their kisses. 'I'm carrying two glasses here. Let me put them down.' As she spoke, Riley was untying the knot of fabric keeping her bikini in place. Their bodies parted slightly and the material fell to the floor, exposing her breasts.

In one rapid movement, Riley took the glasses and threw both into the open fireplace. As the sound of them smashing rang in her ears, Amy took a sharp intake of breath as Riley's mouth moved down to her nipples and began looping his tongue around the rosy peaks. He allowed his teeth to feast on her skin and spoke between light, tender bites. 'I told you not to worry, there's plenty more bubbles in the fridge.' Sinking to his knees, he ran his tongue along the length of the groove lining her toned stomach and pulled the material of her bikini to one side. In an instant he had buried his face deep into her heat, allowing his tongue to explore its interior.

Giving herself up to ecstasy, Amy shut her eyes and wallowed in the sensual joy of Riley's touch. Champagne could wait.

Now, 2015

'This is it, love. You'll have to walk the last bit. I can't reach it by car. That's twelve pounds please.'

Amy was jolted from her retrospective thoughts by the cab driver's words and the slapping of his gum as he spoke. 'Um ... yeah, that's fine, I can walk from here. It's just up that path ...' said Amy. It was true, the last part of the journey to the cottage was a winding, narrow path. It was always part of the cottage's charm that it was so secluded. No-one driving past it would actually know that it was there. Amy couldn't count the times that she'd heard Riley turning the air blue as he dragged his suitcase towards the tiny building, catching it on loose stones as he did so. She couldn't remember a time when she hadn't been smiling at his hot-headed case-rage as they'd opened the door to the cottage. Thankfully her own case today was relatively small.

Amy paid the driver and vacated the cab. It had been over a year since she'd been to the cottage and the first time she'd ever been there in winter. The usual greenness and welcoming colours of the area were strangely absent. Trees that had once been full and alive with their vibrancy seemed gnarled and twisted, as if the youthfulness of their glory days was gone forever. Halcyon days, part of a forgotten era.

Amy felt a shiver of dread wash over her as she walked up to the cottage. There were no lights on, and the dim, dull light from the time of year seemed to cast shadows over the cottage that she'd never seen before. What had once seemed so fairy-tale and beautifully bucolic now seemed to possess an air of menace and dread.

She reached for the flowerpot with the painted yellow sunflower on it just outside the front door and pushed it to one side. There it was, the key. She picked it up and placed it in the keyhole. As she began to turn it her teeth started to chatter together – a result of the mixture of cold and fear running through her body. As the hearty click of the key turning into the unlocked position broke the silence in the air, Amy pushed the door open. Her heart pounded inside her. Amy wasn't sure that this storybook setting would be able to provide her with a happy ending.

CHAPTER 74
Now, 2015

A lone figure watched Amy from afar. This was the moment. She'd come. *Had there ever been any doubt that she would?* No, they needed to be here together. To finally accomplish what needed to be done. Finally she would realise why all of the madness from the last year had happened. Why it had to happen. Why people had died. Life was so precious, but sometimes death was the only answer. She would understand that. There was no chance that she wouldn't.

As the figure watched Amy disappear inside the cottage, they moved out of sight, away from their vantage point behind a tree, careful not to stand on a stray twig or cause any kind of disturbance. The moment had to be right when they finally met. Things were running as planned. Everything was storyboarded to perfection. Now there was just one last scene to play out.

Creeping as quietly as the forest would allow, the figure moved off, a smile painted across their face. Amy had come.

The first thing that hit Amy as she pushed open the door was the smell of the cottage. It seemed musty. It had always seemed so fresh before. During her summer visits there with Riley, the windows had always been open, a light breeze allowing itself to waft through the small abode, the scent of freshly cut wild flowers adding to its magic. Today it seemed devoid of life, a film of gloom coating the air.

She pushed her case out of the way and flicked on the light switch by the side of the front door. Nothing. Even in the dim light she could see that there was no bulb in the overhead light fitting. Her brain fogged with confusion. If Riley was here then surely he would have fixed that. Made 'their place' a home. Were there any signs of life?

Amy's question was quickly answered as she scanned her eyes through the open door off the living area and into the bedroom. There, lying on the bed, was a set of clothes, all strategically laid out. A jacket, shirt, trousers, all arranged in the shape of a body, as if someone was weighing up their options of whether an outfit looked good before wearing it for that special occasion. It was what Riley always used to do. So proud of his appearance, he would place his clothes in front of him, deciding if a 'look' was quite right. The irony was that he looked good in anything.

Walking through to the bedroom, she stared down at the clothes. She recognised the outfit as one of Riley's. A classic fitting Prince Of Wales check wool suit and a crisp white shirt. The suit was one of his favourites. Pure Savile Row. Hadn't she given it the charity shop when she'd cleared out Riley's clothes after the shooting? She was almost certain she had. But obviously not, there it was, right before her eyes. The whole period after the shootings at the Kitty Kat was such a smudged blur that she wasn't really sure of anything anymore.

Amy's eyes drifted from the suit to a folded slip of paper placed on the small wooden table at the side of the bed. Even in the dim light she could see the name written on it. It was her own. The writing was as distinguishable as ever. It belonged to Riley.

Just two words. That was all that was written on the note. It took Amy less time to read it than it did to unfold the sheet of paper. 'At waterfall'. Followed by a kiss. That was all.

CHAPTER 75
Now, 2015

At first Amy didn't spot anyone. All she could see as she walked into the seclusion of the clearing around the waterfall was the bubbling of the water as it tumbled the thirty or so feet from the top of the falls down into the lagoon of water below.

The water was darker than she'd ever seen it before, almost black in appearance, the only disturbance on its surface coming from the semi-circular lines of bubbles marching forth from the tumbling of the falls as they reached their destination. The air was otherwise silent, not even a bird daring to make a sound.

Then it came. A shout from above, at the top of the falls. Amy looked up. A silhouette, bulky and hard to distinguish, was standing there. With the nebulous backdrop of the winter forest behind it, it was impossible for Amy to work out who it was.

The thought of seeing Riley again, of him finally being so close to her once more, coursed through Amy's body like a drug. A wave of nauseating dizziness smothered her. For a moment she thought she was going to be sick, her stomach twisting itself into knots. *Shouldn't she be feeling some kind of euphoria?* Her husband was alive.

The figure waved down at her. Amy narrowed her eyes, attempting some degree of recognition. In the dim light of the forest she was too far away to see clearly.

She was being beckoned, her journey not yet complete. She was being called to the top of the falls. Ignoring the ever-tightening lasso of dread and apprehension wrapping itself around her nerves, Amy began to climb the dirty and precarious set of steps laid out by the side of the falls. Each step was marked with a small piece of wood, spaced between the undergrowth. In summer, either side was festooned with a garnish of riotously coloured flowers. Now the steps were edged with just a few decayed weeds.

The ground was hard beneath Amy's feet, making the climb, short though it was, a tiring one. She'd climbed it countless times before, normally she and Riley together, her squeals of delight ringing through the trees as Riley playfully chased after her, the ground seemingly springy underfoot. When the weather was warm there was nothing more satisfying than the pair of them play fighting in the shallow waters at the edge of the falls. It was a sanctuary of fun, locked away from the world. Was that why Riley had chosen to meet her there, why he was waiting at the top of the falls?

But now, in the biting cold of the December air, the whole place possessed a different feel – one of desolation and foreboding. Something wasn't right. Why would Riley put her through all of this? Why bring her to a place that used to bring laughter after all this misery?

Amy reached the clearing at the top of the falls. Her breathing was fast and disjointed. The sickening feeling of dread within her stomach hadn't quelled. No more than five feet ahead of her, with their back turned to her stood the figure, wearing a long black coat with a hood pulled up over their head.

Now was the time. 'I'm here. Riley?'

The figure turned to face her and pulled down the hood, revealing their face. 'Afraid not. It's me.'

It was then that the lasso became too tight inside her. That was the moment when Amy bent double in fear and felt herself vomit. At the moment when she looked into the face of Grant Wilson.

CHAPTER 76
Now, 2015

Wiping away the traces of vomit from her lips, Amy stared back into the face of Grant Wilson. He was grinning. But this was not the cheeky, roguishly handsome, boy-next-door grin that had won him armies of female admirers nationwide. This wasn't the caring, hand-holding Grant who had spooned Amy in his arms just a few short days before, and this certainly wasn't the dashing medical hero of *Ward 44*, ready to effortlessly save another life teetering on the edge of destruction. No, this was a Grant Wilson that Amy had never seen before. One whose eyes were snake-like and piercing, strangely cold yet burning with hatred, somehow darker than a midnight sky. This was a Grant who had nothing but contempt for the woman standing in front of him.

Terror coursed through Amy as she focussed on the man who had kissed her so tenderly on the cheek in his hotel room. She automatically brought her hand to her cheek at the thought.

'You? What are you doing here?' Like she needed to ask. 'I thought you cared about me, Grant. You kissed me?'

'Never heard of a Judas Kiss, Amy? Classic Oscar Wilde scandal? The David Hare play a bit highbrow for you? No surprise there, I suppose. Let me quote from Wikipedia, I learnt it specially … *A Judas Kiss is an act appearing to be an act of friendship, which is in fact harmful to the recipient.*'

He was playing with her. 'I needed you to believe in me. I've needed you to be on my side all the way along, or else I would never have been able to arrive at this point. I needed you to believe everything that was required.' There was a vile sneer as he spoke, a bravado at finally being able to play out his ultimate role, that of the bad guy in the script of Amy's life over the last six months.

'But I don't understand? This is my special place with Riley. Or it was …' Amy's voice was streaked with fear, her words breaking with each and every syllable. 'How did you even know that this place existed?'

'All in good time, Amy. You can't tell me you're disappointed that Riley isn't really here. Did you really believe for one second that he was still alive? He had his face blown off for fuck's sake, you saw it with your own fucking eyes.'

'But the letters … we saw him … you were stabbed? His clothes at the cottage …' Questions slammed into every corner of Amy's shell-shocked mind, her brain action-replaying everything that had occurred that fateful night at The Kitty Kat Club and all that had happened since. 'You were there when the letter was delivered to me in London.'

A pause. One of enjoyment from Grant. This was his moment. His spotlight. He was centre stage and in no rush. 'I've been there all along, Amy. I was there the night Riley and poor Laura died. I was there at the beginning because I was the one who shot them, and I'll be here at the end when I do the same to you.'

Grant pulled out a gun and pointed it directly towards Amy. 'This takes me back,' he sneered, his finger on the trigger. 'This is how it was supposed to finish in the first place. You're the one who was supposed to receive the bullet …'

A crush of confusion gripped Amy's brain. 'But why me?' What have I ever done to you?' she trembled, attempting to understand.

'You married that cunt of a man. Isn't that enough? You signed your own death warrant the moment he waltzed you up the wedding aisle.'

Nothing made sense to her. 'But why kill me if it's Riley you hated? If I'm about to die then surely I have a right to know.'

Grant nodded with an almost jubilant smugness. There was a madness in his eyes. It was the speech that he'd had been waiting months to deliver. The moment when he could really let Amy know the truth ...

CHAPTER 77
Now, 2015

Grant began to speak, his words as cold as the winter air. 'It all started with Lottie Webber, you know that. Riley crucified me with his humiliation of me at school. I'd never hated anyone as much as I hated him. But I let it pass, bided my time. He stole my first love, but I wasn't going to let him crush me for good. I knew that one day I would gain my revenge.' The gun wobbled in his hand as he spoke, a demonic mask covering his face. He was relishing the theatricality of the moment.

'For years my hatred just kept gently brewing on a back-burner in my brain. I got on with my life, Riley got on with his. I became a massive success in my field and so did he in his. Little did I know what his fucking shifty line of work was, though. I should have guessed – the prick never had an honest bone in his body. He was never a decent man, he could have ruined me.'

'How?' It was a simple question. 'Your worlds never collided, did they?'

'He knew too much about me. About my life, about things I'd done. He could have toppled everything I'd built up with one push.' There was a wobble in Grant's voice as he spoke. 'I made one mistake and suddenly he was the one holding all the aces. But now that's dead too, just like Riley.'

'What mistake?' If Amy was to die she wanted as many facts as possible to take to her grave.

'When I left school I struggled a bit with my acting. I couldn't get a break. It happens to all the big names, ask anyone in Hollywood. Makes you what you are. I needed money. My parents weren't backing me – they were putting me down again, so I made a film. A seedy, dirty romp filmed in some flea-ridden hotel room. It paid well and only took a day. Me, some other bloke and couple of cheap tarts taking it from every angle ...'

'A porn flick?'

'Yes, a skin flick. Me and this other fella degrading two women. Lots of sex and even more violence. Specialist market for Eastern Europe I was told, hence the decent pay. I regretted it as soon as I'd filmed it but what could I do? I just prayed it would vanish off to some far-flung country. I never saw it and hoped I never would. And as luck would have it, it did vanish – it never got released.'

'So, what does that have to do with—' queried Amy.

Grant cut her words off, mid-sentence, his voice angered. 'To do with Riley? Turned out the other guy in the film ended up working for your late husband years later and when Riley mentioned that he'd known me and hated me, the stupid prick told him about the movie. He'd asked for a copy and kept it. Seems he was actually pretty proud of his handiwork. Riley seized the opportunity to spread his poison and bought it off him.'

'How do you know?'

'Because he was trying to fucking blackmail me with it. I'd made it big, he needed more money. He had a copy and said he'd leak it somehow. My career could take a sex scandal maybe, but the violence in that flick ... that's something else. I'd never survive that. Riley needed to suffer. To know he couldn't mess with me.'

'So you decided to kill me? Over some sadistic bit of filth that could ruin your career. Why me?'

'To make him hurt even more. But that wasn't the only reason.' Grant continued, delighting in the unravelling of his tale. 'I started going out with Laura. Yep, your Laura, the girl who was your best friend. I met her at a bar. Such a fun time girl – the ultimate star fucker, we were so alike. She couldn't get enough of me and I lapped it up. She loved it when she found out I was a successful actor and tipped as the next big thing. That was a major turn-on. Reckon she had me down as her fast ticket to a land of celebrity. Still, she was dynamite in bed, I'll give her that ...'

Tears began to flow down Amy's cheeks at the mention of Laura's name, but it was more than just sadness that caused them. 'You and Laura were together? I don't believe you, she'd have told me. We shared everything,' she said. Suddenly Amy doubted herself. She and Laura were complete opposites in many ways. Did she know everything about her best friend? Maybe not.

'But you didn't. She played you for a fool. You probably didn't know about half the men Laura went with.'

There was a pause, sheer melodrama from the actor, before he delivered his verbal killer punch.

'You didn't know about her and Riley.'

Amy heard the words but they didn't compute. All she heard was the sound of betrayal as her memories of her friendship with Laura Cash burst into a million painful pieces.

CHAPTER 78
Now, 2015

'You didn't know about her affair with him, did you?' Grant sneered, keen to watch the reaction on Amy's face as his most brutal blow of revelation so far took hold. The most hurtful. He was crushing the life out of her like a boa constrictor around its prey.

Amy felt like she had been punched in the stomach. Of all the disclosures she'd heard about her late husband, this was the hardest pill to swallow.

She could believe it of Riley, it was merely adding another name to the ever-increasing list of infidelities that Amy had discovered. But Laura? That was something horrifically different. Her one supposed true friend? The woman who had been there alongside her throughout all of her adult life. They'd shared laughter and tears, euphoria and rejection. But sharing Riley? No, that just couldn't be. She wouldn't have. She may have sampled the delights of many different men, but surely Riley was off-limits? The two people who had been at her side when she had buried her parents, the two people who had calmed her nerves about the opening of The Kitty Kat Club and the two people who she loved most in the world, how could those two people betray her so badly?

Suddenly a lifetime of images collaged her brain. Times she had been left alone while Laura ventured off with yet another rich and influential shag. Men before mates, as ever. Moments she had left Laura with Riley – at the club, sorting out her parents' affairs after their deaths … how many times had Riley nipped to Laura's Northern Quarter flat behind Amy's back? It was all feasible and horribly likely now Amy considered the clues. And Riley was Laura's type, rich, influential and given what she now knew about her late husband, as fickle as she was.

'I can't believe it, that's bullshit.' Her voice betrayed her words.

'Stupid, stupid, stupid girl! You really should have seen it coming!' Grant shouted, his voice somehow more amplified within the confines of the forest. The repetition of the same word gave him an increased air of demonic madness.

'Why would I make it up? She left me to be with him. Laura and I were together for a long time. Riley stole her from me. As always he wanted to make me suffer and figured out how to woo her. It wasn't hard. Laura was hardly the settling down type was she? It was easy for him to make her believe that some filthy little bunk-up with him would be more exciting than with a life with me. She wanted excitement and danger and I guess being screwed by the charismatic Riley Hart ticked the boxes. They'd been at it for years behind your back. Yet again, Riley gets one over on me. And he knew it. He planned it. He did it with Lottie, he did it with Genevieve too, it seems, and he decided to do it with Laura. To deliver yet another petty blow. He couldn't wait to try and rub it in at every opportunity. How he was better than me yet again.'

Amy wiped the tears away from her cheeks, they felt cold against her skin. 'But you hadn't seen Riley for ages, not before coming to The Kitty Kat—'

Grant cut her short. 'Wrong yet again! Foolish, gullible girl. It's pretty easy to find out where I'm filming *Ward 44* or which party or awards ceremony I might be appearing at. Pick up any gossip magazine or go onto any celebrity website and there's good old me staring out from the screen. Riley constantly hounded me, threatening me with the porn film and belittling me about his affair with Laura. Handwritten notes telling me how great things were with her, how he was the best man she'd ever had. The greatest lover she'd ever known. He was a bully and he needed to be punished.'

'You could have told me ... I would have been able to stop it ...'

'You? Would you have believed me? Some bloke off the telly who your husband once went to school with and hated turns up and says that the two people you trust most in life are fucking each other. Who would you have believed, Amy? Not me, that's for sure. Plus he said that if I blabbed anything to you then the porn video would hit the internet.'

'So you shot him? Killed him instead?'

The vein running down Grant's temple raised angrily as he yelled, his eyes red and bulging. 'I've told you that wasn't the plan. Do you not see how easy that would have been? I needed to do something much more genius. I wanted to make him hurt like I was hurting. I liked Laura, more than any other woman I've been with. She had something about her. I thought I'd found my equal, but she didn't want us to carry on. She fell under Riley's spell and she left me. My agent wouldn't let me go public with her, said that it was better for me to be single and available to my fans. Laura hated that, so the decision to leave was easy. She went running into his arms like an imbecilic man-hungry fool!'

Amy could see Grant's finger twitching at the trigger of the gun. She knew that she was staring at death.

'But why all this ...? Everything you've put me through. Why kill them?'

'It should have been you. I came to the club to kill you. To make Riley suffer. Despite him not being able to keep his cock in his trousers you were always his number one. I needed to make him realise I meant business and that he couldn't mess with me. Not with my professional life and certainly not with my personal life. That he couldn't play God. He'd made me feel a failure yet again just like my parents used to, time and time again. Relentlessly telling me how pathetic I was.' Grant repeatedly banged the barrel of the weapon against his forehead. The force left a red pressure stain.

'He took Laura, so I had to take you. He didn't love her. He used her, like all men did, apart from me. Laura thought she was happy being single and shagging everything with a pulse, but I was the only one who made her happy.'

Amy couldn't help but feel that perhaps Grant was right. Maybe behind all of Laura's bold, brash exterior was a sad little girl who just wanted to be loved. But she just didn't know how.

'Stealing Laura away was just another swipe at me. I could have tried some Grant Wilson magic on you, schmoozed you into my bed to try and get even, but you're not the type, are you? Dedicated to your man. So I decided to kill you. I had the gun prepared and ready. It was easy to fool you all on the night at the Club, pretend I was drunk and drugged from all that crap Lily gave me. I didn't take any of it. I'm an actor for fuck's sake. It was easy to play drug-fucked and run past you like I was freaking out amid the chaos of the shooting. I needed to keep my wits about me if I was going to make my plan work, and have a steady aim of the gun to kill you. But Laura saw me with it and tried to stop me. I aimed at you and she put herself in the way. Took the bullet for you. She saved your miserable fucking life and gave her own. I killed Laura, the woman I wanted to spend my life with before Riley snatched her. I killed her.' It was now

Grant who was crying, thick floods of tears running down his face.

An assortment of emotions boiled within Amy. Laura had betrayed her with Riley yet she had chosen to take the bullet for her. A selfless act that had cost Laura her own life. She may have killed their friendship with her adulterous actions, but every breath that Amy had taken since that fateful night had been thanks to Laura.

'I watched her die. I couldn't take it. It should have been Riley set to suffer, not me again. So I killed him too. It was simple, the club was in uproar, panic everywhere. I went to his booth and shot him. Stupid black bloke tried to stop it so I shot him too. Then I ran as fast as I could and dumped the gun in the nearest canal. It was easy for me to get away with it, especially when everyone started saying it was a mob killing. Your husband had a load of enemies. Even the police were scared to investigate too much in case they started some gangland warfare. It was all hushed-up and I was scot-free. Winner. Which left me to concentrate on making you suffer again.'

'But why do that to me? Hadn't I suffered enough? I'd lost both my husband and my best friend.' The description of Laura sounded somewhat hollow given what she now knew about her. Their friendship had now so clearly always been a one way street.

'I could have left it there but it didn't feel right. It wasn't the complete picture. You needed to know what had happened. So call it my dramatic flair, Amy, I needed to complete the story. The thrill is always in the chase. To use an acting term, I didn't feel that my little production was "in the can" yet, so I decided to resurrect Riley from the grave. I'd shot the fucker's face off so he was hardly recognisable when the police carted him off was he? We all knew he was dead, really, but I just had to sow a seed of doubt in your vulnerable little mind and hope that you took it, and that was so, so easy. Which is why I wrote the letters.'

'But it was Riley's writing, I know it was ...' spluttered Amy.

'I'm an artist, Amy, a master of my craft,' stated Grant, pushing his tears across his face. 'I can copy people, play a part. I knew Riley's handwriting inside out. I had seen it every day at school, I even have books and production programmes from school signed from classmates and I had Riley's bragging handwritten notes that he wrote to me to gloat about Laura. Copying his writing was no problem. Plus I had six months to perfect every ... how shall I put it? I was able to perfect my writing skills. The letters were easy. As was grabbing a stack of junk mail and sticking it all through your London letter box with the second letter when I turned up at your flat. I just had to make sure that you actually believed that what I'd written could be true. Compiling a list of suspects who would want to kill him off was simple. I just picked a few random names from low-life deadbeats at The Kitty Kat, adding mine in for dramatic effect. That way I knew that if you did believe the letter, even for the merest moment, you would work your way through the cast list, including me. Nearly everybody seems to have a reason to dislike Riley, it was the simplest thing in the world to compile a script of shady characters.'

'You set the whole thing up? But so many people have been involved. And so many of them are dead because of your pathological jealousy and fear of failure. It's pathetic.'

'Not all my fault. Jemima did herself in, I didn't know she was fucking that Winston bloke. Shit happens. She was screwed up obviously.'

'And Lily ...?'

'That was unfortunate, but she had to go. She knew too much. She caught me sticking a knife into myself in that back alley. A beautiful moment to put Riley as public enemy number one. When you play a doctor you know exactly where a blade can pierce your body without any danger of actually dying.'

'She saw you? But you were chasing Riley. I saw him. He was there.'

'All smoke and mirrors, Amy. Classic drama and legerde-main. What you saw was a man I hired. Thuggish thirty-some-things with your husband's build are easy to come by in this city, especially if you pay them well enough. He was so wrapped up against the cold all you saw was what you thought was Ri-ley. Who spotted him first? Yep, me ... but then I knew exactly where he was going to be, didn't I? It was sowing another seed.'

'But Lily didn't need to die ...'

'Wrong place, wrong time. She shouldn't have been there, shouldn't have chased after me and shouldn't have seen me stab-bing myself. But she did ... and became ultra fucking cocky and tried to blackmail me. Invited me to her house thinking I'd quake in my boots if she threatened to tell you I'd lied about Riley stabbing me and cough up some cash. So she had to go. You finding her was a stroke of luck. It all added to your suffer-ing. Just like hiring someone to fire some bullets at you outside the church where your parents are buried. You told me where you were going, so I made a few calls and paid someone to scare you. All part of the game.'

'You're a fucking cold-hearted callous bastard, Grant, and you'll rot in hell for all this.'

'But I won't, will I? No-one will find out. Only you know. It was me who nearly ran you down outside Eruption in a hire car. I just wanted to scare you. I've been following you pretty much since the first letter. I brought the second one with me to your flat and coming back to the hotel to deliver the note telling you to come here was a doddle.'

'But this was *our place* – mine and Riley's – the cottage and the waterfall. Riley wouldn't have told you about this place. How did you know about it?'

Grant swaggered closer to Amy, the gun only inches from her face, the rush of the water as it headed towards the falls bubbling behind him. Another smile painted itself across Grant's now ugly features, but it wasn't one of friendship, it was one of complacency.

'Oh I have the lovely Genevieve to thank for that. She made this final scene for me. I never knew this place existed. I would have been quite happy to kill you off in some dirty backstreet, but you'd be amazed at what a drunk woman can let slip. Riley used to pay for this place and bring her here too. I confronted her and she told me everything. She's just a loose-lipped old lush who was banging your husband too. Those weekends you thought he was away on business, well he *was* on the job ... nuts-deep in Genevieve here at the cottage. She used to organise it, so I knew who to go to for the key, where to leave it, all about this place. How he called it 'your place'. I even saw the suit I laid out on the bed at the cottage in a photo at Genevieve's shop. Good brand, easy to buy another one just like it. He was wearing it in the photo. Her and Riley looking all cosy. Nice touch I thought, leaving the suit on the bed, even laying it out like he used to do with his clothes at school all the time. Old habits die hard, I figured. I wanted to keep you guessing right until this moment.'

Grant held out his arms in full stretch, his actions horribly triumphant. 'I thought this would be the perfect setting for your ultimate demise. Poor Amy, so distraught about losing Laura and Riley and finding poor Lily, comes to the place where Riley used to bring her for weekends of love-making and decides to shoot herself. The flowing waters run red with the blood from a poor, helpless suicide. I'll come to your funeral and cry at your graveside, a bunch of monkshood flowers clutched in my hands. They signify treachery, did you know that? That's why I sent a bunch to Lily's funeral. It seemed kind of apt.'

'You disgust me. You take something as precious as life so lightly. Families, lives have been ripped apart because of you. Even if you kill me here, someday you'll get what you fucking deserve. I know it ...'

'All I know is that you're the reason Laura is dead. You should have taken that bullet, not her. She could have been mine again. But she stupidly chose to save you. So now you have to die too. I need to finish off what I started six months ago.'

CHAPTER 79
Now, 2015

Grant pushed the tip of the barrel of the gun against the side of Amy's head. There was an iciness about it. Amy knew that it might be the last thing she ever felt.

'But I'm not ready to die ...' There was defiance in Amy's words. Inside she was broken, every fibre of her being crushed by Grant's confession, but if she was going to lose her life at the waterfall then there was no way she was submitting without a fight.

She stared into Grant's face – a face that only days before she had found so handsome, yet all she could see now was a monster. Women across the country would have moved mountains to be that close to the TV heartthrob of their dreams, but Amy would rather have been anywhere than just inches from the face of Grant Wilson at that moment.

'... So go to Hell ...' said Amy, her voice calm and without waver. As she spoke she drew her knee up as swiftly as she could, connecting squarely with Grant's groin. She prayed that as Grant doubled in pain, the contact would not make him squeeze the trigger. She cowered, expecting the sound heralding her own demise. Nothing came. It was the slim opportunity she needed. Catching Grant off guard she slammed her body against his, using all of her might to push him towards the water.

Grant stumbled backwards, hands clutching his crotch as the pain in his groin shot through his body. 'You fucking bitch!' he cried, swinging the gun back towards Amy. As he squeezed the trigger, one of his feet slid on a wet rock beneath him. The bullet fired into the air.

Amy watched as Grant's body fell towards the water, his foot twisting on the rock and giving way underneath him. The edge of the river, although not great in depth, hid a myriad of rocks and stones underneath its surface. As Grant landed with a splash, the back of his head smashed against one of the rocks. A trickle of scarlet leaked away from the underside of the actor's skull and flowed with the current of the stream. His hand unclenched, allowing the gun to fall from his grasp into the water. Amy watched as it sank beneath the surface.

For what seemed like an eternity, Amy was unable to move, the truth of all that had happened saturating her brain. The only noise around her came from the gushing of the river. She watched as Grant's body, apparently lifeless, was taken by the current and moved towards the edge of the waterfall. Within seconds it had toppled over the spray of water lining the horizon of the river and disappeared.

Carefully retracing her steps down the path by the riverside she found herself at the edge of the waters below. A body lay face down in the water, a thicker stream of deep red blood flowing from the burst at the back of his skull. There was no mistaking the body this time. It was Grant and he was definitely dead.

EPILOGUE

Ward 44 came off air and all further production ceased forthwith as soon as the news of Grant's death broke. It was never reported exactly how Grant had died. The newspapers said it must have been a horrible accident, the actor slipping to his death at a remote waterfall where he had taken some much needed time to relax away from his busy filming schedule.

There was no weapon found at the scene, Amy had made sure of that, returning to the top of the falls and fishing the gun out of the water. She had disposed of it accordingly after returning to the cottage, grabbing her suitcase and locking the closed door behind her.

She had been careful to wipe away any fingerprints on anything she had touched at the cottage. She wanted nothing to link her to the scene where Grant had, as she saw it, rightfully died.

Having left the cottage, she walked to the train station, not wanting to call a taxi. It was a good two miles, but the journey passed quickly, Amy's mind still crammed with every hideous detail. She was back at her flat in London within hours.

Grant's body was not discovered until a few days later by the man renting out the cottage. When the key wasn't returned he headed there to see what had happened. The near-frozen body of Grant Wilson was found washed up along the riverbank. Amy didn't attend his funeral.

* * *

The Rich family home was put up for sale by Caitlyn Rich. After the death of Lily and the disappearance of her husband, Caitlyn had no reason to keep the house. She hated everything it stood for and couldn't bear to sleep under the same roof where her daughter had so brutally died. If Adam had been there to argue with her, she wouldn't have changed her mind. It was made up, the house was to be sold.

Three months later, when Adam still hadn't been seen, Caitlyn closed the doors on the house for the final time, having sold it to a footballer and his faux-blonde girlfriend. Caitlyn had already set up home with Jona in London, a place that was already filling up with her prized mosaic statues. Some things would never change.

Caitlyn filed for divorce from Adam, having to sign an affidavit swearing that she didn't know the location of her absentee spouse. She didn't. Even after the divorce was made official, Adam Rich never reappeared. He seemed to have simply fallen off the earth.

The only person who knew where Adam had ended up was Jarrett Smith. Not that he would ever tell. He was just elated that justice had finally been served for the killing of his son.

Manchester was now Jarrett's for the taking. The criminal wanted to expand and securing Dirty Cash gave him the perfect opportunity. After the death of both Tommy and Jemima Hearn, the ownership of the casino reverted back to Amy, thanks to a clause that Riley had inserted into the contract when Adam signed the building over to him in order to keep the details of Weston Smith's death a secret. With Tommy and Jemima childless, the ownership reverted to Adam, who had signed it over to Riley. As Riley was now dead, the entire building went automatically to his widow, namely Amy.

The shell that had once been the location of all her dreams, The Kitty Kat Club, was hers again. She didn't want it, it held too much painful history, and Jarrett Smith was the perfect buyer, offering her above the asking price. He wanted the building in order to undertake some renovations before making it the base for his Manchester operations. Amy knew that this meant digging up the floor and searching for Weston's remains and part of her felt that he had every right to do so. Why should anybody, no matter how corrupt they are, not be allowed the chance to give their only offspring a proper burial? The signing of the contract passing the building to Jarrett was the only time Amy returned to Manchester.

Genevieve's business went from strength to strength, with a chain of Eruption stores doing just that – erupting across the country. In the months after finding out that Emily's father was indeed dead, Genevieve was determined to make sure that she could cater for her daughter's every need on her own. She took control of her life and started to attend AA meetings, willing herself to jettison the demons of drink that so often ruled her.

Emily continued to live with her grandma at first while Genevieve stood back on her own two feet and kicked the booze. A year on and the three generations of women were living together in a palatial house deep in rural Cheshire. It was the perfect place for Genevieve to employ a nanny, cook and maid to look after Emily when the demands of her ever-growing and increasingly lucrative fashion empire became too great and took her on trips across the globe, ably assisted by her ever loyal Meifeng. It was all paid for with her own money. There were to be no child-care payments and Genevieve knew that she would never allow herself to feel beholden to anyone else's cash handouts again.

In time, Genevieve would expand her business internation-ally with stores in virtually every major European capital city, and a fully-trained Meifeng would leave her to open her own designer boutiques. But for now, most of Genevieve's time was spent travelling between her two flagship stores in Manchester and London. The Carnaby Street location was a prime site and made Genevieve a massive profit. Life was good, with a never-ending deluge of parties, celebrities to kit out and fashion shows to attend. She was just careful to stay off the booze, avoiding any temptation to slip back into troubled ways.

The one place that Genevieve didn't frequent in London was a new club, just off Carnaby Street, called Anno Domini. Despite being no more than five minutes' walk from her own store, the club was a place she chose to avoid. She had no desire to see the club's joint-owner, Amy Hart, ever again. Her hatred towards Amy had died with the news that Riley was indeed no more. Emily had no connection to Amy any more, and Genevieve just wanted to put the entire sorry affair behind her.

Amy had opened the club with Dolly Townsend, the name of the club shortened to 'AD' after their joint initials. With the money given to the women by Jarrett Smith and the substantial amount Amy was given by Jarrett for buying Dirty Cash, the start-up of the club was an easy process.

Amy liked Dolly but could see that she would spend her money from Jarrett in a matter of months and probably have little to show for it. With a little persuading, Amy coaxed Dolly away from Manchester and the two women went into a seventy-thirty partnership in Amy's favour to open a new London club. The investment money was mostly Amy's after all. Not that Dolly minded. She was more than happy to sit back and watch the thirty per cent of all profits from the club being deposited into her back account. That was still more than her odious sisters would ever have.

The opening night of AD was a huge success. Amy's track record with The Kitty Kat proved that she had kudos when it came to running a nightspot and the queue around the block night after night kept the club well into the black. While Amy and Dolly schmoozed the clientele, the general running of the club was organised to almost military precision by a young lad by the name of Jimmy, who was enjoying his first major job in London. With Dolly and Jimmy by her side, Amy was making new friends.

Within weeks of opening, Anno Domini was receiving major write-ups in nearly every influential magazine, newspaper, website and blog, including one in *Mixmag* which said that 'AD is the kind of happening club London has been waiting for' and that 'it has taken the expertise of Manchester's Amy Hart, former owner of the infamous Kitty Kat Club and its famed theme nights, to make it a reality'. Within a few years, AD would be opening clubs in Ibiza, Hong Kong, Las Vegas and Stockholm and Amy Hart would become a clubbing legend.

Amy was back on top and back in business. And, it seemed, with a new best friend. Despite their many differences, she and Dolly were a good team and it felt comforting to have an ally she could really rely on, one who always wore her honesty on her now-designer sleeve. Perhaps it was Amy and Dolly who were really the two different facets on the same gemstone, now both shining bright in their own unique ways. Amy thought she had achieved that with Laura. How wrong she'd been.

Amy could have crumbled, but after everything she had been through, she was stronger than ever. Invincible. Her parents would have been proud. All she lacked now was a good man to share her newfound life with. She was sure that it would happen with time. When she chose to let it happen. When the timing was right. Yes, she'd look forward to having another man in her life should it occur, but this time around she would definitely find out exactly what he did for a living before committing.

LETTER FROM NIGEL

Hello there everybody! Hopefully you enjoyed spinning around on the dance floor with my latest glam-packed novel, *Deadly Obsession*. I really loved writing it as anything that involves a wonderful set of strong female characters like Amy, Laura, Caitlyn, Genevieve, Lily and the dodgy, devious men around them, all set to a backbeat of pulsating nightclub beats and lashings of murderous action is mighty fine with me!

Writing *Deadly Obsession* was a true blast as it was wonderful to immerse myself in such a gritty story. Did you see the ending coming? Were you able to work out exactly what the story was behind Riley's mysterious letter? And were you rooting for a big reunion or not? I hope you gasped at every page-turning moment of the action.

If you enjoyed the book I would LOVE you to leave me a review on Amazon (UK and USA or no matter where you are around the world). Hearing what avid readers think is one of the many things I absolutely love about crafting a tale and being an author. Who was your favourite character? Could you sympathise with Amy, did you think Laura was a total man-eater and which of the men did you fall for? Personally I have to say I was totally Team Caitlyn, with her fabulous mirrored statues and no-nonsense attitude. And did you spot the characters from any of my other novels popping up too?

If you were entertained by my latest book, then perhaps you'd like to read more of my stories! Plus, let's chat – I'd love to talk all things blockbuster and glamour-soaked fiction on Twitter (you can find me at @Nigel_May), Facebook and Goodreads. The world should always shine with glamour!

Thank you for reading my latest scandalous novel and I'll see you soon with another one – the action is never going to stop, I promise! I'm feeling in a tropical mood for the next one I think …

See you in paradise, love Nigel x

Made in the USA
Middletown, DE
15 April 2018